GUARDED

A STORMFINCH SECURITY NOVEL

HELENA NEWBURY
NEW YORK TIMES BESTSELLING AUTHOR

For mothers everywhere

Cover by Mayhem Cover Creations

Main cover model image licensed from (and copyright remains with) Wander Aguiar Photography

First Edition June 2023

ISBN: 978-1-914526-24-4

1

LORNA

NOBODY HAD EVER TRIED to kill me before.

I'm not pretty, so there are no jealous lovers. I'm not famous, so there are no crazy fans. I'm not important or politically connected.

I'm a single mom. I'm an architect. I'm nobody.

But that day in April, someone wanted me dead, and they were rushing towards me at eighty miles an hour.

It was late afternoon and I was sitting in the back of an SUV as it sped through Mexico City. I don't travel much. Normally, I stay safely huddled behind my drawing board in New York but for this set of meetings, the client had wanted the architect there.

They'd probably expected me to be like my dad, the CEO, with his sharp suits and expert charm. Or my brother, my dad's right-hand man, with his good looks and cocky grin. But I'm...not like that. I'm all pale, soft curves where I should be toned and tight. Instead of their gorgeous chestnut hair, I have an untamable mass of black tresses. And instead of their easy confidence, I panic and clam up when asked to speak to a room full of people.

For three days, I'd *ummed* and mumbled through explanations of the blueprints. All the other women in the room had been ten years younger, lip-glossed, and sleekly efficient, and I'd felt dumpy and ridiculous. But finally, it was over: we won the contract to build the new airport and now I could go back to my safe little world of plans, calculations...and being a mom.

I turned and looked at Cody, my son. He'd dozed off, head thrown back and softly snoring, and it was a rare opportunity to look at him dotingly without him squirming and moaning *Mommm!* He'd inherited my dad's strong jaw and perfect, straight nose, and at nine, he already looked like a mini version of my older brother, Miles. Miles had broken the hearts of every high-society woman on the Upper East Side and once Cody hit high school, I foresaw a lot of weeping teenage girls in his future.

I felt a pang of guilt as I watched him sleep. He was such a great kid, and he'd been so patient, these last few days. But now the meetings were done and I was officially on vacation. I grinned. Cody, my dad, and I were going to stay with Miguel, a wealthy friend of my dad's who lived south of the city. For the next week, it was going to be nothing but lazing by the pool, ping-pong matches, and ice cream.

It was Miguel who'd sent the two SUVs to pick us up: my dad was in the other one, up ahead, no doubt with paperwork spread out over the back seat and his phone pressed to his ear. Hopefully, I'd be able to persuade him to switch off from work, too.

I glanced out of the tinted window. We were speeding through the older part of the city, past little bars and stores. People were fanning themselves with their hats: it was hot for April, pushing ninety. But in the car, everything was cool and comfortable. I stifled a yawn and settled back into the soft leather seat. Maybe I'd have a little doze, too, while we—

There was a *bang* so loud my eardrums ached. My head jerked up and I saw my dad's SUV being rammed sideways by a pickup truck.

Our driver slammed on the brakes but it was too late. I had time to throw a protective arm across Cody and then our SUV smashed into the side of the pickup truck. Cody and I shot forward and our heads came within a half-inch of hitting the seats in front before our seatbelts jerked us to a stop.

I slowly sat back, panting in shock. *Cody!* I checked him: he was white-faced and shaken but okay. The whole front of the car had crumpled and our driver was slumped over the airbag, unmoving.

I craned forward, my chest contracting in fear, to look at my dad's SUV. One side was caved in and with the tinted windows, I couldn't see if anyone was moving inside.

I had to get over there and see if he was okay. I put my hand on the door release—

That's when I saw the men running towards us, guns in their hands and ski masks over their faces.

Oh Jesus. This wasn't an accident.

They were coming towards our car. "Lock the doors!" I yelled. But our driver didn't respond. Either he was dead or unconscious.

"Mom?" Cody's voice quivered. He'd seen the men, too.

I hit my seat belt release, dived forward between the seats, and craned around the driver, frantically searching for the central locking button. *Where is it? Where is it?!*

Just as the men reached the car, I saw a button with a padlock icon and stabbed it. There was a low *clunk*. One of the men pulled at the door handle and cursed. He glared at me through the window and pointed savagely to the door. *Unlock it!*

I shook my head, panting with fear. I knew it wouldn't hold them for long but we had to buy time until the police got there. I got Cody's seatbelt off and pulled him along the seat, switching places so I was between him and the men. His body was stiff with fear and his eyes were unfocused. I took his face between my hands. "Hey! Hey, look at me."

He slowly focused on me.

"We're going to get through this," I told him. "You and me, okay?" Panic was choking me but I tried to make my voice strong. "You and me."

It's a thing we have, ever since his father left. *You and me against the world.* Cody nodded shakily.

I turned to look at the gunman. He raised his gun and leveled it at my head.

My throat closed up. I couldn't breathe. I'd never even seen a gun up close before.

The muzzle swung down for a second, gesturing at the door handle. Then it swung back up to my face, that dark circle sucking all the heat from my body.

I glanced towards the central locking button, debating. Then I heard my dad's voice in my head, his Scottish accent rich and warm. *If they wanted you dead,* he reasoned, *they'd have shot you already.*

I shook my head at the gunman again.

I saw his eyes narrow. Then the butt of his gun smashed the window, showering us with scratchy nuggets of safety glass. He reached in and unlocked the door, then swung it wide. Sunlight and heat blasted us.

One of the men was holding cloth bags, to go over our heads. *Oh God,* this was a kidnapping. Three bags: my dad, me, and—

I looked over my shoulder at Cody. *No. No!* As the gunman reached for me, I grabbed hold of the grab handle above the window and wedged my feet under the seats, making myself a human wall between him and my child. "No!" I screamed. "*NO!*"

But two of the men grabbed my wrists and ankles and hauled me, kicking and screaming, out into the street. One of them held me pressed up against the SUV as the other reached in to get Cody. A third man stepped forward, lifting one of the bags to put it on me—

A bottle smashed over his head and he crumpled to the ground. Behind him was the man who'd hit him: I got a glimpse of blue jeans, a white shirt, and a cream Stetson.

My rescuer grabbed the guy who was trying to take Cody and rammed his head into the car's door frame. As he fell, unconscious, the man plucked the handgun from his waistband, turned, and shot the man holding me.

All three of the gunmen were down and the whole thing had taken no more than five seconds. I stood there hyperventilating, the world going blurry. Then I focused on the boots of the man who'd saved me. They were scratched and worn, boots that had been to the four corners of the earth. And there was something about the way he stood. You know how nervous people shift their weight from foot to foot and can't stand still? This was the exact opposite of that. He stood like a statue built from granite and lead.

My breathing slowed and I lifted my eyes. Blue denim, faded from the sun, the soft fabric stretched tight over muscled thighs. Then a thick leather belt with a silver buckle as big as my fist. The breeze was flattening his white shirt against his body like a lover's hands, showing off flat, hard abs, wide, curving pecs, and shoulders that looked like they could carry the weight of the world.

I was looking straight ahead, now, but I was only up to his chin: the guy was *big*. I tilted my head back...

I'm thirty-seven and he was a little older, forty or so, with just a little silver dusting his black hair at the sides. And he was absolutely gorgeous in a way that jolted me right to the core.

There was something hard about his face, in his rugged jaw and thick black stubble, as if he'd been shaped someplace tough and unforgiving. But there was a softness there, too: he had tiny crinkles in the corners of his eyes like he smiled a lot, and he had the sexiest mouth I'd ever seen, with a gorgeously full lower lip.

I felt my breathing slow to almost normal. I was still terrified but there was something about this man that calmed my panic. He exuded authority: it was in the way he scowled disapprovingly at the men on the ground, in the way he stood, so strong and calm and still.

In the midst of chaos, the law had arrived.

He looked at me and I caught my breath. His eyes were as piercingly pale blue as a prairie sky on a cold, clear day, eyes you couldn't lie to and that couldn't lie to you. They were more than beautiful, they were *soulful*: eyes that had soaked up a lifetime of experience.

The guys I knew back in New York, with their manicures, ski trips, and tennis club memberships, so desperate to impress...suddenly I saw them for what they were: boys.

This was a *man*.

His eyes narrowed, drinking in every detail of me, then flared with a heat that scalded my skin. I gulped and flushed. Guys like him don't look at me that way. *No* guys look at me that way.

He glanced at the scene around us and I saw his jaw harden. Then he turned back to me with a look of such raw, protective fury that I just melted. I stared back at him, open and vulnerable.

And saw his eyes flicker. For a heartbeat, I saw what he hid.

Pain. Unbelievable, soul-tearing pain.

He looked away. Looked back and now he was stoic. *Guarded.* "'Name's JD," he told me in a deep, Texas growl. "And I'm gonna get you the hell out of here."

2

JD

Two Minutes Earlier

I WAS IN HEAVEN.

I'd leaned my chair back against the low wall that surrounded the bar's terrace. The afternoon sun was beating down, warming me to my bones. I had my Stetson tilted forward to shield my face and my eyes were closed. A chilled glass was in my hand and as I inhaled, I smelled fresh lime juice, clean and innocent as a schoolteacher on her way to church. But underneath was the twisting, heady scent of tequila and triple sec, a pair of sultry maidens who'd tempt you into an alley before knocking you over the head...and you wouldn't care at all. This place made margaritas like nowhere else on the planet and I was going to savor this one.

I sipped and gave a long groan of satisfaction. There was a giggle and a waft of perfume as Camila, the waitress, walked past. She'd been flirting outrageously with me all afternoon, despite being half my age. Probably because she sensed—correctly—that this grumpy old gringo wouldn't let things go beyond flirting. A band was on later and hell, maybe I'd even dance, once I'd had a few drinks, but then I'd head back to my hotel alone.

This place: the slow pace, the drinks, and especially the heat, was exactly what I'd needed after Siberia. Earlier that year, I'd wound up captured and imprisoned there in a former Soviet gulag, shivering through the nights under a thin blanket, and this was the first time I'd felt properly warm since.

I'd needed a vacation but stepping away from Stormfinch Security, the private military team I head, hadn't been easy. My best buddy Danny and my little sister Erin had had to poke me for months before I'd finally given in and booked a flight. I told myself it was because I was nervous about leaving Danny in charge but I knew that wasn't it. Danny had proven he could be trusted—hell, I even trusted him enough to let him date my sister, although the way they'd secretly gotten together had driven me crazy at the time.

The real reason I hadn't wanted to go on vacation was because the team had become like a family. And when I was away from them, it reminded me that they were the only ones I had.

At that second, there was the roar of a car engine and a rush of air threatened to suck my Stetson off my head. I reluctantly opened my eyes to see two black SUVs shoot past the bar's terrace. Tinted windows, chrome polished to a dazzling shine. *Money.* Some bigwig on his way somewhere.

I was just closing my eyes again when there was a bang of metal on metal. A pickup rammed the lead SUV aside. Then the second SUV slammed into the pickup and men with guns started swarming out of a nearby building. An ambush.

Gunmen started trying to pull someone out of the second SUV, kicking and screaming. I narrowed my eyes against the sun—

A pair of sneakers emerged from the car. Long, denim-clad legs. Then a white blouse stretched tight by full breasts. Long hair whipping around as she struggled—

A woman. They were kidnapping a woman.

Before I knew what I was doing, I was up out of my chair and halfway across the bar's terrace, reaching for my gun—

My hand closed on thin air. I stumbled to a stop, gaping down at my belt. My gun was back in Colorado. My jaw tightened in fury. *This is why I never take vacations!*

I grabbed a bottle of tequila from the bar and ran towards the crashed SUVs, my training taking over. I brought the tequila bottle down on the head of one of the gunmen. Grabbed the second guy and slammed his head against the car, then took his gun and shot the third. Then I turned to the woman—

And stopped.

I was looking down into the palest gray eyes I'd ever seen, soft as smoke and glittering with intelligence. She stared up at me and it was like she was studying me, mentally scribbling down every angle and line. Her lips were just slightly parted, blush pink and so soft I had trouble tearing my eyes away.

She had creamy-pale skin and long, tumbling black tresses that spilled all the way down her back. Her hair was mussed from when those bastards had dragged her from the car and I had this overwhelming urge to reach forward with one big, clumsy paw and brush it straight, so she was perfect again.

She was a head shorter than me and her body was all lush curves, her blue jeans hugging full hips and what had to be an amazing, rounded ass. Her white blouse was loose, but it couldn't conceal the shape of her chest, the thin cotton stretched tight. I had to drag my eyes away. I've been around the world some but *damn,* I couldn't remember when I'd seen a body that great. And there was something about her...she was soft and beautiful but strong. I couldn't figure it out, but I was fascinated.

The breeze changed and a few strands of that midnight-black hair tickled my cheek, so soft it was like being stroked by wisps of stormy cloud. She smelled like orange blossom and coconut.

She was goddamn gorgeous. I stared down into those pale gray eyes, big with fear and—

It started small but it grew fast, a Texas flood finding a dry riverbed. It surged through me, crashing and thundering, and I felt my chest fill and my fists bunch.

I had to protect her. And that urge came from a place deep in my chest that I normally keep locked up good and tight. For a second, the pain hit me full force and I had to look away and tell myself not to be so goddamn weak.

Just get her safe. Nothing else mattered.

I turned back to her. "'Name's JD," I told her. "And I'm gonna get you the hell out of here."

A gunshot rang out and I instinctively ducked down behind the SUV, pulling the woman with me. Another group of gunmen was headed our way. I dropped one of them with two quick shots, but the rest kept coming.

At that moment, the other SUV's engine suddenly roared into life and it leapt away like a scalded cat. But after less than fifty feet, it screeched to a stop, and the rear door opened. A silver-haired man in a suit leaned out, bleeding from a cut on his forehead. His face looked familiar but I couldn't place it. "*Lorna!*" he yelled. His accent was Scottish. "Get in!"

The problem was, the gunmen were between us and him. They started running towards his car, hoping to grab him before he could close his door. "Go!" I yelled. "I've got her!"

I could see the debate on his face. He didn't want to leave her behind but he was smart enough to see that we couldn't get to him. He said something to his driver and the SUV sped away, leaving the gunmen who'd been chasing it in a cloud of dust. They started shooting at it and I saw the rear window shatter, but it kept going, speeding off into the distance. The gunmen slowed to a stop and started jogging back toward us.

I grabbed the woman's hand. *Lorna,* the guy had called her. We had to get the hell out of there. But as I pulled her towards an alley, she pulled back with surprising force. "Wait!" she told me.

She ran around to the SUV's rear door. She ducked inside the car and hauled out—

I swallowed hard. *A kid.* At first, I thought he was seven or eight because he was just a little thing. Then I got a better look at his face and realized he was more like nine or ten. The same age Max would have been.

Lorna gathered the kid to her chest. She glanced at the gunmen and those soft gray eyes went hard as granite. And suddenly, I knew what it was about her that had me so entranced. Soft but strong. Caring but protective. Beautiful but dangerous. She was a mother.

Jillian had had the same look. The memory woke the pain again and I had to wrestle it down inside before it took over.

"The driver," Lorna said, nodding quickly towards the front of the car. Her accent was New York, rapid-fire and efficient, but there was just a hint of Scottish, too. "I didn't get a chance to check if he's...."

I stared at her, amazed. She must be terrified, but she was still worrying about other people. I fired a shot at the approaching gunmen to hold them back, then leaned into the car and felt the driver's neck for a pulse. I grimly shook my head.

"We've got to move," I told Lorna. "Stay low, stay behind me, and keep a hand on my back so I know where you are."

She nodded mutely, put her palm between my shoulder blades, and pulled her kid close to her side. And together, we ran into the alley.

3

LORNA

I WAS PANTING, terrified, my brain still trying to catch up. Just a few minutes ago, I'd been relaxing in the SUV. Now the driver was dead and people were trying to kidnap us, kidnap my *son*—

The walls of the alley flashed past us as we ran. Buildings painted bright pink, yellow, and white. Graffiti. Garbage bags. And all around us, the shouts of the men hunting us.

With one hand, I pulled Cody protectively to my side. He'd gone sheet white, his eyes huge. He was in shock or something close to it and the fact I couldn't make him safe made me feel more powerless than I'd ever felt in my life.

My other hand was pressed against the only person who *could* maybe keep us safe.

JD advanced down the alley fast but cautious, gun up and eyes everywhere. I'd seen people move like that on TV, in green-tinted news reports about soldiers raiding terrorist strongholds in the dead of night. And JD had taken out those gunmen like it had been nothing. Was he a cop? Military?

JD suddenly twisted and there were two loud bangs, like firecrackers going off right in my ears. When I peeked around JD, I saw a body on the ground up ahead.

We kept moving. The sun was baking me but my skin was icy with fear. I could hear my own shuddering breaths and Cody's shaky gasps but JD was almost silent: under my hand, I could feel his slow breathing. *How is he so calm?!*

Up ahead, the alley curved. As we neared the corner, JD stopped and held up his hand. We froze.

JD put his finger to his lips and I heard voices coming from around the corner. The gunmen were ahead of us. JD looked back the way we'd come. More voices. They were behind us, too. I saw JD silently curse under his breath.

He leaned in close to me. I felt warm fingers move my hair out of the way and then he spoke, his lips almost brushing my ear. Even in a whisper, that deep, Texan growl was strong and rough as granite, and despite everything, I felt my whole body come to attention, a puppet with its strings drawn tight. "We're gonna have to hide. Wait 'till both of them have passed." He looked around, then pointed to a parked truck. "Under there."

He towed me by the hand over to the truck and then motioned for Cody to slide underneath first. Cody lay down on his belly and scrambled under.

Then it was my turn. I got down on my stomach and awkwardly shuffled under until I was pressed up against Cody. There really wasn't a lot of room: my lips were only an inch from the ground and I could sense the underside of the truck claustrophobically close above my head. The voices of the gunmen were getting closer. I quickly beckoned JD in.

He slid in next to me, his muscled chest and shoulders barely squeezing into the narrow space. His body formed a reassuring barrier between us and the alley where the gunmen would pass. He'd put Cody in the safest place, up against the wall, and himself in the most dangerous one, and that spoke volumes about the sort of man he was.

We all went still. But in the quiet that followed, I heard the rasp of panicked, frantic breathing. I turned and looked at Cody. His face was deathly white and his eyes were huge. I understood: this was all just *too much.* But the gunmen were going to hear him. I tried rubbing Cody's back but he just stared back at me, heaving for air. And the gunmen were getting closer and closer: I could hear their boots on the dirt, now.

Then JD reached over my back and put a massive hand between Cody's shoulder blades. He spoke in a low voice and each word felt like a rock, warmed by the Texas sun, strong enough that they built a wall that could hold back anything. "You're gonna be okay, kid. I'm not gonna let anybody hurt you."

On the last two words, JD's eyes flicked to cover me, too, and...I believed him. Maybe it was those eyes, so clear and blue that there was no place for bullshit. I nodded and Cody gave an uncertain little nod, too. His breathing slowed and quietened. I grabbed his hand and squeezed it in mine, proud of him. And then—

I caught my breath as a big, warm hand closed around mine and Cody's. JD squeezed gently and nodded to me and a hot bomb went off in my chest. I stared at our joined hands. It was insane, but...

It was the first time I hadn't felt alone, since Cody's dad left.

I looked across at JD and, for a split second, I saw that pain again, so raw and terrible I just wanted to throw my arms around him. Then that stoic mask returned.

The gunmen who'd been ahead of us rounded the corner. Looking out from under the truck, I saw one, two, *three* sets of boots. They were muttering to each other, tense and foul-tempered. I held my breath. But they walked right past. *It's going to work!*

Then, from behind us, more voices. The other group of gunmen entered the alley...and the two groups stopped as they met, right next to the truck. *Oh no...*

We lay there, barely daring to breathe. The gunmen seemed confused: the plan must have been to pincer us between them and they didn't understand where we'd gone. Their boots shifted in the dirt as they looked around. *Don't look under here,* I begged. *There's no one under here.*

One man wandered closer. His boots stopped three inches from

JD's ear. I dug my fingernails into my palms, staring at the black leather toe caps, holding my breath.

Then the gunmen seemed to form a plan, and the two groups moved back off in the directions they'd come. When the alley was clear, all three of us slumped in relief, going limp against the ground. JD made us wait a full minute still lying there then we crawled out and ran on.

Up ahead, I could hear traffic and bustle. JD turned and spoke over his shoulder. "There'll be people up here. Crowds."

I nodded. Crowds were good, we could disappear. And with so many witnesses, the gunmen might back off.

I had my hand pressed against his back again and I was self-consciously aware of how good it felt. There was something about him, and it went beyond those gorgeous looks and that deep Texas growl.

JD made me think of a massive tree with deep, deep roots that would stand firm even in a hurricane. It wasn't just his big, muscled body or his stubborn scowl. It was what he *did*. He didn't even know our names, but once he'd decided he was going to protect us, *that was it,* no wavering. And that connected with something deep inside me.

When things are bad, I've always taken comfort in things that are solid. As a kid, when a storm was blowing outside the window, I didn't reach for a stuffed rabbit or a Barbie. I used to put my hand on this vintage Tonka truck my dad gave me, so old that it was made out of metal. When my dad was away on business and I was missing him, I used to go into his home office and sit with my back against his desk, which was made from mahogany and needed four people to lift it. Maybe it was my weird brain, even back then, so full of abstract math and physics that I needed something I could touch, for balance. Or maybe I loved the permanence of big, solid things because I sensed, long before my dad explained it to me, that there was a mom-sized gap in my life.

Even now, when I'm overwhelmed by work and people and being a mom, when I feel like I'm going to be swept away, I put my forehead against the cold stone of a wall for a second and soak in its solidness.

I've always needed that feeling. Searched for that feeling.

I'd never known you could get it from a person.

Up ahead, the alley met a busy street, the sidewalk crammed with people. I squeezed Cody's hand. We were almost safe.

And that's when the gunman stepped out of the side alley ahead of us.

4

JD

MY GUN CAME UP. His gun came up. We froze, both staring down a muzzle.

Everything else dropped away. I could still feel the heat of the sun on my bare forearms, and hear the traffic rumbling up ahead, but it was distant. My whole world was the figure in front of me in jeans, plaid shirt, and a ski mask. My brain sucked down every detail, desperate for anything that might give me an edge. He was smaller than the others and lightly built, too. But he was *calm*. I could see his shoulders moving as he breathed slow and deep, the same as me. He'd seen combat before.

If one of us fired, the other one would. We'd both die. He knew it and I knew it.

Without taking his eyes off me, the guy jerked his head to the left. *Move!* He was giving me a chance to walk away. Behind me, I heard Lorna catch her breath.

But I've never been much for quitting. That's why the Army suited me: just a big, dumb ground pounder; point me in the right direction and I'll get there, no matter how many brick walls I have to march through. Jillian used to tell Max his daddy was half man, half mule.

I spoke, my voice filling the alley. "Here's how things are. I don't know what problem you got with this woman and her kid, and I don't especially care. If you want 'em, you're gonna have to come through me. So how about you back away, and I won't have to put a bullet between your eyes?"

The guy didn't speak but I thought I saw his eyes harden and his shoulders set. He was as stubborn as me. I knew in my gut that I was looking at their leader. He wasn't going to back down.

Which was a problem because he could just wait this out and we couldn't. Sooner or later, one of his goons was going to come along and then I'd have two guns on me and it would all be over. I couldn't move but I couldn't stay here, either.

But there was one thing I could do. I could get them safe.

"Very slowly," I told Lorna, "move back down the alley. We passed a door. See if it's unlocked."

I didn't take my eyes off the guy in front of me: even a split second would be fatal. I heard the scrape of Lorna's sneakers in the dirt behind me and I saw the guy tense, pissed that she was getting away. But he didn't dare move his gun to shoot her.

"It's open," Lorna said behind me. Her voice was strained but she was staying calm, doing what I told her. *Good girl.*

"What's in there?" I asked.

"A workshop."

"Does it look like there's a back way out?"

A second's silence while she looked. "There's a window that opens."

"Okay. Take your kid and go. Lock the door behind you, go through the window and *run,* you hear me? Don't stop running 'till you get somewhere safe."

Silence for a few seconds. Then, "Not without you."

My eyes still hadn't left the guy in front of me. "Just *go,* dammit!"

"*No!*" There was panic in her voice. Like the idea of leaving me behind hurt. And that hit me right in the gut, harder than it should have.

I heard her sneakers scrape the dirt again and I relaxed. But then I frowned because her steps were coming *toward* me.

A second later, I caught a waft of orange blossom and coconut, and then her palm was pressing between my shoulder blades. "I can't move," I growled. "Can't take my eyes off this guy."

"I know," she said. "Four steps back."

I hesitated. I didn't like her risking her neck for me. But I got the feeling that arguing with her wasn't going to work, either. I took a deep, slow breath...and stepped backward.

The guy in front of me stepped forwards. A drop of sweat rolled down my forehead but I didn't dare lift a hand to wipe it away.

"Three more," said Lorna behind me.

I walked slowly backward. The other guy matched me, advancing as I retreated.

"There's a step up, a foot behind you," Lorna told me. "About four inches high."

I lifted my foot and felt for it. If I tripped now, it was all over. But it was right where she'd said it would be. And now I was next to the open door. I saw the guy's eyes narrow.

Lorna's hands gripped my shoulders, her fingers cool through my shirt. She guided me as I edged in, keeping my gun on the guy until the very last second—

I slammed the door and locked it, then raced with her through the workshop. There was a window, just like she'd said, high up on the opposite wall. Without asking permission, I grabbed her by the waist and lifted her. She opened the window and slithered through. I grabbed the kid and passed him up and as soon as he'd scrambled through, I jumped and hauled myself up, grunting and cursing as I squeezed my shoulders through the tight gap.

We emerged on a street. I grabbed Lorna's hand, she grabbed the kid's hand and we *ran*. This was our one chance to disappear and we couldn't afford to miss it. We turned corner after corner, losing ourselves. "Is there someplace safe you can go?" I asked her.

"The hotel," she said immediately. "The Majestic."

I nodded. I knew it and it wasn't far. "You got someone there? Husband, boyfriend?"

She didn't answer for a moment. Then she opened her mouth, but the kid got there first. "They're divorced."

"My brother will be there," Lorna said. "And my dad...if he made it back okay."

I nodded. *Her dad,* I thought as we ran. The silver-haired guy in the suit in the other car was her dad.

We rounded a corner and the hotel was right in front of us. The black SUV Lorna's dad had been riding in was parked out front, its bodywork scraped and crumpled, and the police had sealed off the street, probably worried the gunmen would try again.

I ditched the gun in a trashcan. We had to show ID to the cops just to be allowed close to the hotel. As we approached the steps that led up to the entrance, I saw Lorna's shoulders slump in relief. I turned to her. "You're gonna be alright, now. Get inside and—"

She threw herself against me, so hard and fast it took me off guard. Her arms were wrapped around my back, her face was tucked into the side of my neck and she was pressed against me all the way from chin to groin. I could feel the warm softness of her breasts against my pecs and the scent of her hair filled my nose. My cock started to swell and I flushed because I knew she'd feel it. But then all that was swept aside by something stronger.

She was trembling. She'd been so brave, through this whole thing, and now that she was safe, she was realizing how close she and her kid had come to dying. The protective need surged up inside me again. I wrapped her in my arms and crushed her to me, wanting to shield her from the whole fucking world. And...something happened.

Years ago, there was this place, deep in my chest, where *they* had lived. Jillian and Max. My whole world. They were a warm light that kept me going, even when I was far from home. When they were taken from me, that light was ripped out of me.

I'd left that place alone for four years. It was a shrine too precious to touch, a wound too painful to visit. But she was like sunlight streaming through a dusty window and lighting up a dark room, bringing that place back to life. The memories locked up there shook free, a million icy, jagged razors slicing through my body. Max getting lost at the shopping mall. Jillian cutting my hair at the kitchen table. The three of us picking strawberries. Worse were the shadow memories, the ones we'd never got a chance to make. The Star Wars toys I'd had wrapped ready for Max's birthday. The college fund that would never get used.

The pain tore at me, unbearable. But I still didn't let her go.

"Lorna!"

I looked up. Her dad was standing in the entrance of the hotel, a bandage taped to his temple.

Lorna turned, saw him, and gave a groan of relief.

I slowly released her. "Go," I said, my voice ragged. And pushed all the feelings down inside.

She unwound herself from me, those glittering gray eyes big and hesitant. Cops were hurrying down the steps toward us. "*Senorita McBride?*" one of them asked urgently.

She trailed her fingers against mine until the last possible second...and then the cops hustled her and her kid up the steps. At the top, her dad grabbed hold of both of them and pulled them into a fierce hug. He looked at me over Lorna's shoulder and gave a nod of thanks. I nodded back, finally getting myself under control.

The police hurried the three of them inside. I knew I should get out of there before the police started looking for the gringo who'd shot three guys in the middle of their city. But I just stood there like an idiot, staring at the last place I'd seen her. *McBride. Lorna McBride.*

Now I knew why I'd recognized her dad. Russ McBride was always showing up on the business news in a suit and hard hat, standing in front of a part-built skyscraper. Business isn't my thing, but he'd always seemed like a straight shooter, an architect who'd built his company up from nothing until it was worth billions.

And Lorna was his daughter. But she definitely wasn't some spoiled rich kid. She was brave as hell. She'd insisted on trying to save the driver. And she *had* saved me, guiding me back to that doorway when I'd told her to leave me behind. I...

I liked her.

I turned from the hotel and stalked away. Of course I *liked* her, she was hot as hell, with those gray eyes and that luscious, curvy body. I couldn't understand why she hid it under that loose blouse. I kept imagining how she'd look in something tight...and then I was imagining her in nothing at all, her breasts creamy and perfect, bouncing as she walked, or hanging like ripe fruit as I took her from behind. And I didn't *have* to imagine how she felt, I kept reliving the warmth of her waist against my palms, when I'd lifted her up to the window, and the soft press of her breasts against my chest when she'd hugged me.

But it felt like more than lust. There was a strength to her, a determination, that drew me in. And the way she'd protected her kid... The further I got from the hotel, the more it felt like I was marching uphill. All I wanted to do was spin on my heel and run back the other way...

I caught myself and a stab of guilt hit me right in the chest. *What the fuck is wrong with me?*

I shook my head and walked on.

Alone.

5

LORNA

IN THE HOTEL SUITE, my dad clutched me to his chest as if I was a kid again, and I didn't protest at all. I'd gone suddenly shaky, my mind replaying that moment when they'd dragged me from the car over and over, and I buried my face in the soft cotton of his shirt. I had my arm tight around Cody and Cody had *his* arms wrapped around me and his grandpa, and we just stayed in that tight, McBride hug until we all started to breathe a little slower.

"You're okay?" my dad asked when he finally let me go.

I nodded and gently touched the bandage on his temple. "You?"

"That's nothing. I'll have a little scar to impress the ladies."

Despite everything, I cracked a smile and rolled my eyes. My mom died soon after I was born and, for the first ten years of my life, my dad hadn't had anyone else. But when I was a teenager, he'd gradually started dating again, encouraged by me. Now, in his sixties with his classic good looks and Scottish accent, he'd become a silver fox and there were no end of women who wanted to bed him. He'd still never had anything serious, though. No one, he'd told me, could replace my mom.

"Lorna!" A British accent, polished and precise but ragged with sleep. I turned and saw my brother, Miles, stumbling from his room.

His usual three-piece suit had been replaced with a t-shirt and sweatpants and his Monaco tan had vanished, his skin a sickly white-green. "You all okay?"

We nodded that we were. "You look terrible," I told him.

He shook his head, then grimaced and went even paler. "I'm fine," he said through gritted teeth. "It's just a bug."

He'd come down with stomach flu that morning and had been holed up in bed all day: that's why he hadn't been with us in the SUVs. I gently squeezed his shoulder. "We're okay. Go back to bed."

Miles looked indignant: he's as stubborn as the rest of us McBrides. Then he turned even paler. "Give me a minute," he mumbled and ran for his room. We heard his bathroom door slam.

My dad watched him go, his face tight with concern. "Everything okay?" I asked, worried.

"Yeah." My dad sighed, then hugged me and Cody close again. "Just want to be sure everyone's alright."

I was about to press him on it when Paige ran in, clutching so many shopping bags that they formed thick, papery wings. Her long, dyed blonde hair was stuck to her forehead with sweat as if she'd just run five blocks. "Oh my *God!*" she panted in her California, valley-girl drawl. "I'd stopped at a bar and they had the news on. What *happened?!* Are you okay?"

"We're all okay," I told her and pulled her into a hug.

I met Paige three months ago, while I was playing with Cody in Central Park. She'd just moved to the city after breaking up with her boyfriend in LA. We hit it off, went for coffee, and that's when I found out she was a nanny.

At the time, I was working sixty-hour weeks trying to finish off plans for a new high-rise on top of being a single mom. I spent so much time running errands that I'd get behind at the office. I'd bring work home with me to try to catch up, then beat myself up for not spending time with Cody. I was barely sleeping, running on caffeine, and close to burning out. But in the eight years since Cody's dad left, I'd never considered hiring a nanny. I felt like getting help would mean I'd failed as a mom.

But Paige was different. She bonded immediately with Cody and she got on with my dad and Miles, too. She was about my age and she felt more like a friend than a nanny. She had the sort of sleek, toned body men love, with sculpted arms from doing triathlons, and she was fashionable and cool. But unlike the cool kids back in school, she didn't make me feel like a freak for being a math nerd or for not being slim and graceful. She was warm, and she built me up instead of putting me down.

So Paige moved in with us and, immediately, things were transformed. With her handling the school run and errands, I could get my work done at the office and be free in the evenings to spend time with Cody. I started actually getting some sleep and my health improved. Best of all, I'd found a friend. I'd been a shy, lonely geek in high school and I'd never really had a close female friend. I sometimes wondered why Paige had never had kids of her own, but she'd never raised the subject and I sensed I shouldn't ask.

"Tell me about the guy," my dad said. "The one who saved you."

"He was amazing," I said sincerely. "I don't think we'd be here without him."

My dad's lips curled into a smirk. "He likes you."

I balked, feeling my face heat. "*Daaad!*"

"I saw the way he looked at you, when he left," my dad said firmly.

Paige perked up and gave me a sly smile. "Oh really?" She's been trying to find me a man ever since we met.

I shook my head at both of them and tried to change the subject. "I guess the cops want to talk to us?"

My dad nodded and looked towards the door. "They want statements from all of us. I asked them to give us a minute but I'm expecting a knock at any time."

I shook my head, suddenly exhausted. "There's something I need to do, first." I took Cody through to my room and closed the door. Then I sat on the bed, put my arms around him, and just hugged him to me, burying my nose in the hair on the top of his head.

It was the first time I'd had a chance to let go and I sat there shaking as aftershocks rippled through me. *Jesus, I nearly lost him!* I clutched Cody so hard it must have been painful but he didn't complain, just hugged me back as tight as he could. *He* nearly lost *me,* I realized and smoothed my hands over his back. This wasn't like when he woke from a nightmare and I could reassure him it wasn't real. Those men had been ready to kill us, and I had no idea why.

Our breathing gradually slowed until we were just sitting quietly, holding each other. *Me and you against the world,* I thought fiercely. I'd keep him safe, whatever it took.

As my thoughts calmed, they started to circle in on something. A big, warm hunk of granite in my mind, solid and heavy enough that it had its own gravity and roughly textured in a way that made me want to stroke up against it.

JD.

While we'd been running through the streets, I hadn't been able to really register the attraction, but now...

Just the memory of that deep, Texas growl sent little earthquakes all the way to my toes. And the curving slabs of his pecs, so deliciously firm against me when he'd hugged me...the feel of his hand around mine as he pulled me into the alley, his fingers thick and strong and supremely warm...

I flushed, self-conscious. I hadn't reacted to a man in this way in years. But JD was unlike any man I'd ever met, straightforward and uncomplicated and stubbornly determined to do the right thing. The ruggedness of him, the thick black stubble and the frayed jeans and battered boots...he felt authentic. Real. And for some reason, my weird brain, which spends 99.9% of its time thinking about buildings that don't exist, locked onto that realness and wouldn't let go. I kept seeing that gorgeous, full lower lip, imagining those blue eyes scowling down at me as he came in for the kiss....

My dad's words echoed in my head. *He likes you.*

Stupid. Men went for slender little things like Paige, not women like me. I pretty much decided in college that I wasn't destined for romance. Then I met Adrian and, for two glorious years, I felt attractive. *Wanted.*

And then, not long after Cody was born, I found out it was all a lie. And my self-confidence dropped like an elevator with its cables cut, thundering right down to the basement. Now, closer to forty than thirty, with a son and the stretch marks to prove it, the idea that a guy like JD would be interested in me was crazy. Right?

I thought of those prairie-sky eyes gazing down at me, baking me with their heat. And that look of protective fury that had made me feel so safe.

It's irrelevant, I told myself. JD was gone, back to his own life, wherever that was. And I'd never see him again.

6

JD

One Week Later

I WOKE up with her thighs wrapped around me and the hard bud of her nipple against my tongue. But the *beep beep beep* of the alarm was destroying her, turning her to smoke under my hands. I buried my fingers in that soft black hair just as it disappeared.

I opened my eyes and I was alone in my bed. *Goddammit.* Third night in a row.

Lorna McBride had taken up permanent residence in my dreams.

I threw back the covers, twisted around to get up, and—

Fuck! My whole lower back exploded in pain. Every nerve was suddenly a piano wire stretched horribly tight, and someone had thrown a heavy wrench into the whole damn cat's cradle, sending each nerve spasming as it bounced its way down my body. All I could do was lie there panting and grimacing, waiting for it to be over.

Ten years ago, there was a mortar attack on a base I was stationed at Helmand in Afghanistan. I woke in the middle of the night to hear sirens blaring, people screaming and a fire raging. I ran to where a building had collapsed, grabbed hold of a metal beam that was pinning a young soldier to the ground, lifted—

And that was it. After years of dodging bullets and explosions and getting in more fights than I can count, the thing that finally injured me was lifting in the wrong way. I wrenched something in my back and now, every morning, it spasms. Sometimes a little, sometimes a lot. I never sought help for it, afraid they'd move me to a desk job.

When I could finally move again, I got into the shower and turned it on cold. As the freezing water pounded my shoulders, I finally managed to drive thoughts of those soft, pale breasts and luscious thighs from my mind. But something way more dangerous took their place. I started thinking about those big gray eyes, soft and vulnerable but turning harder than diamonds when someone threatened her kid. Something in my chest *lifted*.

Then a wave of guilt crushed it back down. I scowled, furious with myself. It had been a week. I should have forgotten her by now.

I made the bed, tucking the sheets army style until you could have bounced a quarter off them. Then I threw a denim jacket over my plaid shirt because it was cold on a morning, up here in the mountains, and headed out.

Outside, it was weirdly quiet. When the team had first arrived in the little Colorado town of Mount Mercy, some eight months ago, Kian, our boss, had rented us all apartments in this building until we found places of our own. We used to all meet outside each morning and walk to our base—*The Factory*—together. But one by one, all the other guys had moved into places of their own, with their girlfriends. Even Colton, the only other one of the guys who was still single, had moved into a trailer in the woods along with his bear cub. I was the only one still left in the apartment block: I'd started paying rent to Kian because I didn't want to freeload. I knew I should just find a place of my own, but...

That would be making a fresh start. Abandoning them forever.

I grabbed a large coffee and a breakfast sandwich from the cafe on Main Street, together with a box of pastries for the team. By the time I'd walked up into the hills to The Factory, I'd finished the sandwich, the coffee had woken me up and I felt more like myself.

When we found it, The Factory was derelict, with missing

windows and pigeons roosting on the rafters. But after months of work, we'd just about gotten it into shape. As I walked in, my sister Erin was hanging from a pipe overhead, her legs wrapped around it as she secured a bundle of wires with a cable tie. She was an electronics expert and was gradually rewiring the whole place. "Okay, done!" she announced, and let go with her legs so that she dangled by her arms.

Danny, my best buddy, reached up and grabbed her waist. "Got ya," he told her in that rough, London accent. And Erin let go and dropped into his arms. I watched as they kissed slow and deep, eyes closed and big, dumb smiles on both their faces and I felt my mood lift. It was difficult to be down, around these two.

I hadn't been too sure about the relationship at first. Erin's a lot younger than me and I helped to raise her. Danny's always been the cocky charmer, with a different woman in his bed every night. I was sure he'd break Erin's heart. But I hadn't figured on him falling in love with her, maybe the first time he'd ever really *been* in love.

As I watched, Danny carried Erin over to the next section of pipe and lifted her so she could grab it. When I saw the way he looked up at her, watchful and protective and utterly adoring...I knew I didn't need to worry.

At the back of the room, Colton, our hand-to-hand combat specialist, was bouncing around in our new boxing ring, beaming like a kid on an inflatable castle. He'd been wanting a ring ever since we moved in and it had finally arrived late last night. Now, we weren't going to be able to get him out of it.

Cal, our sniper, was climbing wearily from the ring, panting and sweating. Cal's a hell of a big guy, close to seven feet tall, but he had the look of a man who'd just had his ass handed to him.

Colton whacked his gloves together enthusiastically. "Come on, who's next?"

I looked around. Danny was busy with Erin and the others didn't seem to be in yet. *Ah hell.* But I couldn't refuse Colton. He's a big, bearded, intimidating guy who could pass for an outlaw biker, but he's sweet-natured and he's utterly loyal to the team. He was so happy to finally have his boxing ring, I didn't want to spoil it. And it'd been a while since I'd sparred: it'd do me good.

I put down the box of pastries and pulled on some gloves and a sparring helmet. "Go easy on an old man," I muttered as I climbed through the ropes. I was only half joking. At forty-one, I'm easily the oldest guy on the team.

"No problem, boss," said Colton, tapping gloves with me. He dropped into a fighting stance and began to circle me. As always, he was wearing a band tour t-shirt, the edges frayed where the sleeves had been torn off, and his hulking shoulders bulged. Cal was the tallest but Colton was the biggest, a walking wall of lean, hard muscle, and when you squared off against him like this, it was like facing a gorilla. He shuffled towards me, keeping his weight low: he used to wrestle, and you could tell.

At first, I managed to hold my own, throwing fast, hard punches that kept Colton at bay. But the guy was relentless, forcing me to keep moving, making me do all the work, and if I let him get within reach I'd wind up slammed down on the canvas like one of the criminals he bounty-hunted. I tried pushing forward and got in one good hit, but then he ducked under my fists and came at me with a flurry of punches. I stepped back, careful of my footing—

And suddenly, I was back in Mexico, Lorna's soft hand between my shoulder blades, guiding me backward. She'd come back for me, despite me telling her to go—

I dropped my hands just as Colton swung at me. The punch that should have bounced harmlessly off my gloves smacked me right in the jaw and I went backward like a felled tree. There was a glorious few seconds of freefall and then my back smacked into the canvas, knocking Lorna from my mind and all the air right out of me.

"Aw, shit." Colton's Missouri accent came from somewhere above me. "Sorry boss, I thought you'd block that."

I wasn't capable of speech, so I just lifted one gloved hand in response. *It's okay.* It was my own damn fault. I'd dropped my guard because she was in my head. *Goddammit!*

I lay there fuming for a few seconds. Then a wet, rough tongue nuzzled my ear. Atlas, Colton's bear cub, had stuck his head through the ropes and was licking me. It tickled and I chuckled, letting go of the anger. But I knew I had to do something. I couldn't forget this woman and it was messing me up.

At that moment, my phone rang. Colton reached down and hauled me to my feet, I used my teeth to unfasten one glove and then the other and I just managed to get my phone out and answer before it stopped ringing. "Yeah?" I asked, still a little groggy.

"JD Taggert. You're a hard man to find." The voice was male and Scottish, and I'd heard it before.

I scrunched up my forehead in confusion. "Mr. McBride?!"

"I wanted to thank you for what you did," said Russ.

I shook my head, even though he couldn't see it. "It was nothing, sir." My face went hot. I'd called him *sir*, like I was a teenager arriving to take his daughter to prom. "How'd you get this number? How'd you even know my last name?"

"My grandson saw your passport when you showed it to the cops outside the hotel," Russ told me proudly. "Sharp lad. He told me about everything you did. I've made some friends in Washington over the years and they helped me track you down." I could hear him smirking. "Turns out, you and your team are getting a reputation."

I grimaced, remembering the trips to DC after our first mission in Ecuador, senators grilling us while my necktie did its best to strangle me. Then after Berlin, there'd been more questions. Some of the politicians hated us. Some loved us. But it sounded like at least Russ McBride was on our side. "Thank you, sir," I mumbled. *Dammit, I did it again.* I glanced around the room, worried: I hadn't told anyone what happened on my vacation and I didn't want a bunch of questions about Lorna. Luckily, the others had discovered the box of pastries and were crowded around it.

"I want to thank you properly," Russ told me. "There's an event coming up in a couple of days, in New York. It's the opening of a marina we built. I'd love to have you as a guest."

"That's real kind," I told him. "But—"

"My daughter will be there."

I froze, my mind racing. This whole thing was just a dumb crush, I told myself. I'd met Lorna once, while we were both amped up on adrenaline. Since then I'd built her up and up in my mind until she was some curvy goddess. That's why I couldn't forget her. That's why I thought I liked her, in a way that made me ache with guilt.

I needed to meet her again, calm and peaceful. Then I'd realize that this was just lust, plain and simple. I'd be able to forget her and life could go back to normal.

"I'll be there," I told Russ.

7

LORNA

IT WAS A PERFECT DAY. The sky was a rich, clear blue and the sun was warm, for April, warm enough that the women had shown up in gauzy shift dresses and the men were slipping off the jackets of their tailored suits. There was just a sigh of breeze, enough to make the calm surface of the Hudson shatter into tiny, dancing jewels and the scarlet ribbon that hung across the marina's doors dance and swing. Waiters circulated with trays of champagne flutes and pretty little canapés. A string quartet was playing. It was New York high society at its finest.

And then there was me. I sure as hell couldn't pull off a shift dress with my curves so I'd gone for a white maxi dress patterned with big blue flowers. I stood there feeling awkward and huge, an ostrich in a flock of flamingos.

It wasn't just that the other women were slim. They were eye-catching and *glamorous*. They air-kissed each other and took selfies as they basked in the attention the men were giving them. Sure, they were younger than me, most of them mid-twenties, even the ones with forty-year-old husbands. But that wasn't it: Paige was a few years older than me and she was having the time of her life, giggling and flirting effortlessly as man after man asked for her number.

The problem was me: I'd forgotten how to be anything but a mom. The idea of some guy wanting to flirt with me felt ridiculous.

Except for one guy. JD made the New York men in their suits feel flimsy and insubstantial, cut-outs from the pages of a glossy magazine. He'd become the star of all my nighttime fantasies, my ass grinding in circles against the sheets as I guiltily rubbed myself, imagining his muscled hips spreading my legs wide.

I flushed and buried the thought, turning so that the breeze from the river cooled my face. Then I glanced around nervously at the crowd. Everyone was in clusters, their backs turned to me. How was I supposed to break in?

I've never been good with people. My dad's the master of small talk: he can weave these elegant, beautiful threads that pull people together and gently turn the conversation the way he wants it to go. I stand there unable to say anything, afraid I'm going to get tangled.

When Miles was born, he was exactly what my folks expected: a little version of my dad, complete with a winning smile and non-stop chatter. Then, a few years later, I came along and I couldn't have been more different: when our extended family gathered for the holidays, Miles would toddle around and charm everyone while I sat in the corner and stared uncertainly. At daycare, where Miles had made friends on his very first day, I just sat there picking up toys and examining them, slowly turning the wheels of cars and piling up sand in the sandpit. When I showed an interest in the dollhouse, everyone got very excited, but the staff couldn't persuade me to give the dolls names or act out scenes with them. I just kept staring at the house and its walls and floors.

My mom died days after I was born so my dad had to raise me on his own. He tried his best to find a way to bring me out of myself but it was like we were from different planets. He was a born communicator: he'd started out as an architect but he'd built McBride Construction by talking to people and doing deals. My mom had been a rising star in state politics who people were tipping for the US Senate. How could their daughter have turned out so shy? I felt like an utter disappointment. I used to cry myself to sleep at night wondering why I wasn't more like my brother.

Then, one Christmas when Miles was nine and I was six, my dad took us to a huge toy store to choose Christmas gifts. Miles wanted a magician's set but I had no idea what I wanted. We wandered the aisles together until we came to an area where kids sat at tables playing with...what *were* those things? Like brightly-colored little blocks except, when you pressed them together, they *stuck*.

I vividly remember letting go of my dad's hand, something I'd never normally do in a huge, scary store, and walking forward, entranced. For once, I wasn't intimidated by all the other kids. I just sat down at one of the little tables and picked up two Lego bricks. I tried pushing one into the other. There was a satisfying *click* and a light went on in my brain.

I'd always felt lost when I was trying to communicate. I hadn't inherited my mom and dad's people skills and that made me feel nervous and clam up, and that meant I didn't get much practice talking to people and *that* meant I got even shyer, a vicious circle. But for the first time in my life, I realized that there was something I *was* confident in. It had to do with the way the wheels turned on the toy cars in daycare, the way the walls of the dollhouse supported the floor, and the way sand in the sandpit collapsed if you put too much weight on it. My brain understood those things but it hadn't had a way to use that knowledge. Until now.

I put one block on top of another, going diagonally to make a triangular base because *triangles are strong*. No one had taught me that, it just made sense. I clicked in another block. And another. I could feel my brain spinning up to full speed, unleashed at last. Later, as an adult, I'd come to have problems getting it to slow down and stop. But that first time was glorious, like running for the first time.

Some adult was speaking to my dad. Normally, just the presence of another person would be enough to make me freeze but I didn't even look up. I was *busy*. "Oh!" the guy said. "She looks a little young to be, uh...we have bigger, chunkier blocks, with faces and stuff on, for younger kids..."

"Let her play with these," my dad told him firmly.

The tower was up to my chest, now, and growing. I built it narrower as it went higher, because otherwise, it would tip over. I couldn't explain how I knew. I just knew.

"The bigger ones are really more suitable for her age," said the toy store clerk. "They have googly eyes and—"

"*Let her play with these,*" my dad told him, his voice choking with emotion. I had to lean sideways to smile at him, because the tower was up past my head, now.

That's when my dad realized that, for better or worse, his skills had been split between his two children. Miles had gotten all of his charisma and social skills. And I'd gotten all of his engineer's instincts. Finally, he could understand me.

He nurtured me, gradually introducing me to the math I'd need to turn the ideas in my head into reality. I excelled in science while Miles excelled in English and drama. When we were teenagers, he was likable and confident, with an army of friends and female admirers. My body blossomed and I was suddenly all boobs and ass. Without a mom to talk to about it, I just felt huge and awkward, and hid myself away. That meant I didn't make friends, and that just made the shyness worse.

Miles wanted to follow in my dad's footsteps just as much as I did and we complemented each other perfectly. By the time we went to college, our paths were clear: Miles would one day take over running the company while I quietly designed the buildings.

Thirty years on and Miles had become my dad's right-hand man, handling bigger and bigger deals every day and ready to take over in another ten years or so, if my dad could ever be persuaded to retire.

And me? I'd designed apartment blocks, a retail complex, a hospital, and the new airport terminal down in Mexico. Then there was this marina: we'd redeveloped the whole site, creating an entertainment complex and arts center right by the water. And just behind it, Hudson Tower was under construction. Sixty floors of housing wrapped in snow-white stone and shimmering green glass, a sort of sequel to the skyscraper my dad designed and built twenty years before, the McBride Building, where we all now lived. I was one of the company's top architects...but I still wasn't much better with people.

I turned as Cody approached. Over the last few years, most of his friends had shot upward but his growth spurt hadn't kicked in yet and he was the smallest in his class. He wasn't letting it hold him back, though: he was the star of the school's swim team, tearing through the water for length after punishing length. He'd definitely inherited my weird brain: he was a natural at math and physics—but thankfully, in him, it had been balanced by a good dose of social skills. And he was a good kid: last week, he'd spent his Sunday visiting a classmate who was in the hospital with heart problems, taking him a care package of candy, books, and games and spending the whole afternoon with him.

A big swell of mom pride filled my chest but underneath it was the usual flutter of worry, the ever-present feeling of *Am I doing this right?* There was no one to back me up, no one to ask questions. My mom was gone and Paige was great but she was a nanny, not a parent. And soon it would get harder. Cody would start falling in love and dating and then having sex... If he was a girl, I could teach him about the dangers of men, but how did I make sure Cody turned into one of the good ones?

I sighed and looked off into the crowd. And that's when I saw JD, marching determinedly towards us.

My brain struggled to process the image because it couldn't be, not *him,* not *here.* But there was no mistaking that jaw line with its dark stubble, or the way he walked, slow and absolutely certain, unstoppable as an advancing tank.

The image of him flashed from my eyes to my brain and triggered a highlight reel of all my memories of that day in Mexico. The sharp tang of tequila in my nostrils as he smashed the bottle over the kidnapper's head. The protective growl in his voice when he'd told me he was going to get me *the hell out of here.* The amazing solidness against my chest when I hugged him outside our hotel and the cold void when I'd had to let him go. My eyes went to those big, calloused hands and my chest went tight. I was remembering his hand squeezing mine and Cody's, that feeling of not being alone.

My dad sauntered up to stand beside me. "What's *he* doing here?" I croaked, my eyes still locked on JD.

I could hear the smile in my dad's voice as he followed my gaze. "I might have invited him."

I turned to stare at him, my eyes saying what my voice couldn't. *Daaad!*

He grinned and turned to watch JD approach. I turned too and *Oh God* he was really here and close, now. People were shuffling out of his way, the men blinking at his battered boots and faded blue jeans, the women ogling the jutting curves of his pecs beneath his white shirt. In his cream Stetson and mirrored aviator sunglasses, he was the only person who looked more out of place than me. But he didn't seem at all self-conscious. In fact, he didn't seem to register the crowd at all. He stared straight ahead, utterly focused on his target.

I saw a flash of white fabric and blue flowers in his sunglasses.

He was focused on *me.*

The shock earthquaked through me, turning to heat when it reached my skin. No one had ever looked at me like that. It felt insane and wonderful.

I drew in a slow breath, trying to be cool. But then he arrived in front of me, his broad shoulders filling my vision, and the raw presence of him set off a five-reel jackpot in my head. All the secret fantasies I'd had in the week since Mexico clattered out into my mind. JD between my thighs, that hard ass rising and falling as he fucked me with fast, hard strokes. Me riding him, his big hands squeezing my breasts just the right sort of roughly. Me on my knees, ass in the air, and cheek pressed to the pillow as he drove into me from behind. I swallowed and stared up at him. It felt like the fantasies were being projected right onto my beet-red face: he'd see every naked inch of us.

In slow motion, I saw his hand lift away his aviator sunglasses. Then I was looking right into those amazing prairie-sky eyes and they were narrowing, crinkling at the corners: oh God, he knew *exactly* what I was thinking. Surprise flickered over his face. Then lust.

I swallowed and crushed my thighs together *hard*. There was something about him I reacted to, that solidness, that rough *realness*. My mind is always spinning, running numbers and figuring out weights and balance. But JD just stopped it dead. I could feel myself getting wet. *God, what's happening to me?*

But it wasn't just me. JD took a half-step forward as if pulled: he was as out of control as I was, and he seemed to be all *about* control. He loomed closer, towering over me, and I caught my breath. Then he seemed to catch himself and he shuffled back a half inch and tipped the brim of his Stetson to me. "Ma'am."

I just stared up at him, overcome. I'd never had that effect on anyone, including my ex-husband. And the tip of the hat: it was sweetly old-fashioned and charming, especially coming right after that flash of raw lust.

JD turned to my dad. "Mr. McBride," he said respectfully. "Thanks for inviting me."

My dad gave him a warm, double-handed handshake. "Russ," he insisted. "Glad you could make it."

Miles was suddenly beside me and he shook JD's hand, too. "Miles," he told JD. "Lorna's brother. Thank you for keeping her safe." He sounded happy and genuine but I could see how pale his skin was, and he kept his black Ray-Bans on as if the sunlight was painful.

JD turned to Cody. "And how are you doing?" They started talking, Cody full of stories about the flight home from Mexico and the swim meet he'd been to the day before. A lot of adults are awkward around kids, either patronizing or stand-offish. But JD was easy and natural.

Paige stepped forward and introduced herself. Then, as JD turned back to my dad, she caught my eye, mouthed *OMG*, and fanned herself.

"I can't thank you enough for what you did for Lorna and Cody," said my dad. "Look, I've got to go smile for photos while the mayor cuts the ribbon. But as soon as this thing's over, I was going to sail the family out around the bay: my yacht's moored right here. Will you join us? There'll be cold beer and proper food: none of this canapé crap."

JD rubbed at his stubble and looked as if he was trying to come up with a polite excuse for why he couldn't. Then he glanced at me for a second, looked back to my dad, and said, "Thanks. I'd like that."

A silvery ribbon of excitement spiraled up through my chest. *Stop it,* I told myself. God, I was like a teenager around him. I shuffled my feet. I had no idea what to say: it had been years since a guy had shown an interest in me and I'd been awkward even back then.

My dad led the way towards the marina entrance, where the press were waiting. JD fell into step next to me and the looming presence of him there was thrilling. I kept glancing sideways at him, and then *he* glanced at *me* and caught my eye, and his lips twitched into a smile, and I flushed and looked away.

"Oh, just so you know," said my dad, not looking back, "you may need to say a few words."

I stopped in my tracks. "*What?* Don't joke!"

My dad slowed and glanced back. "I'm not joking. Everyone's asking about the architect. So when the mayor sees you, he'll probably want you to make a little speech."

"No!" I could feel my chest going tight. Public speaking is my worst fear. I'm shy just talking to one stranger and there were hundreds of people here. "No, no way!"

"You'll do great, mom," said Cody, ever-loyal.

I bobbed my head in thanks but then shook my head: *no way.* And then, before I realized what I was doing, I glanced at JD for support.

He was looking around at the marina. Then he looked at me, his blue eyes wide with amazement, and he cocked his head to one side. "You designed all this?"

There was none of the skepticism I get from some men. He wasn't shocked and disbelieving because I was a woman, or a mom. He just sounded genuinely impressed and I wasn't prepared for the warm glow that triggered. I nodded. Then, to my dad, "Hard no on the speech, dad."

He sighed. "You two had better stay back here, then, so the mayor doesn't see you. C'mon, Cody." He, Cody, and Paige headed off toward the press. I let out a long sigh of relief, glad that I'd escaped.

Then I glanced across at JD and realization hit. I stared at my dad's retreating back, and mumbled under my breath, "Oh, you sneaky son of a—"

My dad had played me. There'd never been any danger of the mayor asking me to make a speech. My dad had said it so I'd stay here, alone with JD. This was his idea of matchmaking.

We stood there in silence. I stared at my feet, letting my hair fall forward to hide my face. I was thinking furiously. I'd been in mom mode since my ex left, almost nine years ago. *How do you flirt?*

Then a waiter came over and offered JD a tray of miniature cheese soufflés, each one the size of a dime, the tops drizzled with redcurrant jus. JD stared at the tray, bemused, then shook his head politely.

"This isn't exactly your kind of place, is it?" I blurted.

"Is it that obvious?" He glanced down at his jeans and then around at the other men. "Didn't realize everyone'd be all dressed up." His voice was warm with humor: he could laugh at himself and I loved that. If my ex had felt out of place at a party, he'd have been sour and snappy (because somehow it would have been my fault) and we'd have left after ten minutes. I felt myself relax just a little. My eyes flicked between his wide shoulders and the melon-like biceps that stretched out the sleeves of his white shirt and black denim jacket. "You look great just as you are," I said with feeling.

His gaze swept down my body. When he looked at my face again, his eyes were narrowed with lust. "So do you."

I glanced down at myself and I saw what I always saw: there was too much of me, soft curves where there should have been sleek, trim tightness. If I'd been the architect designing my body, I would have screwed up the sketch and started again. I did an awkward little half-shrug and opened my mouth to brush the compliment away.

But when I looked up, I was looking right into his eyes. And what I saw there was *don't you dare*. I faltered, trying to find a way to push through, but the certainty in his eyes was like warm rock and I finally broke and melted against it, flushing. Deep in my soul, the delicate, silvery threads that my ex had stamped into a dirty clump started to uncurl and shine. And that gave me just enough confidence to keep talking.

"It's not really my kind of scene, either," I told him. I nodded toward my dad, who was just about to start his speech. "Parties and speeches and stuff...that's his thing. I'm an architect. I'm usually behind a drawing board or a computer. I'm not good with people."

JD nodded slowly, staring right into my eyes like he wanted to soak up everything there was to know about me. As if he didn't mind me being shy. Liked it, even. I looked away, embarrassed, breaking the spell.

"Your brother looks pretty comfortable," said JD. Miles was standing at my dad's side, grinning from behind his Ray-Bans, and I counted four women who were all looking up at him adoringly. "How come he's got a British accent?"

"Our mom died a few days after I was born," I told him. "My dad was trying to raise two kids and run the company. As soon as Miles was old enough, my dad sent him off to boarding school in England. I went to school over here." It had always been a sore point for Miles: he'd hated boarding school and he resented that I'd gotten so much more time with my dad. He said it was because I was Dad's favorite, which was crazy: Miles was the one my dad was grooming to take over the company. My dad hadn't sent me to boarding school because I was a shy mess who would have imploded there. But I'd never managed to convince Miles of that.

The speech started and we fell silent along with the rest of the crowd. As JD turned to face front, he moved just a little closer and butterflies took flight in my chest. There was something giddily exciting about the hard bulk of him. I wanted to wind around that solidness like ivy.

All through the speech, I kept risking little glances at him. And then, halfway through, I looked across and found *him* looking at *me*. He took a slow breath as he realized he'd been caught. But he didn't look away. Those beautiful, prairie-sky eyes narrowed, urgent and a little hazy. Like I made him crazy.

I'd never made a man crazy before. I turned quickly back to front, breathing fast. I didn't dare look again. But I could feel JD watching me, could feel something building and building in the air between us.

As the applause died away, I slowly turned and found him still staring down at me. He was frowning, as if fighting with himself. Then the words just spilled out. "After Mexico," he said, "I went home to Colorado, figured I'd never see you again." He looked away and rasped his fingers across his stubble. "Didn't like that."

The confession was awkward, halting, as if... *He hasn't done this in a long time, either,* I realized. That made no sense: a guy as gorgeous as him? "Me neither," I blurted.

He moved a half step closer, like he was drawn, like he couldn't quite control himself. The breath caught in my chest. *Say something!* "I'm glad you came. It means a lot to my dad, to be able to thank you."

He cocked his head to the side and pinned me with a look. "That ain't why I came."

I felt as though a thousand watt spotlight had just lit me up. I flushed and shuffled. "I'm nothing special," I mumbled.

JD scowled. "What asshole told you *that?*"

I blinked, speechless.

He stared down at me. I could see him fighting with himself again: he wasn't used to talking this way, wasn't comfortable with it. But he was stubbornly determined to set me straight. "You might just be the most special thing I ever saw," he said in a rush.

I gulped. I felt like my feet were lifting off the ground. I groped for words and couldn't find any.

The wind from the Hudson chose that moment to shift and blow my hair across my face. Thick locks were plastered right across my eyes and mouth and, for a second, I couldn't see at all. I spluttered and clawed blindly at them—

Suddenly, big, warm fingers brushed my chin. As my vision cleared, I saw JD had stepped right up to me and was gently but firmly pushing my hair back and holding it out of the way. I'll never forget the look in his eyes: he was *mad,* like he was giving nature itself a stern dressing down. *No. Stop that. I'm looking at her, dammit.*

He kept his hand there as the wind died away, the edge of his thumb against my cheek. Waves of excitement were rippling out from my core, breaking like waves when they hit my skin. I knew I was probably blushing but, for once, I didn't care. I was locked onto those soulful blue eyes, just falling upwards into them. There was so much experience there, like he'd traveled everywhere, done everything, seen things he'd always remember and some he wished he could forget. And that authority, that *certainty* that made me feel so safe.

He gazed down at me and God, the *need* in his eyes... His hand tensed and his whole palm kissed my cheek. It felt so good, so *right,* that it took everything I had not to nestle into it.

Then his eyes narrowed and I caught a glimpse of that terrible pain. His hand dropped from my face. For a second, the delicious, comforting warmth of him lingered on my cheek...then it shrank down to nothing and disappeared. I followed his hand as it swung down to his side and saw something I'd missed before. A line around his ring finger where the skin had been worn smooth.

He'd been married, once. Is that what left him in so much pain? Had some woman broken his heart the way my ex had broken mine?

And then my dad emerged from the crowd and looked curiously between us. "You two getting along?"

8

JD

I TURNED to Russ McBride and tried to make my face like rock.

Like I hadn't spent the whole speech thinking about his daughter's soft, pale breasts.

Like I hadn't fallen into those big gray eyes and blurted out a whole bunch of stuff that had shocked me...because it was true.

Like I hadn't been seconds from doing something crazy when the guilt had suddenly caught up with me and made me pull back.

"Yeah," I told Russ. "Yeah, we're doing good."

I'm good at hiding my feelings. I've had a lot of practice since I rejoined the world to lead Stormfinch. But I was no match for Russ. He was a pro at reading people *and* he was her father. He smirked and I felt myself flush.

Russ grinned and slapped me on the shoulder. "Alright, then. Let's get out on the water." He turned to Paige and Cody. "Sure you don't want to come?"

Cody shook his head. "Nah, you know I get seasick, gramps."

"I'll take him home," Paige told Lorna. "You go have fun." I didn't miss the look she threw my way.

"Miles?" asked Russ.

Miles pushed his sunglasses up his nose. "Next time. I'm still a bit fragile from the stomach bug."

Russ studied his son for a moment, looking worried, then nodded. "More food for us. Let's go!"

He put his hand on my shoulder and steered me towards the dock, Lorna falling in behind us. I could feel her eyes on the back of my head. She'd be wondering why I pulled away. What the hell was I going to say to her? That now I'd seen her again, this didn't feel like just a dumb crush? That she looked goddamn amazing in that dress, with the vee neckline revealing the upper slopes of those magnificent breasts? That I found her shyness utterly adorable, and it made me feel even more protective?

What's going on? She'd blindsided me, that's what it was. My defenses were down. I'd always figured that if I was going to be attracted to someone again, it would be an outdoorsy, horse-riding, Texas girl like Jillian. Not a shy, curvy New Yorker. The two were different in every way. Except...

Except she was brave, like Jillian. And caring. And the way she protected her son...

The feelings rose again...and with them, the guilt, crashing through me in heavy waves.

We'd only taken three steps when Russ's phone rang. He listened, then sighed. "No, don't call a tow truck, that'll take forever. We'll deal with it." He turned to Lorna and me. "We've got to go on a mercy mission before we go sailing," he told us. "Could do with your muscles, big fella."

I nodded, curious. Russ led us around the edge of the marina. Directly behind it was a huge construction site. "This is another of our projects," he told me. "Hudson Tower." He nodded at Lorna and beamed with fatherly pride, while Lorna flushed. "My daughter designed it. Her first full-on skyscraper. Sort of...passing the baton, you know?"

I craned my head back and looked up at the skeletal skyscraper. Even without its internal walls or windows, it was utterly awe-inspiring, towering over the other buildings. I shook my head in wonder. And it had been designed by this shy, awkward woman standing beside me. Her mind just worked in a whole different way, one I'd never understand: she lived *up there,* somewhere, in the clouds her building seemed to touch, imagining buildings out of thin air, while people like me stomped around on the ground. I shook my head slowly, genuinely amazed. And fascinated. And just a little sad.

Because what could someone whose mind was *up there* want with a big, dumb lunk like me?

"The parking lot at the marina was full," Russ told us, "so I told the string quartet they could park here. But..." He pointed and I followed his finger.

Around the base of the building, the ground had been churned into mud by all the heavy machinery. And stuck hub-cap deep in the mud, spinning its wheels, was an old Volvo station wagon, crammed full of instruments and four worried-looking musicians. The driver, a tiny woman with glasses, was bouncing up and down in her seat, trying to coax the car free, but the wheels just dug deeper and deeper trenches.

Russ chuckled. "This is why people in our business drive 4x4s," he told me, nodding to where a couple of mud-covered off-roaders sat parked. He turned to Lorna and nodded at her wedges. "You stay here, you'll ruin your shoes. Come on, JD." And he marched off towards the stranded car, his shoes squelching in the mud.

For a second, I just stood there, staring. The man was a CEO, his company was worth billions, and he was going to push them out of the mud *himself?* I jogged after him. "Aren't you going to mess up *your* shoes?" I asked. "And your suit?" The cuffs of his pants were already getting coated in mud.

"*Ha!*" He stamped his foot down, happy as a child. "These things cost me a fortune and they go out of fashion before they wear out. About time one of them got dirty."

I decided I liked Russ McBride. He reminded me of my dad, the sort of guy who did his deals with a handshake. The two of us got behind the Volvo, planted our hands on the back of it and prepared to push. "Give it a little gas," Russ told the driver.

The woman behind the wheel touched the gas. We heaved, but the wheels just spun, painting our ankles with mud.

"Again," said Russ. The two of us grunted and pushed for a full minute, but the car wouldn't climb out of the ruts it had dug.

Then we heard a squelching. We looked up to see Lorna marching through the mud towards us, barefoot, the hem of her dress lifted and bunched in one hand. "Make a space," she told us. "And turn around, we need to push *and* lift."

Russ and I made room between us and all three of us lined up, backs to the car, our hands hooked under the rear fender. I followed Lorna's legs down to her bare calves and my eyes locked on the creamy, naked skin. *What's wrong with me?* I finally managed to drag my eyes off her...and looked up to see Russ watching me knowingly. I looked guiltily away.

"On three," said Lorna. "One, two, *three.*"

We dug our heels into the mud, lifted and pushed. The wheels spun, spun...and then found grip. The car surged away, and suddenly, we had nothing to lean against. Russ and I went staggering backwards and just managed to stay on our feet. But Lorna's bare feet were stuck in the mud and she fell—

I twisted and grabbed her just before she hit the ground. The two of us froze there, face to face and bent low, like I'd just dipped her in the middle of a dance. With each breath she took, her breasts brushed my chest. I was lost in the scent of her, the softness of her...

I snapped out of it and slowly hauled her upright, then forced myself to let her go. She gave me a shaky nod of thanks.

Russ caught my eye again, looking amused. "Come on," he said. "We all deserve a beer."

It felt like I'd passed a test. And I wasn't ready for how good that felt.

We trooped back to the construction site's entrance, where the string quartet had stopped to thank us. Lorna picked up her shoes but left them off, saying she'd wash her feet on the boat. I loved that she didn't mind getting dirty: she might be rich, but she was no spoiled princess.

Russ led us down to the dock and over to his boat. I'd been expecting some big, white motor yacht, with leather couches and a hot tub. But it was a sleek, fifty-foot sailboat, built for speed, not showing off. Russ went aboard and started messing with ropes and sails, while we fetched a couple of coolers of food and beer from the marina. I glanced up at the half-finished Hudson Tower again...and stopped. Up close, it had looked huge and impressive. But now we were further away, I could see it as part of the skyline and that brought it to a whole new level. This thing was going to be part of New York culture: in every movie, on every tourist photo. "Wow," I mumbled, stunned. I shook my head. "How do you even..." I trailed off, unable to put it into words, and just gestured at the building.

Lorna ducked her head, letting her hair fall over her face, and shrugged. "Only thing I've ever been any good at. My brain just works that way: loads and pressures and centers of gravity, that all makes sense. Normal stuff, like being good with people...not so much."

I stared at her, my chest aching. She had this amazing ability, this *gift,* but she was so shy, she just wanted to hide away in a corner. Part of me wanted to tug her out into the light, so everyone could see how incredible she was. The other part of me just wanted to hug her tight and keep her safe.

"It's amazing," I told her. But I forgot to look at the tower when I said it.

She flushed. "Building it almost broke us," she said. "The company's leveraged up to the hilt. But if we can get through the next few months, we'll be okay."

The sun was getting warmer so I stripped off my jacket and hung it over one the coolers, then picked the whole thing up. Lorna took the other cooler and we headed towards the boat. "You're military," said Lorna. "Or you *were* military, right?"

I nodded. "Army." I never say *Delta* unless there's a call for it. "Now I'm with this private military group, up in Colorado, doing security and stuff." I smiled, thinking about the team. "Basically, I lead a bunch of reprobates."

"Is there a reason you got out?" asked Lorna gently. And I saw her eyes flick down, just for a second, to my left hand.

Aw, hell. She'd seen the mark where my ring used to be. That question about the military had been a snowball, tossed onto a roof. She was hoping it would roll down, gathering up all my background. *Was I divorced? Did I have kids?*

What happened to your family?

The guilt caught up to me again, hitting me like a freight train. What was I *doing?*

I liked her. I'd only met her a few times but I already liked her more than any woman I'd met since Jillian, even though the two of them were so completely different. And even through all the shyness, I could tell she liked me. I could feel the warmth of her, close enough to touch, and there was an echoing, cold emptiness inside me that craved her. That craved not being alone.

But I was *meant* to be alone. Jillian and Max were my shot and I lost them. *That's what forever means.*

When I didn't answer, Lorna shook her head. "I'm sorry. I didn't mean to—I'm lousy at this stuff." And she hurried on ahead.

Dammit. Now she thought she'd said something wrong. I couldn't be with her but I needed her to know it was nothing to do with her. She was almost at the boat. This was going to be hard enough without doing it in front of her dad. "Lorna!" I called. "Lorna, wait!"

She stopped and turned.

"Look," I said, "I—"

A wall of heat and sound smacked into us as the boat exploded.

9

JD

EVERYTHING WENT BLISTERINGLY hot and then suddenly, shockingly cold. Water filled my mouth and nose and my animal instincts took over: I kicked and tore at the water until my head broke the surface. I inhaled and got a big lungful of smoke. That sent me into a fit of coughing and I twisted wildly around, eyes streaming, trying to get my bearings.

Thick white smoke hung like fog over the water. The air was full of drifting embers that singed my skin and burning chunks of wood floated all around me. Some of it was old, gray wood: the dock I'd been standing on. But some of it was polished teak.

The boat. Oh Jesus. The image replayed in my head, the boat exploding into matchwood. The explosion must have taken out part of the dock, too, and hurled us into the water...

Lorna! I hollered her name but nobody answered. I cursed and threw myself forward, swimming toward where I thought the dock might have been. I pushed burning debris out of my way, squinting through the thick smoke, but there was no sign of anyone.

Wait. There! Floating on her back, bobbing amongst the wreckage. I clawed my way through the water and grabbed her, flipping onto my back and pulling her against my chest. She was breathing but semi-conscious, probably stunned.

I swam her over to a part of the dock that was still standing. By now, the scene was filling up with people, brought by the explosion, and they helped me lift her out of the water. I scrambled up after her and then bent over her. I couldn't see any injuries. "Lorna? Lorna!"

Her eyes slowly focused on me and she came out of her stupor. When she saw the scene around her, she sat up. "Oh God. *Dad!*"

"I'll find him," I told her.

I jumped back into the water and hauled ass towards where the boat had been. The breeze started to clear the smoke and, for the first time, I got a proper look at the wreck.

My stomach knotted. The upper part of the boat was just *gone:* all that was left was a burning, hollowed-out hull. I circled round, pushing slowly through hunks of wood and shreds of sail.

I found Russ facedown in the water. I turned him, just to check, then quickly looked away, cursing. He'd taken the full force of the explosion.

I swam back to shore. Lorna met me as I climbed up onto the dock, her eyes huge and scared. "Is he—"

I didn't have to say anything. She could see it in my face. I watched her buckle and she fell forward against me, burying her face in my soaked shirt.

I wrapped my arms protectively around her and hugged her close. I was in shock, too. *I was just talking to the guy!*

This was going to destroy her. I'd seen how close she was to her dad and I knew what it was like to lose someone so suddenly. I glared at the world over her shoulder. She was a single mom, she had enough to deal with...*Oh God, Cody!* The poor kid was already growing up without a dad and now he'd lost his grandfather, too.

She was shaking. My denim jacket was lying on the dock: I must have dropped it along with the cooler when the explosion hit us. I grabbed it and wrapped it around her to keep her warm, then pulled her close again.

I didn't let go of her when the paramedics showed up.

I didn't let go of her at the hospital.

I didn't let go until the doctors had checked her out and she was standing next to Paige's car in the parking lot, ready to go home. I gave her one last goodbye hug that turned into a full-body embrace, her sobbing against me and me with my arms locked tight around her.

"I needed him," she told me, her voice fractured. "I needed my dad. I can't do this without him."

I closed my eyes and pressed the side of my head against hers. "I know," I told her softly. "I know." My voice firmed. "But you can go on. You will. I've seen how strong you are."

I crushed her to me. And then finally, reluctantly...I let her go.

10

LORNA

"You want a sandwich?" asked Paige. "Or soup? I made soup." I shook my head and she sighed. "Lorna, you need to eat."

As usual, Paige had been a godsend. I wouldn't have made it through the last few days without her and I knew she was trying to help. But my dad was gone and I didn't want to eat or drink or go for a walk.

I just wanted him back.

A gas explosion. That's what had taken him from us. Gas had built up on board the boat and my dad had ignited it with a spark when he turned on a light. The cops and FBI said there was no sign of foul play. Most likely, they told me, it was a leaky hose, a ten-dollar spare part.

I slunk down the hallway. I'd never realized how much I heard my dad around the apartment: his heavy footsteps in the kitchen as he fixed himself a drink, the sound of his voice as he sang to himself while he tied his tie. This was his penthouse, his building: he'd designed the whole thing. Without him, it felt gray and hollow.

I kept thinking of all the things I'd never said to him and now never would. *Did he know I loved him?* I tried to remember the last time I'd said it and worried it was too long ago. There were arguments I wanted to undo, things I wanted to unsay. And things I needed to know, however selfish it was. *Was he proud of me?*

I passed the door to Cody's room. He was inconsolable and had barely come out since it happened. It wasn't just that he'd lost a grandfather: since my ex left and we'd moved into the penthouse of the McBride Building, my dad had been the closest thing to a father Cody had. Cody and I had cried together, I'd held him and we'd done our *you and me* thing...but, for once, I wasn't sure it was going to be enough.

In my bedroom, I closed the door and walked over to the window, looking down at the streets fifty floors below but not really seeing them. I had no idea how we were going to carry on. My dad had always been the immovable center around which we'd all revolved. I was drifting, now, and I knew Cody and Miles felt the same. Who was I going to go to for advice? How could he be *gone?*

And tomorrow would be much, much worse. Tomorrow, I had to say goodbye. Every time I thought about the funeral, it was like I'd stepped off a cliff and was plunging down into nothingness.

Then I saw something reflected in the glass, something dark behind me that shouldn't be there. I turned and saw the black denim hanging on the back of my door. *Shit!* JD's jacket!

I lifted it down from the hook. The denim was rough on the outside but inside, it was surprisingly soft: I remembered how comforting it had been when he'd put it around me. I brought it to my face and inhaled: it smelled of him, of the outdoors and leather and *man.*

I had to get it back to him. It was exactly the sort of simple, practical mission I needed to focus me. He'd given me his number, in case the cops needed to get hold of him.

I took a deep breath and dialed. As the line rang, I stared out of the window at the gray concrete, gray sky and cold, gray rain. JD seemed very distant.

And then suddenly, he wasn't distant at all.

"Hello?"

I gripped the phone hard: it was like the phone line was a tiny tunnel leading out of all the grayness to a bright world where people were still happy, still living their lives.

"It's me," I said, shocked at how shaky my voice sounded. I hadn't said much to anyone in days.

"Lorna." God, my name, in that deep, growly voice... The cold grayness was pushed back a little and it felt so good, I nearly lost it.

Focus, Lorna.

"Um. I still have your jacket," I told him. "If you give me your address, I'll mail it to you."

"How are you and Cody doing?"

I fought to keep my voice level. "We're okay. What's your address?"

"Lorna. *How are you doing?*" It was an order, of sorts, and I couldn't disobey, not when it came in *that* voice, like rock that's been warmed by the sun.

"You know, o—" I started to say *okay* again and shrug, but my voice hitched and the shrug collapsed. "I don't know," I said at last. "It's the funeral, tomorrow."

"You want some company?"

My breath caught. *Him? Here?* That was insane. But it also sounded really, *really* good. It made no sense. I barely knew him, we'd met twice, but when I thought about the funeral, about facing the void where my dad used to be, the person I wanted by my side was JD Taggert.

I pushed the idea away. "That's crazy, JD," I said. "You're in Colorado. It's halfway across the country!"

I could hear something unfamiliar in my voice: it made me think of violin strings, stretched so tight they're about to snap. And he heard it, too.

"It ain't that far," he said firmly. "What's the name of the church?"

I swallowed and debated and finally told him, and he said he'd be on the first flight out in the morning.

"Thank you," I said, my voice ragged. I felt like I'd cracked in two right in front of him, and he could see right to my beating heart.

"Not a problem," he told me. "I'll see you soon."

I ended the call, breathing hard. *What have I done?!* I felt terrible, dragging him all the way back to New York. I lifted my thumb to call him back.

But I knew I wouldn't be able to talk him out of it. And for the first time, I had a tiny shred of hope. When I thought about the funeral, I still felt that sickening, terrifying plunge, like I was falling. But now I knew there'd be someone to catch me.

11

JD

I ONLY OWN TWO SUITS. One of them's gray and I bought it when all my buddies were getting married. I'm past that age, now, and the only time I dig it out is when Kian, the head of Stormfinch Security, drags me to Washington.

Then there's the other one. The black one.

I've worn that one too many times, stood next to grieving wives and parents and told them *it was an honor to serve with him.* Then, four years ago, I had to root in the back of my closet and dig it out again, and that time, Jillian wasn't there to help me get my tie straight and Max wasn't there to tell me *you look sharp, Dad* because it was them I was saying goodbye to.

People say you go through these stages, after someone dies. Denial and anger and a whole mess more. You know what I felt, after I lost them?

Confusion.

I never claimed to be the smartest. Just a big, dumb soldier who does what he's told. The battlefield's where I belong: I know where I am, there. All I wanted was to serve my country and come home and share my life with someone, raise a kid and try to make him a good man. I always knew there was a risk I'd be killed, leaving Jillian a widow and Max without a dad. But the one scenario I never planned for was me surviving them. When it happened, I just couldn't understand it.

I just knew it was my fault. I'd failed to protect them.

Now, under clouds so dark it felt like twilight, I was wearing it again and the tightness of the jacket across my shoulders, the way it bunched up at the elbows, even the smell of the damn thing...it all took me right back to that day.

I took a slow breath in and told myself I was in New York, not back in that churchyard in Texas. But all I could smell was the same scent of wet, freshly-dug earth. I tried to listen to what the preacher was saying but the rain was drumming on the umbrella I held above us, muffling his voice, and every time I closed my eyes, I could see two coffins in front of me, not one. *Goddammit....*

I looked to my right. Lorna stood next to me in a black dress, her hair pinned up. She was crying almost silently, just little quakes of her body as the tears spilled down her cheeks. Cody was pressed tight to her side. His gaze locked on his grandfather's coffin, his eyes huge. I recognized the look: it was all just becoming real to him.

Both of them were in pieces. They needed me. So I told myself angrily to damn well *hold it together*. I set my jaw and forced the memories down inside.

The preacher finished his piece and then said gently, "Would anyone like to say a few words?" He looked at Lorna and I saw her physically flinch, terrified. She glanced around at the crowd: despite the rain, over a hundred people had shown up. Lorna shook her head, then dropped her gaze and glared at her shoes.

I reached out and put my hand on her shoulder. She looked up at me and I nodded gently to her: *it's okay.* She gave me a quick, grateful nod but I could see she was fuming at herself.

Miles stepped forward. For once, he wasn't wearing sunglasses and he looked a little healthier than last time I'd seen him. "Everyone who knew my father," he began, "be it as a boss, a business partner or a friend, knows that he was *a good man*. He had integrity."

People nodded somberly. I could feel the emotion running

through the crowd: they'd really liked Russ. And in the few hours I'd known him, I'd really liked him, too.

"I don't know how we're going to go on without you," said Miles. His voice, normally so confident and controlled, was rough with emotion. "But we *will* go on, because that's what you'd want. And I'm going to do my best to make you proud."

He rejoined us, his eyes shining. The preacher said a few final words and then stepped back and nodded to the pallbearers. They slowly lowered the coffin into the grave as a Scottish piper began to play. I'd never been a fan of the bagpipes but, *damn*, I guess I'd just never heard them played well before, because what came out of them was haunting, beautiful: the hair on the back of my neck stood up.

I heard Lorna give a shaky little intake of breath and when I looked down at her, she'd gone rigid. The coffin had just sunk out of sight and I remembered that moment from four years ago, that single second when it goes beneath the earth and you know the person you laughed and danced and made plans with is *never coming back.*

She turned around and just collapsed into me, sobbing into my shirt. My arms came up around her and I held her to me, patting her back. Cody joined us, pressing into her side, and I dropped the umbrella, reached down, and clutched him with my other arm.

The two of them clung to me and I stood there breathing hard, trying to comfort them while trying to hold myself together. All the memories were flooding back and it felt like my heart was being ripped out of me all over again. I wanted so bad to let them go, turn away, and just be alone until I was back in control. Instead, I held them tighter. They needed me.

I was real glad the rain was streaming down my face.

At last, I felt Lorna inhale, gathering herself. Then she gave me a last squeeze and stepped back. She looked up at me, eyes red and cheeks tear-stained. She couldn't speak yet, so she just gave me a little nod of thanks, and I nodded back. She took Cody's hand in one hand and grabbed mine with the other, squeezing it tight. *Please stay close.*

I squeezed back. *Count on it.*

We began to move slowly toward the waiting cars. The rain was still coming down but we were already soaked so there didn't seem much point using the umbrella now. Cody was blinking hard. He saw me looking at him and turned away guiltily.

I reached down and squeezed his shoulder. "It's okay to cry. Ain't nothing wrong with it."

Cody looked up at me, surprised, then nodded gratefully.

We kept walking and, after a while, Lorna started to speak, her voice small and lost. "He was the one who raised me, you know. My mom...."

Her voice went shaky and I rubbed the back of her hand with my thumb. "It's okay. You don't have to—"

She shook her head. "I want to. My mom...she was in a car crash, just after I was born. Her car skidded on the ice and went off the road, only a few hundred feet from our house. My dad found us. My mom was dead but somehow, I'd survived. He picked up this little thing, practically a newborn... He must have been in pieces, he'd just lost his wife and suddenly he had Miles and a baby to raise on his own. But he did it, he was *the best* dad—" She pressed her lips hard together and shook her head, unable to go on.

I nodded. "I didn't know him long, but he seemed like a hell of a guy."

She nodded firmly. Then she blinked and stopped dead, staring at something ahead of us.

I followed her gaze. A black Rolls Royce had pulled up and a guy in a peaked cap—a chauffeur, I realized—was opening the rear door with one hand while smoothly unfurling an umbrella with the other. A man climbed out, taking up position under the umbrella and tugging on his lapels to straighten his jacket. He wasn't dressed for a funeral. His suit was pebble-gray and it had a silken sheen to it. The buttons on his waistcoat were trimmed with gold thread and his tie was the same violent crimson as freshly-spilled blood. Soft curls of black hair tumbled lazily onto his forehead and he had cheekbones like the model of some classy clothing brand.

The man took the umbrella from his chauffeur and marched towards us.

"Who is he?" I asked.

"Sebastian van der Meer," said Lorna. She sounded exhausted and yet mad. "He's an asset stripper. He's been trying to buy our company for years so he can take it apart and sell the pieces."

"Miss McBride," said the man as he arrived. His accent was old money New York, so polished his family must have been rich before the *Mayflower*. "I was so sorry to hear your news. Are you and your brother free to talk?"

"I have nothing to say to you," Lorna told him. Then she glanced away and took a slow breath: I could tell she was trying to hold it together.

Van der Meer took a half step forward, a shark scenting blood. "It'll only take a moment."

Before I knew what I was doing, I'd let go of Lorna's hand and stalked right up to Van der Meer. "The lady's just buried her father. How about you show a little *fucking* respect?"

Van der Meer winced as if my Texas drawl offended his ears. Then he looked me up and down, taking in my out-of-fashion suit and cheap shoes. He frowned as if he had to think about what to say: I guess he never normally came into contact with people like me. "Get out of my way."

I could feel the protective rage boiling up in my chest. I wasn't going to let this vulture anywhere near Lorna. I stayed exactly where I was.

Van der Meer sighed, rolled his eyes, and tried to walk around me, which was a mistake. I took two quick steps and slammed into him, chest-to-chest. We were about the same height but I had fifty pounds on him and he bounced off me and went staggering backward, only just catching himself before he fell. I stepped forward, keeping him off balance. "I'll give you three seconds to get back in your car," I growled.

"Or what? You'll hit me? Assaulting me would be a very bad idea."

I stepped right up to him again. My voice gets real slow and quiet when I'm mad. "You try to go around me again," I told him, "And I don't care how many fancy lawyers you got, I will *lay you out*."

He gave me a glare that probably put the fear of God into any intern who brought him the wrong coffee. But we weren't on Wall Street and I wasn't someone he could fire, or screw over in a deal. This was about to be a knock-down, drag-out fist fight and that's *my* domain. His glare faltered, then he turned on his heel and stalked back to his car. I kept my eyes locked on his retreating back, the anger thundering through every vein, my breath coming in pants. I was shocked at how mad I was. I hadn't felt so primally protective of anyone since...

Since *them.*

Lorna's hand slipped into mine. "Thank you," she said softly.

I swallowed and nodded, not trusting my voice. We walked over to the limo. Paige and Miles were already inside, sheltering from the rain.

"You sure you won't come to the wake?" Lorna asked.

I shook my head. I was glad I'd been there to support her at the funeral but I'd only just made it through, and at the wake I'd just be in the way. "I'll head back to the airport."

Lorna looked towards the church's small parking lot. "You got a rental car somewhere?"

"I'll call a cab."

"And stand here waiting in the rain?!" I could hear the hint of Scottish in her accent on the r of *rain* and it was so beautiful it hurt.

I shrugged and looked down at myself. "Can't get any wetter."

"Don't be silly. Ride with us, the limo can drop us off and then take you to the airport."

I looked away and frowned at the horizon. I knew what this was: she wasn't ready to say goodbye. I knew because I felt the exact same way. I turned back to Lorna and frowned at her...but found her staring up at me, defiant, ignoring the raindrops running down her face. Jillian used to get the same way when I was stubborn.

And just like with Jillian, I couldn't refuse that face a damn thing.

I sighed and nodded, and we climbed in. I wound up sitting next to Lorna on the back seat. Both of us were soaked and shivering but, as soon as my leg pressed against hers, I could feel the heat of her body throbbing through the layers of wet fabric. The door closed with an expensive *wump,* sealing us off from the outside world, and suddenly, it was very still and quiet.

As we started to move, I glanced at her and couldn't look away. God, she was beautiful. Those gray eyes, glittering in the semi-dark of the car, her lips soft and perfect, her hair all pulled back and pinned up, leaving her neck bare and exposed: an animal part of me just wanted to twist in my seat and kiss all the way down her throat, never mind that this wasn't the time or place, or that Cody was sitting right next to her. *What's wrong with me?*

Then she glanced around and found me looking at her. I froze guiltily.

A cell phone rang, shattering the silence. Both of us jumped and looked away. Miles answered the call and muttered to someone for a moment, then frowned, confused. "That was Dad's lawyer," he told us. "He needs to see us *now.*"

12

LORNA

Twenty minutes later, Miles, Paige, Cody, JD and I walked into a book-lined office. George Parsons has been our family lawyer for as long as I can remember: when I was a child, I thought of him as Humpty Dumpty because he's short and squat, with a bald, polished head. He's normally cheerful and jokey but today he was flexing a pencil nervously between his hands.

Miles marched over to his desk. "George, what couldn't wait until tomorrow? We've got a roomful of people waiting for us."

George nodded. "I know. I'm sorry. But there's something you need to know. I've been trying to figure out when to tell you. I didn't want to do it before the funeral but I thought you'd better know before you talk to everybody at the wake."

"What?" I asked. "What do we need to know?"

George swallowed. "Your father came to me a few weeks before his death." He looked guiltily at Miles. "He changed his will. Miles won't take over the company." He looked at me. "You will."

We all just stared at him. "No, George, that's..." I choked. "No, come on, that's *insane!*"

George just looked back at me sadly. My stomach flipped over. "It's a mistake, it's got to be a mistake. I can't—I don't know anything about running a company!" I could feel the fear rising in my chest, now. I pointed to my brother. "It's Miles, it's always been Miles, my dad's been getting him ready for years!"

George gave a tiny shake of his head. My heart stopped beating. *Oh Jesus, it's real.* I groped blindly, found JD's hand and squeezed.

Miles leaned on George's desk, hands braced on the edge, breathing hard. His shoulders tensed under his jacket and his lungs filled once, twice. I winced, thinking he was about to start yelling, but he couldn't seem to find the words. His head slumped forward and his shoulders dropped. "Why?" he grated at last.

George's voice was tender. "I'm sorry, Miles, he wouldn't say."

Miles gave a quick nod. A moment later, he drew in a long, shuddering breath, straightened up and adjusted his tie. He was doing that whole British *stiff upper lip* thing he learned in boarding school: in fact, I figured that was the only thing holding him together, right now. But then he turned and locked eyes with me and no amount of manners could help. He'd already been fragile from losing his father. Now someone had stuck a knife in him and he just looked betrayed. He looked at me imploringly: *why?*

I shook my head, still in shock. *I don't know! I didn't do this!*

But I could already see the hurt in his eyes turning to anger. He marched to the door, his voice tight with rage. "I'll make my own way there."

I started after him but he was already pounding down the stairs. I cursed under my breath.

"Why would granddad do that?" asked Cody.

"I don't know," I told him softly. I looked at JD and he shook his head grimly, as mystified as me.

I thanked George and we filed back out to the limo. There was no sign of Miles.

As we drove to the wake, I sat there stewing, slowly shaking my head as the enormity of it all sank in. I was going to be CEO of a billion-dollar company. Me. An engineering nerd who can tell you the exact tensile strength of a two-inch steel cable but who stares at her shoes when she has to talk to a stranger. I couldn't chair meetings, or negotiate, or close deals with politicians. I had the exact wrong skillset. And for some reason, my dad had frozen out the guy with the right one.

As we pulled up outside the bar, I blurted, "His entire life, Miles has only wanted one thing. My dad was grooming him for this ever since he was a teenager. Oh God, he's going to hate me." I felt like the entire world was crumbling under me. I'd just lost my dad and now Miles was gone, too. I looked across at JD and my voice cracked. "What am I going to *do?*"

He growled low in his throat, like he was warning the universe to back off, and then he grabbed me by the shoulders and pulled me to him. His arms folded around my back and I was crushed against the warm contours of his pecs. His hands rubbed slowly up and down my back. It wasn't sexual, just caring. It felt good but I was still in pieces.

JD ducked his head and put his lips right to my ear. "Now listen," he told me in a voice like iron. "You're gonna do this, and you're gonna do great. You know why? Because you're smart as hell and you're too stubborn to quit. Just like me." I felt him jerk his head towards Cody. "That's a hell of a kid you raised, over there. That's the hardest thing in the world and you pulled it off all by yourself. You did that, you can do this."

Warmth flowered in my chest, a slow-motion explosion. When JD said something, you believed it. It helped that it sounded like he spoke from experience. *He's got a kid, too?* I nodded nervously, feeling a little steadier.

He gently pushed me back. I looked up...and went utterly still. He was gazing at me with true respect, with belief. I've never in my life seen anyone so *certain.* "You got this, Lorna," he told me.

Something lifted inside me. I'd never felt anything like it before: my chest filled and my back straightened. *Is this how the soldiers he leads feel?* I bobbed my head, overcome.

His expression changed, a little smile touching his lips, like I was cute. *No one ever thinks I'm cute.* And then—

His eyes flared: all that lust I'd seen at the marina, all that need...it was still there, beneath the caring. He still had a hand on my shoulder and his fingers tapped a piano scale, his arm tensing like he was a hair's breadth from pulling me to him in a whole different way.

Then he shook his head to himself and let me go.

I nodded quickly, trying to be all briskly efficient. "We'd better get in there," I said. "The limo will take you to the airport."

We climbed out and, even though it was raining, JD climbed out, too, to say goodbye. He took Cody's hand and shook it solemnly. "You take care of your mother, okay?"

Cody nodded hard. "Goodbye, JD."

"Thank you," I said. *Thank you* didn't cover it, but my voice had gone shaky and I didn't trust it to say more.

JD nodded.

I took Cody's hand, opened the door of the bar and walked into my future.

13

JD

I turned to the limo. "Airport, sir?" the driver asked.

I stood there, one hand on the open door, silently thinking.

I never claimed to be the smartest. But if you make it through enough combat tours, you start to develop an instinct. You know when something's not right.

The police down in Mexico had decided that the attack on Lorna's family had been the work of a local gang: they'd been intending to kidnap Russ and demand a ransom from the company for his release: Lorna and Cody would just have been additional bargaining chips.

Maybe.

Or maybe they'd been planning to murder Russ and his family and make it look like a kidnapping gone wrong.

And maybe Russ's death hadn't been an accident.

I'd been telling myself that I was just being paranoid. But Lorna inheriting the company changed everything. If I was right, if someone had targeted Russ twice, it had to be something to do with the company: any business worth billions had enemies. And now that she was CEO, Lorna would be the one in the firing line.

That deep, protective need filled my chest again. I couldn't leave until I was sure she was safe.

"Change of plan," I told the limo driver. "Thanks anyway." And I closed the door.

As the limo pulled away, I pulled out my phone and scowled at it. No way was I involving the rest of the team in this, but I needed information.

Kian answered on the second ring. He's the one who brought us all together to form Stormfinch: I lead the team in the field and he liaises with Washington and gets us our missions. "JD! What's up?"

"I'm in New York..." I began.

"New York?! What are you doing in New York?"

It was a Saturday, so I'd been able to slip away without anyone knowing. "Do you know anyone here in the FBI?"

I could hear the Irish in Kian's voice: he was worried. "You okay? You in trouble with the law?"

"Nothing like that."

There was a pause while he waited for me to tell him what the hell was going on. But I didn't want to drag him into my problems, and I'm the master of the stony silence. After a few seconds, Kian gave in and sighed. "I do know a guy. Hold on, I'll give you his number."

An hour later, I was squeezing my way into a store in Lower Manhattan. The place sold scented candles and it was so crowded, I could feel the water being wrung out of my soaking suit as I squeezed my way between the shoppers. I inhaled and coughed: the air was a thick fog of scents: apple, vanilla, violets, and about a million others.

There was one guy who looked as out of place as me. His overcoat was stretched across his broad back as he bent to examine the labels on two candles. "You Callahan?" I asked.

He turned around. He was in a suit, too, his tie loose and his hair tousled: I couldn't tell if he'd been in a scuffle, or if he just always looked like that. His eyes met mine and he nodded grumpily at the store. "Don't judge. My girlfriend's crazy about these things and I need to get her something. I've got to meet you, get her a gift, grab a bite and be back in the office in thirty minutes. I'm multitasking." He showed me the two candles. "*Peaches and Cream* or *Unicorns Dancing*?"

"You said you had to get her something...you in the doghouse?"

Callahan rubbed at his stubble. "I'm working a triple murder and I haven't been home much. She's cool about it but I'm not. I want to make sure she knows that *I* know it's not okay." His jaw set, determined, like even a tiny crack in the relationship would be unacceptable.

"Get both," I told him.

He nodded gratefully and we moved towards the registers. "I got a theory," I told him. "About Russ McBride's death."

Callahan winced. "I'm not meant to talk about an ongoing investigation." He ran a hand through his hair. "But Kian vouched for you and that means a lot."

"You and him go back?"

Callahan looked away. "He and his brothers helped me get closure on something. What's your theory?"

"I think maybe someone killed him, made it look like an accident."

Callahan went quiet.

"Tell me I'm wrong," I said, my voice strained. That's what I wanted, for him to tell me I was being an idiot, and then I could go home to Colorado and try to forget Lorna McBride.

"Officially? Our lab people went over the boat. Didn't find explosives. Didn't find a timer or a trigger. So it was a gas explosion. Leaky hose, spark sets it off." He scowled. "Accident."

"But *unofficially?*"

"I didn't buy it. My boss told me to leave it alone." He hesitated, debating. "She'd bust my ass if she found out I'd said anything...ah, fuck it, when did that ever stop me?" He took a deep breath. "Russ McBride *loved* that boat. Spent every spare minute on it. He was loaded, so money for maintenance wasn't an issue. He was a smart guy, architect, understood engineering, he'd have understood a leaky gas line was dangerous."

"Maybe it had just started leaking," I said. I wanted to be wrong, wanted there to be an innocent explanation. "Maybe he kept it well maintained but there was a faulty part."

"And he doesn't smell the gas?" asked Callahan. "Or he smells it and he's dumb enough to cause a spark?" He shook his head. "I think you're right. Someone killed him. But I can't prove it. If they used a trigger, there was no sign of it in the wreckage."

"Which means?" I asked, my chest tight.

"It was a professional job," said Callahan.

I thanked him, he paid for the candles and we headed outside, Callahan making a beeline for a hot dog stand.

Someone had killed Lorna's father. And if they'd done it because he was CEO, she was now a target.

I cursed and pulled out my phone. Lorna answered and I could hear the wake going on in the background. She must be in hell, right now: she'd be the center of attention in a room packed with people, a nightmare for someone so shy. She was suddenly responsible for a billion-dollar company with thousands of employees *and* she'd just lost her father.

She probably thought her life couldn't get any worse.

"JD?" she asked, surprised. "Are you at the airport?"

"No." I took a deep breath. "We need to talk."

14

LORNA

A HALF HOUR LATER, I was standing under the bandstand in Central Park.

The wake had left me emotionally wrung-out and shaky. Remembering my dad and seeing all his old friends had been hard enough. But what was worse had been standing next to Miles, as one person after another told him that he had big shoes to fill. Each time, Miles would wince and nod at me. *Actually, it's Lorna who's going to be taking over.* Each time, he seemed to get a little smaller. It was heartbreaking to watch.

And the way the other person reacted didn't make me feel any better. They'd turn to stare at me, eyes wide, and then give me a fake-cheery smile. *Oh, that's...great,* they'd say. And they were right to be worried. I didn't know how to run a company.

I'd been glad to get out of there. Then JD arrived and I saw his face...and suddenly, I wished I was back at the wake.

He laid it all out for me and the world seemed to spin and tip under my feet. My dad hadn't been snatched away by bad luck or fate. Someone had taken him from us. Now that I was CEO, they'd be gunning for me, too. But more important than any of that—

"Cody?" I asked. "Is Cody in danger?"

"They were trying to pull both of you out of the car in Mexico. At best, these people don't care *who* they hurt."

I remembered arriving home from the hospital with Cody. Every knife in the drawer was a weapon, every chemical under the sink a poison. I'd looked down at the little life in my arms and wished I could lock the two of us away in a cozy nest because the world was just too dangerous. Now I felt that way again but it wasn't just motherly paranoia: someone actually wanted to hurt him.

"Could you be wrong?" I asked in a small voice.

"I can't be a hundred percent. There's no evidence."

I could see it in his eyes. "But you're sure."

He grimaced. "Yeah. I'm sure."

My stomach churned and I staggered as my knees weakened. *Cody!* I could feel an iron band tightening around my chest. Cody being in danger, *me* being in danger, everyone relying on me as CEO...it was just too much.

JD stepped closer and gripped my arm, his face like thunder. He looked ready to annihilate whoever had done this. "Who'd want to kill your dad?"

I almost said *no one.* Everyone had loved my dad. But then I thought about the business we were in and the amounts of money at stake. "We're building a hydroelectric dam in Poland," I said slowly. "If we finish it, their government's going to be shutting coal-fired power stations, so the coal industry's pissed." That opened the floodgates. "We just won the contract to build an airport terminal in Mexico: if we have to pull out, one of our rivals steps in and gets hundreds of millions of dollars. Even right here in New York, the new high-rise we're building is going to affect property prices and there are some serious people in the property game: Konstantin Gulyev, for one, he's meant to be part of the Russian Mob. Or there are the people who want to buy the company, people like Van der Meer." *Jesus.* I was staring into the abyss.

"You need to hire someone," JD said gently. "Protection."

Protection? A bodyguard? Our family had never needed that sort of security: we drove our own cars, walked the streets alone. At events, my dad would chat to anyone, he'd always believed in being open and accessible.

But my dad was dead and Cody could be next. I nodded. I was shaking. I couldn't stop shaking.

"I can make some calls," JD told me. "Find you someone here in New York who knows what he's doing."

Private security. Some smoothly efficient guy in a suit. Sure, he'd protect us if we paid him. But he wouldn't know us, wouldn't care about us. It was a freakin' arms race: some rival had hired men to kill him, so now we had to hire someone to protect us and hope we could trust him. A strange man, in our apartment, in our *lives,* close to Cody... *No.* I didn't trust anyone, right now. Not with my son.

Then I looked up at JD. He was former military, as tough as they come, and an old-fashioned gentleman who couldn't be bribed or bought. And since this thing started, the only times I'd felt truly safe were when I was with him.

"What about you?" I asked. "Would you protect us?"

15

JD

THE ANSWER WAS EASY: *no.*

I was a soldier, not a damn bodyguard. True, I'd escorted some people in Afghanistan and Iraq, but they were government officials making quick trips to warzones, not someone trying to live their normal life in the middle of a city. I wasn't like Kian, with his Secret Service background. And me, a dumb grunt from Texas, would fit into her world of Armani suits and corporate doubletalk like a bear at a tea party. Plus, this wasn't just about guarding her: if the cops weren't going to help us, we had to figure out who the killer was and I wasn't a detective.

Most importantly, I couldn't be close to her. Even now, I could feel myself being tugged towards her, my whole body aching with the need to have her pressed against me again. It wasn't just those big gray eyes and those soft lips. It was the warmth I could feel when we were together, the closeness.

A fresh wave of guilt washed through me. Nothing could ever happen between Lorna and me: it wouldn't be right. And being close to her, feeling that pull and the pain and guilt it caused, would be unbearable.

But when I thought about her and Cody being guarded by a

stranger, my stomach knotted. I just didn't trust anyone else to keep them safe.

I knew that was a bad sign. It meant I was already too close to them. *I can't do this.*

Then I looked down into those pale gray eyes. She was scared. Alone.

I couldn't walk away, either.

I drew in a shuddering breath...and nodded. "Okay."

16

JD

I WALKED Lorna back to the wake and we agreed to meet up at her place in a few hours. I figured she was safe enough in a room full of friends and family and there were a couple of things I had to take care of.

First, I had to go shopping. I'd only come for the day so I had the black suit I was wearing and literally nothing else, not even a toothbrush. I bought some jeans and a shirt and changed into them, and stuffed my soaking suit into a bag. After filling out a lot of forms, pleading my case to the NYPD and getting Agent Callahan to vouch for me, I managed to swing a local firearms license and half an hour after *that,* I had a handgun and a shoulder holster. I sighed in relief, feeling a little less naked.

The sun was sinking between the skyscrapers as I threaded my way through the crowded sidewalks towards Lorna's place. I called Kian. "Uh...I'm gonna need some time off."

"JD, what's going on?" Kian asked. "What are you doing in New York? Why did you want Callahan's number?" He must have realized he sounded a little terse because I heard the rasp of him rubbing his stubble and he said, "Sorry, I'm just..."

Worried. He was worried about me and that made my stomach

twist with guilt. "I'm fine," I lied. I looked up as I crossed a crosswalk and got a glimpse of the McBride Building peeking out between two high-rises. Already, it looked enormous. "I'm just helping someone out," I told Kian, which was at least sort of true.

Kian gave a little sigh that I could tell meant *I don't believe you.* "Of course you can take some time off. We're just training anyway and I can fill in for you. It'll be good for me to get out from behind a desk. Take as long as you need. But JD, *call us if* you need any help."

"Thanks, I will." Another lie. I quickly ended the call. Then I hesitated, the phone still in my hand. Kian knew more about being a bodyguard than anyone. He'd guarded the President's daughter, for God's sake. *Should* I have asked for help?

No. It wouldn't be right to drag the team into something personal. But deep down, I knew that wasn't the real reason. If the team showed up, one of them—probably Gabriel, with his knack for reading people—would soon figure out I had feelings for Lorna, and that wasn't something I wanted to admit. Even to myself.

I scowled. It didn't matter that I had feelings. I was going to protect her, just until I knew she was safe, and that was *it.* I wouldn't slip, like at the marina. I'd keep her at arm's length. I'd be *gruff.*

As I moved through the streets, the McBride Building kept appearing and disappearing. Each time I saw it, it was bigger. Then it went out of view for almost a whole block, until I rounded a corner and—

Wow.

The McBride Building was a New York icon. Its colossal square base rose for twenty floors before tapering up for another thirty. Hundreds of businesses had their offices here but most famously McBride Construction itself—their offices took up the top *seven floors.* And above *that,* right up in the penthouse, was the McBride family home. As the sun sank below the horizon, it turned the building's stone to gold and the thousands of windows to molten, blazing orange. I shielded my eyes and craned my head back. The top of the building really did seem to brush the underside of the clouds. *Skyscraper* was right. Even my dad, who wasn't much for words, would have admitted that the McBride Building was *a heck of a thing.*

I walked through the massive lobby with its coffee stands and sandwich stalls, gazing up in wonder at the silver ribbons of escalators that climbed to the offices above. There was a private elevator that led up to the penthouse, and Lorna buzzed me up. As soon as the doors slid closed, the thing rocketed skyward, leaving my stomach behind. I cursed, almost falling. Everything really *did* move faster in New York.

Just as I was recovering, the elevator stopped and I went weightless for a second. The doors opened and I stumbled out into a hallway filled with bright, natural light. Directly ahead of me was a set of massive double doors in polished red oak that I figured led to the penthouse. I started forward, but glanced left to see where all the daylight was coming from—

My steps faltered and then I stopped and just stared.

The wall was floor-to-ceiling glass and all of New York was laid out before me. At first, it was like being a giant, buildings that I knew were immense reduced to tiny models I might accidentally step on, the cars like swarming schools of colorful fish. Then I looked down the side of the building, to those dots that were people on the sidewalk. I've never been bothered by heights but it made even my stomach flip over. *Good job Colton isn't here.* The poor guy hated heights.

I couldn't get my head around how tall the building was. *How does the lobby not get crushed under all the weight?* The place was incredible. And now Lorna was designing even taller buildings. The woman was a goddamn genius.

I turned back towards the doors...and found they'd opened. Lorna was standing in the doorway, watching me.

She'd changed out of the black dress she'd worn for the funeral and put on a pair of faded blue jeans that hugged her legs and looked incredibly soft, and a big, baggy sweater the color of vanilla ice cream. Comfort clothes. She bit her lip, like she was a little ashamed. Then she lifted her chin defiantly: *I don't care, it's my house.*

She didn't need to worry because I thought she looked amazing. The sunset made her gray eyes blaze like fire and threw amber highlights into her shining black hair. And maybe the big, baggy sweater was meant to hide her body but it had the opposite effect: it gave just enough of a hint of the lush bounty beneath that all I could think about was pushing her up against the door, kissing her hard and sliding my hands up under her sweater to fill my hands with her breasts.

I had it bad for this woman.

And it must have shown on my face because she flushed and did that thing where she ducked her head, embarrassed. Then she stepped back from the door to invite me in. I passed her, inhaling the scent of her, and I suddenly flashed back to all the times women had invited me into their private space. That heady excitement, *do you want to come in for coffee?*

This ain't that, I told myself firmly. *I'm here to guard her. That's it.*

She gave me the tour and I tried to look where she was pointing, and not at her. But it was difficult. It didn't help that her jeans hugged the cheeks of her magnificent ass like a goddamn second skin.

The place was huge. There was a big, open-plan living space with floor-to-ceiling windows giving amazing views of the city, a grand piano, and some fancy art. But it felt like a home, not a catalog picture: the black leather couches look like they'd actually been cuddled up in for movie night, and the bookshelves were filled with a chaotic mix of paperbacks, not leather-bound volumes designed to impress.

There was a scale model of Manhattan, the buildings in white and the McBride projects in blue. I spotted the McBride Building straightaway: it felt weird to be looking at it while standing in it. And there was the marina I'd visited and, behind it, Hudson Tower, the skyscraper designed by Lorna. "What's this?" I asked, pointing at a square blue slab.

"The new hospital. The ground-breaking ceremony is tomorrow." Her face fell as she remembered something. "I've got to give a *speech!*"

That protective need unfurled in my chest and I took a half step towards her before I could stop myself. She was barefoot and that made her smaller and even more vulnerable. I just wanted to pull her into my arms and shield her from everyone and everything. But if I did that, I wasn't going to be able to stop.

I crossed my arms so I couldn't do anything stupid. "You'll do great."

She shook her head. "I'm not my dad."

"No, you're not. You're you," I said sincerely. "And you'll do great."

She cocked her head to one side and frowned at me, utterly confused. *Why?*

And I just stared right back at her. *Because you're amazing.* If she didn't believe in herself right now, I'd damn well believe enough for both of us.

She flushed and gave a little shake of her head, turning away. "This is Cody's room," she told me, knocking and then pushing open a door. Cody was at a desk, doing his homework. He looked up and beamed when he saw me. "JD!"

I grinned back but a cold hand was squeezing my heart. Right above Cody's desk was a huge poster of a Blackhawk helicopter. Max had been obsessed with military hardware, too: for him, it had been jets.

Lorna went in and asked Cody about school, while I stood in the doorway and took in the rest of the room. Swimming medals, video game posters...and one whole side of the room given over to a city made of Legos. A monorail wound around buildings and there were solar panels on all the roofs. *That's the next generation of McBride architects, right there.*

"Paige's room is that one there," Lorna told me, pointing across the hall. "And this is my room." She opened the door just long enough for me to get a glimpse—

A big, wooden bed with soft white pillows and a dark green comforter. There was an old-fashioned, wind-up alarm clock by the bed. Everything was tidy except...there was a bra. A black bra, the cups made of filmy material that her nipples would *definitely* show through. It was hanging off the dresser as if it had been tossed there in a hurry and suddenly, I was imagining her standing there, unhooking the bra at the back as she lifted the cups free from those gorgeous breasts—

I flushed. Lorna closed the door but the image stayed in my mind.

She pushed open the door next to hers to reveal a long room with a double bed, couch and desk. "This is the guest bedroom. You can stay here...if that's okay? She flushed and shook her head. "I'm sorry, this all happened so fast, I asked you and you said *yes:* we didn't talk about all the stuff we should have talked about. Like how this is going to work? And how long can you be here for? And what I'm paying you." Her eyes went wide with horror. "Oh God, you know I'm paying you, right? I'm not expecting you to do this for free! And look, if you've changed your mind or—"

I could see she was spiraling so I grabbed her hands. *"Lorna!"*

She broke off so suddenly and looked up at me so meekly that I swear I nearly lost it and just kissed her right then. One tug on her hands and she'd be against me...

"Now listen," I told her. *"One,* it's fine. We'll figure it out. *Two,* I'll be here as long as I need to be. *Three,* you don't need to pay me. And *four...*" I got distracted staring at her mouth. *"...four,"* I said, rallying, "no, I haven't changed my mind."

She stared up at me. I could see the shock in her eyes and then she gulped, overcome. Jesus, hadn't a guy ever done something nice for her, before? Or had her ex treated her so bad that she thought we were all assholes?

"Thank you," she told me softly. Then her voice grew firm. "I'm paying you, though. That's non-negotiable."

I nodded, and I couldn't stop a smile pulling at my lips. She was beyond cute when she got firm. "Yes ma'am."

She nodded to the room. "I'm sorry it's not bigger. There should be an extra ten feet at the back, but there was a mistake on the plans. The penthouse originally had a private elevator up from my dad's office, one floor down. He changed his mind, figured it was an indulgence too far, but by that point the shaft was already in and he had to just wall it up. This room was going to be a hallway leading to the elevator, that's why it's so long and thin—"

I grinned. "It's great." Hell, it was the same size as my whole apartment, back in Mount Mercy.

"I'll leave you to settle in. I need to spend time with Cody, and then I need to get ready for tomorrow." She took a deep breath and suddenly, she just looked lost. "As ready as I can be."

She walked away and I had to stop myself from marching after her and pulling her into a hug. I couldn't even imagine the pressure she was under, right now. Taking over as CEO of a billion-dollar company, days after losing her dad. Doing it all alone, as a single mom *and* knowing some psycho wanted to hurt her.

My back straightened and my hands closed into fists. I couldn't help her run a company. I couldn't bring Russ back. And I couldn't be with her, however much I wanted to be.

But if someone tried to hurt her again, I was going to make them regret they'd ever been born.

17

LORNA

TEN MINUTES LATER, I was in Cody's room, building.

There's a simple pleasure to building with Legos that's hard to beat. We take turns, one person finding the correct bricks and laying them out ready for the other person to click them together. It's like being a mini production line, a warmly symbiotic relationship that's as relaxing as a hot bath.

"I need three two-by-four thins in red," said Cody.

"Mm-hmm," I acknowledged, rattling through the bricks.

Building with Cody a few times a week was a routine I made sure I never missed. The other moms at his school wouldn't understand but I didn't care. It was our way of geeking out together and I'd learned it was a great way to get him to open up.

"Any blue-tinted window panes left?" Cody asked.

"Hold on, I saw a few," I muttered, sifting through the pile.

"I miss Grandad," blurted Cody.

I looked across at him. His eyes were firmly fixed on the house he was building. I felt my own pain, that tug in my stomach I felt every time I thought of my dad. And chained to that, that ache all moms get, whenever they see their child hurting. "I know," I said softly. "Me too."

We built for another few minutes in sad silence. Then: "I keep forgetting," said Cody with sudden savagery. "And then I *remember* and—" His face twisted and his breathing went tight with pain. "I'm so dumb. I woke up this morning and I was excited because on Mondays we always get pastries with Grandad after school and I was going to show him this idea I had for a robot arm. I've been sketching it out for weeks and then I remembered and *he's never going to see it.*" His voice finally fractured. "He'll never *know!*"

I pulled him into my arms as the tears started, rubbing his back and resting my chin on the top of his head. My eyes were filling up with tears, too. "Maybe we should stop by the grave," I croaked. "You could tell him."

I could feel him quaking against me. "People do that?"

I nodded. "All the time."

"Does it work?"

I didn't know. My mom died when I was only a few days old. As a child, I'd visited her grave, sat there and stared at the name, trying to imagine the woman I'd never known. It hurt, not having a mom, but I hadn't *lost* her, not like this. "It's meant to," I told him.

His sobs softened and gradually stopped, but it was a while before he let me go and moved back. "Are we in danger?" he asked.

My stomach flip-flopped. "No," I told him firmly.

"But JD's here to guard us. Right?" There wasn't much I could hide from Cody. I wondered what else he'd figured out, like *does that mean someone killed Grandad?* I prayed his mind hadn't gone there. This was all too much to be dealing with, at his age.

"Yes, he's here to protect us. But it's just a precaution. Think of him like a sprinkler system." I gripped Cody's shoulders and looked into his eyes. "No one's going to hurt you."

"Or you?"

"Or me," I told him, hoping I sounded a lot more certain than I felt.

～

Late that night, when everyone else was asleep, I slipped quietly out of the penthouse and crept downstairs to my dad's office. I hadn't been able to bring myself to go inside since he'd died. But from tomorrow, it would be *my* office and I didn't want to go in there for the first time in front of everyone.

As soon as I opened the door, I was surrounded by him. The scent of his cologne, the furrows in the carpet worn by him rolling his chair back and forth while he was thinking, the coffee pot on the side table filled with his unbelievably strong coffee... This room had been his for over thirty years. Taking it over meant admitting he was never coming back.

I looked at the chair, steeling myself. I didn't want to, but I had to.

I took a deep breath...and sat down. And suddenly it was real: I was here and he wasn't. I rocked forward, doubling over as if I'd been punched in the gut, and sat there with silent tears rolling down my cheeks for several minutes.

When I had myself under control, I pulled open the top drawer of his desk. God, he hadn't cleared this thing out in decades. I put my hand to my mouth as I pulled out a sketch, drawn on a beer mat, of a building that would now never get built. Further down, I found a poem by Miles, about a troll who floated around in a hot air balloon. Then a crayon drawing by me, of my dad on his boat. I bit my lip, feeling my eyes going hot again. *He kept all this stuff?*

I rooted deeper in the drawer. And right at the back, my fingers touched something that didn't match the rest, something stiff and glossy.

I frowned as I pulled out a photo. A woman, sitting on a couch with her legs tucked up beside her. I didn't recognize her. Some obscure relative I'd never met? But she didn't look anything like my dad. She had long, straight black hair and high cheekbones. And she was smiling at the camera in a way that said *put that thing down and get over here.* I flipped the photo over. Three kisses in blue ballpoint pen, together with a name: Maria.

A lover? My dad had had plenty, over the last few years.

Except...the photo was faded and old.

My heart jumped into my throat. I shoved the photo back where I'd found it and slammed the drawer. Tomorrow was my first day as CEO *and* I had to give a speech. *I have to get some sleep.*

But when I lay down in bed, my mind wouldn't stop spinning. There was the creeping, sick fear that someone was going to hurt Cody, or kill me and leave him without a mom. There was the stress of becoming responsible for billions of dollars and thousands of jobs. But now there was something new. I felt like everything solid, everything I'd thought I could rely on, had crumbled beneath me and I was plunging into darkness.

Maybe she was an old girlfriend. Someone he knew before he met mom. Maybe.

Or maybe my dad had had an affair.

And the guy I'd hero-worshipped my whole life wasn't the man I thought he was.

18

JD

THE NEXT MORNING I WOKE, turned sideways to get up, and grunted in pain. The muscles in my lower back had chosen to rebel again, knotting and twisting like angry serpents. I flopped onto my stomach and lay there cursing into my pillow for a full minute before I dared to move again. The pain died away but my back was going to be throbbing all day, now.

I took a shower, threw on some clothes, and went in search of coffee. The kitchen was enormous, with granite countertops loaded with more fresh vegetables than my place saw in a month. There was a big, vintage coffee machine covered in dials and buttons that I knew I'd have no hope of figuring out. Then I turned and saw something that stopped me dead.

The refrigerator. The refrigerator was covered in *things*, flyers for swim meets and permission slips for school trips and post-it notes, so many post-it notes, grocery items and little jokes and a picture Cody had drawn and—

I'd forgotten what a family home looked like. I'd avoided being in one, ever since it happened. My apartment in Mount Mercy was military-basic, with nothing on the walls, and I'd distanced myself from any old army buddies who had kids. But now, seeing this...*aw crap.* I could see it right now, our big, red, dented refrigerator. Red because the store had been selling it cheap: no one else wanted a bright red refrigerator. Dented because the thing had toppled over as I tried to squeeze it through the door. It had made me mad but Jillian had said it made it ours. I could see the clay model of a cow Max had made, sitting on top: it had a few too many legs, but we loved it anyway. And the photo of the three of us dressed up for Halloween as Superman, Bo Peep, and a pumpkin, which kept falling off the door so the joke was that it was haunted...

I braced myself against the refrigerator, breathing hard. That life, with all its laughs and love and tears, had been so important, and the universe had snuffed it out like it was nothing. Now it only existed in my head and when *I* went, it would be gone forever.

Footsteps in the hallway. A woman's footsteps. *Get it together, JD.* But there was no time. Every breath made the pain in my chest worse, like I was inhaling toxic gas.

The footsteps entered the kitchen behind me. I pulled open the door of the refrigerator and stuck my head in, letting the cool air bathe my face. I took some long, slow breaths and gradually battled the memories back down. "Almond milk," I muttered, playing for time, "oat milk. Where's the damn cow milk?"

A slender arm snaked in from behind me, pulled a carton from the back and waggled it. I grabbed it, took one more deep breath and closed the refrigerator. But when I turned around, it wasn't Lorna behind me. It was Paige.

"Hey," I said awkwardly. "Thanks. I'm—"

"JD," said Paige brightly. "We met." She jumped, nimble as a cat, and sat on the counter, grinning. "Lorna told me what's happening. You want some coffee to put that milk in, cowboy? She twisted and pushed buttons on the fancy coffee machine, then turned back to me as it started to hiss. "So you're going to be her bodyguard?"

"...yeah," I muttered. I had myself under control, now, but she was all blonde hair and bouncy confidence and it made me feel dumb and awkward, a farm boy talking to a cheerleader.

"Guarding her day and night." Paige leaned forward, smirking. "*Close protection.* That's what they call it, right?"

Dammit. She knew I liked Lorna. Or had Lorna said something about liking *me?* I suddenly needed to know but this was Lorna's BFF, everything would get reported back to her... God, this was like being back in high school. I dug deep and managed to make my face an impassive mask.

And then Lorna walked in. And any hope of me hiding my feelings disintegrated.

Those soft waves of black hair were gone: they'd been hauled back and captured in a ponytail, with just two little wisps of hair hanging down to frame her face. It looked classy and businesslike, but it also opened up whole new virgin plains of soft, pale skin down the sides and back of her neck, areas I'd never seen before and now couldn't tear my eyes from. And it made those pale gray eyes seem bigger and even more beautiful. God, she was gorgeous.

I realized she wouldn't be able to hide shyly behind her hair anymore. Then I realized that's why she'd done it. Something tightened in my chest. *Lorna!*

Her suit jacket and skirt were the color of a stormy sky and the sheen of the expensive fabric made it look like armor. A snow-white blouse hugged the sumptuous contours of her chest. She looked like a goddamn valkyrie.

And she was in heels. *High* heels, like every extra inch bought her more confidence, and spiky, like she was going to stamp them through the hearts of her enemies. And between the heels and the skirt and the glossy sheen of nylon...*Jesus,* her legs went on forever. My eyes were drawn up and up until they locked on the ripe curves of her hips, trying to laser through her skirt. I had to know: was it pantyhose she was wearing, or stockings?

I finally managed to lift my gaze and found those big gray eyes looking right at me. "How do I look?" she asked, and she wasn't preening, fishing for compliments. I could hear the fear in her voice. She was about to go into battle and she was terrified.

I felt my chest fill. There was so much I wanted to say. *Amazing.*

Fucking fantastic. I wanted to grab her hand, pull her up against me and just kiss her. But I couldn't. Just thinking about it made an icy blade stab my guts. I'd be betraying Jillian.

But there was something I *could* tell Lorna, right from the heart. "You look like a CEO," I growled.

Her eyes lit up and the fact *I* was doing that to her, just by telling the truth, made that closeness between us grow even warmer. The ruined place in my chest, where *they* used to live, ached, but I held her gaze and the moment stretched on and on...

Paige coughed quietly and we spun, startled, then muttered *thanks* and took the steaming mugs she was holding out. I focused hard on my coffee, careful not to meet Paige's eyes, but I could feel her grinning.

When Lorna had double-checked Cody had his books, lunch, and swim gear and given him a huge hug goodbye, Paige took him to school. I followed Lorna to the staircase that led from the penthouse down to the top floor of the McBride offices.

As we walked down it, I could hear her breathing speeding up. By the time we reached the door at the bottom, she was gulping in air, almost panic-breathing. We could hear the bustle of people on the other side. Hundreds of staff and thousands more spread out around the world, all relying on her.

Lorna swallowed, her face pale, and reached for the door handle. Then she flinched away. "I can't do this," she whispered.

I reached down and gently wrapped her slender hand in my big one. I gave it a little squeeze, then guided it to the handle. "Yeah you can," I told her. I managed to keep my voice firm and level. Just a friend, a bodyguard, giving her a little reassurance. But seeing her so scared sent a tidal wave of protective need washing through me and I was about one second away from just sweeping her up in my arms. *Goddamn it!* This was just the first morning.

With great difficulty, I let go of her hand.

She took a deep breath...and opened the door.

I wasn't ready for what lay on the other side. Long hallways were lined with glass-fronted offices. Men and women in suits hurried back and forth on floors so luxuriantly carpeted, you couldn't hear their footsteps. There were meeting rooms big enough for fifty people, break areas with bowls of fresh fruit, pastries, and fancy coffee. And that was just the executive floor. Below us were another six floors of architects, marketing, sales, finance, IT...

A small crowd of suits saw Lorna and pounced on her, demanding answers to a thousand questions. She was drawn away into a meeting and I was left on my own. So I did what I always did when I was stationed somewhere new: I walked around and tried to get the lay of the land.

But this was more alien than any foreign country I'd ever been to. I was in my usual jeans, boots and white shirt. Everyone else was in suits that cost more than I made in a month and their conversations were all in scales I could barely wrap my head around. Five thousand panes of glass were stuck on a ship in the Suez Canal. Twenty-two *miles* of cable needed to be ripped out and replaced in an office building. Two executives passed me talking about the latest estimates for the new airport in Mexico: *500...no, 520, no, with the new extension, it's going to be 540.* It took me a minute to realize they were talking in millions.

What the hell am I doing here? I wasn't right for this job. Bodyguards needed to blend in but I felt like a big, dumb hick. Maybe Gabriel could have pulled it off: he'd been used to the high life, back when he was stealing oil paintings and robbing banks. But I was used to a military paycheck.

Then I passed a wall-mounted TV in a break area. Some reporter was standing outside the building, talking about Lorna: supposedly he'd spoken to *sources on Wall Street* and they were worried that Lorna was *inexperienced, ill-equipped* and *might make decisions based on emotion, not good business sense.* They were undermining her before she'd even had a chance, while making thinly-veiled digs about her being female. I wanted to put my fist through the screen.

My jaw tightened and I glowered at my reflection on the TV. So *what* if I felt out of place? *Suck it up!* She had it way worse.

As the day went on, I caught little glimpses of her. Sitting at the head of the table in a glass-walled meeting room, her forehead cradled in her hands as she tried to digest the information being thrown at her by twelve different people at once. Shyly shaking hands with the mayor as he grandstanded and peacocked before demanding she slashed costs on the hospital project. Standing between two big, male execs, her small voice drowned out as the two of them screamed at each other that a messed-up concrete order was the *other* one's fault. She looked completely out of her depth. Of course she was: anyone but an experienced CEO would have been. But what knotted my stomach was that Lorna would think it was her fault.

We met up in the afternoon to go to her speech. We stepped into the elevator and as soon as the doors closed, Lorna slumped against the wall and closed her eyes. She looked ready to drop.

"Did you eat lunch?" I asked.

She shook her head.

I stepped closer before I could stop myself, that protective need taking over. "Did you stop *at all?*"

"I don't have time to stop." She sighed, eyes still closed. "My dad wasn't going to retire for another ten years, maybe more. We didn't have any kind of transition plan in place. Projects all over the world are waiting on decisions from him. Work's stalled, we're losing millions each day. So I have to make those decisions, but I don't know people like he did. I know how to calculate structural loads, but I don't know which glass manufacturer in China to trust, or whether a contractor in Delhi is ripping us off. And if I get this stuff wrong, we could lose even more money."

The elevator reached the parking garage and the doors slid open. But Lorna just stood there slumped against the wall, eyes closed. I silently reached out and held down the button to hold the doors open. The last thing I was going to do was rush her.

After another few seconds, she took a deep breath, opened her eyes and pushed off from the wall. "Thank you," she whispered.

"No problem," I told her as I fell beside her. As we walked to the big black Mercedes that would take us to the speech, I could feel the adrenaline starting to flow. Part of me was glad we were leaving the office, even though it meant she was more at risk. Out here, at least I could do some good.

We climbed into the car and the driver pulled away. As we sped through Manhattan, Lorna dug out the notes for her speech and stared at the neatly-printed cards. But I could tell she wasn't really seeing them. Her fingers crumpled the edges and she kept glancing at the window as if she was ready to jump through it to escape. The poor woman was terrified.

"You okay?" I asked.

It was a dumb-ass question but I've had enough scared rookies in my squad to know that you ask *you okay* because it gets them talking.

"I—" She licked her lips, took a breath, then blurted it. "I want my dad." She shook her head. "That's so stupid, it's like I'm ten."

"It's not stupid," I said firmly, twisting in my seat to face her. "It's normal. Especially when you're scared." I wanted to just wrap her in my arms and pull her to me.

She shook her head and straightened up. "I don't have time to miss him."

That damn near broke my heart. Because I knew where she was heading if she went down that road.

I leaned closer. Waited until she looked at me and pinned her with a look. "You gotta *make* time," I told her. "You gotta grieve. Only way to heal."

She swallowed and nodded. But I saw something else, a flicker of concern. She was wondering how I knew this stuff.

I knew I should tell her about Jillian and Max. It would help to know that I'd been through it. But then she'd try to comfort me. She wouldn't understand that my loss was different. I *deserved* to be in pain.

Luckily, at that moment we swept through the gates of the construction site and pulled up beside a crowd of reporters. Lorna jumped as camera lenses pressed against the window like monsters hunting for a way in. Flashes lit up the interior as they tried to get shots of her through the tinted glass. *Bastards!* Couldn't they see she was scared?

"Easy," I told her gently. "Wait for me to come around."

I got out of my side and pushed my way through the reporters, none too gently. Then I opened Lorna's door and took her hand, guiding her out while blocking the reporters with my body.

"Miss McBride, how's the company's debt looking?"

"Lorna, do you feel you have the experience to be—"

"Lorna, what do you say to the shareholders who are worried?"

"Lorna, over here!"

"Lorna!"

They descended on her in a flock. They were used to this game but she wasn't. She was too polite, stopping and turning when her name was called instead of *no comment*ing and pushing past. I put a hand on her back and propelled her forward, using my other arm to clear a path. The reporters were relentless: a few even snapped pictures of me and asked Lorna *who's the guy?* I ignored them.

As we walked, I looked quickly around. The temperature had dropped since that warm day at the marina: the air was bitingly cold and clear and I could see for miles. *Jesus,* we couldn't have picked a worse place for the speech. The site of the new hospital had been bulldozed flat, making a big open space with no cover at all. And all around it was an old industrial area, a maze of twisting pipes where a whole army could hide. The site had a couple of security guards but they didn't even have guns.

Doubts started to creep in. Should I have called in the team? I'd feel a hell of a lot better if we had Cal on overwatch, and Kian with his bodyguarding experience, and Colton ready to tussle any attackers to the ground.

No. I wasn't going to drag them into my problems.

I kept Lorna moving, heading towards the Portakabin that served as the site office. Another ten feet and we'd be safely inside.

Then a reporter lunged in from behind Lorna. He was about twenty, some vlogger looking for his next bit of clickbait. He shoved his phone's camera in Lorna's face. "Is it true you only got the job because some woke PR firm wanted a woman in charge?"

"What?" Lorna recoiled. "No!"

"What do you think your dad would say if he saw you running his company into the ground?"

Lorna's face crumpled. And I saw red.

I roared in anger and the vlogger turned just in time to get my fist in his face. The punch took him right off his feet and he went flying backwards to land in a heap on the ground. His phone sailed through the air and hit the ground with a very satisfying crack.

"See how many likes *that* gets," I snarled.

19

LORNA

THE ASSHOLE vlogger had hit me exactly where I was most vulnerable. I felt myself *break,* and he was getting it all on video. The other reporters closed in, eager for tears—

And then JD was there and the vlogger was just *gone,* like a truck had hit him. All the cameras swung around to point at JD. It gave me a precious few seconds to get my armor back in place. Which was good, because now *he* needed *me.*

The vlogger was trying to get up and JD was marching forward, ready to hit him again. I grabbed his arm and spoke in his ear. "*No! Come on!*" I towed him into the site office.

Thankfully, the press weren't allowed inside. I shut the door and spun to face JD, not mad, exactly, just panicked and worried. "Why did you do that? You can't hit people!"

"He had it coming." JD glanced at the door, ready to storm back out there.

I put my palms on his chest and pressed him back against the wall. "That's not how we deal with things!"

"That's how *I* deal with things."

"You could get sued! It was just words."

He scowled. "Well, those words were upsetting you."

I just...*melted.* No man had ever been so fiercely protective of me, before. And it hit me that protecting people was *what he did.* He'd protect me even if it put him in danger, even if I begged him not to. Getting frustrated with him for that would be like getting mad at a guard dog for barking at an intruder. "Thank you," I told him.

His scowl faded and he gave me a gruff little nod. Then, as his head came up, those prairie-sky eyes locked with mine and a wave of raw heat slammed into me. I saw his eyes flick to the soft skin at the side of my neck. Then to my breasts. My lips.

I realized my hands were still pressed to his chest. The heat of him was soaking into my palms through the thin cotton of his shirt. He pushed off from the wall, his muscles moving under my hands and loomed over me, huge and rough and gorgeous. I caught my breath. "JD..."

"They're—" A female voice from the doorway, abruptly cut off.

JD and I spun and saw one of the company PR people poking her head around the door. Her eyes were big and worried, her cheeks flushing. "Sorry. They're ready for you on stage."

I dropped my hands from JD's chest as if scalded. "Thanks," I mumbled. "Coming."

She retreated into the hallway. When I looked back to JD, he was glaring off into a corner, as if furiously trying to get himself under control. *Had he been about to—* God, what would have happened if she hadn't walked in?

I'd have to think about that later. *The speech!* I could feel the panic starting in my chest. All those people focused on *me...*

A big hand gripped my shoulder. I looked up and his eyes were tender, the lust locked down tight. "Don't worry," he told me. "You'll be great."

We followed the PR woman down a hallway and out of a side door to where a stage had been set up. *Maybe no one will have come,* I thought hopefully. Then I saw the crowd and my stomach dropped. There were at least a couple of hundred people there, plus the press. The PR woman was beckoning me forward but I felt like my feet were glued to the floor.

JD looked me right in the eye and nodded. *You got this.*

I forced myself to walk over to the podium, praying they couldn't see my legs shaking. I spread out my notes.

"Um."

Hundreds of expectant faces looked up at me. Cameras and phones ate up every second of awkward silence, starting a feedback loop in my mind. *I've screwed this up already!*

I looked down at my notes. The PR department had written them: smooth, safe marketing fluff about going *forward into the future.* Miles or my dad could have sold it, because they could sell anything. But there was no substance for my weird brain to lock onto and my mind just stalled, like an engine trying to run on water. I could see the journalists glancing at one another and grinning: *this is a trainwreck.*

I scanned the crowd and found Paige. She'd volunteered to come, just so there'd be one friendly face. She was chewing her lip, her eyes willing me on. I glanced into the wings and saw JD, his body tensed as if he was about to run on, toss me over his shoulder and rescue me, and that sounded amazing, however bad it would look. But I had to do this, for my dad.

My dad.

"I shouldn't be up here," I blurted into the mic.

That made the press sit up.

"My dad was always the one who made the speeches," I explained. "I just drew the plans. I designed this hospital but it was my dad who got us here." The words flowed easily because I was just telling the truth. "You know when he first decided we should build it? It was after the TPS bridge collapse, five years ago."

I almost didn't see the crowd, now. I was lost in the memory. "It hit us hard, just like all New Yorkers. Hundreds dead. Hundreds more injured. My dad heard about the ambulances taking too long to arrive and it made him so angry, it killed him to see people suffer. He said, "This city needs to finally build a new trauma center." I shook my head. "No one thought it was possible. The state didn't have the budget and the land was too expensive. But my dad found this site and figured out a way."

I suddenly realized I'd been rambling on, caught up in thinking about my dad. *Oh God.* "Um, thank you."

And suddenly, the crowd was applauding. I stared at them, bewildered. *But I didn't even give a speech!* I'd just...talked. I looked at the PR woman and she was nodding and applauding. I went shaky with relief. *It's over.*

That's when I saw movement at the back of the crowd. A man in a baseball cap swung his arm up to point at me. A flash of silver in his hand—

"*Gun!*" yelled JD.

He slammed into me as a gunshot rang out.

20

LORNA

My FEET LEFT the floor and for a second I was weightless. Then I crashed down hard on the stage, JD on top of me. He twisted a little onto his side, staring into my eyes from just a few inches away.

There was another gunshot and the noise of wood splintering, right behind JD. I suddenly realized what he was doing: he'd made his body into a wall, between me and the shooter. *No! JD!* I wanted to get us both somewhere safe but my body wouldn't listen: I just lay there, numb.

Two more gunshots and I felt things cut through the air above me, close enough that I could feel the breeze on my face.

Then nothing.

I heard someone panting and realized it was me.

I started to take stock. I was on my back and JD was hunched over me, one knee between my thighs. My skirt was hiked up and JD's arm was pressed tight against the side of my breast.

JD looked over his shoulder, scowling towards the crowd, his whole body tense: I thought of a dog alerting. He clearly wanted to jump down off the stage and race after the gunman. So why didn't he?

Then it clicked. He was staying there to make sure I was safe.

JD shouted to someone in the crowd and they yelled back an answer. JD's body relaxed. "It's okay," he told me. "He's gone." He looked down at me. "Are you hit?"

Hit. He means by a bullet. My mind wouldn't function and I couldn't make my mouth move.

JD didn't wait for an answer. He started patting me down, his big hands starting at my shoulders and tracing quickly but efficiently down my body and under my back. "You're okay," he told me, and I could hear the shaky relief in his voice. "You're okay."

He seemed to become aware of how we were lying and I felt his cock harden against my thigh. Then he was up and offering me his hand.

I tried to take it but my limbs felt like concrete. I stared up at him, panicked.

"It's okay," he told me in that low, Texas growl. "You're in shock. I'm getting you out of here." He bent, slid an arm under my back and another under my legs and—

Suddenly I was lifted into the air. Cradling me protectively in his arms, he marched off the stage and through the last few stragglers - almost everyone had fled as soon as the first shot rang out. Then we were at the car and he was carefully sliding me onto the back seat. Paige was standing nearby, her face white. "You too," JD told her. "Get in."

"But I drove myself here," Paige began. "My car—"

"Paige, *get in the car!*" JD ordered.

Paige jumped in beside me. You didn't argue with JD when he used *that* voice.

JD slammed the door. I saw him point at one of the reporters. "You! You were filming the crowd. I'm gonna need a copy of the footage. You send it to McBride Construction, okay?"

The reporter nodded meekly, not about to argue with a six-foot Texan.

JD jumped into the passenger seat and told the driver to *go,* and I was pushed back in my seat as the car shot away.

As we sped towards home, I started to get...flashes. I'd be looking at Paige or JD or the scenery but I'd see the man in the crowd, or hear the gunshot, or feel myself flying through the air.

It's real.

My feet didn't feel right. I looked down and saw that one heel had snapped clean off my shoe, probably when JD had knocked me down. My hair had slipped partially out of its ponytail and as I tried to fix it, something fell out onto my lap. A tiny chunk of wood: one of the bullets must have hit the podium. The shooter had missed JD and me by inches.

It's real. I'd been hoping that JD was wrong but someone really was trying to kill me. If JD hadn't knocked me down, Cody would be an orphan.

"Pull over," I croaked. My first words since it happened. "Pull over, please."

JD said something to the driver and we pulled over at the side of the road. I scrambled out and threw up.

As I knelt there in the grass, panting, JD squatted down beside me and gently rubbed my back. "Sorry," I managed at last. "I'm sorry." Tears were running down my face and I wasn't sure when they'd started. I wiped my mouth and shook my head. I didn't understand: there'd been gunfire in Mexico and I hadn't reacted like this. "Why —" I blubbed. "Why am I—"

"Because you're human," said JD gently.

I hiccoughed and sobbed, grabbing at the grass with both hands, trying to hang on to a world that was spinning out of control. Someone wanted me dead, someone powerful, and I didn't have any idea who or why—"They're going to kill me," I mumbled. "They're going to kill me."

JD pulled me to him and wrapped me in a fierce hug. "No they're fucking not."

21

JD

BACK AT THE PENTHOUSE, I got Lorna to her bedroom. "Stay with her," I told Paige.

Paige nodded. But I didn't miss the look she gave me. If she'd suspected there was something between Lorna and me before, she was certain, now. I stalked away, flushing. *Goddammit.* How was it that bullets could be flying and I'd be ice cold, but as soon as my feelings for Lorna came up, I felt like a kid with a crush?

As I left them, Lorna's phone rang: Miles was in Miami and he'd just seen the story on the news. She tearfully reassured him that she was okay.

The cops showed up, wanting statements from all of us. Then the FBI swept in, led by a familiar face. "She hated saying it," said Agent Callahan, "but my boss agreed I was right all along. She's put me on the case. Let's start figuring out who's behind this."

The reporter who'd been filming the crowd had sent over the footage and Callahan and I ran through it, slowing down and going frame by frame when we got to the shooting. There he was, at the back of the crowd. With the baseball cap pulled low and sunglasses hiding his eyes, there was no way we were going to ID him. But from the way he aimed and squeezed off the shots, he'd been trained. He might even be former military. A hired hitman, maybe. But hired by who?

Callahan interviewed Lorna for over two hours, going through everyone who might want to hurt her, from former employees with a grudge to rival companies and foreign powers. I had to hand it to the guy, he was thorough. "I'll look into this asset stripper, Van der Meer," he told us. "And the property developer, Konstantin Gulyev."

"Is he really Russian mafia?" Lorna asked.

Callahan nodded. "Oh yeah. And he definitely has the means to pull this off. But he doesn't normally go after civilians and I can't see him targeting a woman, or putting a kid at risk. I'll check it out, though. I've got an inside source I can ask."

"What about protection?" I asked.

'I'll station a couple of agents downstairs, at the building entrance. And I'll have a couple more accompany you when you go anywhere. But the best protection is having *you* by her side." He glanced between Lorna and me. "Keep her close."

I nodded silently. I was really starting to like the guy and it was a huge relief to finally have some professional help. I'd been on the verge of calling in the team a few times but, now the FBI were here, I figured we'd be okay.

I followed Callahan out to the elevator. "So Van Der Meer's your main suspect. You're going to look into Konstantin Gulyev. Anyone else on your radar?"

Callahan rubbed at his stubble. "I got a theory. But I don't want to say anything until it firms up. Hang tight, cowboy, I'll be in touch." The elevator doors closed and he was gone.

When I walked back into the penthouse, I met Lorna coming the other way. She'd put on a fresh suit and cleaned herself up but she still looked pale. I blocked her path. "Whoa there. Where are you going?"

"It's Tuesday," she told me. "I always pick Cody up from school on Tuesdays."

Paige ran up. "I told you, I'll go. You should rest."

I held up my hands. "*I'll* go. End of discussion." I looked at Lorna.

"You're still shaken up, you shouldn't be driving. Go have a hot bath..." An image jumped into my head: her breasts just breaking the surface of the water, the skin shining wetly, nipples hardening as the cold air brushed them. I felt myself flush. *Goddamn it!* "...or something," I finished weakly. "And Paige, please look after her."

Paige nodded, put her arm around Lorna and led her gently away.

I hopped into the big black Mercedes the family leased and drove to Cody's school. As I drew close, I checked my gun. There was another reason I'd wanted to do this myself: if the killer had been watching the family, he might know their routines and be lying in wait.

I pulled up down the street from the school and joined the sea of waiting moms at the entrance. There were only a few guys and they were harried lawyers in suits who'd been told to pick the kids up at the last minute, or stay-at-home dads with baby slings and bicycles. I didn't exactly fit in, with my sunglasses and denim jacket, and when a few of the moms politely said *hi* and they heard my Texas drawl, that drew more stares.

Then Cody ran up to me. "JD! Is my mom okay?"

"She's fine," I told him, eyes searching the crowd. "I just wanted to see your school. C'mon, car's this way."

I got in the front and he climbed in the back. My nose wrinkled as I caught a whiff of chlorine. *Maybe he had swim practice.* But his hair was dry.

Cody got his safety belt on and sat back in his seat, arms crossed. "My mom says you're just a precaution."

"That's right. Just in case." I pulled away and headed for the McBride Building.

"But if someone tries to hurt us, you'll stop them."

"Yeah."

"Why would someone want to hurt my mom?"

Just the thought of it, just the word *hurt* next to my mental image of Lorna, made my shoulders tense. "I don't know, kid."

Cody went quiet for a while as we crept through the traffic. Then, "You're a soldier, right?"

"I used to be."

"You ever killed anyone?"

"Yeah."

He went quiet again. A moment later, as we hit a red light, "This guy that's trying to hurt us...are you going to kill him?"

"If I have to." I met his gaze in the rear-view mirror. The poor kid was staring at me with big, scared eyes. He was too young for any of this. He just wanted to know that everything was going to be okay—

The light was still on red. I twisted around in my seat and let myself be a little less gruff, just for a minute. "Listen. You don't need to worry about this stuff. This guy comes anywhere near you or your mom, he's gonna find out it was a real bad idea. Whatever happens, I *will* keep you safe. Okay?"

"You promise?"

That caught me off guard. It was a long time since I'd promised anything. "Yeah," I said, my voice tight. "Yeah, I promise."

He held his hand out solemnly. I blinked at it for a second, then took his little hand in my big one and shook it. My chest ached, memories of Max flooding my mind.

The car behind us honked. *Dammit.* The light had changed. I twisted back to front and got us moving, then forced myself back into gruff mode. I adjusted the rear-view mirror and noticed that Cody's backpack was dripping, leaving a wet pool on the backseat. "Why's your backpack all wet?" I asked without turning around.

"I dropped it. In a puddle."

I glanced up. There wasn't a cloud in the sky and the sidewalks were bone dry. Now I knew where the smell of chlorine was coming from. Someone had thrown his backpack in the pool. The kid was being bullied.

A hot, vengeful rage simmered up from deep inside and my knuckles went white on the steering wheel. The poor kid had lost his grandfather and he was terrified some psycho was going to hurt his mom: did he not have enough to deal with? Someone was *bullying* him? I wanted to throw the car into a 180, race back to the school, and fucking *annihilate* the asshole.

But I couldn't. *He's not your kid,* I told myself.

I took a long, deep breath...and drove us back to the penthouse.

When we got back, I went to check on Lorna but she wasn't in her room. On a hunch, I went downstairs to the offices and gave a silent sigh of relief when I found her sitting at her dad's old desk. "I told you to rest," I grumbled from the doorway.

"I don't have time to rest." She didn't look up from her screen. "I'm trying to catch up. I was away for half the afternoon."

"You were away because *someone shot at you.*" Before I knew what I was doing, I'd marched over to her. "Go rest. The company will still be here tomorrow."

"Not if I don't keep all the plates spinning," she muttered, tapping at the keyboard.

Worry twisted in my chest. She was working way too hard, especially with everything else going on in her life. My voice turned firm and I put a hand on her shoulder. "You're paying me to protect you. That includes protecting you from yourself. Go upstairs."

She sighed. 'Okay, fine. I want to check on Cody anyway. Thanks for picking him up."

I thought about his wet backpack. "Does he get on well with the other kids?"

"Yeah. He has lots of friends. Why?"

So she had no idea about the bullying. I shrugged. "Nothing." I figured there must be a reason Cody hadn't told her and I didn't want to go blundering in without knowing why.

We went back up to the penthouse and found a guy in his sixties with a soft white beard waiting for us at the door. "This is Marcus McTavish," Lorna told me. "My dad's tailor. I figured he could help you blend in a little better."

I started to protest: I didn't need a tailored suit and I sure as hell couldn't afford one. But Lorna held her hand up. "My treat." And she gave me that stubborn look, the one that reminded me so much of Jillian.

She'd given a little and let me march her upstairs. Maybe I needed to give a little, too. "...okay," I sighed. "Thanks."

Lorna gave me a pleased little smile and it worried me, how much that made my world light up. I led the tailor to my room and for close to an hour, he measured every part of me, showed me fabric swatches and talked me through different styles of suit. I didn't know a damn thing about fashion so I just told him I trusted his judgment, and went to find Lorna.

She wasn't in her bedroom again and when I checked with Cody, he said she'd just finished building Legos with him, and that I'd find her in the room at the end of the hall. I frowned, curious: it was one of the rooms she hadn't shown me on the tour. I opened the door and—

One whole wall of the room was glass, giving a view of New York as the setting sun painted the skyscrapers in shining copper and ruby red. Only there were *two* New Yorks, because the opposite wall was one big mirror, like in a gym. And between the two...

The sunset was so bright, all I could see was a silhouetted figure. One knee was bent at a perfect right angle and the other leg was stretched out dead straight behind it. The arms were high overhead, hands together, like it was raising a sword to the heavens. The figure was so perfectly still, I almost thought I was looking at a statue, some piece of modern art. Then I saw the chest moving in slow, regular rhythm and I realized I was looking at Lorna. *God, is she naked?* I could see the soft globes of her breasts, the firm curves of her ass and hips. Then, as my eyes adjusted, I realized she had a gym top and leggings on, but it was thin enough and tight enough that I could see every damn inch of her. My cock swelled and hardened as my eyes roved over her. God, she was perfect.

She moved, except...she didn't move like I would move, she *flowed,* pushing up into a pose where her legs made a triangle and her upper body hung parallel to the floor. *How does she do that?* I sure as hell couldn't do that. And she made it look effortless.

Music was playing, peaceful stuff that reminded me of things I'd heard when I was out in the Middle East. I realized she hadn't heard the door opening, and I was out of her sight-line. *She doesn't know I'm here.* Minutes passed and the room gradually darkened as I watched, entranced.

Lorna lifted one foot and balanced, her supporting leg rock-steady. She stepped forward and bent at the waist until her forehead almost brushed the floor and her ass was thrust up towards me, a ripe peach. *Jesus.* My cock was like an iron bar against my thigh, now. *Should I leave? Or—*

She lifted up, turned towards me and jumped back, startled. In the dim light, I was just a big hulking shadow. "It's me," I said quickly, and stepped forward so she could see.

The sun had fully set, now, and the skyscrapers outside had transformed into slender black obelisks draped in millions of glittering lights, like debutantes on their way to a ball. The glow edged her in silver light as I found her hands and grabbed them. "Sorry. Didn't mean to scare you."

She shook her head. "It's okay. I just didn't hear you. I kind of go off into my own little world." She looked down at her gym gear and shrugged awkwardly. "I have trouble switching my brain off. Exercise helps but I always hated running and sport and stuff. But yoga...it's all about angles and weight and balance. I think they designed it for architects. You focus so hard on getting everything lined up and balanced, you forget to think. And I need to not think, right now."

I nodded. I couldn't even imagine the stress she was under. "You looked good." *Shit.* It just spilled out before my brain had a chance to vet it. "I mean, you make it look good." *Not much better.* "I mean, you make it look easy." *Smooth, JD, real smooth.*

Her gray eyes glittered in the darkness, analyzing everything, probably realizing I'd been staring at her ass. She ducked her head and I couldn't see, in the darkness, if she was blushing. "You should try it."

"*Me?!*"

"I could show you. It might help your back. Your back hurts, right?"

How did she... Sure, my back hurt, but I just pushed on through, like you were meant to. No one else had ever been able to tell, not even the Stormfinch guys I worked with every day. She must have studied me as I walked, locating that knot of muscle in my back the same way she'd find the stress point in a building or a bridge. "Thanks. But I don't think I can see myself in Lycra."

She nodded meekly. My eyes were adjusting to the dim light, and I could make out more details. Her gym top was cherry red and it must have some sort of built-in bra because I couldn't see any bra straps, but I couldn't see any nipples, either. *Stop staring at her boobs!* And her tights were sea green and outlined every luscious curve of her rear. *And her ass!*

I stalked out, closed the door and leaned against it. From now on, I'd make damn sure I stayed out of that room because if I saw her in that tight yoga gear again, I was going to do something dumb. I let out a long growl of frustration, my cock still rock hard against my thigh. Being this close to her was torture.

And it got worse. For the next week, I never left her side for more than a half hour.

The days fell into a routine. I got up early, went up to the roof and ran a few laps around it, looking out at the city as the dawn broke across it. Then I'd grab a shower and eat breakfast with Lorna, Cody and Paige. Usually it was oatmeal and toast and stuff but one morning, Cody got me talking about food and I mentioned I used to make blueberry pancakes. He'd never had them. And before I knew what I was doing, I'd asked Paige to pick up flour, eggs and extra milk when she went grocery shopping. The next day I made a batch of them, hot and fluffy and drowning in maple syrup, and Cody thought they were the best thing ever. Lorna—who kept telling us she was too busy for breakfast—even tried some and just for a second...

Just for a second, I felt like I had a family again.

Paige took Cody to school each day, with one of the FBI agents riding shotgun. I went downstairs with Lorna and watched over her all day, either at the office or on-site visits. She was managing to keep everything running but as fast as she tackled one problem, a new one would come up. The latest thing was pay negotiations with the workers building the hydroelectric dam in Poland. "We have these negotiations every five years," Lorna told me. "My dad always handled it and it always went fine. But with me, their negotiator's just digging his heels in, holding out for more and more money. It's like they're seeing how far they can push me."

I was worried about her. She was working twelve hour days, barely eating and I guessed barely sleeping, either. Each day, she looked a little paler and more drawn. Meanwhile, business journalists were writing clickbait articles about how she was a mom, not a CEO, and it made me mad. They didn't realize that all those feminine qualities they thought were weaknesses were strengths. Yeah, she was a mom. It meant she cared about every employee like they were her kids. And just like a mom, she'd sacrifice her own health to look after them.

Early one morning, the tailor showed up with a whole pile of clothes for me: two suits, one gray and one blue, and eight tailored shirts. I stared at them, trying to get my head around clothes that cost as much as I made in a month. But when I pulled them on...*holy shit.* The shirts were the softest thing I'd ever felt and they fit like a glove: suddenly all my cheap shirts felt uncomfortable and scratchy. And the suit...wearing one still felt unnatural but this one kind of flowed around me, moving when I did, instead of pulling and catching, and when I took a look in the mirror...dammit, I thought I actually looked *good.*

I scowled at myself. I was turning into Danny. But I couldn't resist taking another look.

When I met Lorna in the hallway, she stopped in her tracks and just stared. I saw her eyes flick over my shoulders, my chest, my waist, my thighs. She took a shaky little breath that made my cock harden. "Do I look okay?" I asked.

Lorna looked away and I saw her cheeks flush. "You'll do."

In the evenings, Lorna would help Cody with his homework,

build Legos with him and then do a quick yoga session before putting in a few more hours of work. One time, Cody asked if I'd seen any sticky tape anywhere. I hunted around for him for a while, finally found some in a kitchen drawer and took it to him in his room. When I walked in, he panicked and tried to hide what he was repairing: someone had torn one of his math textbooks almost in half. Protective rage blossomed in my chest and I stepped forward before I could stop myself. "Who did this? Same kid who tossed your bag in the pool?"

Cody ducked his head, just like his mother, hiding behind his hair. Then he nodded.

"Does your mom know?"

He shook his head.

"Kid, you've gotta tell her. Let her help."

"No!"

"Why not?"

Cody lifted his head and glared at me from between locks of hair. "Because I don't want to run to mommy."

I gazed at him sadly. I remembered being that age, loving my mom but getting ready to turn into a man. What he needed was to talk to a guy about this stuff—

Don't, I told myself fiercely. He wasn't mine. But *fuck,* every fatherly instinct was firing, unleashing a flood of jagged, painful memories. Max falling and skinning both hands and knees, while we were playing tag in our yard. Max in tears after he left his toy dog in our car when we went on vacation, and me racing through the airport to rescue it before our flight left.

Max on the phone, that one time.

I was holding the doorpost in one hand as I leaned into the room and my hand *squeezed,* knuckles white. "Okay," I muttered to Cody. "I get it. But you're okay?"

"Yeah," said Cody. "I'm okay." We both knew he was lying. He looked at me. "Are *you* okay?"

"Yeah," I told him, my voice rough. "I'm okay."

We both knew I was lying, too.

~

The week passed quietly: no more attacks, nothing suspicious. But I knew Russ's killer was still out there, somewhere, waiting and planning. I called Callahan. "You any closer to figuring out who it is?" I demanded.

"Look, I know you private military guys just do whatever the hell you want but we're the FBI, it's got to be by the book. I have to find evidence, get warrants for wiretaps, it takes time." He sighed, as if he didn't like it, either. "Hang tight, cowboy, we'll get this guy."

I growled that I understood, and ended the call.

That night, I lay in my bed, unable to sleep. All week, I'd been unable to get the image of Lorna in that skintight yoga gear out of my mind. It wasn't just that it showed off those full breasts and ripe ass. It was that it showed off the way she moved, graceful and feminine, breasts bobbing as she bent and arched and... I realized my hand had snaked into my boxers and I was slowly stroking myself, something I'd been holding back from doing all week. *Dammit...* But maybe it'd help me sleep. I thought of the way she'd bent over, ass thrust in the air—

My door opened. *Jesus!* I sat bolt upright in bed like a guilty teenager and stared at Lorna, framed in my doorway by the hall light. "Sorry, did I wake you?" she asked.

I grunted noncommittally. *How much can she see?* The covers had fallen to my waist and I was bare chested. Could she tell that my cock was hard? "What's up?"

She leaned against the doorframe. "Remember the dam in Poland, the pay negotiations? They've completely broken down. The workers are threatening to strike. If they do, we won't complete the next stage of the dam on time. We won't get paid and we need that money for our other projects: the company's leveraged up to the hilt."

I nodded, trying to get my brain out of raw lust so I could have a conversation. But it wasn't easy because she was in a nightshirt, some pink thing with a cartoon kitten on the front, and it only reached about an inch below the bottom of her panties. My hand was still around my cock under the covers and I didn't dare move it in case she saw. "What do we do?"

"We've got to go there and see if we can thrash it out in person," she said. "We'll have to fly out tomorrow." She stepped back from the door. "I'll let you sleep."

The door closed, leaving me in darkness. But now I was wide awake, replaying her words over and over. Had there been a tiny pause, before *sleep?* Had I seen her glance down at my lower body?

Did she know that I'd been jacking off? Did she guess it was her I was jacking off to?

I groaned, punched my pillow into shape and lay down. I needed to get some sleep. A foreign trip. Just the two of us, alone on a plane for hours. God, this was going to be unbearable.

On the plus side, Poland was a stable country and whoever the killer was, he was *here,* in New York. The trip should be safe.

Right?

22

LORNA

I WAS LEANING SO low over my drawing board that the white paper was all I could see. The lines seemed to draw themselves and I could feel myself frowning as my pencil moved. It wasn't a skyscraper or an apartment complex. This was smaller, modern but traditional, with lots of wood. It felt warm, safe...*cozy*.

A shadow fell across the white expanse. A rugged jaw, a Stetson. I spun around on my stool. *JD!* But why was he back in jeans? We had to leave for Poland any minute.

He marched closer. I saw his blue eyes narrow in lust and there was a sudden, silent detonation deep inside me, shockwaves rippling out to every part of my body. I was pinned by that stare, unable to get up or speak or do anything except breathe faster and faster—

He leaned down and put both hands on my waist, the heat throbbing from his palms through my turtleneck sweater. I sat there breathing hard, our faces inches apart. Then he let out a low growl and—

I groaned as his lips met mine. That hard upper lip spread me and I flowered open under him, then his tongue was seeking mine. His hands slid up my sides, pushing up my sweater as he pressed me back against my drawing board.

I glanced towards the glass walls of my office. *Everyone will see!* But then he pushed my bra up and lightly squeezed my breasts, thumbs brushing my nipples, and I didn't care. "Don't stop," I panted against his mouth.

"Don't stop what?" asked JD in a curious voice.

I opened my eyes. He was in his dark gray suit and the ceiling behind him was curved. And my drawing board had turned to soft leather under my back...

I blinked a few times and fought my way up through sleepy brain fog. We were on the jet. I must have dozed off and dreamed. And JD had heard me say—

"Don't stop *what?*" he repeated. He was looming over me, arms braced against the ceiling, eyes crinkled as he frowned down at me. I sat there panting. My brain had flashed to hot embarrassment but my lips were still tingling from the dream kiss, my breasts still aching where his hands had squeezed them. Half of me wanted to curl up and die, the other half wanted to grab the collar of his shirt and pull him down on top of me.

"Stirring," I said, not very convincingly. "I was watching you mix concrete."

JD raised one eyebrow and pinned me with a look, just like in the dream. Those blue eyes *burned*...oh God, did he *know?*

Then he nodded and turned away. "Sorry I woke you." He pointed to the window beside me and I realized that that's why he'd been leaning over me, to raise the shutter. "We're landing in a few minutes."

Already? "What time is it?"

"About one in the morning, our time."

My brain fog started to clear. That's right, we'd got on the plane at five in the evening. I'd wanted to leave earlier but I'd been caught up in meetings all day. Plus, Paige's mother had broken her leg so Paige had to go see her which meant I'd had to arrange for Cody to stay at a friend's house for the night. It was about an eight hour flight to Poland: no wonder I'd dozed off, it was the middle of the night. But then how come a sunrise was blasting me? I shielded my eyes "What time is it *here?*"

"Six in the morning," JD said apologetically.

I groaned. I'd only had a few hours of sleep and now I was about to start a whole new day. I wasn't even sure what day it *was*. I ran my hands through my hair, trying to make myself look as if I hadn't slept in my suit. "How do I look?" I asked, without much hope.

JD's gaze swept slowly down my body, the heat of it soaking into me. I caught my breath, every inch of me waking and standing to attention. It felt like my clothes were disintegrating, leaving me nakedly exposed, skin throbbing. But it felt reverent as well, his eyes staying on my lips and eyes for as long as my breasts and hips. "You look great," he said at last.

I broke his gaze and fastened my seatbelt for landing, but it took my shaking fingers three attempts to slot the buckle. I wasn't used to anyone looking at me like that. I'd been in mom mode for years: all that had mattered was Cody. But it was more than that. Being a mom was just an excuse. I hadn't felt attractive since Adrian left me.

I risked a glance across the aisle to JD. I liked him. *More* than liked him. He was hot as hell, he had an old-fashioned charm and he made me feel safe like no one else. He grounded me in the physical world, making my brain spin down and stop for a while: he balanced me. And for some reason, he liked me. But then why did he keep pulling away? I bit my lip. Cody already liked him. I didn't want him to get close to JD and then have him up and leave: he'd already lost his dad *and* his grandfather. I wasn't sure if he could take losing JD and I wasn't sure if I could, either.

At the airport, we climbed into an SUV and a driver was soon speeding us through the countryside. It was a cool, crisp morning and shafts of golden sunlight were chasing pools of mist out of the valleys. With the mountains in the background, it was unspeakably beautiful. My dad had spent a lot of time here when he was setting up the dam project and I could see now why he'd loved it so much.

Then the dam came into view, a two-hundred-foot sloping wall of concrete that would one day hold back millions of tons of water and bring clean power to this whole area. As we started to descend into the valley, the wall grew and grew, until we felt like mice looking up at a refrigerator. JD craned his head out of the window and cursed in amazement.

The head of construction was waiting for us, a big Polish guy in his sixties called Michal with white, mutton-chop sideburns. He took me to the small site office. JD waited outside, watching for trouble.

Michal took me by the hand. "I was sorry to hear about your father. Russ was deeply respected by the whole team."

I nodded, trying to stay composed. I should have expected this: the project had started almost forty years ago. When my dad had first come over here, he'd been a young man. It had taken many trips and over thirty years to finally get the Polish government to sign off on the project and then there'd been five years of construction. Of course Michal and my dad would have been close. Michal brought out a bottle of vodka and two shot glasses. "A toast," he said. "To Russ."

I didn't generally drink at eight in the morning but I clinked glasses and we drank, the vodka icy-smooth but with a long, fiery tail.

"Your English is very good," I told Michal.

"It's got better," he said modestly. Then he chuckled, remembering. "When your father first came out here, I could only say *hello* and *very good.*"

"How did you manage?"

He froze. Then, "We had to get someone in to translate. A local woman." He stood up and busied himself putting the vodka away. "Now to business—"

But my mind was spinning, remembering the photo I'd found. "What was her name?"

Michal blanched. His jaw tightened determinedly. I recognized that look: the look of one man protecting another.

"Please," I said, my voice a little strained.

Michal cursed under his breath. "Maria," he said at last. "Maria Burski."

It *was* her. I stared at Michal. *Go on.* He rubbed the back of his neck, then sighed in resignation and sat back down.

"Your father was here for some weeks. Maria translated for him, not just with me but with the government officials. The two of them became...close."

Jesus. It had that sensation again, like I was plummeting into space. My dad had cheated on my mom, while he'd been in Poland. *Why would he... How could he?!*

Michal saw my expression and shook his head viciously, muttering something. "Don't worry about that *czarownica*."

"*Czarownica*?"

"*Witch*," Michal said darkly. "Russ was a good man. Maria, she..." He mimed clawing at something, sinking talons into it. "She was trouble, right from the start. Beautiful, but she drank, she used drugs. She was...unstable."

My mind was spinning. I'd never thought of my dad as the sort of man who'd have an affair. I wanted to run. Get the hell out of that room and go somewhere I could be alone and just process. Instead, I had another problem to solve. "Let's go talk to the workers and try to get things worked out."

Michal nodded. "I will get their negotiator to come in here."

He reached for his radio but I put my hand on his. "Stop, no. I'll go to them." I needed to make peace with the guy, not summon him to the office like a naughty schoolboy.

Michal stared at me. "You want to go into the site?" He looked me up and down.

"I brought work boots," I told him. "And jeans." Why was he so surprised? My dad must have walked around the site all the time.

I changed, JD joined us and then Michal handed out hard hats and high-vis vests and we went into the site, our boots squelching in the mud. I could see JD watching for danger: when a truck or bulldozer thundered by us, he'd shift position so that he stayed between me and it. I was pretty sure he didn't even realize he was doing it, but it made me feel warm inside, *safe* in a way I wanted to last forever.

The dam was a towering wall of huge concrete blocks, covered in scaffolding and crawling with workers. Already, it was two hundred feet high and it was still growing. Workers blinked in shock when they saw me. Then, instead of nodding hello or shaking hands, they made a point of turning their backs. *Not a good sign.*

Michal showed us to the man who was representing the workers in the negotiations, a gruff little guy called Bolek. He, too, looked surprised to see me marching through the mud. He shook my hand politely but, as soon as I tried to talk money, he crossed his arms and stonewalled me, just as he had in all our conference calls. "We want an eight percent rise."

"Six," I told him gently. "That's more than generous." And it was.

He stuck out his chin. "Eight."

Eight was ridiculous and he knew it. *What's going on?* "Six and a half," I tried.

"Eight."

I stared at him, bewildered. I was lousy at this kind of thing but even I knew that wasn't how you negotiated. You had to give *some* ground.

Then I glanced around at the other workers. They'd stopped work to watch and were smirking and nudging each other.

I suddenly knew why they'd all been so surprised to see me down here in the mud when my dad had visited all the time. Why Bolek wouldn't negotiate in good faith with me, why they had no respect for me. My dad had been one of them. But I was a woman.

I looked across at JD and saw the fury in his eyes. He'd realized what was going on, too, and his shoulders squared like he wanted to thump Bolek. But he knew I had to fix this myself.

"I have work to do," Bolek told me. "Give us eight percent or we strike tomorrow." And he turned his back and marched off.

I stared at him, open-mouthed. There was nothing I could do. The company couldn't afford an eight percent rise and even if I gave it to him, he'd just ask for nine and then ten. He'd push and push because even though I was CEO, I was beneath him.

There was a rising chorus of panicked yells, off to my left. I turned to see one of the big, yellow bulldozers thundering towards me. I tried to get out of the way but there was no time: the thing was going full speed. *Why doesn't he slow down? Doesn't he see me?*

I looked up at the cab. *Oh Jesus!*

There was no one at the wheel.

23

LORNA

I RAN but there was just too far to go. The bulldozer was terrifyingly wide, much wider than a car, and it was almost on top of me. Its huge metal shovel was going to slice right into my legs.

I threw myself forward...and JD's big hands grabbed mine. He pulled and twisted and my feet left the ground as he swung me out of the way. The bulldozer flashed past less than a foot behind us.

He clutched me close and stared down at me, those prairie-sky eyes full of fear. I could feel his heart pounding. For a second, all the stoic gruffness fell away and he just squeezed me, harder than he ever had. A big, warm swell broke in my chest and I clutched him back, speechless.

A crash of metal made us look up. The bulldozer had smashed into the bottom of the scaffolding, knocking down several support poles. It came to a stop up against the dam and someone managed to shut the engine off, but the damage was done. The whole scaffold tower sagged and began to lean sickeningly. And there were at least thirty men still on it, some of them a hundred feet off the ground. "Oh God," I moaned aloud.

The scaffold tower tilted towards us and people scattered, fleeing the site. JD tried to pull me away but I tugged back against his hand. "No! We've got to help them!"

"The whole thing's coming down!" JD snapped, still pulling.

I pointed to the men on the scaffold. "They're—" I tried to explain that they were my responsibility. They'd signed up with McBride Construction, trusting us to keep them safe, and if they didn't come home to their wives and kids tonight, that was on me. But there was no time. "I'm not leaving them!" I blurted.

JD stared at me. Then his face softened and he stopped pulling on my hand.. He got it. He was a leader. You don't leave people behind.

I turned to look at the scaffold tower. A lot of the ladders had fallen over. People were trying to get them back into place so their friends could climb down but there was no time. The whole thing was collapsing in on itself. I looked at the shifting, trembling boards and the straining poles and my weird brain kicked in: I could see the stresses, see the weakest point. It needed support...*there.*

I ran to a fallen support pole but it was too heavy for me to lift. "Help me with this thing!" I yelled, and JD raced over and picked up the other end. "We've got to cram this underneath," I told him, pointing. "Right *there,* where that board's sagging. Come on!"

We ran up to the dam, dodging the people running the other way. I got my end of the pole up and under the collapsing tower and JD helped me force it into place. The scaffold tower stabilized and there were shouts of relief from above. But there were worrying creaks and groans, too. Tons of weight were now resting on this one pole.

I grabbed hold of it. "We've got to keep it vertical," I panted. "It's strong when the weight's coming straight down but if it leans, it'll bend and snap." I glanced up. We were right under the scaffold tower: if the pole *did* snap, it was all coming down on top of us.

JD nodded grimly and grabbed hold of the other side of the pole. We leaned inwards, using all our strength to hold the pole upright, our faces inches apart.

There was a creak of tortured metal above us, then a crash as something gave way. The foot of the pole skittered across the ground.

"Push!" I said through gritted teeth. My boots dug trails in the mud as I pulled and JD pushed.

We got the pole vertical again and I heard running feet above us as the men raced to ladders and climbed down. That was good, but as their weight moved around, it made the tower teeter even more. The pole started to lean towards me and I heaved against it. JD raced around to my side and pushed with me, his chest against my back, his hands on mine. The tower stabilized again, but I could feel it getting more precarious every second. We braced our legs, putting everything we had into keeping the pole straight...

"They're all off!" yelled Michal. "Get out!"

As soon as we let go of the pole, we heard the metal groan. We sprinted away from the dam, scaffold boards falling all around us. I looked over my shoulder and saw the pole we'd been holding twisting and rocking as the forces built up. Then it started to lean... and I winced as it suddenly snapped clean in two. The entire scaffold tower collapsed, sending up a huge cloud of dust that engulfed everyone.

I coughed and choked. "Everyone okay?"

Michal repeated it in Polish and the work crews started sounding off, checking they had everyone. But as the dust cleared, there were nods and cautious smiles. *Yes.* Everyone was okay. I slumped in relief.

In the quiet that followed, I heard someone start to clap. Then another, and another. I looked around and saw Bolek, the negotiator, leading the applause. I realized they were clapping *me*. I flushed, embarrassed but pleased.

Bolek walked right up to me and gripped my shoulder hard. Then he gave me a firm little nod of respect.

24

JD

LORNA STAYED at the site for two hours, helping with the clean-up, and agreeing a six and a half percent pay deal with Bolek. I stayed within touching distance the entire time, scowling suspiciously at anyone who came close.

I almost lost her. *I almost lost her!*

As soon as the bulldozer had been dug out of the scaffolding wreckage, I'd checked the cab. Someone had wedged a plank of wood on the gas pedal. A few guys had gotten a glimpse of someone jumping from the cab, but in a hard hat and high-vis vest, it could have been anyone.

On the plane on the way home, I sat watching her sleep, fuming at myself. I'd completely underestimated the danger she was in. I'd thought she'd be safe, thousands of miles from home. But either the killer had followed us here or, more likely, he'd hired locals to do his dirty work. That meant it was someone with serious money and international reach.

Her hair was still full of dust and I leaned closer and brushed a little of it out, then cursed under my breath when she nearly woke up. *Dumbass!* I stared at her in the dim light of the cabin. I couldn't take my eyes off her. I'd thought she was special before but the way she'd risked her life to save those men...my feelings had grown to a whole new, dangerous level.

But as that need, that *pull*, tugged at me, it made that ruined place in my chest resonate, echoing with memories of the first time I'd felt like this.

She's Merv's granddaughter, my mom had told me, her hands covered in bread flour. *She's going to help him with the ranch.*

I'd known even then, standing in the kitchen with her, that I was being matchmade. But I didn't take it seriously. I was 28, serving with Delta Force. Didn't imagine myself settling down soon or ever. But when my mom got an idea into her head... So I agreed to go to the church picnic, just to help my mom carry the food.

And that's when I saw her. White summer dress with a blue ribbon belt. Sun backlighting her and turning her long, blonde hair into a glowing halo like she was an honest-to-god angel, while silhouetting her body in a way that made my thoughts anything but pure.

Back then, I was even more of a big, dumb grunt. Didn't know what to say, didn't even approach her. But I spent half that night awake, thinking. I'd heard she had a fence down, on the edge of her ranch.

Before the sun had even crept over the horizon, I was riding over there with a sledgehammer and a bag full of fence posts. I worked away fixing her fence until, near noon, I heard a horse approaching. She rode up in blue jeans and a blouse, a flask of coffee in her saddlebag in case I was friendly and a shotgun across her back just in case I wasn't.

She looked at me.

I looked at her.

And I *knew.*

We were married a year later. She was my everything. My *forever.* For me, the Army had always been about protecting my country. But for the first time, I had a personal stake. When I went overseas, I knew I was doing it to keep her safe. And when Max was born, when I looked down at the fragile little wrapped-up bundle, I knew that I was doing it to make sure the world he grew up in was a good one. I was happy. Complete.

And then they were gone and I didn't think I'd ever feel those things again. Until...

I stared down at Lorna.

She made me feel the same way Jillian had. The thought was wonderful and terrible. The guilt mixed with the need until I could barely breathe.

I sat there silently watching her until we landed.

Back at the penthouse, Lorna scooped up Cody and hugged him, jamming the Polish army hat she'd bought him onto his head. And then suddenly, Miles scooped them *both* up from behind, making them yelp in surprise as he gathered them into his arms. He started to say something, but Lorna gave him a warning look. She gently asked Cody if he'd give us a minute and he ran off to his room. *She doesn't want him to know what happened,* I realized. Only when he'd gone did she turn back to Miles.

"I'm so glad you're okay." Miles's voice was shaking. "It should have been me."

Lorna hugged him again, hard. When they finally released each other, she looked up at him and her expression was heartbreaking: eyes full of hope, praying that now the tension between them would be over. But Miles turned away and I saw Lorna's shoulders slump in disappointment.

Miles ran his hand through his hair and made his voice fake-light. "Are you ready for the ball tomorrow? Got a dress?"

Lorna grimaced. "Do I really have to?"

"Dad would want you to go," said Miles. "I'll be there, too. And Paige is coming as my plus-one."

Lorna sighed and nodded. *Why doesn't she want to go?* I thought all women loved balls and fancy dresses.

My phone rang and I checked the screen. *Callahan.* I excused myself and went out onto the balcony, closing the doors behind me. "Yeah?"

"Heard about Poland," said Callahan. "If this fucker hired hitmen in Mexico and Poland, he's got money."

I stared out at New York. "Van der Meer," I told him. "He's got plenty."

"Is there any way he could have known you'd be in Poland?" Callahan asked.

I thought about that. "No. It wasn't a PR trip. The press didn't know about it. *We* didn't even know we were going until the night before. Only some high-level people at McBride knew."

"Hold that thought," said Callahan. "Remember I said I had a hunch? Well, my girlfriend's a hacker. She got me into a certain someone's bank account. Guess who's been making some serious cash withdrawals, starting a few months before Mexico?"

"Go on," I said, my voice tight.

"Miles McBride."

I spun around, my heart pounding. I could see Miles and Lorna talking inside. The thick glass blocked their voices but I could watch their body language. Lorna pleaded with him, her hands out, while Miles stared sullenly at the floor.

"You think he'd kill his own father? His own *sister?!*" The words felt alien in my mouth. I thought of my own sister, Erin. Nothing in the world could make me hate her.

"I can tell you've never been a cop," Callahan told me. Then his voice softened. "When a woman's killed, about one time in four it'll be a family member who did it."

No. Come on, no way. But then Lorna said something, Miles looked up and just for a moment, the anger in his eyes was open and unguarded. He stormed out, leaving Lorna close to tears.

"Miles wasn't in the convoy in Mexico, was he?" asked Callahan.

"No," I said reluctantly. "He had a stomach bug."

"And he didn't go on the boat with Russ, either."

"No..." It was a beautiful spring day but suddenly, I couldn't feel the sun on my shoulders at all. An icy dread had started to creep through me. I didn't want it to be real.

"Wanna hear my theory?" asked Callahan. "Miles has been working with Van der Meer for months. The plan was to kill Russ, have Miles take over as CEO, then Miles would sell the company to Van der Meer. They hire the hitmen in Mexico but they fail, thanks to you. Then they get someone to blow up Russ's boat and this time it works...but then they find out Miles isn't inheriting the company after all. Russ must have found out they were working together, that's why he changed his will."

I shook my head, even though he couldn't see it. I was *determined* for this not to be true. "Your theory doesn't make sense. Why would they try to kill Lorna? If she's killed, the company would pass to Cody, not Miles."

I heard a chair creak and imagined Callahan leaning back in smug satisfaction, waiting for me to catch on. But I wasn't smart like him. "*What?*" I begged.

"Think it through, cowboy. How old is Cody?"

I looked towards Cody's room. I could see him through the window, building with Legos. "Nine."

"Can you inherit a billion-dollar company at the age of nine?"

"No," I said tiredly. "Some adult would hold it in trust until—"

I broke off.

"I bet you a million dollars," said Callahan, "that Lorna's will says Miles holds onto all her assets—including the company—until Cody's eighteen."

Oh Christ. The ice had spread through my whole body, now. I struggled for something, *anything* that would make it not true.

Then I remembered the hug. The way Miles had held Lorna and Cody so tight, just a few minutes ago. No one was *that* good a liar. Relief flooded through me. "No," I told Callahan. "He loves her. And I spoke to him at the marina, he really did seem sick."

"Here's a funny thing about Miles McBride," said Callahan. "I'm looking at his school records and do you know what he was good at? I mean off-the-charts good, so good his teachers were pushing him to go into *this* instead of business?"

"What?" I asked.

"Acting. He even got offered a place at The Hessington School of Performing Arts - that's like the British Fenbrook Academy."

And finally, reluctantly, I lowered my instinctive resistance and let the idea in. And the more I thought about it, the more it all made horrible sense. Miles had inherited all of Russ's people skills. But he'd lost his mother, then been sent away to boarding school in England when he was still young. If he was bitter, resentful...is it possible that he'd grown up to be almost the reverse of Russ, equally charismatic but utterly cold inside?

I closed my eyes. "What do we do?" I asked.

"I can't do much," said Callahan. "The bank records I obtained illegally. Can't use 'em. I don't have enough evidence for a warrant. So it's your call, pal." He took a deep breath. "Do you tell Lorna that her brother's trying to kill her?"

25

LORNA

I'D GONE DOWN to my office to try to get some work done. But I could feel the pull of the photo through the wood of the desk. After an hour, I finally gave in, hauled open the drawer and grabbed it.

I stared into Maria's eyes. *Why?* Why had my dad done that? She was beautiful: had it just been lust? Or something else?

A noise in front of me. I looked up to find JD standing in the doorway. I slapped the photo face-down on the desk. "What's up?"

He stepped slowly into the room and shut the door behind him. His eyes went to the photo, then to me. "Nothing that can't wait. What's *that?*"

I shook my head. "Nothing. An old photo."

JD sat down across from me and pinned me with those soulful blue eyes, patient but firm. I held out for about four seconds before I gave in. I flipped over the photo and told him everything I'd learned in Poland. "I don't get..." I leaned my elbows on the desk and ran my fingers through my hair, staring at the photo. "Why do men *cheat?*"

"'Cause sometimes, our dicks go hard and we follow like they're pointing us to a well. 'Cause we spend so long looking across the street that we forget what we've got at home." He sighed. "'Cause we're dumbasses, I guess."

I looked up at him. "You must have been away from home a lot, in the army. Did you ever cheat?"

He shook his head and I saw a flash of that soul-deep pain again. Then he looked away.

"Sorry," I mumbled. When had he gotten divorced, and why? Had she cheated on him: is that what broke his heart?

JD looked at me again. "This isn't just about your dad," he said quietly. "Is it?"

I stared at him. Opened my mouth to say *yes*—

"He cheated on you?" JD said tightly. "Your ex?"

I froze. *How did he...* Then I nodded.

"You want to talk about it?"

I shook my head. I could feel the pain and hot humiliation filling my chest, the way it always did. I'd swallow it back down. It wasn't fair to offload it onto someone else. I'd managed, all these years.

But JD leaned across the desk and closed his big, warm hand around mine. He looked right into my eyes and gave me a tiny nod, offering to soak up all the pain I could throw at him.

I hesitated, biting my lip...and then I started to speak.

"I was a dork. God, you've seen me with people. I sat huddled down on the planning floor, with the other architects. I didn't go out, I didn't meet guys, let alone date. I didn't think anyone would want me."

JD's hand squeezed mine and his eyes burned, furious.

"Then..." I took a deep breath. "I was at this dinner thing, my dad was picking up an award. And there was this *guy*..." My voice softened and I shook my head in wonder. "Adrian was good-looking and sophisticated and he was so, *so* charming. He took me to one side and right there, he asked me out. Less than a year later, in The Hamptons, he asked me to marry him."

"My dad never liked Adrian. But he wanted me to be happy. We had this enormous wedding, I had a huge white dress...I felt like a princess. It was amazing, I'd always thought..."—she looked down at herself—"I'd always thought people like me didn't get the fairy tale." She swallowed. "At first, everything was great. My dad set Adrian up with a lot of his connections and Adrian started doing all these deals. I had plans to start my own architecture firm: I figured I'd work for my dad for a few years, then strike out on my own. I got pregnant with Cody and I was awed and scared and just over the moon. But Adrian...it didn't seem to affect him the same way. He started working away more. I figured it was just different for men."

I saw JD's jaw tighten. Like it hadn't been different for him, like he'd felt all those things I had.

"I had Cody," I said. "He was perfect. Amazing. I thought that Adrian would want to spend more time with us, now we were a family, but he just threw himself into his work even more. I barely saw him. It was like he had no interest in me or the baby." I could hear my voice starting to fracture. "And then, when Cody was one, there was this..." I shook my head and dropped my eyes, glaring down at the desk. "God I'm so stupid."

"No." JD's voice was so firm, so unshakeable in its belief, that it broke through all the self-hate. "That's one thing you're not." He put his finger under my chin and lifted it so I had to look at him. "You're the smartest goddamn person I've ever met," he told me. "Tell me what happened."

"He played tennis," I said. "Like, *a lot.* He went to this fancy tennis club every week. So I'd been learning how to restring a racquet because I figured that was something nice I could do for him, maybe it would make him—"—the words caught in my throat—"want to spend time with us. And it appealed to me, I mean, it's engineering. I got all excited about it: I'd ordered this really top-quality, state-of-the-art line from the internet and I'd watched all these videos on how to get the tension *just* right but..." I sighed. "Every time I checked his racquet, it hadn't gotten loose at all. Even after months and months, like he wasn't even using it. It didn't make sense. So eventually, I followed him... all the way to his mistress's house. The same mistress he'd been fucking the whole time we were married."

I took a shaky breath. "The—The worst part was, he wasn't sorry: he was *relieved.* He'd already gotten what he wanted out of the marriage. He'd made millions from the deals he did with my dad's friends." I shook my head. "He never loved me. I don't—"—my breath hitched—"I don't think he even *liked* me. But he put up with being married to me, in return for getting rich." She gave an awkward shrug. "Turns out, I was right: people like me *don't* get the fairy tale."

JD's chair scraped as he jumped to his feet. "Now you listen to me," he ordered. "He was a fucking asshole. He didn't deserve you."

My chest was shaking, tears close. "I should have left it alone. Why didn't I just *leave it alone?* Cody could still have a father and I'd still think—" I hiccoughed and my eyes went hot. "I'd still think that somebody—that somebody could—"

JD grabbed me by both shoulders and leaned in, looming over me. "Somebody—"

He bit it back. I looked up at him through a sea of tears. *Somebody what?* I blinked and—just for a second—I saw it in his eyes. And all the self-doubt and self-hate that Adrian left me with just got freakin' *annihilated* by a warm wave that took my breath away.

Then the pain returned to JD's eyes. He screwed them shut and when he opened them again, he was stoic and gruff and back under control. "Somebody *will*," he growled.

"Thank you," I whispered.

He turned and stalked out, leaving my office door swinging wide. I watched him all the way down the hall, barely daring to breathe.

I knew what I'd seen. What he'd been about to say.

Somebody does.

26

JD

I NEEDED SOMEWHERE I could be alone so I took the stairs up to the roof. It wasn't luxurious, like the rest of the penthouse: if you wanted to see the views, you were meant to use the balcony downstairs. But unlike the balcony, it was private.

I crashed through the door and staggered out into the open, breathing hard. The sun was just starting to go down, painting long fingers of shadow from the forest of air conditioning duct and turning the satellite dishes into crimson flowers. I glared left, then right. I'm usually the last one to lose my cool but right now, I just wanted something to break.

I've killed plenty of people, more than I'd like, but always because I had to, not because I wanted to. But if Lorna's ex was here in front of me...it scared me, what I'd do to him. The fucker had used her, stolen her chance at happiness, robbed Cody of a loving dad. And he'd destroyed her self-confidence so completely that she'd spent the last eight years alone. I was *trembling*, I was so angry with him.

But I was still more angry with myself. I'd so nearly said it, so nearly let slip everything she meant to me. I knew she knew, or at least she must have some idea. But as long as I didn't say it, we could both keep pretending. And as soon as the words had come into my head, the guilt had hit. I'd seen Jillian's face, not angry but heartbroken, not understanding how I could betray her.

I stalked around a corner, fuming and—

Cody was in his school uniform, sitting with his back against an air conditioning unit, looking up at the sky. He must have recognized my footsteps because he didn't look surprised. "Hi," he said.

I blinked at him. "Your mom know you're up here?"

"No." He brushed back his floppy hair and looked at me. "Does she know *you* are?"

"...no." I looked around, scowling, then leaned against an air conditioning duct.

"I guess we both had the same idea," said Cody.

"What's bothering *you*?" I asked, getting in first.

Cody shrugged, then seemed to wince. "My mom. I'm...worried that—" He broke off, not wanting to say it.

My anger disappeared, pushed aside by something more important. I crouched down. "I'm not gonna let that happen," I told him firmly.

"But there's only one of you."

"Yeah, but I'm from Texas."

Cody gave me a weak smile but I could see how close to tears he was. My chest ached. The poor kid was worried sick. I couldn't tell him not to worry: that's what you *do,* when someone you love is in danger. "You talk to your mom about this?"

Cody shook his head firmly. "She's got enough to worry about." He looked at me, concerned. "Don't tell her. She's already got me seeing the school counselor. I'm not crazy."

I sighed. "It doesn't mean you're crazy. Talking to a counselor can help people."

"Have *you* ever been to one?"

I hesitated. He was way too smart to lie to. "No." *Dammit.*

Cody adjusted his position against the air conditioning unit and winced again.

I frowned, suddenly remembering the wet backpack. "Something wrong with your back?"

Cody shook his head.

"Let me see," I ordered.

Cody hesitated. Then he scooched forward and lifted his school blazer and shirt. Bruises in purple, green and muddy yellow covered his back. I'd seen the aftermath of enough beatings to recognize the shapes. Someone had knocked him down and then kicked him, again and again.

Hot rage blossomed in my chest, stealing my breath. I felt my hands curl into fists. "Who did this?"

"Taylor. A kid at school."

"What's Taylor's problem?"

Cody stared at the ground. "I know the answers, in math and science. Back at the start of the year, I put my hand up a lot." He shook his head. "I don't anymore but it's too late."

My eyes narrowed. He was targeted for being smart, for being different, like his mom. And already, he'd started to hide how smart he was, hide *himself,* hoping no one would notice him. A life on the sidelines, in the corner...

I wasn't going to let that happen. I couldn't stop him worrying about his mom but this, *this* I could fix. "Stand up," I told him.

"Why?"

"Because I'm gonna teach you how to fight."

Cody stared at me, then looked down at his small form. "Have you seen me?! Taylor's a head taller than me!"

"Well, you gotta use what you've got."

"What have *I* got?"

"You're quick. You can use that. Come on, *up.*" He stood up. "Now, this asshole comes at you from behind, right?"

"Yeah."

"Well next time, what you're gonna do is whip around and slug him right in the guts. Here, let me show you."

For the next hour, I taught him how to punch, with all his weight behind it, and how to dodge and sidestep so he could get in the couple of good hits he needed. By the time we'd finished, our shadows stretched all the way to the edge of the roof and Cody was smiling.

"What about you?" he asked me suddenly. "What's bothering *you?*"

I froze and tried to think of a lie. But he didn't give me the chance. "It's my mom, isn't it? You like her."

Dammit. I rubbed my stubble. Then nodded.

Cody came closer. "My dad was shitty to her," he told me. "If anyone does that to her again, I'll kill them."

I nodded soberly. "Cody?" I said, looking him right in the eye. "I'd never hurt your mom."

Cody gave me a tight little nod and we went back downstairs. As Cody headed off to his room I stood at the bottom of the stairs, scowling, brooding. I knew I was getting attached and I knew that was a mistake.

And I knew that if I wanted to protect Lorna, like I'd told Cody I would, I had to man the fuck up and have the conversation I'd meant to have earlier.

I marched down another floor and found Lorna still in her office. "I know, I know," she mumbled, staring at her screen. "I need to take a break but I've got all this—"

"It ain't that," I said, closing the door. "You *do* need to stop working so hard, but it ain't that."

She looked at me, worried. "What?"

I sat down, took a deep breath and laid it all out for her. How Callahan and I thought Miles was working with Van der Meer. The cash taken from his bank account. The way he'd always been somewhere else, when the attacks happened. The fact only a few people knew we'd be in Poland.

I thought it'd be bad. I wasn't ready for *how* bad.

Lorna stared at with an expression I never wanted to see: she looked betrayed. "How could you believe that?" she asked. "How could you even *think* that?"

"Look, I know you don't want to think it," I said gently. "But try to take a step back. Think it through logically—"

"I don't need to think it through. He's my *brother!* He'd never hurt me." She stared at me. "Callahan *hacked his bank account* and you're okay with that?"

I was getting frustrated. "We're just trying to protect you."

She glared at me, those beautiful gray eyes like diamonds. "You don't need to protect me from *him!*"

I could feel myself digging in. "I know you love him, but it's a billion-dollar company. That much money can make people—"

She jumped to her feet. "*No!* Not him!"

"Lorna—"

"*No!*" She shook her head. "Just—JD please get out. Just get out, I can't talk to you right now."

Too late, I realized I'd gone too far. I fumbled for words but she just stared back at me, trying to keep her composure. *Aw crap,* I hadn't realized how close to tears she was. I got up and backed out of her office, nearly knocking my chair over, and closed the door behind me. When I was two paces away, I heard the tears start and I stopped, pinching the bridge of my nose. *Shit.* What had I done?

I'd been stubborn, that's what I'd done. I'd dug my boots in when I should have given. I should have been gentle, subtle, but I'd waded straight in there and now I'd hurt her. Jesus, she'd lost her mom, then her dad: Miles was the only family she had left and I'd just tried to tear them apart. Of *course* she was mad. And I had no idea how to fix it.

I marched up to the penthouse and into my room, then started pacing. It had been four years since I was even in a relationship and even with Jillian, I wasn't exactly Mr. Sensitive. *I'm not good at this stuff—*

I stopped pacing.

I wasn't good at this stuff. But fortunately, I knew someone who was.

I pulled out my phone. Glowered at the screen.

And then I called Danny.

27

JD

THE PHONE RANG for so long, I thought it was going to go to voicemail. Then Danny's rough London accent filled my ear. "JD?" he said breathlessly. "Sorry, mate, I was in bed."

I frowned. *In bed?* It was seven in the evening, which meant it was only five in the afternoon in Colorado. Why was he—

'Is that JD?" A soft, female voice, also out of breath. "Tell him I said hi."

Oh. I closed my eyes and took some deep breaths. Was it possible to get used to the idea of your best friend fucking your little sister? If it was, I wasn't there yet.

"Erin says hi," said Danny. He at least had the decency to sound embarrassed. "What's up?"

"Go somewhere Erin can't hear you," I muttered.

I heard him clump down some stairs. "Alright, I'm in the workshop. What's up?"

I drew in a deep breath. "How do you say you're sorry?"

Maybe it was my tone or maybe it was because I was calling *him*, but he got it immediately. "To a woman?"

"Uh-huh."

"A woman you *like?*"

"Uh-huh."

"Let me guess, you got on your high horse about something and wouldn't back down and left her in tears?"

"That's about the shape of it,' I muttered.

"You going to let me ask who she is and what the fuck is going on in New York?" asked Danny.

"Nope."

He sighed. "Okay. This thing you said: can you tell her you were wrong?"

I'd already thought of that. But I was pretty sure Callahan was right about Miles. I'd told Lorna to keep her safe. Lying to her would just put her in more danger. "No. What I told her was right. I just did it all wrong." I grimaced. "What do I say to her?"

"Tell her you were trying to do a good thing but you messed it up. Tell her that you know you can be a stubborn, grumpy arsehole. Tell her that you're sorry, that you're a work in progress, but you're trying to be better because she's worth it. And then ask for another chance. And most of all, show some vulnerability."

I rubbed at my stubble, saying nothing.

"Shit. I forgot who I was talking to," said Danny. "Okay, look...if you can't tell her all that, show her."

"How?"

"Make a sacrifice. Do something she knows you don't want to do."

An hour later, I gently pushed open the door to the yoga studio. Lorna was bent in an inverted V, her ass high in the air. It was fully dark outside and she'd lit some candles around the edge of the room. When the flames flickered in the draft from the door, she looked up. She saw it was me and the air in the room froze.

Then she took another look at me...and stared.

I shuffled my feet. I drew the line at Lycra but I'd been down the street and found a sportswear store. I was in a pair of running shorts, a t-shirt and bare feet.

"I figured I'd take you up on that offer," I said. "If it's still good."

We studied each other in the candlelight. God, she was beautiful. Those big, pale gray eyes searched my face, asking if I was going to hurt her again. And I did my best to look humble and sorry.

"Sure," she said at last.

She unrolled another yoga mat and I stood next to her, my hulking body dwarfing hers. And for the next hour, she coached me through a whole bunch of poses that looked easy but turned out to be sheer hell. She flowed through them like her body was made of taffy while I felt as clunky and awkward as one of the stone trolls in Erin's fantasy books. All the muscles I'd been ignoring for the last forty years suddenly had to start working and after a half hour, I was aching like I'd done two hours of weights. I'd thought that the army had hardened me into steel but when we lay on our backs with our legs in the air and did core work, it turned out my core was made of Jell-O.

But it was worth it. Because with every minute I endured, the tension between us unwound a little.

"How do you feel?" she asked me when we'd finished and I lay panting on the mat.

"Like I got run over by a truck," I said truthfully. "But thank you."

We stared at each other in the candlelight for a moment.

"I'm sorry," I said. "Didn't mean to—"

She nodded. "I know." Her voice was calm, pained...and resigned.

And I suddenly realized that she hadn't been upset before because she thought I was wrong. She'd been upset because a little part of her thought maybe I was right. She hated the idea, maybe even hated herself for doubting her brother. But she didn't hate me anymore. And that meant we could fight this thing together.

I nodded in thanks, relieved, and then got out of there before I screwed it up.

~

The next morning, I woke up, stretched and frowned. Something was different. It took me a moment to figure out what it was.

For the first time in years, my back didn't hurt. Maybe there was something to this yoga stuff after all. More importantly, I'd patched things up with Lorna. I grinned.

Then I caught my reflection in the mirror and it was like I'd stepped outside my body and was seeing myself with fresh eyes. With *their* eyes, Jillian and Max.

What the hell was I doing?

My feelings for her were getting stronger and stronger. When she'd been mad at me, nothing had mattered except putting things right. And Cody, too...when I thought about the two of them, it triggered echoes deep in my chest, right where Jillian and Max used to live.

And that made me feel like the worst husband and father in the world. Because no one, *no one* was allowed to replace them.

I had to get out, now. Walk away before things went any further. But I couldn't. She needed me.

So what the hell was I going to do?

28

LORNA

I LEANED low over Cody's math book, the sides of our heads pressed together. "Almost," I prompted gently. "Remember what we said about solving it when you have a negative constant?"

I waited patiently. Three breaths, then Cody gave an *ohhh* of understanding and feverishly wrote in the correct answer. "Attaboy!" I said, squeezing his shoulder.

"Enough work," Paige told us. "Eat your eggs!"

I sat down and quickly buttered some toast, even though I probably wouldn't get time to eat it. Cody had to head to school any minute and I should really already have gone if I wanted to make a dent in the mountain of work I had. But I loved helping him with his math homework: it was one of the few parts of being a mom I felt confident in. And it let me forget, just for a few minutes, that iron band constricting around my chest, the stress of everything that was going on. "What else have you got today?" I asked.

"History," said Cody despondently. "I've got to discuss which of General Lee's officers failed him."

"Trick question," rumbled JD as he walked in. "Whatever they did or didn't do, Lee's biggest problem was that he thought his men were invincible."

I loved the way he walked. Some guys strut, chests puffed out, but JD had this way of moving, unhurried and quiet but absolutely sure, like he knew exactly where he was going and he had nothing to prove. And with me seated, he looked even bigger, his shoulders huge as they rocked gently from side to side. He hadn't put his suit jacket on yet and as the morning sunlight blasted through his white shirt, it silhouetted the hard lines of his torso. God, I could just reach out and touch him, trail my fingers along the hard ridges of his obliques as he passed... I grabbed my coffee mug with both hands and gripped it firmly.

"Where'd you learn *that?*" Cody asked.

"First hand," said Paige, before JD could answer. She turned to him, eyes mock-innocent. "What was life like, back then?"

JD gave her a glower, she handed him a mug of coffee and they both grinned. This had become part of our breakfast routine: her teasing him about his age and him playing the grump. I was glad they got on so well.

Cody finished his breakfast, I gave him a kiss and he and Paige headed for the elevator, Cody fist-bumping JD on the way out. *They* were getting on well, too, but that made a hard knot tighten in my stomach. I liked JD so much it scared me. And he would so obviously make a great father: calm, patient and honorable, a great role model. But every time the two of us got close, he pulled away. And if we couldn't be together, if he was going to be gone as soon as the danger passed, I didn't want Cody to get attached and have to lose *another* man in his life.

The danger. I glanced out of the window at New York and suddenly, the band around my chest was back, making every breath tight. Since Poland, I hadn't had cause to leave the building, but tonight was the charity ball in aid of injured firefighters and my dad hadn't missed it in twenty years. He'd have wanted me to go and I wasn't going to let him down.

I needed something to wear so I'd blocked out forty-five minutes that afternoon for a lightning shopping trip. I spent my life in jeans and sneakers so I'd had to research on the internet where women bought ball gowns and we had an appointment at a specialist boutique.

As we sped through the city in the back of a car, I thought about Miles. I'd forgiven JD for what he said: I knew he was only trying to protect me. But I hadn't expected his crazy theory to take root in the dark depths of my mind.

I'd tell myself it was insane: this was *Miles.* Miles who used to do magic tricks and I knew secretly still did. Miles who'd camped with me in a little two-man tent in the backyard when we were five and nine, and who'd volunteered to sleep in front by the door so I'd feel safer. Miles who, when one of my Lego towers fell over and knocked a glass paperweight from our dad's desk, shattering it, lied and told my dad it was his fault so I wouldn't get in trouble. *Miles.*

But then I'd start thinking about how he wasn't there in Mexico, or on the boat at the marina. How he'd seemed differently, these last few months, withdrawn and moody. How he'd known we were going to Poland. And my mind would slowly see-saw the other way and suddenly it felt obvious, and I was stupid for denying it. *Argh!*

"We're here," said JD.

He got out first and looked up and down the street, jaw set, brooding and silent. Then he frowned at the buildings across the street and my stomach knotted when I realized he was checking the windows for shooters. Finally, he opened my door.

I looked at him, worried. *Is it safe?*

He nodded and offered his hand. I took it, feeling myself relax. If JD said it was safe, it was safe.

He led me into the store...and my jaw dropped. It was like no store I'd ever been in. The floor was glossy black tiles with tiny, glittering flakes of silver trapped in them. The lighting was low and a path wound back and forth through a forest of mannequins in ball gowns, each one on a raised pedestal and lit by a spotlight. The dresses were stunning: there were fabrics I'd never seen before: a pale red one so gauzy it looked like smoke, a dusky pink one that looked soft as rose petals. There were patterns picked out in gold and silver thread so intricate I could have stared at them for hours. And there were designs that hugged the mannequin's bodies like lovers, and used ribbons, spaghetti straps and laced bodices to tempt and taunt and hint. It was breathtaking.

And I couldn't imagine myself wearing any of it. I looked up at a dress that seemed to be the star of the whole store, the mannequin hanging on wires and lit from above as if she was an angel ascending to heaven. The dress was a delicate pink that reminded me of a dawn sky. It was made of hundreds of super-thin panels, stitched together with silver thread, and it was the most beautiful and intricately-made thing I'd ever seen. But it was insanely over-the-top glamorous, made for someone who was twenty-three and a movie star.

Two assistants hurried over...then tried to hide their surprise when they saw me. Maybe it was my thrown-on make-up, maybe it was my curves or the way I stood, shyly ducking my head. I so obviously didn't belong there.

But my suit and the Mercedes parked out front said *money* so they pasted on smiles. I told them apologetically that I had no idea what sort of dress would suit me, so one of the assistants ran off to find me some choices. The other asked, "Would your boyfriend like a coffee while he waits?"

We turned to each other. JD was so surprised, he forgot to be gruff for a second. He looked innocently sweet and the longing in his eyes made me catch my breath.

Then he turned to the assistant and the mask came down again. "I'm just her security," he told her. "And no thank you."

The other assistant returned with a huge green dress and I followed her to the fitting room. *JD!* What was it that kept making him pull away?

I pulled off my clothes and hauled the dress up around me. Then I turned to the mirror...and winced. It was beautiful, the fabric an iridescent sea-green. But with the huge, thick skirt I felt like a flamenco dancer. It would look fantastic on someone who knew how to move and twirl and make the most of it, but I just felt overwhelmed. "No," I said sadly.

"No problem," said the assistant, and passed another one over the door.

This one was very different, a long blue tube of clingy fabric covered in tiny sequins that caught the light. But it was designed for someone without curves...or with curves and bags of confidence. "Sorry, no," I said meekly.

And so it went on, dress after dress. The assistant, who'd started off chirpy and upbeat, became awkward and embarrassed. By the tenth dress, I was close to tears. What was I *doing?* This was *me:* big, shy, geeky *me.* I wore sneakers and jeans and had concrete dust under my fingernails. I was curvy, not some willowy thing who wore ball gowns. That's why Adrian had only pretended to love me long enough to get his claws into my dad's clients. Most of all, I was a mom pushing forty. Any tiny shreds of glamor I'd had when I was young had been stripped away by years of diaper changes and getting PlayDoh in my hair.

I pulled on my clothes and stomped out, heading for the door. JD's hand caught mine just before I got there and he gently turned me around to look at him, looming over me and mercifully blocking me from the shop assistants. "What's the matter?" he asked, and the caring in his voice almost tipped me over into tears.

"There's nothing I can wear here." I told him.

"You want to go somewhere else?" He sounded so patient, like he'd happily take me to thirty dress shops if that's what it took.

"It's not the dresses," I told him. "It's me."

He stared at me. The hand that gripped mine squeezed and then pulled me a little closer. "No it's not." His words were like huge, heavy rocks, immovable. "If they ain't got the right dress for you here, that's their fault 'cause there ain't a damn thing wrong with the woman they're putting it on."

And just for a second, I *did* feel pretty and special.

"But I tried all the things they thought would look good on me," I said helplessly.

"*Forget* them," growled JD, and it sounded like he'd nearly used a different word. "Is there anything *you* like?"

I looked around. Then I looked up and saw the angel dress. I loved it because it was beautiful, but also because I could see how it was made: I loved it as a piece of engineering. But it was *pink,* and so elaborate...I could never pull something like that off.

JD followed my gaze. He nodded firmly, then turned to march off towards the assistants.

I put a hand on his arm. "Stop," I said, uncertain. "Wait..."

But for once, he shook off my hand and marched on.

"Why?" I called after him helplessly.

He looked back over his shoulder. "Because you *do* get the fairy tale," he growled. And then he was asking the assistants, politely but firmly, to get the dress down for me.

A few moments later, I was back in the fitting room, pulling it on. It *was* clever and there was something about the way it clung to me that I liked: it almost felt like part of me. But it was so big, with an almost floor-length skirt that fanned out like magic when I turned. And it was both tight *and* revealing, with a lace-up bodice and a criss-cross halter neck that showed more cleavage than I was used to. *I'm thirty-seven. Do I just look ridiculous?*

I took a deep breath...and opened the fitting room door.

JD was waiting right outside. His eyes widened in shock and then I saw that big, wide chest fill as he drew in a slow breath. I'd never seen him go so still before, like he was entranced.

My whole life, I'd never entranced anyone.

And then he just nodded. A big, hard, definite nod. And I melted. "I'll take it, please," I squeaked to the store assistant.

It was only when I was changing back into my suit that I realized that JD would need to be at the ball, too, and if we wanted him to fit in, he'd need a tux. Fortunately, the store knew of a place just down the block, and fifteen minutes later, JD was turning back and forth in front of a full-length mirror, cocking one eyebrow at me: *is this okay?*

I nodded just as firmly as he had. God, he looked amazing, the classic lines of the jacket accentuating those powerful shoulders and the hard power of his waist, the snow-white shirt stretched tight over his broad pecs. He looked like a Texas billionaire from the oil boom, powerful and gorgeous but with a dash of old-fashioned honor.

I knew he was going to the ball to guard me. But just for a moment, it was like we were a couple, going together. And God, it felt good.

~

We got back to the penthouse just as Paige arrived home with Cody. Cody handed me a folded note from his school. I got plenty of them, usually praising his work. But this one looked different and when I unfolded it, I saw why. It was from the principal and— "You got in a *fight?*" I asked, horrified.

Cody was grinning, happier than I'd seen him in months. "You should have seen Taylor," he told JD. "He doubled right up and nearly lost his lunch!"

I remembered the fist-bump that morning. "What did you do?" I asked JD.

"I just taught the boy how to fight," he muttered, and looked down at his shoes.

I stared at both of them. "Go to your room," I told Cody. Cody did as he was told, throwing an apologetic glance back at JD.

"Don't be too hard on him," said JD. "This is my fault."

'You taught him how to *fight?*" I demanded.

"This Taylor kid has hit him plenty of times. *And* wrecked his stuff. He had it coming. This way he'll leave Cody alone."

"He's being *bullied?!*" Suddenly, the anger was gone and I just felt like a terrible mom. "Why didn't he tell *me?*"

JD shrugged. "'Cause I'm a guy. 'Cause *he's* a guy."

My shoulders slumped. I felt wounded. But was that just dumb? Would JD have been hurt if we had a daughter and she'd come to me instead of him with boy troubles?

I shook my head guiltily. "He's never had a father. Adrian left when he was so young..."

"That ain't your fault," JD told me firmly.

I went quiet and leaned back against the wall. "You're good for him," I said at last.

JD said nothing.

I pushed off from the wall and went right up to him. I stared up into his eyes and he stared down into mine. "You're good for *us*."

Those prairie-sky eyes heated until I could feel the furnace blast of them. They flicked down to my lips and then up again, and the raw need I saw took my breath away. A need that went beyond lust. I recognized it because I'd felt it, too, for so long now.

Then he started to turn away and I couldn't take it, anymore. "Why?" I blurted. "Why do you keep—Why *can't* we?"

He froze, his broad back turned to me, a wall.

"Did she hurt you?" I asked in a small voice. "The way Adrian hurt me? Did she take your kid, when you divorced, do you not see them? Or—"

"They're dead."

It wasn't just the enormity of the words that stopped me cold. It wasn't just the scalding flash of raw humiliation that lit up my cheeks, the *oh God what have I done* as I realized how badly I'd messed up. It was his voice. He didn't sound like him. The words weren't comforting, warm rocks, they were thin and fragile as old paper.

I stared at his back with no idea what to say. I lifted my hand but I wasn't sure if I should touch him.

"Jillian and Max," he said. "They were murdered. Four years ago. Max was five years old."

Now I understood and I wished I hadn't pushed. "*JD...*" I whispered. "God, I'm so sorry."

He was silent for a few seconds. Then, "I'll talk to the FBI about tonight. Make sure we have a couple of agents with us at the ball."

And he walked away without looking back.

29

LORNA

I sat down with Cody and had a long talk about how *we don't solve our problems with violence,* but I couldn't be too hard on him: this Taylor kid had had it coming and Cody was so much happier, now that he'd stood up for himself. JD really was good for him.

Paige helped me do my hair, somehow taming my black mane into ringlets that spilled down my shoulders. She also worked wonders with make-up brushes and eyeshadow, giving me elegant cheekbones and big, smoky eyes. But as I sat in front of the mirror with her, all I could think about was JD. How was I going to help him?

Paige left to get changed herself: she and Miles were meeting us there. I pulled on the angel dress, put on my heels, and went to meet JD in the hall. He was looking out at the lit-up city and I braced myself. "JD?" I said quietly.

He turned and saw me. His chest slowly filled and he slowly shook his head, as if he didn't even have the words. "You look...like a goddamn dream."

He met my eyes and, for just a second, the stoic mask flickered. A flicker that said *please.*

Please leave it alone.

I gave a tiny nod, and saw him relax. *That's* how I helped him, at least for now.

"You look amazing, too," I said with feeling.

He crooked his arm, I slipped my arm through it, and we set off for the ball.

The car slowed as we joined the line waiting for valet parking. I hunched down in my seat so I could look up at the massive building we were approaching. One of New York's oldest venues, the entrance of the Hattendorf Ballroom had marble pillars the size of redwoods and a three-stage staircase leading up to towering wooden doors. Tonight, the stairs were a waterfall of color running in reverse as a constant stream of women in beautiful ball gowns swept gracefully up them. There was a throng of press clustered around the arriving cars and the camera flashes were going so fast they were almost continuous.

As our car crept closer, I could feel my chest going tight with panic. It wasn't just the thought of some guy out there with a gun or a knife. It was the thought of being in the spotlight, instead of safely in the corner.

JD must have seen my face because his low, Texas rumble came from next to me. "If you want, we can just get out of here."

I looked across at him. He'd driven me there himself, with the two FBI agents tailing us in a separate car. I knew he really would just get me out of there, no judgment, no questions asked, and I loved him for that. But I shook my head. I was thinking of my dad: this was his favorite night of the year. He'd have wanted me to be there and I wasn't going to let him down. "No. Let's do this."

The car in front moved up, but JD held my gaze for a second, looking at me with something like wonder. I flushed and looked down at my lap. Then we drove forward and it was our turn.

JD got out first, looking like a Texan James Bond in his tux. He scowled at the press, his eyes everywhere, watching for trouble. Then he opened my door and helped me out. Camera flashes blasted me and all I could see were glowing negatives of everything. But JD slipped his arm around my waist and guided me up the stairs.

We moved through a short hallway and then, up ahead, I could hear the big, echoey space. I looked down at myself and my steps slowed. "Everyone's going to be looking at me," I mumbled uncertainly.

JD looked at me and his eyes gleamed as if I was the best thing I'd ever seen. "Yeah they are," he said with feeling. And I felt something in my chest just *lift,* almost lifting me right off my feet. I took a deep breath and, together, we walked into the ballroom.

At least a hundred couples were there: bankers and business people, actors and politicians. Miles was there with Paige, who looked amazing in a long silver dress, her golden hair in an updo. She was grinning and wide-eyed, squeezing his hand with excitement. He'd given up his plus-one so she could have a night of glamor, when he could have used it for one of his hundreds of female admirers. That decided me: of *course* Miles wasn't the killer.

A ripple went through the room and then the crowd just parted, people melting aside as someone approached from the far end of the huge room. People who a second ago had been arrogantly preening suddenly couldn't move out of the way fast enough. Hedge fund managers who'd been crowing loudly about their gains fell silent. People who'd come to the party to be seen ducked their heads as if wishing they were invisible.

There was something regal about the man: his face, with its sharp cheekbones and full, pouting lower lip, was like something you'd see on a marble statue of an emperor, handsome but mercilessly cold. Familiar, but I couldn't place it, at first. His tuxedo was immaculate and he wore it with the sort of casual ease that suggested he attended a lot of parties. But as he came closer, I could see the black shadows of tattoos under his white shirt, and not the clean black patterns some Silicon Valley CEO with a rebellious streak might get. These were sprawling and complex, a web of dark violence. And suddenly, I knew who it was. "Konstantin Gulyev," I thought out loud.

The Russian Mafia boss. And he was heading straight for us.

By Konstantin's side was a woman with wavy brown hair in a beautiful scarlet dress. Two men I assumed were bodyguards followed at a discreet distance. I looked left, looked right: there was nowhere to run. JD took a step forward but, on instinct, I grabbed his shoulder. "Don't," I warned. He was Kostantin's equal, physically. But this man's menace went way beyond what he could do in a fist-fight.

Konstantin stopped just a few feet away and I could feel it rolling off him, breaking in waves against us. I wanted to turn and bolt...or duck my head and curtsey. I knew now why everyone had gotten out of this man's way. All those people had money. But this man...he had *power*.

"Miss McBride," said Konstantin. His voice was calm and unhurried, his Russian accent turning the words into silver-edged slabs of cold stone. "Your father was a good man. I was truly sorry to hear of his death."

He sounded sincere...but then I was the world's worst person at reading people. JD clearly didn't buy it: I could feel his muscles tensing under my hand. Konstantin glanced at him and then gave both of us a wan smile. "You suspect I am responsible," he said lightly.

"It crossed my mind," muttered JD.

"I assume Agent Callahan of the FBI has weighed in," said Konstantin. When we blinked at him, amazed, he exchanged a smile with his date. "Oh yes, we know him. What did he say?"

"That killing civilians isn't your way," I said.

Konstantin nodded soberly. "And he is correct."

"But you *are* in property," I said. My heart was thumping in fear and a voice in my head was screaming at me to *shut up, don't antagonize him!* But I'd been living in fear for over a week. I had to know if this was the man responsible. "If we finish Hudson Tower, it *will* affect the prices your buildings fetch."

Konstantin looked at me sadly. "Miss McBride, I can see you're concerned so let me speak plainly." He stepped closer and I felt JD bristle...but Konstantin did nothing more than speak softly into my ear. "If Hudson Tower was a threat to my plans...I would never have allowed it to be built."

He stepped back and the two of them swept away. "Tell Callahan I said hi," Konstantin's date threw over her shoulder.

I stood there shaking, gulping in air. And as my heart slowed, I realized I knew two things for certain. I was right to be scared of Konstantin Gulyev. But he was telling the truth. This man operated on a whole different level. If he hadn't wanted us to build Hudson Tower, the project never would have gotten off the ground.

By now, everyone had arrived and people were mingling and chatting. All my shyness returned: this was exactly the kind of thing I was lousy at. But JD had seen my fear. He slipped his arm around my waist again and started to lead me around the room.

He had a way of just wandering up to a group and joining the conversation. He wasn't like Miles, who'd say exactly the right thing at the right time and weave himself into the banter. JD just stood there calmly, radiating quiet confidence, not afraid to be silent. Within seconds people would welcome him into their group. I went from feeling like I was drowning to beginning to float. I started to join in the conversations and, after an hour, I realized I was having a good time.

I took a break to go to the bathroom and I was on my way back to JD when there was an announcement, and the music changed. The knots of people dissolved into pairs and I quickly scurried off the dance floor as some kind of waltz began. I saw Konstantin dancing with his date—they were surprisingly good—and Miles dancing with Paige. My chest tightened. I had no clue how to dance and the idea of everyone staring at me made me want to sink through the floor, but they looked so happy... Just for a second, I wished I was there *with* someone, so we could try it.

I glanced to the side...and there, also at the edge of the room, was JD, looking for me. He visibly relaxed when he saw I was safe. Then he cocked his head to one side and frowned, reading my expression. He looked away, brooding for a moment. Then he straightened up, his shoulders set and he marched through the crowd towards me, more determined than I'd ever seen him.

"C'mon," he said, grabbing my hand. "It ain't right that someone like you is on the sidelines."

I stared and flushed red. "But...I can't dance."

He led me onto the dance floor. "Neither can I."

He turned to face me and settled one big hand on the small of my back, the warmth of him throbbing through my dress. Then he *pushed* and the distance between us closed. My breasts brushed his body and I felt my nipples peak and harden under the dress. All I could see was the solid wall of his chest and then I looked up and those prairie-sky eyes were blazing down at me.

JD looked at a couple behind me, copying, and lifted his other hand up and out to the side, lifting my arm with it. He stared at our joined hands. And then he squeezed my fingers decisively.

We started to move. I didn't know what I was doing and neither did he, but it didn't matter. He was decisive and strong and he didn't give a fuck what anyone else thought and that meant I could just relax and give myself up to it...and it was *amazing*. We dipped and spun, twirling around the dance floor. The skirt of my dress swirled out in slow-motion waves and the spotlights turned the golden thread into glittering magic.

I felt like I was flying. I felt like some fairy-tale princess. And for the first time in a long time, I didn't feel like a mom.

The music died away and another piece started, with a faster rhythm. We looked at each other and, without words, we decided *we're staying*. JD swept me off around the dance floor and I giggled. I *never* giggled.

I felt that iron band around my chest loosen and then, gloriously, it slipped away entirely.

We danced on and on. We stepped on each other's toes and bumped into other couples and were hysterically bad at it. But it didn't matter. The lights of the room and the other people all faded away and all I was aware of was him: the protective press of his hand on my back, the warm solidness of his body against mine and the firm confidence with which he moved us.

The music died away and we finally slowed to a stop. I looked up at him, smiling...

And went utterly still, because I suddenly saw the way he was looking at me.

He looked helpless. My heart fluttered.

The other couples flowed past us, leaving the dance floor. But JD stood like a rock, his breathing quick and his eyes locked on mine, that pale blue burning hotter than any flame.

I'd never seen him like this. *Oh my God...*

His hand released mine and a ripple of disappointment went through me. Then his palm cupped my cheek and my whole body tensed, giddily excited. His thumb stroked the edge of my hair once, twice. His eyes flicked down to my lips—

"Hey," said a voice from beside us. "Lorna. I need a minute."

I blinked. *What?* I saw JD blink, too, and felt it all slipping away. *No! No, God, no, not now!*

Too late. JD frowned like a man waking from a dream, turned to look...and the moment was lost.

In despair, I turned to look too. The man standing next to us was in his fifties, heavyset with gunmetal gray hair and an arrogant, sly grin, like he'd enjoyed interrupting us.

"Henry Creel," said the man, and jerked his head. "Come on, I want to talk to you in private." And he took a step away, expecting me to follow.

JD took a step towards him, his face thunderous. I didn't like the guy's arrogance, either, or the way he'd called me by my first name, like it was a way of putting me in my place. But as the shock died away, his name sank in. Henry Creel was the head of the New York planning association. I quickly put a hand on JD's arm. "It's okay. Give us a minute."

I followed Creel, feeling that iron band tightening around my chest again. I wanted to weep: escaping it had felt *so good!*

Creel led me up a flight of stairs to where a balcony overlooked the main floor. It was dark up there, and when he turned around I could barely make out his face at all. Then he grinned and his white teeth made a floating, Cheshire Cat smile. "I brought you up here to discuss approval for your hospital."

"We went through planning months ago. Everyone signed off!"

"*Wellll*...actually my committee only granted *provisional* approval. The final paperwork is still sitting on my desk."

I had that unsettling feeling I get, like I was getting tangled in threads of meaning I couldn't even see. "Okay, so...what is it you want us to change? Do you want more parking spaces? Is it about the solar panels?"

He gave a single, throaty chuckle and then passed me a folded slip of paper. I unfolded it and stared at the lazy, looping swirls of handwriting. $100,000.

I was naive enough that it actually took me a second to understand.

"We don't—I'm not paying bribes," I managed.

"I know you're new to this," he said sourly, "but all construction companies do it." I could hear the anger in his voice. I'd made him feel dirty and he didn't like that.

I shook my head. "Not us."

He leaned closer, a looming black mass in the darkness, and I smelled whiskey and cigars. He jabbed a finger at the note I held in my hand. "That was your father's *standard rate,* you pious bitch."

I swallowed. *No. No, my dad wouldn't—* Then I remembered Maria and wilted. *Oh crap.* What if Creel was telling the truth? What if I'd just been blissfully unaware, all these years, of what my dad was really like?

Creel's grin returned as he saw my reaction. He patted me on the shoulder. "*There's* a good girl. You'll soon learn how the game's played."

He strolled away and I stood there shaking. *Shit!* I was so, so far out of my comfort zone. *What do I do?* Why couldn't it be my dad, or Miles making this decision?

My fingers found cold stone in the darkness. I curled them

around the wide, satin-smooth handrail and the weight and solidness of the building filled me, calming me. It had stood here for decades, an icon...

I stopped thinking about what my dad would do, or what Miles would do. I thought about Cody, and him having this conversation with someone in twenty years, about me.

I took three deep breaths. Then I turned and called after him. "No!"

He stopped, looked back in confusion, and then marched back to the balcony. "Don't get all holier-than-thou with me, Lorna, your father—"

"It's *Miss McBride*. And it's not my father's company, anymore. It's mine." Saying that last part was like trying to swallow razor blades, but I got through it. "And I don't care what my dad did or didn't do, *I'm not paying you.*"

And I walked off towards the stairs.

He was so shocked that, for a moment, he didn't move. Then I heard his footsteps coming after me. I sped up, but he caught up with me at the top of the stairs and grabbed my arm. "Don't walk away from me, you bitch!"

A stab of fear went through me: he was bigger than me.

And then a huge, shadowy form rose out of the darkness of the stairs like a leviathan walking out of the ocean. When it was two steps below us, it was already taller than Creel, and it kept coming, not stopping until it was looming over both of us, six inches from our faces.

"Let go of her arm," said JD.

"Back off, farm boy—" snapped Creel.

JD used *the voice*. "Let go of her arm *now*."

Creel faltered, went silent...and let go of my arm. I took two steps down the stairs and turned back.

"Sign off on the approval," I told him. "Or I'll ask the mayor to launch a corruption investigation and we'll find out who *has* been bribing you."

And I turned and walked away, not looking back. JD followed, one step behind so that he could guard my rear. As we reached the lights of the dance floor, I glanced around and saw him smiling at me. "I think your dad would have been proud."

I nodded gratefully, not able to speak yet. I couldn't believe I'd stood up to Creel like that. Where had *that* come from? Aftershocks of fear were still making me shiver and suddenly, I felt exhausted. The ball was coming to an end. "Let's get out of here," I said.

JD nodded and we said our goodbyes: Miles was heading out as well, but Paige was going to stay for a little while and get a cab home: I was guessing she had her eye on someone.

Outside, we climbed back into the car and JD checked that the two FBI agents were ready to follow behind us. As we pulled away, I slipped off my heels and gave a groan of relief. I looked up and saw JD's eyes locked on my stockinged legs.

The quiet of the car became a silence that grew and grew. We had to talk about what happened and JD was doing his gruff, stoic thing.

I took a deep breath. "JD," I said gently. "When we danced...*after* we danced..."

He swallowed. Turned and looked at me...

The world flew sideways as another car slammed into ours.

30

JD

FOR A MOMENT, I thought it was my fault. I'd taken my eyes off the road to look at her and gotten lost in those pale gray pools. I'd been thinking too hard about what I was going to say. *After we danced. When I almost kissed her.* Then I'd smashed into something.

I looked frantically around through the cracked windshield. We hadn't crossed an intersection. So how had someone—

We were rammed sideways again and this time, I saw what did it, a black SUV. It managed to push us into oncoming traffic and Lorna screamed as headlights lit up our faces. I hauled on the wheel and we slewed back across the street, missing the oncoming car by less than a foot. *Shit!* This wasn't an accident, it was an attack.

Where's the FBI? I checked the rear-view mirror and my stomach flipped when I saw their car on its side, further back down the street. We were on our own.

The black SUV came in to sideswipe us again and I braked hard. It passed in front of us, but that put it on Lorna's side. I cursed and sped up again, pushing sixty and swerving so it was back on my side: I wanted to be between her and it. *Who's driving that thing?* The windows were blacked out so I couldn't see. Then my chest went tight. *Miles. Miles left the ball just as we did.*

There was a brutal crunch of metal as the SUV hit us again and we swerved, only just missing a lamppost. The adrenaline was flooding through me, now, my hands shaky on the wheel. I had no idea what to do. If I stopped, the SUV could crush us against a wall. If I kept going, we were going to wind up in a crash.

We screeched around a corner and I felt one side of the car lift sickeningly. I pawed at the wheel, panting in fear, and only just managed to keep us from rolling. *Dammit, I wish Danny was here.* Danny's driving would leave the other car in the dust.

And that's when I knew I'd made a mistake, a bad one. I should have called in the team after Poland, or after the shooting. Hell, I should have called in the team from the very beginning. But no, I'd had to go it alone, just because I didn't want the guys to see that I'd fallen for Lorna.

And now, thanks to that mistake, I might lose her.

We skidded around another corner and into the docks. I tried to do what Danny would do, weaving between the shipping containers that lined the dock, but it was a lot harder than it looked. I had to keep going faster and faster to stay away from the SUV, the containers whipping past. And then, ahead of us, the dock just *stopped* and there was nothing but black water.

"Oh God," croaked Lorna.

I took a chance and stamped on the brake. I heard a tire blow and then we were spinning and spinning and I closed my eyes, smelling hot metal and burning rubber...

We stopped. I slowly opened my eyes.

We'd stopped in time...just. We were side-on, right at the end of the dock: if I opened my door, I'd be stepping out into space. I blew out a long sigh of relief.

Then headlights lit us up from the side and I heard the roar of an engine. I hit the gas but the ruined wheels just spun in place. "No," I panted, "no no no no no—"

The SUV rammed into us and our car shot sideways...and fell into the dark water below.

31

LORNA

FOR A MOMENT, we were weightless. Then the car hit the water and my head hit the ceiling so hard I saw stars. We rolled crazily and then we were dropping, dropping—

The headlights went out. The lights of the dock dimmed and then there was only blackness. I heard our panicked breathing and the terrifying rushing sound of water.

There was a bump that shook my teeth and my throat closed up in fear as I realized what that meant. *Oh Jesus, are we on the bottom? Are we on the bottom of the bay?!*

I could feel things under my stockinged toes: a lipstick, keys...my purse must have dumped out its contents at some point during the crash. I ducked down, groping for my phone. But nothing made sense, the footwell wasn't where it should be and I kept putting one hand into the freezing water that seemed to be getting deeper and deeper...

My fingers finally closed around the smooth plastic of my phone and I turned on the flashlight. The car lit up in dazzling whites and deep black shadow. Now I saw why nothing had made sense in the dark: the car had landed on its side. Water was pouring in from cracks in the windshield, through air vents, through any hole it could find. It was already a few feet deep and rising fast.

I turned the light on JD. He was hanging limply in his seat but as the light hit him, he came awake and looked groggily around. "Get unstrapped," he told me. "And get out of that dress, we're going to have to swim."

By the time both of us had got our seatbelts off, the water was up to our waists. I could feel myself starting to panic breathe. "It's okay," JD told me, stripping off his tuxedo jacket. Even now, his voice was calm, certain, and I clung to his words like they were life preservers. "We've got to wait for the pressure to equalize, so we can open the door." He pointed to the driver's door, which was above our heads. "Then we're going to swim straight up, okay? Just follow the bubbles." He unzipped my dress and I shimmied out of it.

The water was up to my armpits, now, and I started to shiver, half from the freezing water and half from fear. "*Hey,*" said JD, rubbing his hands over my bare arms to warm me. "You're gonna be okay." And he squeezed my shoulders.

The water rose higher and we rose with it, treading water, until our heads were pressed up against the driver's door. The water crept up my neck, up my chin, and I felt my ears pop as the pressure changed—

"Here we go," said JD, squeezing my shoulder. "Take a deep breath."

I exhaled and took the biggest breath I could.

The water rose over my mouth and face, filling the car completely.

JD pulled on the door release.

Nothing happened.

He yanked on it again, and pushed the door with all his strength, the muscles in his shoulders standing out. The door didn't move. *Oh God...*

JD pointed to the back of the car. I was closer, so I swam to the rear door and pushed on *that*. But it wouldn't give, either. JD and I looked at each other, both realizing the problem at the same time.

The doors that were facing upwards were the side that had been rammed over and over by the SUV: the metal had caved in and jammed them. And the doors on the other side were pressed against the bottom of the bay.

We were trapped. And the gulp of air I'd taken was running out: already, my lungs were starting to burn.

The flashlight on my phone was somehow still working, but the screen was starting to flicker and corrupt. JD started to pound on the windshield with his fists and I got in next to him and tried kicking it.

If we'd been in air, we could have smashed it easily. But the water dragged on our limbs, killing the momentum and cushioning the glass: I was kicking as hard as I could but it felt like I was barely tapping it. And the effort used up what little air I had left. My chest was screaming now, begging me to exhale and gulp in fresh air, but all there was to breathe was water. As the cold chased the last of the heat from my body, reality hit me with a startling, horrible clarity.

We were going to die, down here.

JD turned to me and read what was on my face. His expression darkened, I could see him raging at himself and my stomach lurched as I realized what he was thinking. *He'd failed me.* That was going to be his dying thought.

No! I grabbed his shoulders, stared into his eyes. *No! No, you didn't! This isn't your fault!* My lungs felt like they were going to explode but I kept my eyes locked on his, willing him to understand. *This isn't your fault!*

The flashlight on my phone finally went out and we were in pitch darkness again. I could feel my body straining to breathe and my brain going spacey from lack of oxygen. Another few seconds and I'd gulp in water and that would be it. My fingers dug deep into JD's shoulders, trying to hold back—

And then I felt his hands on my cheeks and his lips mashed against mine, forcing them apart.

Rich, warm, life-giving air filled my lungs. My brain snapped awake as I realized what he was doing. He was bigger than me, could hold his breath longer than me. He was giving up his last seconds of life to buy me a little more time. *JD! No!*

He broke the kiss. I felt his shoulders tense under my hands: now *he* was running out of air. I threw my arms around him, pulling him close. *JD!*

A light lit up the car, blindingly bright. I twisted and saw a flashlight blasting through the windshield and a figure silhouetted behind it. Then something hit the center of the windshield, spider webbing it. A tire iron. Another blow and the windshield crumpled inward. Another and it broke free and floated loose. The figure reached in and grabbed my hand and I grabbed JD, and the three of us kicked and swam, out through the hole and up, up, up.

My face broke the surface and I sucked in glorious, stinking New York harbor air. A second later, JD surfaced next to me, lungs heaving. It was several seconds before we blinked the water out of our eyes, looked around and saw who'd rescued us.

"You okay?" panted Miles.

32

JD

THE COPS and paramedics arrived and bundled us all off to the hospital to get checked out. Lorna and I had picked up some bruises and scrapes but otherwise we were okay. Agent Callahan arrived, looking even more tousled than usual: from the look on his face, he'd been in bed when he got the call. Sitting on the edge of hospital beds, wrapped in blankets, Lorna and I gave statements. Then we all listened as Miles gave his: he'd been a few cars behind us when the killer started ramming us, and he'd followed us to the docks.

Callahan and I exchanged sheepish looks. Miles obviously wasn't on the killer's side. Then we looked apologetically at Lorna. Lucky for us, she was too relieved to give us a hard time about it.

But Miles picked up on all the furtive looks. "What?" he asked in that refined British accent.

Callahan quickly stood up. "I'll give you all some space." He left, leaving the three of us looking at each other.

I tried to figure out what to say. But Miles figured it out from our guilty faces before I could even open my mouth. "You thought it was *me?!*" He stared at his sister, not so much angry as wounded.

"Don't be mad at her," I told him. "She defended you the whole time, she wouldn't believe it was you. This was all me and Callahan."

"You thought I'd killed my *dad?* Why?!"

I sighed and looked at the ceiling. Then I laid it all out for him.

Miles hung his head. *"Fuck!"* It was sudden, venomous: I saw Lorna flinch.

But it wasn't us he was mad at. We watched as all his smooth charm and confidence collapsed.

He took a breath but the words wouldn't come. He tried again: nothing. Lorna put a hand on his arm. He finally dredged the words up and spat them out like something stinking and toxic. "I have a problem."

"What sort of problem?" Lorna asked innocently. Miles just stared at her, humiliated and broken, and she slowly inhaled, realization hitting. "How?" she asked. "Why?"

Miles shook his head tiredly. "Gradually. I don't know, no one plans on becoming an addict." He sighed. "You take something to help you relax after an eighteen hour day. Then you need something to get you going the next morning. Then you need something to let you sleep." He looked at me. "I didn't have a stomach bug in Mexico. I was going through withdrawal because I hadn't dared bring anything over the border. And I didn't come on the boat because I'd been at a party the night before and I was coming down, I knew I'd throw up if I went out on the waves."

"What about the cash you withdrew?" I asked, rubbing my stubble. "Can't all have been for drugs."

"Rehab." Miles looked at Lorna. "I wanted to get clean but I didn't want anyone to find out, so I took the money for the clinic out in cash." He shook his head. "I never checked in. We were too busy. There was never a good time."

"Dad found out you were using drugs," said Lorna slowly. "That's why he changed his will."

Miles nodded. "I didn't know he knew, until that day in the lawyer's office. That's why I was so mad. He died worrying I was an addict." His eyes filled with tears. "If I'd known he knew, I could have talked to him about it, I could have got clean!"

"I thought you were mad at *me*, because he made me CEO," said Lorna in a small voice.

Miles shook his head. "I was mad at myself because I knew it was my own fault."

Lorna grabbed his hands, blinking through her own tears. "I never even *wanted* the job."

Miles leaned closer, "I know! I know that! I've seen how hard it is for you and I knew it was because I'd messed up."

Lorna threw her arms around her brother and the two of them crushed each other close, tears spilling down their cheeks. I could feel the tension between them melting away.

When they finally released each other, Miles wiped his face on the corner of his blanket. "I'll check into a rehab place tomorrow," he said solemnly. "I might not be around for a few weeks."

"Whatever you need," said Lorna. "We're here for you." She hugged him again and I leaned forward and patted his back.

Lorna and I got a cab back to The McBride Building and stumbled through the doors of the penthouse. Both of us were in just our underwear beneath our hospital blankets: I had my soaking tuxedo in a plastic bag and Lorna's dress was still at the bottom of the bay. The place was mostly in darkness, with just a few lamps throwing out warm pools of light. Cody was staying over at a friend's house and Paige must have hooked up with someone and gone home with them because her room was dark and empty. We were alone.

And in the dark stillness, the adrenaline drained away and the feelings I've been crushing down inside me for the last few hours finally broke free.

That moment at the ball. As the music came to an end, I'd looked down at her in my arms and I was suddenly overcome. The dance was over but I didn't want to let her go...*ever*.

I'd fallen for this woman completely.

And tonight, I'd nearly lost her.

Lorna had wandered over to the big floor-to-ceiling windows and was standing with her back to me, looking out at the lights of New York. Her hair was in damp tangles and she was wrapped in a blue hospital blanket. She'd never looked more beautiful.

I dropped the plastic bag containing my wet clothes and took a silent step towards her.

The pain and guilt took hold. *Don't.* I didn't deserve another shot. *It's my fault they're dead.*

Lorna gave a little shiver and hugged the blanket tighter around her. *She's freezing.* My chest went tight. She needed to be wrapped up in my arms, to be warm. I took another step.

Don't. I couldn't abandon them. They were my *forever.*

I was close enough now to see the pale skin on the back of her neck, jeweled with water. One more step, and I could kiss it.

Don't—

My foot lifted to take the final step...

My hands tightened into fists, my whole body tensed...and I stopped. I forced my eyes away from her, made myself stare out at the city. My heart was slamming against my ribs. Just a few seconds, then I'd be under control enough to march off to my room.

That's when I saw her reflection in the window. Her pale curves, revealed by the split of the blanket. Her soft lips. Those gray eyes, glittering in the darkness, beautiful and liquid and so very, very lonely.

Something gave way inside me.

I grabbed her shoulders, spun her around, and kissed her.

33

LORNA

THE ROOM BLURRED as I was whirled around. For a second, all I could see was JD's broad chest. I frowned, looked up...and his lips met mine.

The kiss had all of his brute determination in it, all of his raw power. Everything he'd been bottling up since the day he first met me. His hard upper lip forced me open and spread me, his lower lip gorgeously soft against mine.

The kiss rolled and moved, scarlet pleasure earthquaking from my lips down through my entire body, and I panted against his mouth. The force of the kiss was bending me backward a little and with his big hands still gripping my shoulders, I felt deliciously small and helpless.

He broke the kiss for an instant, growled and kissed me again. And again and again, lifting his lips just enough to break contact each time, so fast and urgent that it left me breathless. It was like he'd been waiting to kiss me for so long that now he wanted to experience it over and over.

I reached up and grabbed for support and my hands found the veined hardness of his forearms. My fingertips swept through the soft hair on the backs of them, following them upwards as they thickened and thickened, until I hit the huge, solid bulges of his biceps. I went weak, my groin tightening at the sheer, solid size of him.

My eyes had closed but I could feel him looming over me, could feel the heat from his body throbbing against me. Then, as he bent me back and back, our bodies touched. The contact was gloriously warm and it stretched all the way from the tops of my breasts to just above my groin. And where our blankets hung open, there was a sinful ribbon where bare skin pressed against bare skin. I drew in my breath as the hard ridges of his abs kissed my naked stomach.

His tongue toyed with me, tracing the edge of my upper lip. Trembling pleasure broke in silvery waves, washing down through my body, and I rose up on tiptoe, needing to be closer to him, needing *more*.

He broke the kiss for a second and I reeled. I was so drunk on him, it took me a couple of seconds to open my eyes. When I did, I saw those prairie-sky eyes blazing down at me, flicking over my hair, my eyes, my cheeks, drinking in every detail of me.

"You're the most beautiful goddamn thing I ever saw in my life." That sun-kissed, Texan growl, deliciously rough and so heavy with certainty that the words sank straight to my core. His hands squeezed my shoulders and he took a step forward, forcing me to take a step back. His leg went between mine, pushing aside the blanket, and the muscled warmth of his thigh pressed against mine. I caught my breath, remembering how close to naked we were, under the blankets.

"I can't take my eyes off you," he said. "Do you know that?" He took another step forward, pressing me another step back. I was shaky with excitement, my breathing ragged. My hands stroked his biceps and I could feel the need thundering through him: God, he was like a bull, unstoppable. Something had made him crazy. I stared up at him, panting, and he gazed back, his eyes clouded with lust. It sank in that this was *me* doing this to him, and a wild rush of shock and pride swept me up and lifted me.

He rubbed his thumb along my lower lip. "Every time I look at you, *every* time, I'm thinking about kissing you. Thinking about tangling my hands in your hair and tearing that suit right off you." The excitement was a pounding, violent drumming, now, vibrating through my body. He took another step forward, pressing even harder against me, and this time I could feel the hot throb of his cock against my inner thigh. I stepped back...and my back pressed against the wall.

"I have to see you," he growled. And his hands closed on the neck of my blanket.

A sudden wave of fear hit me and my hands closed on his.

He cocked his head to one side. "I've seen just about every part of you."

But I didn't move my hands. "I don't have the sort of body men like."

"Well I'm a man," he told me. "And you're *exactly* what I like."

My chest filled and a warm wave soaked down through my body. I released the blanket and he pushed it back off my shoulders so that it fell to the floor. He looked down at my body and the raw lust in his eyes chased the last of my insecurities away.

He let his own blanket fall and my eyes roved over the firm curves of his pecs, the heavy globes of his shoulders and biceps. Then lower...I'd seen him topless, before, but I hadn't seen all of him, hadn't seen the brute power of his muscled thighs, dusted with golden hairs, or the hard globes of his ass and the outline of his cock, revealed through the clinging fabric of his wet boxers. God, he was *big*.

As he stood there gazing at me, he smoothed his hands over my bare shoulders in slow rhythm. Then he slid his hands inwards, to the sides of my neck, then *outwards,* and I drew in my breath as he hooked the straps of my bra off my shoulders.

His palms moved down my upper arms, taking the straps with it. The straps pulled tight and then began to tug my bra down with them. I was breathing hard, now: watching him watching me was the hottest thing I'd ever seen, the lust in his eyes so strong I could feel the heat of it on my skin. The cups of my bra flipped down and I felt my nipples harden under his gaze. He kept pushing on the bra straps, flattening my arms to my sides, until the straps fell free of my hands.

Then he reached behind me and freed the bra's clasp and it fell around my feet.

He leaned in and kissed one breast, then the other, closing his lips around it and skimming his tongue over the nipple. "God, I love your breasts," he growled. "They're just perfect." Each word was a hot little gust that made the aching, spit-wet flesh tighten even harder.

He kissed his way down my stomach. When he reached the top of my panties, he hooked his thumbs into them and then very slowly tugged them down. I gasped and leaned my shoulders back against the wall, the heat slamming through me, now. He pulled the panties lower, lower, and I could feel his breath on my pussy as he completely exposed me. Then the panties were falling at my feet and I was completely naked in front of him.

For a moment, he just crouched there, gazing at me, his eyes narrowed in lust. Then, in one quick movement, he stood and scooped me up, one arm under my legs and one under my back.

I yelped in shock as my feet left the floor. In three big strides, he carried me over to the grand piano and sat me on the keys with a dramatic, discordant crash. He dropped to his knees before me and his elbows spread my knees wide. Then he leaned forward and—

I sucked in a huge, shuddering breath as his tongue drew a line up the length of my dewy lips. Then he licked down and I rocked back on the piano, bracing myself on the smooth mahogany top. He began to lick me steadily, his tongue whipping up to flick over my clit on each stroke, igniting silvery, glittering fireworks that detonated low in my belly, building towards something bigger. My thighs tried to clamp closed: I was overwhelmed. But JD's elbows pinned them open: I might as well have been pushing against a stone statue. He looked up at me and the smirk he gave me, together with the feeling of being so easily overpowered, sent a dark, twisting thrill through me.

His tongue began to tease my lips apart, the pleasure turning to slick wetness as he pushed deeper, spearing up into me. I threw my head back and my legs kicked out to either side of him. Piano notes filled the room, low then high in a quickening rhythm as I rocked from side to side.

His upper lip rubbed at my clit as his tongue plunged to the root again and again, fucking me. My back arched, my fingers dancing along the edge of the piano as the pleasure built and built. And the more he felt me losing control, the more turned on *he* got, growling in pleasure in a way that sent vibrations right through my groin. It was a feedback loop and I spiraled breathlessly higher and higher until I was panting and straining, my skin scalding against the keys, my folds sopping. "God, yes, *please,*" I begged.

He drew his tongue from me and circled my clit, hard and fast. Two fingers plunged into me, curling to find that secret spot just as I began to spasm. The pleasure rocketed straight up to my brain and exploded there, rolling down through my body in shockwaves that made me rock and jerk against him, my hands mashing keys either side of me as I cried out long and loud.

While I was still twitching and dreamy, he picked me up again, carrying me effortlessly. He set me down on my feet, facing him, then pushed me back a little as he kissed me slow and deep. I felt a touch against my shoulder blades, smooth and gloriously cool against my scalding skin. Then another, against my ass, and then my whole back was pressing against it.

His hands cradled my cheeks and I moaned as his tongue entwined with mine. I flexed against the surface behind me and realized we were up against the window. There was a little rush of fear: I knew the glass was toughened and wouldn't break even if we threw a chair at it. But I was naked, pressed up against a window in front of the whole city. The lights were off, I knew that really, no one could see, but...

JD broke the kiss for a moment, retrieved something from his bag of wet clothes, then shoved his boxers down his thighs and off. His cock sprang out, long and thick, a gorgeous tan with an arrow-shaped, silken pink head. He stepped closer and it slapped against my stomach, weighty and hot. We both looked down and I swallowed: with it pressed against me, I could see just how deep he'd go.

Something inside me let go and suddenly, I didn't care if anyone saw us.

He nudged the inside of my feet and I quickly opened my legs. He rolled on the condom, guided himself to me and then...

My mouth opened wide as the head of him spread me. I rose up on my tiptoes with him...and then stopped moving while he kept going, filling me in one long, satiny stretch. He pressed closer between my thighs and I took hold of his shoulders. Then he grabbed my ass and lifted me off the ground, pinning my body between him and the glass.

For a moment, we just hung there, staring into each other's eyes. There was something about the way he lifted me so easily, I felt *small*, delicate. My palms traced the slabs of his pecs and the heavy swells of his shoulders, reveling in the solid power of him. Then I wrapped my arms around his neck and my legs around his waist, gasping as his cock moved inside me.

He began to fuck me. Slow strokes at first, letting me feel every hard inch. I panted into the side of his neck: my own weight was impaling me on him, grinding my clit against the root of him on each stroke. "God," he muttered, staring deep into my eyes, "you feel incredible."

I was beyond speech. Every thrust of his cock inside me sent a tight wave of pleasure rippling up through my body to coalesce in my core, where a new climax was building. Then he leaned closer and the very tips of my nipples started to stroke against his chest as we moved. The pleasure tightened and twisted, throbbing hotter and hotter. He was strong enough that he could lift and lower me, moving my body to meet each thrust, ensuring he hilted himself every time. I locked my ankles together behind him and my hands went crazy on his back, roving over his muscles as I clung to him.

The room filled with the sound of my panting as the sensations built and built, carrying me up toward my peak. *God*, I'd never felt anything like it. The brute strength of him, the hardness of his body against me. The exquisite friction as his cock pumped into me in hard, fast strokes. The little jolts of sensation as my breasts bounced against his chest, my nipples achingly hard. I'd never felt so open, so tightly close to someone.

The pleasure spiraled and tightened until it was too much to contain: my toes danced and my fingers tangled in the dark curls of his hair. I stared into his eyes from just a few inches away as the orgasm overtook me. *"God JD yes,"* I gasped in a rush.

I felt myself spasm around him and feeling me come sent him over the edge. He growled and his hands squeezed my ass hard. He gave three more savage thrusts and then buried himself, holding me tight to him as he shot and shot inside me.

He held me as we both shuddered and twitched, kissing me again and again. Then he walked me carefully to my bedroom and eased me down onto the bed. As he shifted around to spoon me from behind, I felt sleep coming up to meet me in a warm black wave. I was utterly exhausted. But before we slept, there was something I needed to know, something I kept wondering.

"JD?" I asked quietly in the darkness. "What's your full name?"

He gave a low chuckle. Then he sighed and, with just a hint of embarrassment, he said, "John. John Dusty."

It was perfect. Strong and solid and old-fashioned, just like him. And with that mystery solved, I pulled his arm around me and fell asleep.

34

JD

I struggled up through the blackness and opened my eyes, some soldier instinct pulling me awake. I lay there silently listening for what had woken me. A siren that meant we were under attack? Weapons fire? The stealthy footfall of someone creeping up to gut me as I lay in my sleeping bag?

Then my other senses started to wake and I felt the warm, female body snuggled against my chest and the soft squish of the pillow beneath my head. I was home. Safe in Texas with Jillian. I felt my whole body relax and I almost went back to sleep.

But something scratched at my half-asleep brain. The house didn't smell right. There was always a scent of hay on the wind, and horses, and damp wood from where the boards hadn't quite dried out after the last storm. It wasn't there.

I inhaled and smelled orange blossom and coconut.

And that's when I remembered that my wife was dead.

That warm, safe place in the center of my chest was ripped out of me all over again and I sat bolt upright with a groan of raw horror. I glanced around the room, some part of me still trying to cling onto the illusion. I willed the foot of the bed to morph into our battered old iron bedstead. I willed the lights outside to be fireflies and not a city.

But everything stayed as it was. Jillian was gone. Max was gone. And I was in Lorna's bed.

I looked down and saw her mutter and shift in her sleep. *Oh Jesus, what have I done?*

It wasn't just the sex. The sex was cheating and cheating only made me feel like a piece of shit. It was the way I felt when I looked at her. The way I felt when I looked at Cody. I'd let them into that cold, raggedly-torn place where Jillian and Max used to live and that was way, *way* worse. *You bastard. How could you forget them?*

Lorna mumbled and came awake, feeling for me behind her and tracing my torso, then opening her eyes when she realized I was sitting up. "What's up?" she asked sleepily. Then, when I didn't answer, "JD?"

I turned away, staring out at the city lights.

"JD?" She put her hand on my shoulder, worried, now. "Talk to me."

I knew what I had to do. I just didn't want to do it. I thought back to when I'd taken pieces of shrapnel. It was always better to pull it out fast, right?

"This was a mistake," I told her.

Her hand jerked back as if bitten. I turned and saw her face crumpling. *Shit.* Why was I so bad at this?

I grabbed her hands. "I want to. I'm crazy about you." My hands squeezed hers. "And I'll protect you and Cody with my dying breath but I can't do..."—I looked at the bed, at the two of us—"...this."

She stared at me, utterly wounded, and the guilt tore even deeper. "Why not?"

"Because being with you means letting go of them."

It was a lousy explanation but she got it. She nodded. Turned away and just sat there on the bed for a few moments, processing. Then she got up, dug in a drawer and started pulling on some pajamas.

"Lorna..."

"I'm fine." She had the bottoms on, now.

"Lorna—"

She pulled the top on. "Just give me some space." She hurried out into the hall, leaving me cursing.

35

LORNA

I MANAGED to get out of the bedroom before the tears started. I had to blink my way down the stairs as my vision swam and by the time I reached my dad's office, shut the door and leaned against it, my chest was heaving with deep, painful sobs. But that was okay. The sun wasn't even up yet and no one else was here. No one would see.

I looked around at my dad's office: I wasn't sure I'd ever start thinking of it as mine. But the pain of losing him was starting to change, the brutal dislocation of him not being there slowly being replaced by sadness. It didn't hurt any less but I felt like I was on a path to somewhere where it would.

But JD...from the pain I'd seen in his eyes, from the way he'd spoken about his lost family...his pain was as fresh and horrifying as the day he lost them. God, the poor guy. He hadn't moved on, maybe hadn't even grieved. So of course, when he met someone he cared about, he felt disloyal.

The last thing I wanted to do was force him to let go of them. But if I didn't, if *someone* didn't, JD was going to be alone forever. I crossed my arms, hugging myself, as hot tears rolled down my cheeks. I felt guilty for thinking of myself but...God, for a moment, I'd really thought the two of us had a chance and that Cody had a shot at having a father.

Cody. I really hoped he hadn't figured out that there was something between us. Even if he hadn't, he'd gotten attached to JD and now JD would be leaving as soon as this whole thing was over. It was going to break his heart. And mine, too.

I had to do something, or I was going to go crazy. I swiped at my face with the sleeve of my pajamas and sat down at my dad's desk.

Ever since the party, I'd been worried about what Henry Creel had said. What if he'd been telling the truth about my dad bribing him? I needed to know if the guy I'd hero-worshipped all my life had really been dirty. I felt like I was already as broken as I could be: if there was more bad news, I wanted to get it out of the way now, when it couldn't push me any lower.

For the next few hours, I dug through every bit of paperwork my dad possessed, everything that he hadn't entered into the official accounts. But as I reached the bottom of the last drawer, I dared to hope. I'd found nothing: no bribes, no secret deals. My dad really had played it straight, just like I'd hoped.

I lifted out the very last file: just paperwork from the early days of the dam project in Poland. Nothing suspicious...but as I took it out, a yellow slip of paper that had gotten stuck to the back fluttered down and drifted under the desk. I rooted around and brought it up into the light.

A receipt from the currency exchange at my dad's bank. He'd changed US dollars into Polish Zloty. Nothing strange about that, he'd want some spending money for expenses he couldn't charge to the company: beers, maybe gifts to bring home to us. Except...the receipt was for a hundred thousand dollars. Why the hell would he need to take that much cash with him? *Had* he bribed someone after all, maybe some Polish official? But—I checked the date—this was way too early for that. My dad was just looking at the site to see if a dam was even possible, they were still years away from trying to get planning permission. It was less than a year after my dad first went over there and had his affair with Maria.

I checked the date again...and my heart stopped.

It was just over *nine months* after my dad's affair. And suddenly, I knew what I was looking at.

My dad had paid Maria off because he got her pregnant.

36

JD

I GOT IN THE SHOWER, turned the spray on cold and stood there head bowed as the icy water hammered my body. I'd messed up. I should never have allowed myself to get close to Lorna and Cody. Now I'd hurt her, after promising Cody I wouldn't. And I had no idea how to fix it, or if I could.

But there was one thing I could fix. I'd made another mistake, right back at the start, and it was time to put it right.

I got out of the shower, wrapped a towel around me and grabbed my phone.

Danny answered on the third ring, his voice tight with worry. "JD?"

"I need you," I told him. "I need all of you. Here. Right now."

~

Just six hours later, they trooped in, laden with bags and flight cases. I introduced them to Lorna as they came through the door. Gabriel, our reformed thief, looked smart and smoothly charming in a black shirt. Colton, pushing a huge flight case, could have passed for a roadie with his beard, muscles and band t-shirt with the sleeves torn off. Bradan followed, quiet and watchful, his hands in the pockets of his leather jacket. Our giant sniper Cal, in his plaid shirt, had to stoop to get through the door. Then, from behind him, there was a scuffle of paws and—

Cal's big German Shepherd, Rufus, shot through the open door, jumping and licking at my face, fluffy tail wagging so hard it swept a vase off a side table. As Gabriel neatly caught the vase, Rufus bounded over to Lorna and jumped up at her: *new person! New person!* She shrieked in delight and ruffled his fur. Rufus pushed the side of his head towards her and she got the message and scratched behind his ears. Rufus pounded a paw on the floor in ecstasy.

"Figured it didn't hurt to bring him," said Cal.

I nodded, pleased. The big guy always missed Rufus when we were away on missions so it was nice they didn't have to be separated for once. Plus, Rufus would be useful: if you want security, you can't beat a big dog with sharp ears and a protective streak.

Last through the door was Danny. He gave me the sort of hug only a best friend can. "What have you got yourself into now, you pillock?" he muttered.

I said nothing, just hugged him back, a lump in my throat. I hadn't realized just how much I'd missed him, this last week. How much I'd missed all of them.

I went to close the door...and almost got hit in the face when my sister, Erin, threw it open. She hugged me, too, and I patted her back, staring in shock. "What are you—It's great to see you, but—"

"You want security, right?" She showed me her electronics toolkit. "This is what I *do.*" She looked at Lorna and pushed her glasses up her nose. "Please don't take this the wrong way, but you could use an overhaul."

I ran my hand through my hair, frowning. "It's that bad?"

Erin looked embarrassed. "How do you think we got up to the penthouse just now? You didn't buzz us up. I bypassed the keycard system in the elevator in thirty seconds."

Lorna went pale.

"Don't worry," Erin told her quickly. "I brought cameras, motion detectors, the works. Give me twenty-four hours and this place will be Fort freakin' Knox."

I went to close the door again but it pushed open again. I blinked at Kian. He usually stayed behind a desk because he had to keep his name out of the headlines: the price of dating the President's daughter. "You're here too?!"

"Well, for once we're not leaving the country so it shouldn't ruffle any feathers. Emily's here, too."

"Stacey's here as well," said Bradan. "We all checked into a hotel down the street."

Kian pulled me close as I shook his hand. "I think the two of them were going stir crazy in Mount Mercy. They're both city girls at heart. And Stacey's stressed because she still doesn't know what she's going to do for work in Mount Mercy. They're going to binge on shopping and cocktails. If this job takes more than a few weeks, they may bankrupt us." He looked at Cal and Gabriel. "*Their* other halves wanted to come, too, but Bethany's got med school classes and the hospital couldn't spare Olivia."

I grabbed his shoulder with my other hand and squeezed, delighted. Kian knew more about being a bodyguard than I ever would. He was going to be invaluable. And it was great that Emily and Stacey had come. It was rare that we had a job that let them stay close to their men. I'd figure out shifts so that everyone got some downtime and the couples could enjoy being together. "Okay," I said, finally nudging the door closed with my foot. "Now that we're all—"

"*Ow!*" The door bounced open again, revealing a figure in aviator sunglasses rubbing her nose. "Don't shut me out of the party!"

"*Gina?*" Even our grumpy but lovable pilot had come. I pulled the door open and carefully checked the hallway in case there was anyone else, then finally closed it and turned to look at them all, amazed. "You *all* came?"

"'Course we bloody did," said Danny. "Now do you want to tell us what we're dealing with?"

Lorna excused herself and went downstairs to work. And I started at the beginning and told the team everything: Mexico, Russ's death, the shooting, Poland and the two of us nearly drowning the night before. When I'd finished, Gina raised her hand. "So there's a kid? Can I go on record as saying I *hate* children?"

Colton sidled over to the floor-to-ceiling windows, took a cautious look out and grimaced. "Did she have to live so fucking high up?"

Cal was leaning against a wall: even leaning, he was taller than the rest of us standing straight. "Who do you figure's trying to kill her?"

"Best guess is this son of a bitch, Sebastian van der Meer," I said, showing them a photo. "He wants to buy the company and break it up. Lorna's dad wouldn't sell, neither will she." I rubbed the back of my neck, embarrassed. "I thought Lorna's brother was working with him but I was wrong."

"And you and Lorna?" asked Gabriel.

I did my best poker face. "Me and Lorna?"

Gabriel lifted his eyebrows just a little.

"Goddammit," I muttered. "When did you know?!"

"The moment I walked in the door," said Gabriel. "The body language. The way your voice goes soft when you talk about her."

"No it doesn't," I snapped.

Everyone nodded sadly. *Yes it does.*

"*Goddammit!*" They all knew?! I sighed and glowered out of the window. "I got...attached to them. Her and the kid." I caught sight of my reflection in the glass and glowered harder. "It was a mistake."

"You sure?" asked Kian gently.

I nodded firmly. "We're gonna protect them. We're gonna find out who's behind this and stop them. Then we're out of here."

And I gave them all their orders.

Two hours later, I was pacing the penthouse, on the phone to Callahan. "C'mon," I pressed. "There's got to be something you can do about van der Meer. Can't you get a warrant or a subpoena or *something?*"

Callahan sighed. I could hear office noise in the background and imagined him lounging at his desk in the FBI building. "Look, this guy's smart. Too smart to leave anything pointing to him. There's nothing tying him to the boat explosion or the shooting at the speech. The SUV that rammed you into the water was stolen, so no clues there. And as for Poland, van der Meer does business over there, but he does business *everywhere.*" He lowered his voice. "I even took a chance and got my girlfriend to take a look at his bank accounts. The guy likes his $5000 cognac and his Rolls Royces but there's nothing criminal there. I agree, he's our best suspect. But we don't have anything we can pin on him."

I cursed, thanked him and ended the call, then went to check how everyone was doing.

I started down in the underground garage. The leasing company had just delivered a new Mercedes to replace the one that the police were lifting out of New York Harbor with a crane. Danny was elbow-deep in the engine, getting everything tuned to perfection in case we wound up in another chase. From now on, he was going to handle all the driving.

Erin was sitting in the driver's seat so she could run the engine when he needed her to. Her laptop was on her lap and she was typing furiously between tests. "I've put cameras in the lobby and motion detectors in the stairwells," she told me. "We'll be able to monitor them on this laptop, or even on a phone. Then I'm going to upgrade the security on the elevator so you can't hack it like I did. No one's getting upstairs without us knowing."

"Try it now," Danny told her.

Erin fired up the engine. It roared like a raging lion, then settled down to a softly purring cat. Erin leaned out of the window and she and Danny fist-bumped. I smiled. The two of them made a good team.

Next, I met up with Bradan. He took me on a tour of the building, showing me all the weak spots he'd found just by quietly hanging around. "There are takeout delivery people coming and going all the time," he told me. "And the reception staff just buzz them up without ID. Easiest thing in the world to just steal a uniform, or even get a job with one of those places for a day, and then stroll right up to Lorna's floor and pull a gun out of the pizza box. Or I could just swipe an ID badge, look..." And he showed me the three he'd taken from people without them noticing. "I could get right up to the McBride offices, then wait until she's on her own, like when she goes to the bathroom. Do it with a knife, put the body in a stall, I could be out of the building before anyone finds her."

I turned to him, horrified. He gave me a helpless shrug: *this is what you wanted.*

I sighed and nodded, patting him on the back. This *was* what I'd wanted, for him to put all those years he'd spent as an assassin for the cult to good use, so we could plug the security holes. But it was still disconcerting to hear it. "Good job," I told him. "I'll talk to the security guards and tighten everything up."

As we walked the rest of the way up to the penthouse, I watched him out of the corner of my eye. I could tell he was hurting. He'd been that way ever since we started Stormfinch, wracked with guilt over all the people he'd killed while he was brainwashed. I'd tried talking to him and so had Gabriel and his brother, Kian, but all we could offer was sympathy. We didn't have any answers.

And then it hit me that maybe there was someone who did.

"Can you help Cal?" I asked Bradan. "I asked him to look for sniper spots." Bradan nodded and I watched his retreating back, rubbing at my stubble. *I hope this works.*

I met up with Kian and he gave me a crash course on bodyguarding. We walked around the block with him as the bodyguard and me as the subject. "We turn the corner and I'm checking the windows of the building on our right," Kian narrated. "Those two guys coming towards us in the crowd, the one on the left has something under his jacket. That van: why is it parked there? Are the guys unloading looking at what they're doing or looking at us?"

I suddenly realized how much I'd been missing. "I should have called you in from the start," I muttered.

"Yeah," said Kian reproachfully. "You should have." He glanced sideways at me. "You've really fallen for her, haven't you?"

I looked away, not answering. Which was an answer in itself.

"I know a thing or two about falling for the person you're guarding," said Kian slowly. "You sure you're doing the right thing, pushing her away?"

I scowled at the sidewalk and shook my head. "I can't be with her."

Kian let me cool down for half a block. Then he murmured, "I know a thing or two about losing people, too."

I turned to him. "You gonna say something about moving on?" I said tightly. "Letting go?"

Kian looked at me sadly, which made me even madder. I didn't want his sympathy. Didn't deserve it. "No," he said, and patted me on the back, and we carried on with the training.

Back at the penthouse, Colton was checking the doors and figuring out which locks and hinges needed to be upgraded. As a bounty hunter, he kicked down enough doors to know what would hold and what wouldn't. Meanwhile, Gabriel was sitting on the couch with Erin's laptop, checking each of the new cameras and sensors in turn.

I headed up to the roof and saw Cal and Bradan standing at the edge. Both had binoculars to their eyes and they were talking quietly as they looked at the roofs of neighboring buildings.

"I know what you mean," Cal said. "There isn't a day that goes by that I don't think about those kids in the SUV. And all the rest."

"I keep thinking...they were someone's brother," Bradan said. "Or dad. Or son. And I just took them out of the world. *I'm* the reason they're not there anymore. And I didn't even know why, most of the time."

I saw Cal's massive body stiffen. "They never told me, either." There was a long pause. "You know what Bethany told me? She said no one's irredeemable." He finally lowered the binoculars from his eyes and Bradan did, too. "She said you can't change the past, you can only change what you are now."

They looked at each other for a moment. Then they put the binoculars back to their eyes and went back to work.

I quietly retreated before they saw me. I knew it wouldn't be a magic solution, because there were no magic solutions for what those two had gone through: Cal, killing for the CIA, and Bradan killing for the cult. But maybe it would be a start.

Everyone was doing their jobs and I felt better already for having the team there. But now I had to do what I'd been putting off all day.

When Lorna finished work, I took her into my bedroom, where we could be alone. It was worse than I'd been expecting. She wouldn't even look at me, just glared at the floor. *Aw crap.*

I'd rehearsed what I was going to say about a million times but now it came to it, none of the words sounded right. I wound up just blurting out what I felt. "I'm sorry I hurt you."

She nodded. Then glanced up and met my eyes for a second to see if she could go, now. Her eyes were starting to swim with tears and I felt my heart breaking. All I wanted to do was wrap my arms around her and pull her into a hug, and maybe kill the bastard who'd upset her. But the bastard was *me* and hugging her would only make this harder. I sighed. "You know this place. What's the room with the thickest walls, and no windows?"

"Why?" she asked, struggling to control her voice.

"I want you to have a safe room to go to, just in case."

Her head jerked up again and this time, she was panicked. "You think someone could get in here?" The penthouse had always been a sanctuary, the one place we knew was safe.

I put my hands on her shoulders to calm her—and just that touch of her body was enough to melt me. *Dammit.* "No. We'll make sure that never happens. But just in case." I squeezed her shoulders and Lorna gave a little intake of breath. Everything stopped.

I needed this woman in my life.

But I couldn't. I couldn't replace Jillian and Max, couldn't push them away into the darkness. I forced myself to let go of Lorna's shoulders. She slumped a little in pain and my chest ached.

She turned and walked out of the room and I followed her. She led me through her bedroom and *God,* the bed, the bed was still rumpled where we'd slept. She stalked past it, not looking, and showed me into her bathroom, tidy and feminine, with big fluffy white towels and the scent of her shampoo in the air.

"Here," she said, still avoiding my eyes.

"Okay," I told her. "Anything ever goes wrong, you grab Cody and Paige and you run in here and lock the door. Don't come out until I come for you. Okay?"

She nodded. "Anything else?" I could hear her fighting for control again.

I felt like something that had crawled out of a drain. "No," I said at last.

She showed me out of her bedroom and closed the door behind me. I leaned back against the door and ran a hand over my face. An instant later, I felt the door shift just a little, and realized she'd done the same, on the other side. We were back to back, with just the slab of wood between us.

I heard her start to cry. I rocked my head back against the door and stared at the ceiling. *Fuck.* I put my palm flat against the door, wishing I could touch her. *I'm sorry.*

37

LORNA

THE NEXT MORNING was good-natured pandemonium.

JD had set up shifts so that only he had to be at the penthouse full time and the others rotated. But the shift change happened at eight, so right in the middle of the morning school and work rush, we had a whole team of big military guys—plus Gina and Erin—yawning and stretching after a long night awake or laughing and joking as they arrived for their shift. "Donuts are here," I yelled above the bustle. I'd ordered two dozen, plus eight coffees, because our coffee machine couldn't keep up with so many people. I put the donuts down in the kitchen and before I'd even lifted the lid, Colton had appeared, his nose twitching.

"Cody, do you have your bag?" I called. "Danny's going to drive you."

"Yup." Cody was playing with Rufus. He'd throw a bouncy red ball down the hallway and Rufus would race off, woofing and barging his way past people and finally leaping to grab it, then trot back to Cody and deposit the ball at his feet: *again, again!* Cody had never been around a dog before and he was besotted.

I dodged around them and walked through to the living room, where Marcus, the tailor, was measuring the team for suits so they'd fit in a little better around the office and at events. "Better order an extra roll of fabric," he muttered to his assistant as he looked up at Cal.

I started passing out coffees. "Could I get a secret pocket in the lining of mine?" I heard Gabriel ask the tailor.

Marcus wrote it down. "And what did *you* have in mind?" he asked Bradan.

Bradan looked embarrassed. "I dunno," he mumbled, his Northern Irish accent hard but beautiful. He looked at Danny. "All those years, I never bought clothes 'cos I liked them. I bought what I needed to fit in."

Danny, who I thought of as *The British One,* grinned. "Well, you came to the right man. How about a nice three-piece, single-breasted..." He gave Marcus a detailed description and Bradan smiled, relieved.

I handed them each a coffee, then turned and passed one to Cal, who was standing with arms outstretched, being measured. "Thanks," he rumbled. He kept glancing out of the windows at New York, looking a little disconcerted. He felt out of place here, more than the others, and it wasn't just his plaid shirt and worn jeans. "You okay?" I asked gently.

He looked out of the window again. "Eight *million* people," he muttered, then shook his head. "It's a little more than I'm used to."

After a few days, things had fallen into a routine. By day, JD and two or three others would keep watch around the office, or come with me if I had to go out to a meeting or an event. At night, the ones who'd been on duty would go back to the hotel and some fresh team members would watch the penthouse. I got used to hearing Rufus's collar rattling as he patrolled the hallways with Cal, and to the way Bradan tended to lurk unseen in corners. I bonded with all of them, from the coolly professional Kian in his designer suits to the rough, bearded Colton (who I had to ask to tone down his cursing around

Cody: I got a shame-faced *yes ma'am).* I found them all a lot easier to get along with than the corporate types I had to deal with at work. And I felt much, much safer having them all there. The constant stress, that ache around my chest, eased a little.

The only problem was JD and me. Whenever I saw him, I felt this deep, brutal ache for what could have been, made worse by the fact I knew he was hurting, too. It would have been easier if I could have been mad at him, but I wasn't. I just wanted him to be okay.

And it wasn't like the attraction had gone away: whenever we were in the same room for more than a few seconds, I could feel it building: I'd catch him stealing little glances at me when he thought I wasn't looking and then become aware that I was doing the same. He'd brush against me in the hall and I'd feel my whole body come alive, every inch of my skin throbbing under my suit. I'd feel his hand on my back when we were out at an event, and I'd close my eyes for a second, luxuriating in his touch, savoring it because it was all I'd get of him all day. It was agony.

One evening, while Cal was teaching Cody how to whittle a stick, I walked past the kitchen and saw Danny on his own in there, brewing tea. I checked no one else was around and then sidled in.

Danny turned around and gave me a big, wide grin. He really was charming. I could completely see why JD's little sister had fallen for him.

"You're JD's best friend...right?" I asked.

He turned back to his tea-making. I could feel him debating, not sure if he should get involved. Then he slowly turned around, opening himself up to me. "Tea?" he asked.

I nodded. "Please."

He started to make me one. "I'm sorry for what happened. For what it's worth, he didn't mean to hurt you. He can be a grumpy, stubborn bastard but there's not an evil bone in his body."

"I know," I said quietly. Then, "Jillian and Max...he hasn't let them go, has he?"

Danny crushed the teabag mercilessly against the side of the mug, extracting every last drop of tea from it, then dropped it in the trash. "No. He hasn't." He added milk, passed me the mug and then sighed, hanging his head. "His family was his whole world. He used to be lighter. He'd *laugh*. But when he lost them, the way it happened...he changed."

I thought about the pain I saw in JD's eyes, a wound that was still raw. And the advice he'd given me, on the way to my speech. "He didn't grieve properly, did he?"

Danny's lips tightened. "I don't reckon he grieved *at all*." He went quiet for a moment, turning his mug around and around in his hands. "He ever tell you about his dad?"

I shook my head.

"Real tough Texan rancher. Not abusive or anything, just the sort of bloke who was up every day before the sun, throwing hay bales around, breaking the ice in the troughs with his bare hands so the horses could drink...not a man who moisturizes, you know what I mean? A *man's man*. Anyway, when JD's twelve, his dad gets thrown by a horse. Breaks his back. That's why JD had to step in and help his mom raise Erin. So his dad, this rancher who's spent every day of his entire life riding and ranching and doing physical work...suddenly, all he can do is sit on the porch in his wheelchair." Danny paused for effect. "And he *never. Complains. Once.* Never talks to anyone about it, never accepts any help adapting to his new life." Danny shook his head, then lifted his gaze to look me in the eye. "That's why JD never grieved. He'd learned from his dad that you can't cry, can't show weakness. *That's not what men do.*"

My chest ached. *Oh, JD...* I thought about what he'd said to Cody at the funeral. He *knew* this kind of stoicism was bad. But that didn't mean he could change.

"Ever since it happened, it's like he's not really been living," said Danny. "Just...surviving." He looked at me. "Until he met you."

"How do we help him?" I asked.

Danny shook his head. "I'm not sure we can. I think maybe he has to figure this out on his own."

~

That night, I was still at my desk at one in the morning. It wasn't just that there were a thousand decisions that I needed to make as CEO, it was that every one of them came with millions of dollars worth of consequences. I was learning that executives made the easy decisions themselves so they could take credit. The hard decisions, they sent upstairs to me, so that it would be my neck and not theirs if things went wrong. I stared at my screen and groaned, my head in my hands. I'd been circling around and around on five big decisions for two hours, unable to decide on any of them.

I got up, legs aching from sitting still for so long, and stumbled out of my dad's office in search of coffee. I turned towards the break room...and slammed straight into someone, so hard I bumped my nose. My pulse shot through the roof and I jumped backward, tripped in my heels and went down on my ass. I lay there panting on the carpet, my heart slamming. Most of the lights were off and the guy was hidden in shadow. All I knew was that it wasn't JD.

I made out heavy black boots and immense, denim-clad calves and thighs. The guy was *big,* a walking wall of hard muscle. Then, as he stepped into the light, I saw a soft cotton t-shirt stretched across his chest, with silvery-blue gothic letters spelling out what I guessed was the name of a band. A thick, black beard and then—

"Sorry," rumbled Colton. "Didn't mean to scare ya."

I slumped in relief and then flushed, embarrassed. I'd seen him around plenty over the last few days and I should have known that JD would have someone down on this floor while I was down here. But in fairness, Colton *was* pretty intimidating. He was gorgeous in a rough, brutish way, but with his muscles and beard, he looked like an outlaw biker.

I took the massive hand he offered and he hauled me to my feet like I weighed nothing. "I was just going to get coffee," I told him, straightening my skirt. "You want some?"

He shook his head. "Nah, I'm good." But he walked with me to the break room, his big body filling the small space. Now that my heart had slowed, his strength felt comforting, like a friendly grizzly was looking after me.

He watched as I poured myself a mug of coffee. "You planning on getting *any* sleep?" he asked.

I rubbed the back of my neck. "Probably not." I sighed and braced my hands on the counter, suddenly exhausted. "I'm trying to make all these decisions but I can't."

"Why not?"

I shrugged, which made me realize how tense my shoulders had gotten. "I don't have any right. My dad put me in charge but I'm around all these people who've been doing this stuff for years. I shouldn't be here."

Colton grunted and crossed his arms. His brows lowered and he stood there thinking, "Yeah," he said at last. "I know what that's like."

I turned to him, shocked.

He nodded towards the ceiling, to the penthouse above us. "All those other guys, they're Delta or Marine Raiders or Secret Service. Me? I was just regular Army, and military police." With his Missouri accent, it sounded like two words, *poh-leece.* "I come to Stormfinch and it's all fake passports and secret missions and working with the CIA and shit. And they're all used to it but I ain't. I'm just used to following orders, cuffing guys and throwing 'em in a truck. I'm glad to be here, y'know? I need this job. I love what we do. But I keep thinking that sooner or later, someone's gonna turn round and realize I don't belong."

I stared. *Colton,* the big, scary ox of the team, had a touch of imposter syndrome? "That's not going to happen," I told him. "The others respect the hell out of you. I've seen the way JD talks to you when he's handing out orders. He trusts you. He knows you'll get the job done."

Colton nodded gratefully, embarrassed. And I nodded back to him, because I felt better, too. Maybe we both just needed to believe in ourselves.

I took my coffee back to my dad's office, took a deep breath, and started plowing through the decisions one by one.

∽

The next day, Marcus returned with everyone's new suits and the men disappeared in turn to try them on. At the same time, Emily, Kian's girlfriend, and Stacey, Bradan's girlfriend, stopped by, bringing cupcakes. I took to both of them immediately: Emily was warm and down-to-earth, not at all how I'd imagined the President's daughter would be. And Stacey was a whirlwind of efficient energy: I found her intimidating until Emily shared how she'd fallen off her stool in a cocktail bar the night before.

"I didn't *fall off*," protested Stacey. "I went to sit down and *missed my stool*. Someone must have moved it."

They'd taken Erin out shopping and she'd returned with a whole new look. The baggy, shapeless hoodie she'd shown up in was gone and she was sporting a green angora sweater that hugged her body and a pair of tight black jeans. When Danny walked in and saw her, he stopped dead in his tracks. The soft *wow* he finally whispered made me go melty: he was so obviously crazy about her. He grabbed her by the waist, picked her up and spun her around, then hugged her against him and we all *Ahh*ed.

"I bought other stuff as well," Erin told him excitedly. "Some strappy tops and a skirt and—" She put her mouth close to his ear and whispered something.

Danny's eyes went wide. *"Like in the book?"*

Erin nodded, blushing.

"Excuse us," said Danny and marched off, still carrying her.

"She found this leather corset," Emily whispered to me. "Sort of *Lord of the Rings* meets Victoria's Secret. We may not see them for a while."

At that moment, Bradan walked in, in his newly-tailored suit. Stacey's eyes went wide. *"Ohmygod!* I haven't seen you in a suit since the double wedding! You look *amazing!"*

And he did. The suit was midnight blue, subtle and refined, but as he moved you caught little glimpses of the silk lining which was the bright cyan of a Caribbean bay. The jacket was perfectly cut to show off his powerful shoulders and the tight lines of his waist, and the pants were just tight enough to let you see his muscled ass. He looked like the CEO of a company that made space weapons, about to play high-stakes poker. Bradan grinned, pleased but nervous: he'd always sort of blended into the background but now, suddenly, he stood out.

One by one, the other men filed in, in their new suits. They didn't look *respectable,* exactly, but they did all look gorgeous. Colton, in particular, was transformed: with a crisp white shirt stretched across his chest, you realized just how wide and strong those pecs were and with his dark beard and brooding good looks, he looked like some underworld billionaire. But I only had eyes for JD. As he straightened his jacket, I could see the exact curve of his chest where I'd laid my head as I dozed off. As he adjusted his tie, my eyes locked on that soft lower lip and my own lips tingled, remembering his kisses. And then our eyes met and there was so much there, sadness and regret and that agonizing pain...

I tore my eyes away and took a deep, calming breath. I'd managed before him. I could manage after him.

Except...after was so much harder because now I'd always be thinking about what could have been.

"You all look badass," said Gina, leaning against a wall. "I'm sticking to my flight suit, though." She was trying to stay upbeat but I knew she must feel like a fifth wheel. She'd taken turns on guard duty and watching the cameras, but there wasn't much for her to actually do, and I felt sorry for her.

So I'd done something about it. "Come with me," I told her.

She followed me up to the roof, curious. As soon as she saw the gleaming, blue-and-white helicopter on the helipad, her eyes lit up.

"My dad bought it a few years ago so we could get to sites faster, but we so rarely used it, we wound up storing it at the airport," I told her. "I thought, now that you're here..."

Gina ran over to it, opened the door and inhaled. "It still has that new chopper smell!" She turned to me, beaming. "I never get to fly anything as new as this, it's always rentals or old military stuff!"

I grinned. I couldn't do anything about me and JD but at least I'd made someone happy.

A week on from the team arriving, things were going well. There'd been no more attacks, the office and penthouse security had been tightened up and I was even starting to feel like I was getting a handle on work. I still didn't have the people skills that my dad or Miles had, but my confidence was gradually improving. When I chaired meetings, I was actually making my voice heard and when an architect messed up and nearly cost us a million dollars, I did something I never dreamed I'd be able to do: I took them aside and had a calm but firm talk, and made sure they'd learned from the mistake, just like my dad had once done.

It helped that we'd had a couple of big wins: Henry Creel, the creep from the ball, had caved and granted planning permission for the hospital and the dam in Poland was back on schedule. The work was still punishing, though. I was working sixteen-hour days, seven days a week, barely sleeping or eating, and I worried that I wasn't getting enough time with Cody.

One night, after I finally finished for the night, I snuck into his room and just stood there watching him softly snoring. Overcome, I bent down and kissed his chestnut curls. *I won't be able to get away with that for much longer.* He was growing up so fast.

I started to sneak out...but a glint in the darkness made me stop. Sitting on his desk were the mirrored aviator sunglasses he'd begged me to buy him a few days before. It wasn't lost on me that they were identical to the ones JD wore. My chest ached. JD was so great for him and the two got on so well, but unless JD could find a way to let go of his past, we couldn't be together...and Cody was going to lose another father figure.

Then I saw something else on the desk, hidden under a sheet of newspaper. I checked Cody was still asleep, then lifted one corner to peek...

Cal, the huge sniper who'd lived alone in the woods for years, had been teaching Cody how to make things with wood. I'd been aware that Cody had been working on something, but I hadn't known what until now.

It was a letter rack, to organize paperwork. It was beautifully carved and sanded: it must have taken him days. He'd painted it ocean green, my favorite color, and MOM was picked out in raised letters. He was trying to help me, any way he could.

I just melted. I wanted to gather him up into my arms right then and tell him how lucky I was...but he needed his sleep. I quietly put the newspaper back in place so that the letter rack could stay a surprise, then crept quietly out. *Just a few more weeks,* I told myself. Then Miles would be out of rehab and could take over as CEO. And as soon as that happened, Cody and I were taking a vacation. Just a few more weeks and everything would be okay.

The next morning, Paige came running into the kitchen as we were eating breakfast. "Have you seen the news?"

JD and I followed her through to the living room. The early morning business news was on and the ticker tape along the bottom of the screen told the story. While we'd been asleep, one of the big European banks had decided to close our line of credit. We couldn't borrow a dime more.

"What does that mean?" asked JD.

"It means..." My throat closed up. "It means we're going out of business."

38

LORNA

MY PHONE STARTED to ring but I ignored it, watching as the talking heads on-screen started to calmly discuss the end of McBride Construction. They put a photo of my dad in the corner of the screen. "What I can't get over," one pundit said, "is how quickly things have fallen apart since his daughter took charge."

My head went swimmy and I had to put a hand out and brace myself on the wall. *This isn't happening.* My phone was still ringing and I stared numbly at the unknown number. JD finally grabbed it out of my hand and answered for me. He listened. "No comment," he snapped and stabbed the *end call* button.

"Paige?" I said, my voice quavering. "Would you please get Cody to school? I need to get downstairs."

Paige nodded, her face pale. I hugged Cody very tight and told him to have a good day, trying to be normal. But Cody was tense and worried. "It'll be okay, mom," he told me. "You'll fix it.'

I forced a smile and hugged him again. But my insides had cinched down to a cold, hard knot.

JD and I went downstairs to my dad's office and I started making phone calls, trying to get a handle on things. As people heard the news, they rushed to my desk and soon my desk was surrounded by a crowd of executives three-deep, everyone talking at once. JD stayed right by my side, silently protective.

Miles called, asking if I wanted him to come in. "Thanks," I croaked, "but no. Stay put. You're where you need to be, right now. Focus on getting well."

I talked to the bank. They were apologetic, but they wouldn't explain why, after forty years, they'd suddenly decided to stop lending to us, or why they'd announced it publicly. I called all the other banks, asking and then begging, but they'd been spooked by our bank dropping us. No one would lend us money. And without money, we couldn't keep things running until we were paid for our current projects. I wanted to scream in frustration: we were so *close:* in just a few weeks, we'd finish the next stage of the dam in Poland, get paid and our bank account would be back in the black. But we wouldn't last that long.

"Why would they do it?" demanded JD at last. "It doesn't make any sense!" I could see the frustration on his face. He knew he didn't understand business stuff and he probably thought he was asking a dumb question. But he was right, it *didn't* make sense.

Unless...

I turned to our top financial guy. "Find out if anyone's been buying shares in our bank. A *lot* of shares."

He ran off. He was back less than five minutes later. A huge chunk of the bank had been bought just a few days ago by a hedge fund. A hedge fund run by Sebastian van der Meer.

"Christ." I put my head in my hands. "He took control of the bank and forced them to drop us."

"How long till we're bankrupt?" asked JD quietly.

By now, I knew the figures by heart and the math was simple. "Four days."

There was a chorus of cursing and then everyone started talking at once. Panic filled the room, squeezing out all the air until I could barely breathe. I stared down at the polished surface of my dad's desk. He'd spent forty years building this company and I'd destroyed it in just a few weeks. Thousands of people were going to lose their jobs. Couples and young families who'd sunk every penny they had into a deposit for one of our apartments were going to be screwed over. The hospital would never be built.

Everyone was yelling, a thousand different questions but they all boiled down to the same thing: *Lorna, what are we going to do?* And I had no idea. I wasn't my dad. I wasn't a leader—

"I can't do this," I muttered.

People stared at me, frowning. I slowly got up and started pushing through them to the door.

"Lorna?" one of them asked.

"What—Where are you—" demanded another.

I shook my head and moved faster, panting and desperate.

"Lorna, you can't—"

I hit full-blown panic. I barged my way to the door, stumbled out into the hall—

"*Lorna!*" yelled JD.

...and ran.

39

JD

I took the stairs to the penthouse three at a time. Burst through the door, hoping to see Lorna sobbing in Paige's arms. But Paige hadn't seen her. I checked the whole penthouse, just to be sure. Lorna wasn't there.

Gabriel, who was on day shift, looked uneasy. "You check the roof?"

"The *roof?*" I frowned at him, confused.

"You said she was pretty upset."

My stomach lurched. *Oh God.* Cal was on a neighboring rooftop, keeping watch with his rifle. "Cal!" I yelled into the radio. "Cal, has Lorna gone up on the roof?"

"No one's been on the roof all morning," Cal reported.

I slumped in relief. But then where the hell was she? She was scared and panicking. *Where would she go?*

I rubbed at my stubble, thinking. I'm not some psychologist with a couch and a room full of books. But if you work in small teams for long enough, you get a feel for what makes people tick.

I went all the way down to the lobby and then down to the parking garage. Then I went down to the very lowest level of *that.* I hunted around in the gloom until I found one of the enormous, circular pillars that held the building up.

And there, sitting in a tight bundle with her back pressed against it, was Lorna. I crouched down next to her and she looked up, her eyes red from crying. "How did you find me?" she croaked.

"Folks get upset, they reach for what comforts them." I slapped the pillar.

She sniffed. Hiccoughed. "For someone who claims they're a big dumb cowboy, you're pretty smart, you know that?"

I eased myself down next to her.

"Thousands of people are going to lose their jobs because of me," she said. "*Thousands.*"

"It's not your fault."

"Of course it's my fault, I'm CEO! I'm responsible for them!"

My heart ached. I knew she meant it. Just like in Poland, she cared about every employee.

"I've destroyed everything he built," she said bitterly. She was silent for a moment. "You know I'm pretty sure he got his mistress in Poland pregnant? My whole life, I idolized him. Now I feel like I didn't know him at all."

"We all do things we regret," I said slowly. "Doesn't mean he was a bad guy."

She slowly turned to me. I stared into her eyes and hoped she knew I wasn't just talking about Russ.

She looked away. "I'm not the right person for this. I don't know what to do."

I knew what she was going through. I knew what it was like to be the leader, to have everyone looking to you. All I wanted to do was hug her, but I couldn't: once I touched her, there'd be no stopping. And I couldn't fight this for her. All I could do was support her, just like Danny always supported me. "Your dad picked you for a reason," I began.

"My dad picked me because Miles had a drug problem!" she said savagely.

I waited a few seconds, letting her calm a little. Then I spoke slowly, my voice like iron. "That's not true. He could have left it all to some executive he trusted. He chose *you*. He had faith in you. And *I* have faith in you." I lowered my voice. "You can do this."

I reached out and took her hand. Nothing happened. She just sat there, broken and miserable.

But I wasn't going anywhere. I sat there in the darkness, just letting her know that.

And at last, her hand moved in mine...and then squeezed, and I squeezed back.

I felt her steeling herself, building herself back up. Then she drew in a long, shuddering breath, sniffed and lifted her head. I could tell she was thinking: she looked like Russ, when she was deep in thought. Finally, she stood up.

"I have to go see him," she said firmly. "I have to go see Van der Meer."

40

JD

I GAPED UP AT HER, then climbed to my feet. "I'm trying to keep you safe," I told her. "You're talking about walking right into the lion's den."

"He isn't going to murder me himself, in front of witnesses," she countered.

"We don't know *what* he'll do. Why would you want to go to him?"

"He did this," said Lorna. "He's the only one with the power to undo it. Maybe I can persuade him, if I do it face to face."

I narrowed my eyes. I wasn't *that* dumb. That bastard wasn't going to change his mind just because she asked nicely. She had something up her sleeve. Well, fine. I didn't need to know every damn detail. I just had to protect her. "That son-of-a-bitch tries anything..." I warned.

Lorna made the call on our way upstairs. I scowled as I heard Van der Meer's sneering voice. "I'm on my yacht, off the coast. I'll send you our position."

In the penthouse, I called in the whole team, even the ones who were resting at the hotel, and explained the plan. Everyone grabbed their gear...and then I frowned because I saw Paige pulling on her jacket. "You're not coming," I told her. "This could be dangerous."

Paige grabbed me by the sleeve and dragged me off to the kitchen. "Now listen,' she told me. "I know you have to protect her. And I know *why* you have to protect her." I felt myself flush down to my collar. "But I'm her *friend*. She's in pieces right now and she needs some moral support, not just guys with guns and the man who just broke her heart. If that prick says *no* to her deal, she's going to lose everything and if that happens I'm not going to be hundreds of miles away!"

I nodded, chastened. She was right: women need their besties.

We all trooped out to the chopper. It was a gorgeous day, the sun warm on our faces and the sky a deep, flawless blue. Bradan was next to me and he seemed different: a little lighter, like a weight had been lifted. That talk with Cal had worked.

We opened the rear door of the shining, blue-and-white chopper. "Wipe your feet!" yelled Gina over the roar of the rotor blades. "Colton, no eating!"

We flew out to sea and over the endless blue ocean for more than a half hour. Then the yacht crept into view on the horizon. Gina whistled and we all pressed our noses to the glass to look. It was huge, a floating palace five decks high with a helicopter pad and a hot tub.

Gina brought us down on the pad and we were met by Van der Meer's own bodyguards, sour-faced men in suits. They led us to where Van der Meer lounged on a couch, his cream suit dazzling in the sun. I felt the anger flash through me, tightening my muscles and heating my face. It took everything I had to keep from punching him.

Lorna stepped forward and we all formed a protective wall around her. Paige's purse hit a side table, nearly knocking over a crystal decanter, and she had to grab it before it fell. "Careful," said Van Der Meer mildly. "That cognac costs more than you make in a month." Paige glared at him.

It was meant to be Lorna who did the talking, but I couldn't help it. "We know it was you who killed Russ," I snapped. "And the shooter at the speech, the attack in Poland, ramming our car into the water—"

Van der Meer chuckled and held up his hands. "I had nothing to do with any of that."

"*Bullshit!*" I spat, stepping forward.

Lorna put a hand on my chest. "But you *did* buy a stake in the bank so you could cut off our credit," she said.

Van der Meer smirked. "That...I *did* do. And you must know that appealing to my better nature isn't going to work. Therefore I take it you've come here with an offer?"

I turned to Lorna, frowning. *An offer?*

She nodded stiffly.

Van der Meer turned to the side table, shooing Paige out of the way. "I bought this especially for the occasion. I knew you'd come crawling to me sooner or later." He poured two glasses of cognac and offered Lorna one. She grudgingly accepted the glass and sat down across from him. Van der Meer raised his glass in a toast. "To the root of all evil!"

God, I hated this guy.

Lorna waited until he drank, then did the same. She stared wretchedly at her glass, taking little sips to try to delay the inevitable. Van der Meer grinned, enjoying her misery. At last, her glass was empty and she couldn't delay any longer.

She put her glass down and took a deep breath. "I'll sell you the company," she told him, her voice ragged.

The whole team stared at her. That was giving him exactly what he wanted. It went completely against her dad's wishes. "But he'll break it up and sell off the pieces!" I told her.

She turned to me. "I know. But this way, we can at least negotiate a grace period. We can give the workers settlement packages. People will have some warning and they won't all be laid off at once so they'll have more chance of finding a job."

My heart was breaking for her. The company was doomed no matter what: most CEOs would have let it die rather than sign it over to their rival, just as a matter of pride. But Lorna was putting her ego aside to look after her workers. I couldn't stop myself: I put my hand on her shoulder and squeezed. I needed her to know she wasn't alone in all this.

We all looked at Van der Meer. He made us wait until he'd finished his cognac. Then he smiled, savoring his victory, and...

"...no," he said.

"*What?*" croaked Lorna. "But it's what you've always wanted!"

Van der Meer leaned forward. "It's simple math, darling. Yes, I could buy your company now. But in...what, a week, you'll declare bankruptcy. I can sweep in and buy your assets for a pittance. No need to pay for any settlement packages. I'll make two, three times as much."

Lorna jumped up from her seat. "Jesus, don't you have any—" She broke off and tottered a little.

"Lorna?" I asked, worried.

She shook her head. "I'm fine, I just stood up too fast." But she was turning pale. Then one leg crumpled under her and she fell sideways into me. I caught her and lowered her gently down so she was sitting on the deck. "*Lorna?!*"

Sweat broke out across her forehead and her breathing turned raspy. I passed her to Danny and jumped up, cold terror crushing my chest. "*What did you give her?*" I yelled at Van der Meer.

"You think I *poisoned* her? On my own yacht, in front of witnesses? *I* drank it too!"

Gabriel stepped forward, furious. "The glass," he said. "He must have put something in her glass, so that only she got it."

Lorna was panting frantically, now, as if she couldn't get enough air. *Oh God.* I grabbed Van der Meer by the collar and drew my gun. Van der Meer's bodyguards drew theirs but they were loose, sloppy. By the time they had their weapons out of their holsters, my team were already pointing guns at their heads. Van der Meer turned pale.

I rammed him up against the wall and pressed the muzzle of my gun to his temple. I could hear Lorna straining to breathe behind me and the sound stripped away what little self-control I had left. "If she dies," I said, "I swear to God, I'll put a bullet through your head. So you better tell me what you gave her..."

I trailed off. Something was wrong. Van der Meer was clutching at his shirt collar, fighting for air. I let him go and he slumped forward onto the deck, his breathing as frantic as Lorna's.

"Oh *shit*," said Danny.

41

JD

THE FEAR SURGED up inside me, paralyzing me. I stared down at Lorna and Van der Meer's helpless forms. *Oh Jesus.*

"Get her to the chopper," yelled Gina. "I'll get it started." And she ran off towards the helicopter.

I scooped up Lorna and ran after Gina, the rest of the team forming up around me. "I'll call Olivia," said Gabriel, pulling out the satellite phone. Olivia was his girlfriend, the prison doctor he'd fallen for and who we'd all gone to South America to save. "Her specialty's toxicology. She'll know what to do."

He had a hurried conversation with Olivia, then wedged the phone between my ear and shoulder for me. Olivia's voice filled my ear, quick and efficient. "We've got to narrow down what poisoned her. Any blistering or swelling of her lips?"

I looked down at Lorna. God, she'd gotten even paler. "No."

"Is she convulsing?"

I looked up at the chopper. Gina had the blades spinning, now, but it would be another minute before she could take off. "No. She just can't breathe, and she can't stand, her muscles are weak—"

"Smell her breath for me," interrupted Olivia. "Is there a scent?"

I sniffed. "Yeah. Kind of like almonds, but bitter."

"It's cyanide," Olivia said immediately. "You've got five, ten minutes to get an antidote into her."

I opened the pilot's door. "What's your flight time to the nearest hospital?" I yelled over the roaring blades.

Gina had already programmed it into the GPS. "Forty-three minutes!" she yelled back.

I froze. I thought I'd been scared before but now the fear rose up inside me in a freezing wave. We weren't going to make it in time. She was going to die in my arms on the way.

The fear washed away all the guilt and toxic self-hate, letting me see things clearly. I loved this woman. I had to have her in my life, no matter what. I'd been wrong to ever push her away and now it was too late.

"JD?" said Olivia in my ear. "JD, what's happening? Are you on your way to the hospital?"

I've never felt so helpless. "We can't—" I struggled to speak, my voice fracturing. "We're not going to get there in time."

I heard Olivia take a deep, shuddering breath. Then she spoke, steady and reassuring. "Okay, then. We're just going to have to figure out how to treat her where you are."

I nodded like an idiot, forgetting she couldn't hear me, and stepped back from the chopper, slicing my finger across my throat to tell Gina to kill the engines. I laid Lorna back down on the deck. Her skin was deathly white and she was limp as a ragdoll. *Please,* I was begging, *please let me have her back. Just let me have her back, I'll figure out how to be with her, I don't care how much it hurts.*

"We're treating her here!" I yelled to the team, and they gathered round. A tearful Paige pushed her way to the front and dropped to her knees beside Lorna, grabbing her hand. I knelt on the other side and put the phone on speaker.

"We need an antidote," said Olivia. "What do you have where you are? Is there a pharmacy? A veterinarian's?"

"No," I said, my chest tight.

"How about...a factory, some kind of industrial unit?" asked Olivia. "They'll have chemicals."

"We're on a yacht in the middle of the sea," I said desperately. "We've got—" Colton had found the first aid kit and passed it over. "A first aid kit...fuck, it's just bandages and dressings!" My hands were shaking with panic.

Olivia went quiet as she thought. "Okay, okay...we don't have nitrites, we don't have thiosulfate, we don't have hydroxocobalamin...*glucose!* There's some anecdotal evidence that glucose can work!"

I nodded at Bradan and Kian. They grabbed one of Van der Meer's bodyguards as a guide and ran off.

"What else can we do?" I asked desperately.

"I'm thinking, I'm thinking," said Olivia. "In the ER we use activated charcoal for poisonings. It doesn't bind all that well with cyanide but if you gave her enough of it, it might buy you some time. But that's not something you'd have there."

I looked across at Gabriel. He was staring at Lorna but his eyes were distant and I could tell his mind was working overtime. *C'mon, Gabriel, think of something, please.*

"Water filters," he said at last. "The galley will have water filters and those are made of activated charcoal. Would that work?"

"If you could grind them up and mix them with water, maybe," said Olivia.

"A blender," said Colton. "We put 'em in a blender."

"Go!" I told them. "Go!"

They ran off and I sat there stroking Lorna's hair, listening as her breathing grew more and more desperate. "Hold on, baby," I whispered. "Hold on."

Minutes passed that felt like hours. Then Gabriel came running back holding a blender filled with black sludge. At the same time, Bradan and Kian raced over to us, clutching a wad of fruit-flavored glucose gel packs. "One of the bodyguards is a distance runner," Kian told me. "He had a whole load of these in his cabin." We ripped them open and squirted the contents into the blender.

I got Lorna sitting, tilted her head back and we poured the mixture down her throat. She coughed and choked weakly but swallowed it down. When the jug was still half full, though, she pulled away, shaking her head.

"Come on," I said gently. "You've got to drink it."

But she shook her head again and pointed. I followed her finger to Van der Meer.

"*No!*" I told her, panic squeezing my heart. "*No,* I don't know if there's enough, *you* have it, have all of it!"

But she shook her head again. Cursing, I passed the rest of the jug to Colton and he marched over and poured it down Van der Meer's throat, not being gentle about it.

"Now get her to the hospital," Olivia told us. "Fast as you can."

I picked up Lorna and we ran towards the chopper. But as we bundled her inside, her eyes closed. "Lorna?" I patted her cheek but she didn't respond. "*Lorna!*"

42

LORNA

I became aware of voices, muffled and distant. Voices I recognized. I focused and swam upwards towards them. My eyelids felt like they were made from lead but I forced them open...

Light and sound and JD's prairie-blue eyes, crinkled at the corners as he beamed. "*Hey!*" he breathed. "There she is!" There was something different about him.

Then Cody threw his arms around me, pressing the side of his face to my stomach. "*Mom!*"

I reached down to hold him and an IV drip pulled tight against my arm. I looked around: a hospital room. Paige and Gina were there, and I could see more of the team standing guard in the hallway. Memories started to come back to me. The yacht, the terror of not being able to breathe. I tried to speak but my mouth was desert dry. JD passed me water and I sipped through a straw, then tried again. "*Van der Meer?*" I husked.

"Doing fine," said JD darkly. "He'll recover and so will you. You'll be in here for a few days, though." He took my hand and knitted his fingers with mine. There was definitely something different about him. "No arguments, you're staying put."

"He hasn't left your side," Paige told me. She gave JD an approving glance and he flushed.

"And how about you?" I rasped to Cody. God, I was so weak! I could barely get the words out.

"Gina's been showing me the chopper!" Cody told me, grinning. "I'm learning what everything does!"

We all looked at Gina, who looked away, embarrassed. "Yeah, well, no one needed flying anywhere, I had to kill time somehow."

JD looked at Cody. "You think you could give me a minute alone with your mom?"

Cody nodded and headed outside with Paige and Gina. JD sat down on the edge of my bed and brushed a stray lock of hair back from my face. I looked into his eyes...and suddenly, I knew what was different about him. Ever since I first saw him in Mexico, there'd been a battle going on in those soulful blue pools. It was gone, and in its place was a need so strong it took my breath away.

He leaned closer and that deep, Texan growl filled the room. "I messed up," he told me. "Guess I've been messing up since the first day I met you. I wanted you, soon as I laid eyes on you. But I thought I couldn't have you, couldn't have anyone, ever again. That's why I tried to let you go. Except..." He squeezed my hand. "Except, when I thought I was going to lose you, I realized...I can't *ever* let you go. You're the most incredible damn thing I ever met and I want—I *need* —to be with you. With you and Cody. If you'll have me."

I gulped, tears filling my eyes. *He chose us!* And then I realized he was waiting on me for an answer, like there was any answer but *yes,* and I nodded madly. His chest filled and his eyes lit up with excitement: for a second, he looked like a teenager. He took my hand in both of his and kissed it. Then he looked away and his voice went tight. "Guess that means I need to deal with some stuff. *Talk* about some stuff. But—"—he looked around at the hospital room, at the team outside—"Not here."

I nodded quickly. "Whenever you're ready," I whispered.

He squeezed my hand, then leaned forward and rested his forehead against mine. With my free hand, I stroked the huge, hard muscles of his shoulder, overcome. This beautiful, broken man had a rough journey ahead, but I'd help him. My heart swelled: we were *back together!*

I wanted to stay in that safe, warm silence forever. But another memory had caught up with me and it made me grimace and speak. "The company."

JD gently pulled back and took hold of my shoulders, scowling and shaking his head like a big, protective bear. "Don't worry about the company. You need to rest."

"How long was I out?" My voice was a weak rattle but I stared at him stubbornly.

He sighed and gave in. "A day."

My stomach flipped. While I'd been lying here in bed, the company had gotten a day closer to collapse. And...I fell back against the pillows as something else sank in. We'd been wrong about Van der Meer. He was an evil bastard, but clearly he wasn't the one trying to kill me. He'd said he'd bought the cognac especially for when I came to him offering a deal: the killer must have bugged him or something, found out about the cognac and intercepted the bottle in transit. That meant the killer was more resourceful, more dangerous, than we ever thought. And we still had no idea who he was.

43

LORNA

I PERSUADED JD to let me have a laptop and a phone so I could work from bed. He didn't like it and neither did the doctors but I refused to just lie there when thousands of people were about to lose their jobs. For two days, I desperately called banks, trying to scrape together enough money to keep the company afloat another week, another *day*. But no one would give us a dime.

JD brought me food, made me take breaks, and kept Cody occupied. Watching them together made me melt: JD was gentle, patient, and he so obviously loved spending time with Cody, even though it must have brought back memories. They planned a camping trip for when I was better, together with a road trip to Texas to do some horse riding.

The team took turns guarding my hospital room. At one point, while Colton was on watch, he asked if he could use my laptop on the hospital WiFi to call home. "I want to check on my bear," he told me.

Bear? I let him login and make the video call. An image of a beautiful, pale-skinned woman with black hair a little like mine filled the screen. She seemed to be in the kitchen. "Hey, Colton!" She had a wonderfully gentle, relaxing voice...but there was a faint edge to it. I thought of a kindergarten teacher trying to maintain her composure with an unruly class. "Atlas is doing fine."

There was a crash from off-screen and Bethany's head whipped around. "*No!* You've already had enough of that." She looked back to the camera. "It's all good," she told us, not very convincingly. "All under control."

We heard a snort and something that sounded almost like a growl. Then a rounded, hairy back shot past the bottom of the frame. "No. No, Atlas, *no refrigerator!*" There was the creak of a refrigerator door opening, then the clink of glass. "No! Stop that!"

The camera suddenly rocked. "No!" Bethany bent and huffed and seemed to be wrestling with something. "No, we don't go up there!"

I watched, transfixed, as a paw came into shot. Then another paw. Something furry was trying to haul itself up onto the table where Bethany's phone was perched. "No!" Bethany told it, panicked. "No, Atlas, you're too heavy—"

There was a crash as the table collapsed and the camera suddenly dropped. It bounced and we saw the ceiling for a second. When it landed, it was tilted at an angle and we were looking at a young bear, the size of a large dog. It sat back on its ass, blinking at the camera, then lifted a carton of milk in its paws and glugged from it, milk gushing over its snout, its chest, and the floor. My mouth dropped open, silently *ahh*-ing. Colton grinned sheepishly.

A hand retrieved the phone and we saw Bethany again. "Let me call you back," she panted.

On the third day, the doctors said I was well enough to be discharged. "But no work. You need to rest and eat, rebuild your strength," they told me.

I nodded obediently, already thinking about which meetings I needed to hold first. But JD must have seen the look in my eyes because he leaned close and growled in my ear. "You *are* gonna take it easy. Don't make me make you."

I sighed, frustrated...but feeling warmly protected.

There were a million forms I had to sign, then I collected up my stuff and started to climb out of bed. "Wait," said a nurse. "We can't let you walk to the parking lot. You'll have to wait until we can get you a wheelchair."

"Thank you, but I'm fine," I told her. "I can walk."

The nurse shook her head. "It's the rules."

I sat back down on the bed and we waited. Ten minutes. Then thirty. "Goddamn it," muttered JD. "It's okay as long as she doesn't walk, right?"

"Yes," said the nurse cautiously.

JD marched over to the bed, slipped his arms under me...and then I was lifted into the air and cradled against his chest. I snuggled in there, looking up at him, my chest bursting, and he stomped off towards the parking lot with the team falling in behind.

Back at the penthouse, I got into a fresh suit, wincing when I saw myself in the mirror. My skin was still worryingly pale, almost translucent, and my eyes had huge, dark shadows under them. I put on make-up but I still looked half-dead. "How do I look?" I asked JD.

"Beautiful," he said sincerely, putting his hands on my waist and pulling me close. "But you shouldn't be working."

"I've got to do this," I told him. "Then I'll take a break, promise."

Downstairs, I'd asked all the hundreds of people who worked in our New York office to gather on one floor. The ones who worked in offices around the world were watching on a video link.

I stood at the front of the crowd and took a deep breath. These were our workers, our family. It was heartbreaking.

I told them that we'd be filing for bankruptcy tomorrow. That I'd tried everything and that there was nothing more I could do. That I was sorry.

Some people cursed. Some started to cry. I saw people looking at friends they'd worked with for years, knowing they were going to have to move to a different state or a different country to find another job. That they might not find another job at all.

"*Now* take a break," JD told me.

"I will," I said. "But I've got to tell the others. They should hear it from me."

Danny drove us to the hospital construction site and I spoke to the workers there. Then we drove to Hudson Tower and I did the same again. As we walked back to the car, it hit me that I'd just made three speeches in one day. *I couldn't have done this a few weeks ago.*

Then my head went floaty and I tripped over my own feet. JD caught me, his big hands warm on my waist. "You're taking a break," he told me. "And getting something to eat. There's a diner right over there."

I nodded. "Just let me make some phone calls, then I'll—"

"*Lorna,*" said JD in a voice like iron, "*now.* I'll hogtie you and carry you if I have to."

He stared down at me, worried and smoldering and stern and I just melted. I nodded meekly and he steered me across the street.

The whole block was pretty run down, with a hotel that looked like it had been shuttered for years, an apartment building and a small garage. But in the middle of it all was an old-fashioned, art deco diner, all polished chrome and curved glass. JD marched me to a booth, slid me along the vinyl seat to the wall and then sat down next to me so I couldn't escape. "You're not moving until you've had something to eat," he told me. And I decided to just let myself be taken care of.

Danny, Colton, Gabriel, Kian and Cal were there, too, and it was like a small army of big guys in suits had invaded the place. We took over two booths and started ordering. It was already late afternoon but none of us had had a chance to eat breakfast or lunch so we wound up ordering a massive brunch from their all-day menu. Tall glasses of orange juice and huge plates of crumbling, golden waffles, topped with salty bacon and drowned in maple syrup. Eggs sunny-side-up basking on beds of crunchy whole wheat toast slathered with butter. Bowls of granola, still warm from the oven, sticky with melted sugar and topped with velvety, slowly-sliding spoonfuls of yogurt which in turns was topped with strawberries and blueberries. And coffee. Big mugs of strong coffee, refilled each time a waitress passed by. I ate, surprised at how hungry I was. And gradually, I started to feel better.

An hour later, JD walked me down the stairs of the diner. His arm was around my waist and he snuggled me protectively to his side. Behind me, Danny was talking to Cal about how Cal's girlfriend, Bethany, was doing in med school. "She's acing it," rumbled Cal. "I miss her during the week, but it's not so bad. I got Rufus, and lots of work on the house to keep me busy. Got that bench finished now, we sit out on that and watch the sunrise when she's home. Might make a new henhouse, next."

It was a happy moment. As we reached the final step, I glanced down at myself...and winced. There was a big splodge of ketchup on my blouse right between my breasts. I touched it, but it wasn't wet. Then the red *moved,* sliding downwards. "JD?" I asked, worried I was hallucinating. He turned to look. Then he threw himself against me just as a shot rang out.

44

JD

MY BRAIN KNEW what it was straight away: the red dot of a sniper's laser sight. But all that worrying about her health, followed by the long, happy brunch, had made me slip from bodyguard mode into boyfriend mode. It took me a full second to react and I knew that was too slow. Even as I felt myself start to move, I was wincing, waiting for the shot.

But it didn't come straight away. The red dot crawled lower, moving from her chest to her stomach. It stabilized there...

I slammed into her, knocking her to the side. and the sharp crack of a gunshot echoed off the buildings. I heard the bullet hiss past us and bury itself in the wall of the diner.

The team surged down the stairs, their training taking over. I grabbed Lorna and we all took cover behind a parked car.

"On our left!" yelled Gabriel. He already had his gun out and started firing at two men in black combat gear who were advancing down the street towards us.

"Two more on my side!" called Colton. He started firing, too. "We've got to move, boss!"

He was right. In a few minutes, they'd easily overrun us. Except as soon as I peeked around the end of the car, another shot rang out, making me pull back. The sniper had us trapped. "We've got to find out where he's shooting from," said Kian, reading my thoughts.

"Someone's got to be bait, draw him out," I said. "I'll go."

"No," said Danny firmly. "Your job's to stay with her." He nodded at Lorna.

I shook my head stubbornly. I couldn't let him put himself in danger for me...for *us*. I'd gotten them all into this mess, it should be me.

"Let's be honest," said Danny. "I can run faster than you anyway, *old man*." He turned to go. "I'll head for that car across the street. You watch for the flash, figure out where he's firing from." He took a deep breath, readying himself.

I stopped him with a hand on his arm. Then I squeezed, unable to speak.

Danny put his hand on mine. "I know."

Then he ran. Out from behind the car. Across the street, dodging left and right—

A shot rang out. My heart stopped beating. But the bullet hit the street a foot to the left of Danny and he kept running.

"Got him," said Cal. "Roof of the hotel. I can get him from the top of the apartment building. Give me two minutes." And he set off at a dead sprint.

Danny was almost across the street, now. A few more steps and he'd reach the shelter of a parked car.

Then another shot rang out and Danny flew backwards as if he'd run into an invisible wall. He landed sprawled on his back on the street, a sea of red spreading across his white shirt.

45

JD

"*No!*" I sprang to my feet and would have run, but Colton and Gabriel muscled me back down behind the car.

Lorna, white-faced, dialed 911. "Ambulance," she said breathlessly.

I stared at Danny through the car window. He wasn't moving and his whole chest had turned red. Worse, a dark slick was starting to spread across the asphalt beneath him. "He's bleeding out!" I yelled, and tried to get up again.

Kian had to help push me back down this time, the Irish thick in his voice. "That's what the bastard wants, to make you run to him, then he'll get you, too! We can't go out there 'till we kill the sniper."

Gabriel put his hand on my back. "Cal'll get him. He's the best."

I couldn't answer. I just crouched there, guts twisting, watching the pool of blood beneath Danny grow and grow.

46

CAL

I CRASHED through the double doors of the apartment building and sprinted over to the elevator, dodging a bucket in the middle of the tiled floor. I hit the button and stood there primed, ready to slide around the door as soon as it was open wide enough, my thumb ready to punch the button for the top floor. I'd seen Danny get hit and all I could see was that spreading red stain on the front of his shirt. *Thirty seconds,* I told myself. That's all it would take for the elevator to get up to the tenth floor. Then I'd find the service stairs up to the roof. One quick shot. Less than a minute, and JD and the others would be free to help Danny.

Five seconds passed. *Come on. Come on!* Then it sank in that I couldn't hear any clunking and whirring from the lift descending. I hit the button again and, this time, I noticed that it didn't light up.

I twisted around and looked at the bucket I'd dodged. Water was dripping into it from a leak in the roof. The place was falling apart.

The elevator doesn't work.

Fuck.

I bolted for the stairs and started pounding up them.

47

LORNA

"Where the *hell* is Cal? It's been more than two minutes!" JD was beside himself, his eyes wild, his voice rough with pain. I put my hand on his arm, but there was nothing I could say. I knew he blamed himself for getting the team into this but it was *my* fault, they were all risking their lives for *me*.

"Cal'll drop that guy, any second," Kian told him. "It'll be okay."

Then a shot rang out and Danny jerked on the ground and let out a heart-rending scream of pain. I put my hands to my mouth in horror. The sniper had shot him again, just to lure us out.

And it worked. JD took two quick steps towards the end of the car. Gabriel and Colton were busy trying to hold back the gunmen who were still advancing from either end of the street. Kian tried to grab him but JD shook him off.

I lunged forward and grabbed JD's hand just before he stepped out into the open. "*No,* no, John, please. He'll kill you!"

JD pulled savagely against my grip. I was about to lose him. I grabbed his hand with both of mine and grimly hung on. "*Please,* please we need you here!" I was sobbing, now. "We need you here!"

JD tugged against me, raging and straining, but I hung on,

pleading with my eyes. And finally, he stopped. For a few seconds, he just crouched there, staring at the red lake surrounding Danny. Then he bellowed in rage, pounding his fist on the car door hard enough to leave dents. I pulled him to me and clung to him.

Cal, I begged silently, *where are you?*

48

CAL

I WAS THUNDERING up flight after flight, fast enough that they didn't seem like stairs anymore, fast enough that I just saw floor numbers flashing by.

Five.

Six.

I hadn't run like this since Idaho and that hadn't been up stairs. But I didn't have time to be out of breath, didn't have time for my lungs to hurt. I was running on pure adrenaline...adrenaline and hate. *Move your ass, you big dumb fuck. How could you pick the one building with an elevator that wasn't working? It's your fault if he dies.*

Seven.

Eight.

I wasn't used to cities. All the right angles didn't sit nice in my brain like the soft contours of the woods. But I still had that hunter's instinct that stops me getting lost. As I corkscrewed up through the building I knew that now I was facing north, now east, now south... and I could picture where the sniper was.

Nine.

Ten.

I burst onto the tenth floor and straight up the service stairs that led to the roof. There was a locked door at the top but I didn't even slow down, just shoulder-charged it.

The sound carried across the street and I saw the sniper look up and raise his rifle. But I already had mine up to my shoulder, the scope to my eye. I got a close-up glimpse of the guy's face and the tattoo on his neck and then I squeezed the trigger and he fell.

49

LORNA

A SINGLE SHOT rang out from behind us, echoing off the buildings, and the whole team was up and moving before Cal even hollered from the rooftop that it was clear. They trusted his shooting *that* much.

Gabriel and Colton took up better positions and started forcing back the advancing gunmen. JD, Kian and I ran to Danny.

"Oh crap," whispered JD. Danny was deathly pale. We could see the ragged wound in his chest, now, and the second wound in his leg. And there was so much blood, God, a whole spreading pool of it around him. JD grabbed my hands and pressed them to the leg wound. "Press on it!" I pressed hard, tears filling my eyes. JD did the same with the chest wound and I flinched, expecting Danny to cry out in pain. But he barely reacted, and that made my stomach drop.

Gabriel and Colton stopped firing. A moment later, they jogged over to us. "They pulled out, boss," said Colton.

Then Cal staggered over, chest heaving. "Elevator was out," he managed.

Gabriel patted his arm. "Not your fault," he said gently. But Cal wouldn't acknowledge him, just stared down at Danny, his jaw tight.

Kian had been feeling up and down Danny's neck, pressing with two fingers. "I can't find a pulse," he said quietly.

"Where's that ambulance?" roared JD. There were tears in his eyes.

I pressed hard on the leg wound, tears rolling down my cheeks. And prayed.

50

JD

AT THE HOSPITAL, the whole team waited in silence. They'd rushed Danny into surgery three hours ago.

I sat in the center of the long row of chairs, with my arm around Lorna on one side and Erin on the other. My mind was playing an endless loop of all the ways in which this was my fault. I should never have involved the team. I should have checked out the area better before going to the diner. I should have been the sniper bait, not Danny...

Lorna was hunched over next to me, staring at the floor. I'd told her, again and again, that this wasn't her fault, but she was convinced it was because we'd all been protecting her.

Erin had her head on my shoulder, her eyes closed and silent tears trickling down her cheeks. She'd cry for a while, then just go quiet and stare at the wall, haunted. Imagining a life without Danny. Stacey and Emily were there, silently gripping the arms of their men.

Cal paced up and down, his size and the fury on his face making the other patients and relatives shrink back each time he passed. Gabriel, Kian, Bradan and Gina kept trying to comfort him, but the big guy was tearing himself apart for not taking out the sniper faster, even though there was nothing he could have done differently.

The doors to the surgical area opened and Danny's surgeon came out. All of us instantly swarmed him, nine of us throwing questions at him at once. The surgeon staggered back and raised his hands in surrender. *"He'll live!"*

We all slumped in relief and Erin began sobbing, hanging onto me for support.

It would be another few hours until we were allowed to see Danny, so we grabbed coffees from the vending machines and sat back down to talk.

"The cops have taken the body of the guy Cal shot," Kian told us. "I've talked to Callahan, the FBI haven't identified him yet."

"He had a tattoo," said Cal. "A dog's head, on his neck." He was calmer, now, but still determined to make amends. "Not like a picture of a pet. Stylized. Like it meant something."

Gabriel sidled over to the nurse's station, leaned over the counter and spoke to the nurse there. His voice was too low for us to make out the words but, a moment later, the nurse was flushed and giggling and he returned with a pen and a wad of printer paper. "Tell me what you saw," he told Cal, sitting down next to him. And he began to draw.

Now that I was calmer, I could think better, and a cup of coffee helped, too. I sat there silently sipping, brows furrowed, running over what I'd seen again and again. The sniper had put his red dot right on Lorna's chest. If he'd shot then, I wouldn't have had time to save her. But he hadn't. He'd moved his aim down to her stomach before he took the shot.

There was only one reason to do that. The shooter wanted Lorna to die slowly and painfully. But that made no sense, unless...

I lifted my head and looked Lorna right in the eye. "It's personal."

She cocked her head to one side. "What?"

"I've had this wrong from the very beginning," I said. "I just *assumed* it was to do with McBride Construction. But it's nothing to do with the company. This is about *you*. You and your family."

Lorna stared at me. "But..." Her face fell and she looked down at herself, horrified. *Someone hates me that much?*

I grabbed her, pulled her to her feet and crushed her to me, wrapping her in my arms, then stood there trembling in protective rage, scowling at the world over her shoulder and daring it to come near her. Suddenly, everything was different. I'd worried that I didn't understand all this corporate stuff, that I was a dumb soldier up against some billion-dollar conspiracy. But now it was simple. Primitive.

Someone hated her. Hated her enough to kill her. But they weren't going to get her, they weren't going to *fucking* touch her, because...

Because they had an opposite. Someone who loved her as much as they hated her.

Something released inside me, and I closed my eyes and pressed the side of my head to hers. It was time. If I wanted to be with her, I had to go through the pain and hope I made it to the other side.

I gently unwound myself from her, went over to where Kian was sitting and put a hand on his back. "I need some time with Lorna."

He looked up at me, then patted my hand. "Go. There's nothing you can do here until they let us see Danny. I'll keep you posted."

Gabriel looked up from where he was sketching. He was already several sheets into the wad of printer paper, drawing based on Cal's instructions, like a police sketch artist. "We'll keep working on the tattoo," he told me.

I hugged Erin tight and made sure Stacey and Emily were distracting her with girl talk. Then I went back to Lorna. "Come on," I said quietly. "We gotta talk."

I took the big black Mercedes and drove Lorna across the river to New Jersey. Storm clouds were building overhead, but the weather was holding for now. I stopped on a deserted bit of waterfront and we climbed out and looked across the river. The sun was just going down and, as it slid behind the skyscrapers of Manhattan, its glow was sliced into shining ribbons of gold and scarlet, stretching out across the water.

I turned away from her for a moment, breathing hard, glaring at the ground. Then I took a deep breath and faced her. "I never told anyone what happened to my family. Not the whole thing. Not even Danny. It hurt too much." I looked her right in the eye. "But I've got to. I gotta get it out of me because it's stopping me being with you. And I love you."

She pressed her lips together tight, eyes shining. "I love you, too," she whispered.

I bowed my head...and told her.

51

JD

Four Years Ago

I WAS SUNBATHING.

We were in Venezuela, on a rock-strewn plateau halfway up a mountain. The mission—reconnaissance for the CIA—was done, no one got hurt, and we'd reached our extraction point an hour early. I had two men keeping watch but that was just a precaution: we'd slipped in and out without the bad guys ever knowing we were there. Most importantly, I was bringing all my men home safe. That was reason to celebrate and I was celebrating by stretching out on a big, smooth rock with my shirt off, basking in the sun like a lizard. There was only one more thing I needed to make things perfect. "Pass me the sat phone," I said to Danny.

He gave me an indulgent smile and passed it over, and I dialed. Then I closed my eyes and lay there, listening. There was a long series of clicks and pauses, a reminder of how far from home I was. Then—

"Hello?" Jillian's voice was excited, like she was hoping it was me.

My chest lifted and I knew I must be grinning like an idiot. Suddenly, I wasn't in Venezuela: I was right there, in the kitchen, putting my arms around her from behind, kissing the side of her throat in that way that made her giggle and squirm. "Hey, gorgeous. It's me. Wanted to let you know I'm on my way home. Should be there tomorrow."

I heard her take a slow breath in, "*That's good,*" she said, and it was like she was releasing all the worry she'd been bottling up. I squeezed the satphone, overcome with emotion for a moment. I hated being away, hated worrying her. But at the same time, hearing her voice made all the time in the jungle worthwhile. It reminded me of what we were protecting.

"Is Max around?" I asked.

"Hold up." She took the phone away from her mouth. "*Max!*" She came back on. "I got him the spaceship that shoots the foam darts but you've gotta help me wrap it, okay? It's the most awkward thing in the world."

"Good work, and deal," I told her firmly.

Feet hammering on the stairs. Then an excited, "*Dad?!*"

I still remembered the first time Max made a noise that kinda sounded like *Dada.* That primal sense of pride: *I did that. I helped make him.* That stomach-dropping moment of fear as the responsibility sunk in: he was mine to raise right or screw up. And that tidal wave of raw, blind love. It still got me every time and I hadn't heard him say it in a week so it hit me extra hard. "Hey pal," I managed around the lump in my throat. "I'll be back for your birthday."

"Really?!"

I was so glad I didn't have to disappoint him. And I felt so bad that I nearly had. "Yeah."

"Can we have a water fight?"

I grinned. We'd had an *epic* water fight the week before: squirt guns, water balloons and even a few buckets of water. Jillian had ventured into the yard to call us for dinner and had gotten hit by a stray water balloon. She took the nuclear option and turned the garden hose on both of us, but we joined forces and unloaded all the balloons we had left on her. By the time we were done, all three of us looked like we'd gone swimming, and Jillian had to excuse herself because her summer dress had turned damn near transparent. As soon as I'd gotten Max into some dry clothes, I went and found her in the bedroom, her body still gleaming wetly, and...well, dinner wound up being pretty late. "Yeah," I told Max. "We can absolutely have a water fight."

He put Jillian back on. I could hear a whistling in the background. "Is that the wind?" I asked.

"Yup. It's really picking up out there. Don't worry, I've got everything battened down good and tight."

I could hear rain lashing the windows, too. It was gloriously hot where I was and the disconnect was jarring. That feeling that I was right there in the kitchen with them slipped away. "I'll be home tomorrow," I said, as much for me as for her. "Maybe late, but tomorrow."

"Well, I'll be here waiting," she said softly. "With a plate of sandwiches in the refrigerator, a bottle of red on the table and me in that green silky robe and the black underwear with the little gold chains." I growled appreciatively and she giggled. "Is someone getting excited?"

"Hell yeah. You know how long it's been since I had a good sandwich?"

She burst out laughing. "You're an *ass!*" she told me, mock-angry. Then her voice changed. "That's weird."

"What's weird?"

"I swear Max went back upstairs but I just heard him coming in the back door. Hold on..."

I relaxed, listening. Then her scream tore through me.

I sat bolt upright, saying her name, but there was no answer. I reached for her, opening my eyes...and the green jungle and bright sun reminded me I was thousands of miles away.

On the phone, I could hear her pounding up the stairs. "Come on!" she said and grunted, and I heard Max's breathing very close: she must have scooped him up. She ran again. Then a door slammed. "Help me push this!" she told Max. And the sound of something heavy moving.

"What's happening?" I begged.

I heard thunder echo outside the house. "Guy in a ski mask," she said. "He has a gun."

My skin had gone ice cold. I was going to throw up. I looked around and saw Danny frowning at me, worried. "Where's the chopper?" I demanded. As if the chopper could somehow magic me back to Texas in a few minutes.

"Twenty minutes," Danny told me. "What's wrong?"

I didn't answer, too busy listening. There was a crash of wood, then another and another. My stomach dropped. *He's trying to break through the door.*

There was an electronic beeping. *The gun safe. Good girl.*

Jillian cursed and the beeping started over again.

"Four-five-three—" I began.

"I know, I know!" She was panting with fear. Then I heard the clunk as the safe door opened.

Wood splintering and falling. There was so much I wanted to tell her: that I loved her, that I loved Max, that I was sorry I wasn't there. But there wasn't time. I had to tell her what she needed, not what I needed. "You can do this," I told her. "Safety off. Aim for the torso."

A howl of wind from outside. A crash of wood. Then two gunshots, deafeningly loud over the phone. It was quiet for a second. "I don't know if I hit him," she said softly.

Then, out of nowhere, two more gunshots from a different gun. Jillian gave a grunt of pain.

"*Mom!*" yelled Max. I could hear the tears in his voice.

I pressed the phone as tight to my ear as it would go. "Jill?" I begged.

She didn't answer but I could hear wet rasping as she struggled to breathe.

Wood breaking. The sound of something heavy being scraped along the floor. Then footsteps.

"*Daddy?*" cried Max, near-hysterical.

"Don't hurt him!" I yelled. "Don't hurt him, he's just a kid. I'll pay you, I'll give you whatever you want, just don't hurt—"

Another shot rang out and I jerked the phone away from my ear and stared at it in horror. I put it to my ear again. "Max? Max? Jill?"

Nothing. Just footsteps, walking off down the stairs.

Then, in the quiet that followed, I heard a faint, ragged breathing. One of them was still alive. "Hold on," I told them. "Hold on, I'm gonna—I'll call an ambulance..." I looked at the satphone, furiously debating. We only had one. I'd have to end this call to make another one. "Just hold on."

Jillian's voice, terrifyingly weak. She was trying to say something. "Mor— Mor—"

"Don't talk," I told her. "Don't talk, save your energy." I could feel tears running down my cheeks.

"Mor— Mor— *Morkret,*" said Jillian. And then her breathing stopped.

52

LORNA

JD WAS CRYING, those beautiful, prairie-sky eyes awash. It was scary, to see this rock of man finally crumple and show his vulnerability. Scary and wonderful because I knew, in my gut, that this was the first time he'd let himself cry since it happened.

I was in pieces, listening to him, silent tears running down my cheeks. I needed to throw my arms around him but I didn't want to risk him stopping: he had to get this out of him.

"The CIA rushed me home," JD told me, "but it still took nearly twelve hours. By the time I got home, the place was a crime scene and the cops had taken them to the morgue."

"Did they catch him?"

JD shook his head bitterly. "Never even figured out *why*. Nothing was missing from the house. The name Morkret didn't lead the cops anywhere. I spent years trying to figure out what she was trying to tell me but I never did." He drew in a shaky breath. "I didn't know how to deal with it. They were *gone* and It hurt so bad and I just couldn't..."

Couldn't let it out, I realized, my heart breaking for him. He'd just bottled it up, all these years. He hadn't let himself grieve. That's why he felt like he was still with them. That's why being with me had felt like cheating on them.

But now the wound was open. It was agony, but all the poison could finally come out. "It was my fault," he spat. "My fucking fault. I should have been there!"

"No!" I told him. "No, it wasn't!"

"I didn't deserve them. She was just the sweetest, funniest...and Max was...Jesus, he was a really good kid..."

"I know," I sobbed. "I know." And I meant it. From the way he'd described them, I liked them both. "But you *did* deserve them, you're a really good father. A really good guy."

"They were— They were—" He took big gulps of air, fighting to get the words out. "They were meant to be my forever and they're just *gone*. And I don't know—I don't get what I did wrong."

I threw myself against his chest. "Nothing. Nothing, you didn't do a thing wrong." I hugged him tight and he hugged me back even tighter.

"I miss them," he sobbed. "I miss them *so much*."

Oh JD... I'd always drawn strength from how big and solid he was. Now I lent him my strength, willingly, clutching his muscled body to me as it shook and shook. The sun blazed down below the horizon, the sky burning orange then red and finally succumbing to cool, soft darkness.

JD's sobs died away and he just held me, emotionally wrung out. But he felt lighter, somehow, as if something painful had been extracted. I knew he wasn't healed but it felt like he was in a place where the healing could finally start.

He pushed me gently back so he could look at me. His voice had lost that granite certainty: he was venturing onto unfamiliar ground. "When I started to get attached to you and Cody, it felt like you were replacing them."

I shook my head, thinking of my dad. "Nothing can ever replace them. They'll stay with you always. What we have..." I knitted my fingers together.

"This is something new."

He nodded, then pulled me into another hug. And as he held me, I felt his strength gradually returning.

Manhattan was lighting up, becoming a glittering, night-time kingdom. He drew back and looked at me in the glow of the lights. The pain in his eyes wasn't gone, but it didn't rule him, now. And when he spoke, he was certain, again.

"I'm sorry I hurt you," he told me. "I won't do it again."

I nodded. I knew he wouldn't.

He cupped my cheek with his palm and ran his thumb along my cheekbone, staring into my eyes. He went to speak and then frowned, frustrated, like he was trying to find the words. "From the first time I saw you, that day in Mexico, I was just blown away. Not just 'cause you're beautiful. Not just 'cause you're a great mom. You're special, damn near magical. The way you think…" He gestured helplessly at the skyscrapers across the water. "You imagine your way right up into the clouds and then you build your way there with math I could never understand." His voice slowed down. "You're starlight and dreams. And I don't know what you see in a big dumb grunt from Texas—"

"*Everything,*" I said quickly.

That made those gorgeous lips twist into a smile. "…but I do know I never want to let you go."

And he leaned down and kissed me.

The first kiss was soft and sweet. Just a gentle brush of his lips on mine: a fresh start, deliciously free and full of promise. Silvery tremors rolled all the way down to my toes.

He drew back and looked at me, as if confirming that this was real. Then he pulled me to him and the next kiss was urgent and fierce, a breathless, fearless, making-up-for-lost-time kiss, his hands crushing my softness to his muscled chest. The old-fashioned maleness of him hit me full force, even stronger for seeing that moment of vulnerability. I inhaled him, got drunk on him, my hands sliding over the hardness of his forearms and the smooth globes of his biceps. He took my head in both hands and kissed me even harder, and I felt myself disintegrate, just dissolve into a Lorna-shaped pillar of silvery glitter that was being sucked in a shimmering twister right up to heaven.

We both came out of the kiss heavy-lidded and slow. He looked down at me and I saw his gaze run over my body. When his eyes came back up to my face, they were clouded with lust. And suddenly, my gaze was flicking over him: the brute power of his wide shoulders where they stretched out his suit jacket, the contours of his chest under his white shirt, his darkly stubbled jaw and that hard upper lip...

We both leaned in and this time, he growled and demanded entrance, spreading me open, and I melted and submitted. He pulled me full-length against him, and together we fell against the car. The kiss took on a rhythm, pulsing through both of us as we twisted and moved. We emerged from it panting, staring at each other in the darkness. We couldn't carry on, out here on the street. But this felt way too special to be put on hold while we drove back to the penthouse.

JD, as always, was decisive. He threw open the rear door of the car, grabbed me by the waist and lifted me onto the back seat, then jumped in after me and slammed the door.

53

LORNA

I SCOOCHED along the seat to make room for him. My heart was suddenly racing, shock mixed with excitement. *Are we really doing this? How far are we going to,,,*

The door slammed, sealing us off from the outside world. It was suddenly quiet enough that I could hear my breathing, fast and trembling, and his, slow and steady.

He slid next to me, his hip pressed against mine. Then he took my face in his hands, the tips of his fingers sliding into my hair, and tipped my head back for his kiss. I could feel the brute power of him as he pressed up against me, that cowboy roughness: the size of his palms on my cheeks, the rasp of his stubble when it brushed me. In the luxurious, refined cabin of the Mercedes, with its hand-stitched leather and chrome vents, he felt even more deliciously raw and real. It didn't matter that he was in a tailored suit: underneath he was denim and granite and I fucking loved it.

The kiss turned open-mouthed and hungry, every press of his lips sending ribbons of silvery excitement rippling down to my core. Then he started kissing down my jaw, down my throat, and I tangled my fingers in his hair and panted. Each kiss was a hot little explosion on my skin, sending out scorching shockwaves, and he drew a trail all the way down to my collar bone, as low as he could reach without undoing my blouse. Then he moved back a little and we opened our eyes and looked at each other.

We had to decide: were we going to be sensible, respectable, and drive back to the penthouse? We were in a parked car right out on the street, for God's sake. The street was quiet and it was pretty dark, but what if someone walked by? Sex in a car was something teenagers did. I was a mom and close to forty.

I looked at JD's hulking silhouette, at those prairie-sky eyes gleaming in the darkness...and nodded.

He smirked and then he was on me, tipping me back on the seat until I was flat on my back. He leaned down and kissed me again, pushing me down into the sumptuously soft leather. He put his hand on my calf and started to work his way up my leg, rubbing in slow circles through the nylon of my stocking, and my breath tightened, the anticipation building with every inch

I bit my lip as his hand slid under my skirt. He stroked my upper thigh and then growled as he found the top of my stocking and the bare skin above. My eyes flew open and I stared up at him as his fingertips circled higher and higher. Then they nudged the silky material of my panties and the soft warmth of my pussy, and I moaned.

He started to rub me there. His fingers were strong and expert, working up and down the length of my lips with firm strokes that made me buck my hips and pant. But he kept it teasingly slow, enough to drive me crazy but not enough to get me off. With his other hand, he started to unbutton my blouse, kissing my bare skin as it was revealed.

My hands came up and started to stroke his sides through his shirt, fingertips running over the deep ridges of his obliques. Touching him opened the floodgates: I couldn't get enough of the feel of him, of that sculpted, hard maleness. I tugged his shirt free of his pants and my hands dived beneath the soft cotton. I smoothed my palms over the tight flatness of his stomach and then slid them upwards, tracing the intoxicating V where his torso flared outward to his chest.

JD had my blouse open to my stomach, now, and that was enough for him to flip the cups of my bra up and free my breasts. His tongue lapped at my nipple and I cried out, arching my back, pulses of heat sliding down to my groin, where they turned into wetness. His tongue licked and teased, swirling around the base of the nipple and drawing it up to aching hardness. Then he went to work on the other one, opening his mouth wide to take in the soft flesh and licking with slow, hard strokes. He began to rub the first nipple between finger and thumb, squeezing just enough to make the pulses of heat go silver-edged and fluttery. I groaned, feeling myself getting wetter and wetter, my ass grinding against the soft leather.

The fingers rubbing my pussy slowed. Then he nudged aside my panties and a finger slid up inside me. I took a deep, shuddering breath as it filled me: thick, knobbly perfection. My toes tap-danced in my heels as he pushed into me to the limit and then he hooked his finger and began to rub and I hissed, my head going back and my eyes screwing closed as the pleasure spiraled tighter. I was running my hands up and down his naked back, now, but it was awkward, with his shirt still on and bunched up around his chest, so I scrambled to undo it, blindly fumbling the buttons open.

He started to tease my clit with his thumb and I clamped my thighs together around his arm, riding his hand, desperate for friction. His breathing went tight, as if seeing me so needy turned him on even more. He kept licking at my breasts but now, with his other hand, he pushed my skirt up around my waist, baring my thighs to him. Then he slid a hand under me and started squeezing my ass as he finger-fucked me. The pleasure was spiraling tighter and tighter, a black hole that sucked in everything else, even thought. I got his shirt open at last and my hands went crazy, stroking the hard muscles of his back, his pecs, roving down to his six pack, desperately trying to vent what was building inside me. I was *his,* under the command of his lips and tongue and those big, rough hands. "Oh, God," I panted. "D—Do it. I need you."

I could feel his cock through his pants and it twitched, then swelled even more, an iron bar against my thigh. "Need me where?" he growled, his words hot little hurricanes on my wet breasts.

I was in a thick fog of pleasure and had to struggle to think. Then I realized what I'd said and flushed, going quiet.

His fingers moved a little faster. His hand on my ass squeezed and I went weak inside: "Need me *where?*"

"I need you inside me," I croaked.

He lifted himself from me and his finger withdrew, leaving me aching and empty. My eyes slowly opened and I watched, heavy-lidded and dreamy, as he unbuckled his belt and pushed his pants and boxers down around his thighs. His cock sprang out, rock hard and weighty, and he rolled on a condom. He hooked my panties down my legs and off, tossing them away. Then he spread my thighs, pushing one leg tight against the seat back and nudging the other off the seat and onto the floor to make room for him. He lowered himself, the muscled bulk of him spreading me more.

I drew in my breath as I felt the head of his cock nudge at my sopping lips: *God, are we really going to do this, right here?* Then he was sliding up into me and all thought ceased. With one long push he went deep inside me. He used his forearms to brace himself so that he didn't crush me but that didn't stop the heady thrill of feeling him on top of me, the solid weight of him pinning me down.

He drew back, a long, silken motion. Every slickened inch he glided over threw out streamers of silvery, crackling pleasure that fed the building, glowing center. Then he pushed forward again and *Oh God* tight perfection: with my legs so close together, I could feel the shape of him, the thick head and every bulge and vein. I clutched at his shoulders, drawing him down to me, needing more. He drew back again, thrust again, fast, taking me by surprise, and buried another inch inside me. He slid his hands under my ass, lifting me a little to meet him, drew back and thrust a third time, and I cried out, eyes wide, as I felt the root of him against me and his balls brushing my ass.

He began to pump at me, each stroke making that glowing center inside me compress and tighten. He had his hands planted either side of my head and I began to stroke up and down his forearms, loving the chiseled hardness of him. We stared deep into each other's eyes as he fucked me: I could see the way his eyes narrowed in pleasure as he sank deep into me, the tightening of his lips as he withdrew, fighting for control. And he could see the way my eyes widened and my lips parted each time his cock filled me, how I bit my lip and moaned each time it left me.

His thrusts got faster, harder, the raw power of them pushing me along the seat until he had to wedge his elbows against the tops of my shoulders to pin me in place. That made the tight friction of him even better, each pump of his cock ratcheting me closer to orgasm. I could hear the blood rushing in my ears, I was helpless, going crazy: *God,* it had never been like this before, not even when he'd fucked me up against the window. I pulled both my feet up onto the seat, bending my knees and opening them wide, my hands clawing at his shoulders.

My climax was building fast, now rushing towards me. He fucked me faster, faster, slamming into me, and my hands slid down his back to his ass, shamelessly pulling him into me. He leaned down and kissed me and I panted against his lips as I got closer. Then he reached down, captured one of my nipples between thumb and finger and squeezed just a little—

I came, the orgasm thundering through me. My legs scissored around him and my hands clutched his ass hard as I arched and spasmed. My breasts rubbed his chest and I heard him growl low in his throat. I shuddered and shook, riding the climax on and on, until I finally went limp.

JD was breathing hard. He reached down and cupped my cheek, then brushed back a lock of hair and kissed my sweat-damp forehead. As I came back down, it sank in that he hadn't come, yet: that growl had been him holding himself back.

He let me recover for a moment and then he put his hands on my waist and gently lifted me, keeping himself inside me as he rolled over and turned, until he was sitting in the middle of the back seat and I was riding him. Gravity pulled me down and I groaned as I sank onto him.

He leaned right back in the seat, wrapping his arms around me and pulling me close. With my blouse and his shirt open, my breasts could stroke against his naked chest and I drew in my breath as my nipples dragged against his pecs.

His hands smoothed my hair back so that he could see all of me. Then, gazing into my eyes, he took my ass in his hands and lifted me, sliding me up his cock until the head of him almost popped free of me. I gasped, eyes wide, and my fingers played piano scales on his shoulders: I was still super-sensitive. Then he slowly pushed me back down and I inhaled as I took all of him.

I sat there for a moment with him rooted in me. I was still recovering, wasn't sure I could go again so soon. But that taste he'd given me, that single, slow stroke up and down, had been too addictive. I began to move: at first, it was almost just rocking back and forth, just enough to make his cock shift inside me. But then it became a grinding in his lap and then I couldn't resist: I shuffled my knees either side of his legs, braced my hands on his shoulders and pushed, lifting myself up...and then dropping myself down. *God,* it was incredible: the hot hardness of him so deep, and the way I could control it, setting the rhythm I needed. I began to fuck him, slow bounces that became faster and faster, another climax already starting to glow.

Because of the roof of the car, I had to press tight to him and hunch over, my mouth pressed to his ear. With every rise and fall of my hips, my nipples raked up and down his chest, the pleasure wrapping around the growing climax and cinching it tighter and tighter. I clung to him, writhing against him as I rode him, hands smoothing over the firm globes of his shoulders, knees squeezing against the hard muscles of his thighs, lost in the feel of him. And as I spiraled towards my peak, something happened. In the dark privacy of the car, pressed as tightly to him as I could be, I found the confidence I'd lost and some I'd *never* had. I forgot about being curvy, about being a mom, about pushing forty. I *let go,* panting out how good he felt, how much I needed him and how hard I wanted him to fuck me. And that finally took him beyond control. His hands closed on my hips and he began to move me, lifting me up and then pulling me down on him, while stabbing upwards with his hips. I began to circle my hips on him and the climax wound in on itself and *shook,* incandescent...

"God, JD, *yes,*" I moaned.

He pulled me down, impaling me on him, and we came together, the orgasm ripping through me as he groaned and shot in long, hot streams inside me.

I flopped against his chest, weak and shaky. He held me tight until our breathing had slowed. Then he gently lifted me, turning and repositioning us so that we were lying on our sides on the seat with him spooning me from behind. He wrapped his arms around me and we lay there in the darkness, together for good.

54

LORNA

WE WERE HALF DOZING when JD's phone rang. He answered it sleepily, then cursed when he realized it was a video call. I scrambled to pull my blouse closed. Luckily, it was Cal who'd called, and he hadn't quite gotten the hang of video calls, yet: all we could see was the ceiling and by the time he got the phone pointed at his face, I was decent.

"Sorry," rumbled Cal when he saw JD's open shirt. "We got the tattoo. Gabriel drew this from my description and he nailed it: this is exactly what I saw on the shooter's neck."

He held a piece of paper up to the camera. Picked out in heavy, black ink was a vicious-looking dog, its leash gripped in a stylized fist.

Colton leaned into shot. "I saw this on a guy, once. Scary-looking dude. Accent sounded like Eastern Europe."

JD took a screenshot of the drawing, thanked them and ended the call.

"Eastern Europe," I said slowly. "Do you think it *is* the Russian mafia? Maybe Konstantin *is* behind it all?"

JD frowned and shook his head. "Still doesn't feel right to me. I think Konstantin was telling the truth. And I still think it feels personal. But I know someone we can ask." He dug through his phone, searching for a number. "There's a hacker group we use, the Sisters of Invidia. One of them has a boyfriend who used to be Russian mafia."

Hacker groups, Russian mafia boyfriends: it was a reminder that he lived in a completely different world to me. He found the number, buttoned up his shirt, and started a video call.

A beautiful, curvy woman with hazel eyes answered. She was wearing an apron and had flour on her nose. "JD?"

"Hey Gabriella. Is Alexei there?"

The camera bobbed and we got a glimpse of a kitchen. Then it focused on a dangerously handsome man with sharp cheekbones and dark stubble. The edges of tattoos were just visible in the open collar of his white shirt. He would have been scary as hell but the apron and the fact his hands were covered in dough softened him a little. He glanced down at himself, looking embarrassed. "Yes?" he asked in a heavy Russian accent.

JD sent him the screenshot. "You ever seen that before?"

Alexei showed us his sticky hands apologetically and instead of taking the phone, he let Gabriella keep hold of it and just leaned closer. He frowned. "Yes. Once."

"Is it a Russian mafia family?"

Alexei shook his head. "I saw it when I was in military." His English was fractured. "Is Special Forces. A very particular group. Assassination squad, a brutal bunch."

"Why would the Russian military be after me?" I asked in a small voice.

Alexei shook his head. "Is not Russian. I met them when they try to cross our border. Is Polish."

"Son of a bitch," muttered JD. "I know who's trying to kill you."

55

JD

THE STORM WAS MOVING in and rain was pattering on the roof of the car as we sped back into Manhattan. Lorna was desperate to know what I'd figured out but I stubbornly refused to share my theory until I could back it up.

We headed back to the hospital. The second Gabriel saw us, he looked me in the eye and lifted his chin, grinning knowingly. I flushed. It didn't matter that we'd fastened up all the buttons and Lorna had untangled her hair, he could tell we'd fucked. And that something deeper was different, now. Kian was giving me a similar look. Hell, all of them were.

I put my arm around Lorna and pulled her close, giving them their answer. Both of us went red, but at least it got it out of the way.

"Aw, shit, boss, you too?" said Colton. "Y'all pairing up faster than raccoons in winter."

"Don't worry." Gabriel patted his back. "We'll find you someone."

To my relief, a nurse told us that we could finally go in and see Danny, but only two of us and only for a few minutes. I went in with Erin.

Danny was shockingly pale and most of his torso and one leg were wrapped in bandages. But the grin he gave us was still cocky.

"*Get over here, you two,*" he rasped. Erin rushed over and he touched his forehead to hers, both of them closing their eyes in relief. He reached out with his hand and I took it and squeezed, a lump in my throat.

"You seen sense and got back together with her, yet?" Danny managed.

I sighed in defeat. "Yeah."

A satisfied grin spread over Danny's face. "Took you long enough."

The nurse said that was enough and herded us out of the room, saying we could visit again in the morning. I managed to persuade Erin to go back to the hotel and get some sleep, and the rest of us headed back to the penthouse. The storm was right overhead, now, the wind picking up and the rain hammering the windshield so hard I could barely see to drive.

As soon as we arrived, I called Lily, another of the Sisters of Invidia. She's the best there is when it comes to hacking databases. I asked her to get into the Polish military and check their Special Forces records for a certain surname. Lily being Lily, it took her less than five minutes. "Got him. No photo, but a whole string of commendations and a *lot* of kills. Special Forces, then recruited as a spy by military intelligence. Head of some sort of elite unit: all that stuff's redacted."

"And his mother's name?"

She told me. I had her pull the mother's death certificate, too, then thanked her and ended the call.

The whole team was waiting expectantly, lounging in couches, sipping mugs of coffee Paige had brought them. Rufus was curled up in Cal's lap like an overgrown puppy, dozing while Cal stroked his head. I glanced at the windows and was glad we were all inside and safe: I could hear the wind howling past the building and the lights of the city had turned to shimmering blurs through a curtain of torrential rain.

I dropped into the last available seat, beside Lorna, and rubbed my stubble while I figured out how to explain. "We've been wrong from the start," I said at last. "This was never about the company. The guy trying to kill you is Polish Special Forces. A spy, an assassin. He's brought his team to America to kill you."

"But *why?*" asked Lorna.

I took her hand. "Because the guy's name is Radoslava Burski. Son of Maria Burski." I looked around at the team. "Lorna's father had an affair with a Polish woman, almost forty years ago. He got her pregnant." I looked at Lorna. "The man trying to kill you is your half-brother."

Paige handed me a mug of coffee, her eyes wide. I nodded my thanks.

"He's angry because my dad abandoned them?" asked Lorna. "Because he paid off Maria?"

"According to the death certificate, Maria died four months ago," I said gently. "Drug overdose. We don't know what she told her son about your family. Maybe she poisoned him against you." I took her hand. "Look, everything's going to be okay, now. We'll find a photo of this guy and the FBI will track him and his team down. We got him."

At that moment, Rufus suddenly sat up. He looked around and then gave a single, short bark.

"What is it?" Cal asked him.

The lights went out. The hum of the air conditioning faded away to nothing.

I stood up, my face grim. "They're here."

56

JD

THE EMERGENCY LIGHTING KICKED IN: tiny, harsh white lights in the ceiling that were enough to guide you to the exit but that left most of the place in deep shadow. In the sudden silence, we could hear the screech of the wind and the rain lashing the windows.

Gabriel grabbed a laptop and brought up the feeds from the security cameras. *Thank God for Erin.* But I was glad she was at the hotel and not here.

We saw four guys in combat gear moving through the underground parking garage. A moment later, one of the motion detectors went off. "They're in the stairwell, heading up," said Gabriel.

Kian and I exchanged worried looks. We couldn't use the elevators because they'd cut the power. If we tried to go down the stairs, we'd run straight into them. We were trapped up here, fifty floors above the street.

I called Callahan and told him what was happening. "I can scramble a SWAT team," he told me. "Twenty minutes."

"They're on the tenth floor," reported Gabriel. "Eleventh. These guys can really move."

"We don't have twenty minutes," I told Callahan. "*Hurry.*" I turned to Lorna. "I want you in the safe room."

I went with her to get Cody. Lorna had gone pale, her gray eyes huge. As we passed the kitchen, I glanced at the pictures on the refrigerator and my stomach twisted. This place had always been the family's haven and now the killer was *here,* about to knock down the door.

Lorna scooped a sleepy Cody up from his bed, together with the comforter, and carried him in a bundle to her bedroom, then into her bathroom.

"Paige, you too," I ordered. "And Rufus as well." I herded them all inside.

Lorna turned and reached for me. "But—"

I took her hand and quickly kissed it. "I know. But I need to know you're safe. Lock the door."

She bit her lip...then closed the door and I heard it lock. I looked at the door, wishing it was ten feet thick and made of steel. Then I ran back to the living room. "They're on the thirty-second floor," reported Gabriel.

I looked around the living room and saw the heavy oak table. "Colton, Cal, help me move this thing." Together, we dragged it into the center of the room and then flipped it onto its side to give us something to shelter behind.

"Fortieth floor," Gabriel told us.

I looked around at the team. "We make our stand here. We have to hold them for twenty minutes, until Callahan gets here with the cavalry." I pointed at the double doors that led out to the hallway. "We *do not let them through that door!*"

Everyone nodded grimly. They'd all bonded with Lorna and Cody over the last week. We took up our positions. Bradan and I knelt behind the table, right in the center of things. Gabriel, Colton and Kian crouched at the sides of the room, ready to take down anyone who got through the door. Cal crouched right at the back, rifle raised.

"Forty-five," said Gabriel, his voice tight.

The adrenaline was flowing now, just like it always did when we were about to go into action. But there was something new, too. My heart was slamming against my ribs and I kept glancing down the hall towards where Lorna hid. This time, it wasn't just a mission.

"Forty-eight," said Gabriel.

I thought about how this guy had killed Russ, and so nearly killed Danny and Lorna and Cody.

I thought of Jillian and Max, and how I hadn't been there.

I savagely worked the slide of my assault rifle, putting a round in the chamber. *Well, I'm here now.* And this Radoslava guy was about to find out how Texans defended the people they love.

"Fifty!" said Gabriel.

The door exploded inwards.

57

LORNA

GUNFIRE SPLIT THE AIR, shockingly loud. I hugged Cody to my chest, clapping my hands over his ears. There were two doors between us and the living room: how loud must it be out there?!

More gunfire. I flinched at every shot. Any one of them could be the one that ended someone's life. I imagined JD falling to the floor, or Kian, or Cal...all of them were putting their lives on the line for *us*. And there was nothing we could do to help, we just had to sit here and wait. I suddenly understood a little of what military wives went through.

Then I looked down at my phone. Erin had shown me how to access the cameras she'd put up around the apartment. I could at least check how the fight was going. I logged on and brought up the one in the living room.

The double doors had been blown to pieces and the air was thick with what looked like snow. It took me a moment to realize that it was paper, from the bookshelves, and shreds of furniture upholstery. Our home was being torn apart.

Flashes of gunfire lit up the scene like lightning. I could make out JD and the team, firing towards the doorway. It didn't look like anyone had gotten inside.

Just to be sure, I cycled through the other cameras. There were none in the bedrooms but Erin had put a few in the hallways. Everything was quiet. I was just about to go back to the living room camera when something caught my eye. What was *that?*

The door into JD's bedroom was open and the camera could see inside. Down at the far end of the room, the wall was...it almost looked like it was moving. Shaking. Then a black line appeared. I frowned. Was the camera glitching?

The black line grew steadily longer. I squinted, confused...and then my architect's brain overlaid the structure of the building over the scene and I realized what I was seeing. My stomach dropped.

I was watching someone cut through the thin, drywall partition at the end of JD's room with a drywall knife. It was a partition wall because it was only there to block off the disused elevator shaft that ran down to my dad's office.

My head jerked up and I stared at the bathroom door and the gunfire we could hear outside. The attack at the front door was a decoy. We'd seen four guys arrive in the parking garage and we'd just assumed that all four had come up to the fiftieth floor. But some of them must have stopped on the floor below, broken into my dad's office and climbed up the old elevator shaft. They were going to cut their way in through JD's bedroom, walk up behind the team and... *Oh God, they'll kill them all!*

The black line had changed direction, now forming two sides of a square. Another minute and they'd be inside.

I called JD. He didn't answer. Either he'd turned his phone off so it didn't ring and give away his position, or he couldn't hear it over the gunfire.

Three sides of the square were cut, now. *They're going to die. All of them are going to die, shot in the back, unless I do something.*

I looked down at Cody, my heart ripping in two. I couldn't leave him.

But I couldn't let JD and the others die, either. *Oh Jesus...*

I leaned down and kissed Cody on the head. "I'll be back in one minute," I told him, trying not to let my voice shake. Then I passed him to Paige and stood up.

Paige balked when she saw me unlocking the door. "What are you *doing?!*"

"Take care of Cody," I told her.

Then I took a deep breath...and slipped out of the door

58

LORNA

I crept out into my bedroom, then quietly opened the door to the hallway and peeked out. All quiet. I was just about to run to the living room to warn JD when I saw a figure emerge from JD's room. *Shit!* I was too late!

I ducked back inside my bedroom and pressed myself against the wall, holding my breath. One, two, *three* sets of footsteps went past. Three of them were sneaking up behind the team. They'd slaughter them unless I could get there first and warn JD. But how? I stared helplessly at my bedroom wall and my weird brain did its thing: I could see the structure of the building, the rectangular rooms and the snaking hallway that connected them. It was no good. The bad guys were ahead of me, blocking the only path.

But...what was that dark space *above* the rooms, where all the walls stopped?

I looked up. The penthouse was built with a suspended ceiling, just like the offices downstairs. Between it and the next floor, there was a crawlspace...

I grabbed a chair and put it on my dressing table, then pushed up the tile in the corner of the room. Above was a dark, cavernous space. It was only a few feet tall, but it extended across the entire penthouse.

Everything was thick with white dust: no one had been up here in decades.

I heaved myself up, panting and struggling: I wasn't built for gymnastics and I was trying not to make any noise. I knew the brittle plasterboard ceiling wouldn't take my weight, but the metal support struts should. I inched forward, wincing, and the struts creaked...but held.

I started crawling along the struts, heading for the living room. Within seconds, I was sweating. If I went too fast and made a noise, Radoslava's men would hear me and I was dead. But if I went too slow, they'd beat me to JD.

One advantage I had was that there were no walls up here, so I could go in a straight line instead of following the winding hallway. But there were no landmarks, either: I was completely reliant on my mental blueprint of the building. *Ten more feet on and I'll be over the kitchen. Twelve feet after that and I'm at the living room wall...*

Halfway there, I passed an air vent and peeked down. I froze when I saw Radoslava's men creeping along the hallway, guns raised. I was crossing their path.

I held my breath until they'd passed, then looked ahead of me, estimating how much further I had to go. At this rate, they'd get there first.

I set my jaw, grimly determined. I wasn't giving up. I forgot about stealth and just crawled as fast as possible.

59

JD

I FIRED A BURST, then ducked back down behind the table as they returned fire. Bradan and I looked at each other, then glanced around the room at the devastation. Anything not behind cover was getting destroyed by the hail of gunfire coming through the double doors. I watched as the model of Manhattan, with its mini versions of the McBride projects, was shredded. The big floor-to-ceiling windows shattered one by one as bullets hit them, the glass frosting for a second and then crashing to the floor like water.

I frowned. The guys outside the double doors were doing a good job of keeping us pinned down, but why weren't they pushing forward and trying to get into the penthouse? Then I shook my head. *Who cares?* We could just hold them off like this until Callahan showed up with a SWAT team.

Then Bradan nudged me and pointed silently at the ceiling. At first, I didn't understand. Then I saw the ceiling flex, ever so slightly. *They're up there!*

Bradan already had his rifle pointed at the ceiling. I did the same. We'd fire a long burst and shred whoever was up there.

I mouthed a countdown. *One...*

Two...

Th—

Lorna fell through the ceiling in a cloud of dust and broken tiles. Bradan had already squeezed his trigger but I slammed his rifle sideways and the shots went wide. Lorna managed to grab a metal strut and dangled for a second, then fell the last few feet and landed on her ass. I grabbed her and hauled her behind the table.

"What the hell are you doing?!" I yelled. "We nearly shot you!"

She was panting too hard to speak. She pointed towards the hallway that led to the bedrooms. I looked, and saw a flicker of movement as someone peeked around the corner. "On our six!" I yelled.

Cal kept up his watch on the door. Everyone else whipped around to face the new threat behind us and started firing. I counted three guys there: God, they'd been seconds away from shooting us all in the back. Lorna had saved us, but now she was caught in the thick of the fight. I pressed her to the floor, covering her body with mine as bullets hissed overhead.

With all of us firing at them, the three who'd been trying to come up behind us were gradually forced back. Then Kian took out one of them, and Cal managed to pick off the guy outside the double doors. The final two pulled out, retreating the way they'd come. It was over.

I let Lorna sit up and quickly checked her over for wounds. She was shaking, disheveled and covered in white dust, but she was okay. I grinned in relief and hugged her tight.

We slumped against the upturned table, gazing around at the remains of the living room. Wind and rain were blowing through the place, spreading the piles of broken safety glass across the floor. The black leather couches had been shredded and were disgorging their foam interiors like fluffy blossoms. The air was still full of gun smoke and drifting scraps of paper and the once-pristine cream walls were peppered with dark holes. But Lorna and Cody were safe and the danger was over. In another ten minutes, Callahan would be here and he could start the hunt for Radoslava. I drew Lorna into a hug. "It's gonna be okay," I told her.

One by one, the rest of the team slumped down, exhausted,

sitting on torn couches or just on the debris-strewn floor. "You're gonna need some new furniture," said Colton, looking around.

Which raised a question. Now that it was all over, what did we do next? I'd been so focused on just keeping her alive, over the last few weeks, that I hadn't thought about the future. I had a sudden stab of panic. New York? Mount Mercy? How the hell were we going to make it work?

I stroked Lorna's hair, sending a shower of dust down over her clothes. She looked up at me shyly with those big gray eyes and the swell of protective love that hit me was like getting body slammed by Colton.

My panic melted away. I didn't know what the future would look like, but it was going to be together. I pulled her close and she cuddled in, resting her head on my chest.

My phone rang: Lily. I had a missed call, too, from Lorna: I must not have heard it over the gunfire. "What's up?" I asked Lily.

"I fucked up," she said. "That military record, Radoslava Burski…I only looked at the main section, the part with all the commendations and kills. I never thought to look at the basics. And in my defense, there was no photo. It just never occurred to me—"

"Whoa, whoa. Slow down. *What* never occurred to you?"

Lily sighed, embarrassed. "Alexei pointed out that Radoslava is a girl's name. I checked the record and he's right: Radoslava's a woman."

I sat there blinking, my mind trying to catch up. Russ's secret child was a girl, not a boy.

I'd just assumed all along that a man was behind this. Now I felt like an idiot. In Mexico, I remembered thinking that the leader of the gunmen was small and lightly built. It had never occurred to me that she might be female, under the ski mask.

And then I froze, remembering another moment.

In Lorna's office, when she'd shown me the photo of Maria. I remembered thinking the face was familiar. The cheekbones, the smile.

I'd just realized where I'd seen them.

I bolted for Lorna's bedroom. Kicked open the door to the bathroom.

As soon as Paige saw my face, she knew. I raised my gun but she was quicker. She pulled Cody in front of her, whipped out a knife and put it to his throat.

Lorna ran through the door and froze, horrified. "What the *fuck?* Paige, what are you doing?"

Paige said nothing, just stared back at me, watching my eyes. Just as she had in Mexico. Cody had gone pale and was struggling but Paige kept him mercilessly pinned to her chest.

"Paige, *please!*" yelled Lorna, almost hysterical. "Put the knife down! This isn't funny! You're scaring him!"

"Her name isn't Paige," I told her. "This is Radoslava Burski. Maria's daughter."

60

LORNA

I THOUGHT I'd known fear. Standing on stage, seeing the gun swinging up to point at me, or trapped in the car feeling the water rise over my chin. But I hadn't. I hadn't known *true* fear until I saw a crazy woman holding a knife to my son's throat.

My mind refused to accept what JD was telling me. I pushed past him, putting myself between him and Paige and held my hands out like a teacher trying to stop a schoolyard fight. It had to be a mistake, a misunderstanding. "*No!*" I yelled. "*Stop!* She's a *nanny!* She's from *Los Angeles!* I checked her references, I talked to families she'd worked for!"

"Yeah," said JD, his eyes locked on Paige. "You asked about their nanny, Paige. And they told you how great she was. But did any of them show you a photo of her?"

The knife was so tight against Cody's neck that the skin was indented. I could see a vein on his neck bulging, a millimeter away. I was so scared I could barely think. "No," I said at last.

"There really *is* a nanny called Paige somewhere in New York," said JD. "Radoslava stole her identity."

"But..." My mind still wouldn't accept it. "No. No, I met her by *chance*, in Central Park!"

"No you didn't. When did you say you met her? Three months ago? Her mother died four months ago. I figure that was what started all this. She came over here, probably watched your family for a month. Figured out that you needed a nanny. Stole the real Paige's identity and then approached you in the park."

The rest of the team arrived, drawn by the shouting. When they saw what was happening, they froze, crowded in the bathroom doorway.

I looked between JD and Paige. It was crazy. JD had to be wrong. But then why wasn't Paige denying it? Her gaze was fixed on JD and there was a raw hatred in her eyes I'd never seen before. "Paige?" I asked, my voice fractured.

She shuffled back a step, getting some distance from JD and, for the first time, she looked me in the eye. The hate was so intense that I took a stumbling step back. I felt instantly dirty, I felt like bugs were crawling all over me.

I'd never been *loathed* before.

And my blood turned to ice water because suddenly, I knew JD was right. Paige was the killer. *She killed my dad!* And I'd invited her into our lives, I'd let her take care of my child...

"*Why?*" I croaked. "Why do you hate us? Because my dad had an affair?"

"An affair?" hissed Paige. Her sun-kissed, California drawl was gone: her real voice was quick and vicious as a flick knife, with a strong Eastern European accent. "He got my mother pregnant then paid her off like she was a whore. She'd never had money before. She spent it on booze and drugs. He destroyed all our lives. My whole future."

Destroyed their lives? There's more. There's more I don't know. I felt like I was falling again, just like when I first found the photo of Maria. I felt my eyes filling with tears. "Please, Pai—Please, Radoslava, just take the knife away, *please!*" She didn't move a muscle. In fact, despite how angry she was, her hand wasn't even trembling. That was scarier than the knife itself, in a way. "Why didn't you just kill me?!" I sobbed. "Why come into our lives, why *all this?!*"

"Because I wanted to see you suffer," said Radoslava. "I wanted to see you lose your father and mourn him and finally envy him because he didn't have to live in fear. I wanted you to know it was coming."

Oh God. There was something in her voice, an undertone that was like nails-on-a-chalkboard to a mother, the trigger that makes you snatch your child away from someone. Radoslava was unstable. And she had a knife to Cody's throat. *How could I not see this?* Jesus, her *arms*, muscled and lean from being in the military, not from triathlon training.

"That accent," said JD, shaking his head in wonder. "And *Jesus,* you got the best poker face I've ever seen." He jerked his head towards the ruined living room. "I sat there talking about Radoslava Burski, I said your *name*...and you just handed me a mug of coffee."

I suddenly started running through it all in my mind. The attack in Mexico...Paige had said she was shopping but she'd been *there,* in a ski mask with the other gunmen, hunting us down. And then, after JD saved us, she'd changed and raced back to the hotel, clutching shopping bags. She'd come to the speech, not to support me but so she could watch me get shot. "Poland," I thought out loud. "You said your mom had broken her leg so you had to fly home to California. But you flew to Poland, didn't you? You were there, at the dam, watching, while one of your men drove that bulldozer into the scaffolding?"

"And she was driving the car that rammed us into the water," growled JD. "And now I know why she insisted on coming to meet Van der Meer. I thought someone had intercepted that bottle of cognac before it was delivered, but it was her. When she bumped the table, she dropped the poison in the bottle."

I stared at Radoslava in horror. I remembered lying there on the deck, feeling like my insides were on fire, and Radoslava shoving people out of the way so she could kneel beside me and hold my hand. She'd pretended she was in pieces, terrified for her BFF. She'd been enjoying watching me die.

That was the biggest betrayal, in a way, the one that made me want to crawl into a deep, dark hole and never come out again. After years of being a lonely, awkward geek, I'd thought I'd finally found a friend. But it had all been a lie. All my teenage self-hate came back, only a thousand times worse. *Of course no one wants to be your friend!*

But none of that mattered. Only one thing did. "Please," I begged, tears coursing down my face. "*Please,* if you want to kill me, kill me. But let Cody go."

Radoslava shook her head. "This isn't over yet." And, dragging Cody with her, she moved towards the door.

I wanted to throw up. "No," I sobbed, near-hysterical. "No, no, please no. Take me, take *me!*" But she kept moving.

"*Mom!*" sobbed Cody.

I stepped forward: I couldn't stop myself. Radoslava glared at me and scraped the knife against Cody's throat, leaving a red scrape mark. I froze.

JD was in her path. He'd kept his rifle leveled at her this entire time, never letting it waver.

"Move," said Radoslava.

Cody was full-on blubbing, now, his face shining with tears. "*JD, help, I don't wanna go.*"

JD stood like a rock. "It's gonna be okay," he told Cody. "It's gonna be okay, pal."

"*Move,*" Radoslava repeated. The knife twitched...

"*JD!*" I begged.

JD cursed under his breath...and stepped aside.

Radoslava pulled Cody through the doorway and backed away through my bedroom. I saw Colton step up behind her. He raised his arm as if to grab her and looked at JD: *should I?*

JD gave a quick, bitter shake of his head.

Radoslava dragged Cody out of the room, out of the penthouse... and they were gone.

61

LORNA

THERE's a feeling only a mother knows, that primal panic that claws at you when your child is missing. From the moment they leave your body, you always know where they are, even if they're at summer camp, or at a friend's house, or with grandparents. So when you *don't*, when you turn around in the store and there's an empty space where they should be, your stomach drops. And this was a thousand times worse because I knew he was in danger.

It had been almost a half hour. My instincts were screaming at me to go full tigress: I needed to run, to scream, to kill anyone who stood between me and him. Instead, I just had to stand there...and wait.

JD pulled me into his arms. "She'll call."

He wrapped me up, but I was stiff and wide eyed, huffing air in quick little gasps. "What if—What if she doesn't? What if she just kills him?"

JD squeezed me harder. "She won't." His voice was as firm as always, but I wondered how much he was trying to convince himself. "She loves him. I've seen the way she looks at him, I think that was real. We were wrong about everything else about her, but we weren't wrong about that."

I stared at the ruined living room. Gabriel and Kian had been down to the basement and gotten the power back on and with the lights on, the damage looked even worse. How did this all go so wrong, so fast? Just a few weeks ago, everything had been normal. Now Cody was gone, my dad was dead, the company was about to collapse and even our home was wrecked.

What if she just kills him? She was determined to hurt me and she was unstable. What if JD was wrong, what if—

My phone rang. I snatched it up.

"Put it on speaker," JD told me. He was staying strong but I could hear a father's fear in his voice.

Radoslava's voice filled the room. "Are they listening?"

"Yes," I croaked. "Is Cody okay?"

Radoslava said something to someone in Polish. Footsteps. Then—

"Mom?"

"Cody!" It was almost a sob, my voice was shaking so much. "Are you okay?"

"Yes." His voice was so small, so terrified, that it felt like a knife in my stomach.

"What do you want?" I begged. I was ready to give her anything, absolutely anything.

"I'll contact you," Radoslava told me coldly. "Just you. Or I *will* hurt him. You know I keep my promises, Like when I told you I'd return your dress."

And she ended the call. I stared at my phone in horror. I've never felt so helpless. I realized my cheeks were wet with tears. I hadn't realized I'd started crying.

JD stepped towards me but I put a hand up. "Give me a minute," I told him, and went to my room. My legs went shaky and I had to sit on the edge of the bed or I would have collapsed. *She has him.* And he'd sounded so scared...

Think, Lorna. Crying won't get him back. I swiped at my face with my sleeve.

She'd said she'd contact me, *just* me. She wanted to talk to me privately. *Why?* Because she wanted *me,* not him. She wanted to arrange a trade, my life for Cody's, and JD would never let me do it. *How?* How would she contact me privately?

I replayed the conversation in my mind. That last part about borrowing my dress...at the time, I'd thought she was just being mockingly playful. But...

I poked my head out of the door and checked the coast was clear. JD was still in the living room, talking to the rest of the team. I sneaked out of my room and into Paige's. I still couldn't think of her as Radoslava.

Months ago, Paige had borrowed an old dress of mine, a scarlet, strappy thing that was way too small for me. She'd only been going to wear it once but it looked so good on her that she'd hung onto it for another night out, then another. It had become a running joke between us: I'd kept saying she could have it, it didn't fit me anyway, but she kept insisting she'd return it any day now. She told me where I could find it, if I ever needed it: in a box under her bed.

I felt ill, remembering all the times we'd laughed together, all the secrets I'd told her. The whole friendship had been a lie. Just another way of hurting me when I found out the truth. It brought back every ounce of geeky paranoia I'd ever had. All shy introverts worry that *my friends don't really like me*. Imagine finding out that your one friend, your best friend, was acting all along.

Focus. I dropped to my knees and pulled the dress box out from under the bed. Behind it was a smaller, unmarked box. I pulled that out and opened the lid...

Cellphones. Eight of them, still in their packaging. And a ninth, already opened and charged. I picked it up and pushed everything back under the bed, then crept back to my room. Just a few minutes later, the phone buzzed. *Number withheld.*

I answered, my heart racing. "I'm here," I whispered.

"Were you stupid enough to tell JD about this?" asked Radoslava.

"No."

"Good." And she told me where to go. "If you come alone, I'll let Cody go. If you bring the others, I'll kill him."

"Don't hur—" I said, but she was gone. I disintegrated into tears again. *Oh God.* I hadn't even gotten to speak to him. What if she—

The door burst open. JD looked at the phone. "Was that her? What did she say?"

I went to speak...and then said nothing.

JD slowly shook his head. "Lorna, you've got to trust me. Whatever she said, she's trying to manipulate you." He took a step forward.

I took a step back.

JD froze, going pale, and indicated the space between us. "No. No, no, this is what she wants. We've got to stick together, it's the only way we'll get him back. What did she say? Did she say to come alone?"

I bit my lip, torn.

JD's voice shook. "If you do that," he told me, "she'll kill you."

I knew he was right, but I had to get Cody back. Even if that meant me dying.

"Come here," said JD gently, and held his arms out.

I shakily stepped forward. Put my own arms out, ready to take his hands and be crushed against that big, warm chest...

And then I ducked under his hands and ran past him.

62

JD

I SPUN AROUND, big and dumb and slow. By the time I got myself moving, she was already in the living room, dodging around the rest of the team. I chased her through the gaping hole where the double doors used to be, both of us slipping on spent bullet casings. But she had twenty feet on me and the elevator was already there, waiting for her. She hurled herself inside and hit the button and the doors closed in my face. *Shit!*

The others spilled out into the hallway. "What the *feck* is going on?" asked Kian.

There was no time to reply. I ran for the stairs and started pounding down them, jumping the last five or six stairs of each flight, pinballing off the walls. Every few floors, I'd glance at the elevator indicator and see her pulling ahead of me a little more.

If I lost her now, I'd lose her forever.

Going down was a hell of a lot easier than going up but it was still fifty floors and I'm not as young as I used to be. By the time I reached the parking garage, I was dripping with sweat and my legs felt like limp noodles. I slumped against the wall for a second, heaving for air, then stumbled on. The elevator was empty and I could hear her heels hurrying across the concrete ahead of me.

Where is she? I passed the big company Mercedes we normally drove her around in, then her own car, a BMW. She hadn't taken either of them.

Headlights went on at the very back of the garage, blinding me. An engine roared into life and then she was swerving past me in an old, mud-covered pick-up truck. She raced towards the exit and I put everything I had into chasing after her, knowing she'd have to stop for a second at the exit.

She slammed on the brakes, stopping with her bumper an inch from the red-and-white barrier. As I got closer, I could see the tension in her body: she was staring at the barrier, ready to floor it as soon as it rose.

I staggered up beside her and slammed my hand against her window. "*Wait!*" I begged. "Lorna, *please!* She'll kill you!"

She turned and looked at me and I could see the tears in her eyes. But I was between a mother and her child. She shook her head.

The barrier rose. And she roared away down the street.

63

JD

THE ELEVATOR DOORS opened on the fiftieth floor and I found everyone waiting for me. Their faces fell when they saw that Lorna wasn't with me.

I was in pieces. She was out there, somewhere, on her way to meet that crazy woman. And there wasn't a damn thing I could do about it. When Radoslava ran off with Cody, I'd called Callahan and told him to hold off on the SWAT team, since we didn't know where to send them. I could call him again and get an APB put out for the pick-up truck, but in a city the size of New York, there was no way they'd find her in time.

I shook my head as I walked into the living room. "I should have known it was Paige," I growled, kicking at a mound of shattered glass. "I was living under the same fucking roof with the woman for two weeks. I should have spotted it."

"She's a spy," said Bradan. "Lying's what she *does*. None of us saw it, either. It's not your fault."

Isn't it? If I'd kept my distance from Lorna and just been a damn bodyguard, maybe I'd have been more objective. Every time I was around Paige, I'd gotten embarrassed and awkward because she was the BFF of the woman I was falling for. I'd wanted her to like me. I'd been worried she'd come between us. I'd never had time to be suspicious.

Kian put a hand on my shoulder. "We'll get her back."

I glared, about to snap at him. But he just looked at me levelly, not flinching, and my shoulders sank. He was just trying to help. And he knew what I was going through, from when Emily was in danger.

Gina arrived, her face pale and drawn. "That psycho bitch took *Cody?*" She was in a flight suit, ready to fly us wherever we needed. The problem was, I had no idea where Lorna had gone.

Gabriel led me over to one of the couches, its cushions shredded by bullets. He sat me down, then squatted in front of me. When we'd started the team, he'd been the last person I'd have wanted advice from. I'd seen him as a criminal who couldn't be trusted and he'd seen me as a boy scout: we'd endlessly butted heads. But when the shit went down, he'd shown that he'd sacrifice everything for the team. He'd come to be a good friend and he was the smartest of all of us. If anyone could help, it was him.

"You've been there for everything Radoslava's done," said Gabriel. "Mexico, the marina, everything. You know her better than anyone. You've got to get inside her head. Where would she meet Lorna?"

I shook my head. Gabriel was a charming thief, a master con man. He was the one who was good at reading people, not me. "I'm not like you."

"Bullshit. You knew where to find Lorna, when she ran off upset. You knew when Cody was being bullied. You're good with people: that's what makes you a good leader. You just don't think about it, you do it on instinct. Now what can you tell us about Radoslava?"

I wasn't sure he was right, but I had to hope he was. I thought about it for a long time. "It's about her family. Whatever happened in Poland scarred her for life, turned her crazy. She *hates* the McBride family. But she hasn't tried to kill Miles, or Cody. It's all about Russ and Lorna."

Gabriel nodded. "Okay. What else?"

I scrunched up my brow. "It's like she's trying to taint the legacy they'll leave behind. At the marina, they were opening a new building...but now everybody will remember that that's where Russ McBride died. She tried to shoot Lorna when she was at the site of the hospital they were building." I looked around. "She attacks us *here,* even though it's well protected, because it's the family home and the building that Russ built."

"Alright," said Gabriel slowly. "So what else connects Russ and Lorna? What's their legacy?"

I had no idea. I scowled and turned away, glancing around the wrecked room. Then my eyes fell on the model of Manhattan, with its McBride buildings picked out in blue. They'd been torn apart by bullets but I still recognized them. The skyscraper we were in right now, the hospital, the marina...

I froze. I was staring at a blue skyscraper that was lying on its side. Hudson Tower. The first skyscraper Lorna had designed. The one that passed the baton between father and daughter. Was *that* it? Or was I just grasping wildly?

I racked my brains, remembering looking up at the half-finished building, just after we helped the string quartet get out of the mud...

The mud. The ground had been all churned up. Russ had said you needed a four-by-four. I looked at the rain hissing down outside. The whole site would be a swamp, tonight. That's why Lorna took the pick-up truck, when there'd been other cars closer.

I jumped up. "I know where they are! Everyone in the chopper!"

We grabbed our gear and ran up to the roof. On the helipad, the rain was crashing down in sheets and the wind was gusting and howling, blasting our faces with water and nearly knocking us off our feet. It took me right back to four years ago. Another storm. Another family.

I climbed into the chopper, grimly determined. I wasn't going to lose them. Not again.

64

LORNA

I TURNED off the road and into the construction site, the wheels slipping in the mud. I skidded to a stop and looked up at the half-finished building. Radoslava had said to meet her on the roof but there were no elevators in the building, yet: it was just a skeleton with open, gaping sides. There was only a construction elevator: a basic box with mesh walls that climbed up the outside of the building on a track. I ran over to it, pulled the door closed and reached for the *ascend* button.

A hand slammed against the mesh wall. I jumped and spun around—

JD stared at me through the mesh wall. "You go up there, she'll kill you."

"I know," I whispered. And reached for the button again.

"*Wait!*" he pleaded.

I hesitated, my hand still hovering over the button

Rain was coursing down his face. "I know you're scared," he said. "But you gotta trust me. Me and the team...this is what we do."

What if he's wrong? My palm traced the plastic circle of the button, my heart tearing in two.

JD pressed his face closer and his words were as solid as huge hunks of granite. "Lorna, *I swear to you. I swear,* I will get him back."

My arm tensed, ready to press. I stood there panting, debating, my eyes filling with tears.

Then I dropped my hand from the button, hauled the door open and JD pulled me into his arms.

65

JD

WE PULLED BACK to the marina, out of sight, to plan. I looked up at the building, then looked around at the team. Radoslava and her men had had time to dig in and prepare. She'd told Lorna to come alone but she'd be prepared for us to show up, too. Whichever way you sliced it, we were walking into a trap and the people we were up against were Special Forces, too. There was a good chance not all of us would come home from this one. And this was *my* mess I'd involved them in.

"Look," I began. "I *have* to do this. But the rest of you—"

"Yeah, yeah," said Gabriel. "We get it. We don't have to do this."

"JD," said Kian. "Can you just, for the love of Christ, accept that we're all here for you and skip to the part where we shoot the bastards?"

I stopped and looked around at them in amazement. And I realized we'd become more than a team. And I'd become more than their leader. I should never have shut them out.

I had to look away and clear my throat before I could speak again. "Okay. Lorna, tell us about the building. How can we get to the top?"

She sketched on her phone screen. "The building elevators haven't been fitted yet. There's the construction elevator on the outside of the building and there are two stairwells. When we get to the roof, there's a separate structure, a restaurant, in the middle that goes up one more floor."

I thought. "They'll be expecting Lorna to come up in the elevator. I'll go up with her. Kian and Bradan, you go up the north-east stairwell and stop one floor from the top. Gabriel and Colton, you do the same on the south-west stairwell."

Colton looked up at the building: sixty floors, with open sides and the wind whistling through it. "Why d'you have to build these things so fucking high?" he muttered. But he nodded: he'd suck it up and get it done, and I nodded in thanks.

"When we're all in position," I said, "I'll give the go and you can rush them from two directions at once while I grab Cody. Cal, you find a place where you can watch over us."

Cal looked around and saw a crane that towered over the whole area. He grabbed his rifle and loped off. Kian, Bradan, Gabriel and Colton headed for the stairwells. Gina had taken the chopper back to the penthouse after dropping us off, so that left me alone with Lorna.

I reached in my pocket and took out a radio earpiece, then gently brushed back her hair and carefully inserted it. I could feel her shaking. "It's gonna be okay," I told her.

She looked at the ground and swallowed, then looked me in the eye. "If it comes down to him or me, you save him. Okay?"

I stared at her, speechless. I hadn't been ready for that. "It won't come to that," I said at last.

She shook her head. "Promise me."

I glared at her. I didn't want to say it, didn't want to give that idea life. But she stared back at me, those gray eyes hard as diamonds.

"I promise," I said at last, my voice rough. Then I grabbed her and pulled her into a tight, tight hug, kissing the top of her head. Without letting go of Lorna, I touched my earpiece. "Kian, how are you doing?"

Kian's Irish accent sounded in my ear. "In position."

"Gabriel, where are you?" I asked.

"Nearly there," said Gabriel. "One of us ain't built for speed."

"Fuck you, pretty boy," panted Colton. "It's sixty floors!" A few moments later, he came on the radio again. "In position, boss, one floor from the top."

I looked up at the crane, high overhead. It was so tall, I couldn't even see Cal. "Cal, you ready?"

"All ready," said Cal, "got a good view of the roof but I don't see anyone. They must be lying low."

I pushed back from Lorna and took her hands in mine. "Alright," I said gently. "Let's do this."

66

LORNA

RATTLING AND SHAKING, the construction elevator crawled slowly up the side of the building. With every floor we ascended, my heart rate ratcheted a little higher. I hugged myself, shivering: the mesh walls didn't do much to stop the wind and rain and my suit was already soaked.

We passed the last floor before the roof and I glimpsed Kian and Bradan through the open side of the building, crouched and waiting at the bottom of the final flight of stairs. Then we were on the roof. I slid open the door and looked around. It was a mess: the big, open area was scattered with construction equipment. Work lights threw out blindingly bright, cold white light and left everything else in an inky shadow. Generators to run the lights and other equipment were scattered around, surrounded by barrels of diesel fuel. At one end of the roof, steps led up to a boxy, concrete building that would one day be a fancy restaurant with amazing views.

I couldn't see anyone. *Where are they hiding?* Then a male voice, heavily accented. "You alone?"

"Yes," I managed, my voice tight with fear.

Two of Radoslava's men appeared from the shadows and came

over. They looked inside the elevator and confirmed I was alone, then motioned me forward.

JD's voice in my ear, warmly reassuring. "Don't go with them. Tell them you want to see Cody."

"Where's my son?" I asked.

One of the men scowled. "Will take you to him," he told me in fractured English, and motioned impatiently.

"*Don't,*" said JD in my ear. "We need to know where he is. It could be she's got him stashed somewhere else. Insist."

It was so hard not to glance up. JD was three feet above me, stretched out under a tarpaulin on the roof of the elevator. I planted my feet. "I'm not moving until I see my son."

The men looked at each other. Then one of them spoke in Polish into a radio. He listened to the response, then pointed.

I followed his finger. In one of the windows of the restaurant, Cody's face had appeared. My legs buckled in relief and I had to fight the instinct to just run straight towards him. Then I saw another face, peeking out from directly behind him. Radoslava.

"Cal?" JD asked instantly. "Can you take her out?"

"No," Cal told him. "Wind's changing too fast. I could hit Cody."

"OK," said JD. "Then we'll run in and take 'em. Everybody ready?"

The team sounded off one by one. It looked good: Radoslava and her two men were all looking my way. The two stairwells were behind them so the team could take them by surprise.

"On three," said JD. "One. Two—"

"*Hold! Feckin' hold!*" Bradan's Northern Irish accent cut through everything.

Radoslava's men motioned me forward again. I walked slowly forwards, out of the elevator and into the full force of the pouring rain and howling wind.

"What's the problem?" demanded JD.

"Tripwires," said Bradan breathlessly. "They've booby-trapped the top of the stairwell. Claymore mines, you can barely see 'em in the shadows."

"Gabriel, check yours," JD said quickly.

Silence for a second. Then Gabriel whistled softly. "He's right, they're on our stairwell, too. We touch a tripwire and we'll be blown apart."

My heart was crushed with a cold fist. Four of the team were now trapped and useless, stuck one floor below us. Our careful plan was in tatters.

"I'll do it on my own," snarled JD.

"That's suicide," Cal told him. "They're all looking right at the elevator. You'd be cut down as soon as you stood up. There'd be no one to get to Radoslava. She could kill Cody."

I could hear JD panting, debating. He didn't want to risk Cody but he couldn't let me go to my death, either. I kept walking, and looked down at the ground so that Radoslava's men couldn't see my lips move. "You promised," I whispered.

JD didn't answer but I could hear his breathing go shaky as he fought for control and my heart broke. He knew he was about to lose me, just like he lost his wife. There was so much I needed to say to him but I couldn't risk more than a few words.

"Take care of Cody," I whispered.

And I followed Radoslava's men towards the restaurant.

67

LORNA

THE RESTAURANT WAS BARE CONCRETE, echoey and stark and it didn't provide much shelter from the storm outside. Rain poured in through a huge hole in the ceiling where one day a massive skylight would be. The wind shrieked as it blasted down a set of stairs that led up to a VIP roof terrace and through the gaping window holes that would eventually give diners the best views in the city. Barrels of diesel fuel were everywhere.

Radoslava was dressed in black combat gear. She was facing away from me, looking out through one of the empty window frames, with Cody right in front of her. The whole city was laid out before her, a glittering, magical map. I'd spent so much time in New York, I'd kind of forgotten how beautiful it could be.

"I used to think about you," she told me without turning around. "Every night, when I went to bed. Other little girls go to sleep dreaming of princesses. But I knew there really *was* a princess, called Lorna McBride, growing up *here*." She swept her hand at the skyscrapers, the stores, the riches.

I'd known there was more to her story than she'd told us. Was that what it was really about, jealousy? She hated me because my family were rich? "I'm sorry," I said sincerely. "I didn't even know you existed until a few weeks ago. I'm sorry my dad abandoned you. I think he was trying to do the right thing, giving your mom the money."

Radoslava spun around, pulling Cody with her. "He fucking cursed us with that money! My mother burned through it in ten years. She did so many drugs she couldn't work. By the time I was a teenager, we had *nothing*, we couldn't afford *food!* Do you know what happened *then?*"

I glanced down at Cody's tear-stained face. He was flinching each time she yelled, absolutely terrified. The woman he'd trusted, who'd been part of his life for months, suddenly turning into *this... You and me,* I mouthed to him. *You and me together, we'll get through this.*

Radoslava was still waiting for my answer. I shook my head.

"That's because you grew up rich." Her voice was like a blade made of ice. "You don't understand what happens to teenage girls who need to eat and have no money."

Light dawned. *Oh. Oh shit.*

"I spent every night on my back," Radoslava told me. "Man after man. Just so we could afford bread, and blankets, and heat in the winter. I could have gone to college, Lorna. I'm smart. My mother was smart. She was a math prodigy when she was young. She could have been someone, but she burned out and dropped out of college."

"I'm sorry—" I began.

"When I was fifteen, I got chlamydia," Radoslava interrupted. "By the time I found out, it was too late. It had left me infertile. As soon as I was old enough, I joined the army. I thought that if I couldn't bring life into the world, I might as well bring death."

I stared at her, horrified. Now I understood why she hated us so much. "I'm sorry," I said, walking towards her. "I'm *so sorry.* I'm sorry my dad fathered you and left you there—"

"*That's* what you think?" she asked, her face twisted in disgust. "You think that bastard was my father?"

Wait, what?! I gaped at her. Suddenly, I didn't understand anything.

"I was two years old before your father ever met my mother!" she snapped. "My father was a local man who ran out on us before I was even born!"

My mind was spinning, trying to catch up. So Radoslava *wasn't* my dad's child. "But my dad got your mother pregnant," I said. "What happened to the baby? Did it die?"

Radoslava stared at me as if astonished I could be this stupid. "The baby didn't die. Your father stole you from us."

68

LORNA

THE WORLD SEEMED to dissolve beneath my feet and I plummeted sickeningly into the void. Radoslava wasn't my father's secret love child: *I* was.

The truths I'd known for thirty-seven years skittered past my fingers as I clawed for a handhold. "No," I said weakly. "No, my mom was Catherine McBride. She died in a car crash. I was in the car, I—"

I broke off. I'd been about to say, *I survived.* The same miracle story I'd been told my whole life. But with an awful, creeping certainty, I knew what had really happened.

I pictured my mom, driving home with the baby in the car. Then crashing just a hundred yards from the house. My dad opening the door and finding his beloved wife dead. Checking the baby...and finding her dead, too.

My dad, heartbroken, inconsolable. And in his grief, he'd come up with a desperate plan. He knew that Maria had just given birth to his baby in Poland. He knew that she was unstable, that she drank and did drugs. He'd probably been planning to give her money to raise the baby but now there was another way.

He must have buried the baby's body in secret. Then, some time in the next few days, when everyone thought he was taking care of the baby at home, he'd secretly flown out to Poland, given Maria the hundred thousand dollars to let him raise me in America, and brought me back home, substituting me for the baby who died. In those days, airport security was much lighter. With a few bribes to officials, it wouldn't have been difficult to get me into the country surreptitiously. And once I was there, who would know the difference? I was the same age as the baby who'd died, give or take a few days.

Now I knew why I was so different from Miles. We shared the same father but while his mother had been a politician, mine had been a math prodigy. And I knew why my dad had kept me close, instead of sending me off to boarding school: he was overcompensating after losing his first daughter. He probably thought he was doing a good thing, making up for his affair by giving the baby the best life he could give it. But to Radoslava...this American had snatched her baby sister away to raise in paradise, while giving her mother the money that would wind up making Radoslava's life a living hell. "Oh Jesus," I whispered. "I'm sorry. I'm sorry, Radoslava."

"I don't want your apologies," she said coldly. "Upstairs." She motioned me to the steps that led up to the roof terrace and I slowly climbed them. She followed, pulling Cody along with her.

I stepped out into the pounding, freezing rain and had to blink just to see properly as the water sluiced down my face. I turned back to Radoslava and she nodded me onwards. "To the edge," she told me.

The roof terrace ran right to the back of the building. One day, there'd be a parapet for safety but for now, there was nothing, just a raw, concrete cliff and a sixty-floor drop. I knew what was coming. I looked helplessly at Cody, who'd started to cry. He was all that mattered. "You've got me, now," I told Radoslava. "Let him go."

"I'm not going to hurt him," she told me. "But I'm not letting him go, either."

I stared at her, confused, and she stared back at me, a tiny smile on her lips. She was waiting for me to realize. And suddenly, sickeningly, I did.

This wasn't just about my dad. It wasn't just about me. It was about Cody, too. I knew now why she'd come up with this complicated plan and inserted herself into our lives as his nanny. I started to hyperventilate. "No," I begged.

"Mom?" asked Cody. "What is it? What's happening?"

I stared at him in terror, every motherly instinct surging up inside me. As Radoslava saw it, my father had robbed her of the ability to have children. So she was going to take my son and raise him as her own, just like my dad had taken me. That's why she'd become Cody's nanny: it had been about motherhood, all along. "You *can't*," I sobbed.

"Don't worry, I'll give him a good life." said Radoslava. "He'll grow to love me, in time." She pointed to the edge of the building. "Now I want you to walk out on there."

I followed her finger. A metal beam stuck out into space from the edge of the roof. "No," I pleaded. I didn't care about myself, but the idea of Cody being brought up by her...

"Do it," she told me. "Or I'll kill you both."

I looked desperately between Cody and her. Would she do it? Or had JD been right, did she love him?

I couldn't risk it.

"Cody?" I said, my voice shaking. "I love you."

"*Mom!*" Tears were streaming down his cheeks, now, and he was fighting against Radoslava's grip, but she held him tightly against her. "Don't make her! Please, Paige! Mom, don't!"

I walked slowly to the metal beam. It was so narrow, I couldn't even put both feet side-by-side on it. I took the first step, the smooth metal slick under my heels.

"*Mom!*" yelled Cody.

I looked back over my shoulder. "Don't make him watch," I said through my tears. "Turn him away."

Radoslava nodded. She twisted Cody around so that he was facing her and pulled him tight against her chest. "To the end," she told me, raising her voice over the wind.

I took another careful step, then another, trying not to look at the yawning gulf below me. The wind was plucking at my suit jacket and tugging at my hair so hard it hurt. One gust in the right direction and I'd be gone.

Another step. And now I was at the end. I swallowed, then finally looked down at the grid of streets and the glowing, red-and-white snakes of traffic far below.

"MOM!" bellowed Cody, hysterical. *"MOM!"*

Please, God, don't let him be watching.

"Good," said Radoslava. "Now jump."

69

JD

I WATCHED from the top of the elevator as Radoslava led Lorna up onto the roof terrace. I was breaking inside. *I'm going to lose her.* She was about to be ripped away from me, just as Jillian and Max were. Only this time, it was worse. This time, I had to watch it happen and there wasn't a fucking thing I could do about it. If I stormed in there alone, Radoslava would kill Cody and I'd lose both of them.

My breathing shuddered as I watched Lorna walk out along the support beam. *Please.* My hands gripped the roof of the elevator so hard the edges cut into my palms. *Please, God—*

God didn't answer.

But Cal did. "JD, I still don't have a shot on Radoslava," he said. "But I think I can hit one of the claymore mines on the north-east stairwell and set it off."

I drew in a breath of hope and spoke fast. "*Kian! Bradan! Get clear of the stairwell! Gabriel, Colton, get over there! Cal, you take that shot the second they're clear. As soon as the mines are gone, everyone move!*"

My eyes were glued to Lorna. She was right at the end of the support strut, now, about to jump.

"We're clear!" said Kian.

The sharp crack of a rifle shot. Three sharp, hard, detonations pounded my ears, so close together they were almost one, as one mine set off the others. The entrance to the north-east stairwell disappeared in a cloud of white smoke. Then there was a second, bigger explosion that belched out orange flame and thick, black smoke. Some of the diesel barrels must have been hit when the mines went off. Burning fuel spilled across the rooftop.

Everyone; the two soldiers, Radoslava, even Lorna, turned to look. And now, at last, I had a chance.

I surged up from under the tarpaulin and jumped down, then started running towards the restaurant. Meanwhile, the two soldiers cautiously approached the stairwell. They were expecting to find bodies. Instead, four big guys with guns came charging out of the smoke at them, forcing them back.

The burning diesel was spreading out into a lake, setting fire to more fuel drums. As I ran into the restaurant, I could hear drums starting to explode outside.

I sprinted straight up the steps and up to the roof terrace. Radoslava had her back to me, looking down to where her soldiers were fighting the team. Lorna was out at the very end of the support beam, trying to keep her balance as the wind howled around her.

I put my head down and charged, slamming into Radoslava. We went crashing to the ground together and she lost her grip on Cody. "Cody! Run downstairs!" I yelled. Smart kid that he was, he didn't ask any questions, just ran down the stairs into the restaurant.

As I tussled with Radoslava, one of her soldiers fell, hit by a shot from Gabriel. Then the other one was taken down by a shot from Cal. Now it was only Radoslava left and I had her pinned down. "It's okay!" I yelled to Lorna. "Cody's safe, come in!"

Lorna carefully turned around to start back along the beam. But at that second, a gust of wind pushed her sideways and she fell.

70

LORNA

MY HEELS SKIDDED SICKENINGLY on the smooth metal and I dropped. The beam whacked into my stomach, knocking all the air out of me, and for a second I hung there, draped over it like a wet sack of cement. Then I started to slither off, sliding faster and faster, clawing at the metal but not finding any grip.

Just as I lost contact completely, a big, warm hand closed around my wrist. I looked up into prairie-blue eyes. JD had thrown himself full-length on the beam and had me safely in his grip. "Gotcha," he panted.

I just hung there gasping, tremors of relief rolling down my body. I made the mistake of glancing down at what was beneath my dangling feet and went dizzy.

"Hold on," said JD. He shuffled along the beam, getting himself in position to haul me up.

Then someone came into my view behind him. Radoslava was up, and drawing a handgun. She stalked towards us. "*JD!*" I screamed.

He looked back over his shoulder and I saw his body tense. But there was nothing he could do to defend himself, not while he was holding me.

Radoslava raised her gun and JD flinched, waiting for the shot.

An explosion rocked the whole rooftop and a dirty red fireball rose into the air. The fire had reached the fuel drums inside the restaurant. Tongues of flame leapt up through the hole in the ceiling. And then we heard a scream.

Cody! Cody's in the restaurant!

Radoslava turned and ran towards the steps. JD heaved on my arm and hauled me up onto the metal beam, then pulled me back onto the roof. I clambered to my feet and we ran.

Fire had completely enveloped the restaurant and smoke and flames were shooting up through the hole in the roof. The team had run over to it and Colton was trying to get in through the door but he kept being forced back: the flames were just too intense.

"Mom! JD!" Cody's cries came from inside, somewhere near the back.

The only way left into the building was the stairs. Radoslava was standing right by them. She turned, locked eyes with me for a second—

And then she ran down the stairs into the flames.

JD and I ran after her. But just as we reached the stairs, a gout of flame shot up through the opening. We staggered back, then ducked down and tried to push forward. But burning fuel had spread all over the steps: they were completely impassable.

"*Cody!*" I screamed.

Then JD grabbed my arm, pointing down through the hole in the ceiling. I stumbled closer. The heat was so intense, every breath scorched my throat and oily smoke made my eyes burn and tear. I choked, squinted against the brightness of the flames...and saw Radoslava struggling across the restaurant, forcing her way through the inferno with Cody clutched tight to her chest. She looked up and saw us and lifted Cody up. I fell to my stomach and lunged down through the hole in the ceiling...but he was well out of reach. "No," I sobbed. "No, no, no—"

The flames roared higher, whipped up by the wind, and Radoslava was forced back, away from us. I saw her look around desperately. Then her eyes locked on a concrete counter. That would give her enough height to pass Cody up. But the top of it was awash with burning diesel.

She set Cody down for a second, took two quick breaths and climbed up onto the burning counter. Flames immediately licked up the sides of her military boots and the cuffs of her pants.

She quickly bent down and grabbed Cody under the arms, heaving him up to her chest. She turned towards us and took a staggering step closer, the flames already climbing her thighs. Her legs shook, her face a mask of pain. She lifted Cody up into the air and held him out towards us. *"Take care of him,"* she grunted.

JD and I grabbed one of Cody's hands each and we hauled him up onto the roof terrace. As soon as he was safe, we lunged back down again to try to grab Radoslava. But the flames had already climbed to her hips. She screamed and crumpled, falling down into the fire, and was gone.

JD pulled me back from the edge. I grabbed Cody and crushed him against me. Then JD wrapped both of us in his arms and we lay there in a tight, three-way hug in the rain. It was over.

71

LORNA

WE LAY there for a long time, physically and emotionally exhausted. The flames roared higher and higher as the fire reached its peak but there was no diesel, up on the roof terrace, and we were safe as long as we stayed put. JD called Callahan and told him where we were.

Then the fuel began to burn out and the rain damped down the flames. By the time we heard the wail of sirens, the fire was mostly out. JD led the way down the stairs and through the blackened, smoking restaurant. "Keep your eyes on me," he told Cody and me, and we did: I focused on that broad, strong back and I kept Cody in front of me, my hands on his shoulders, making sure he didn't glance over towards the counter.

We rejoined the team and looked down at the streets below. A convoy of fire trucks was approaching from one direction and a cluster of police cars was approaching from the other, "It's gonna be a long night," predicted Gabriel.

"I don't care," said Colton, scowling at the drop, "'long as we get to do it on the ground."

We all headed down in the elevator. Cal loped up just as Callahan's car screeched to a stop. "Everyone okay?" asked Callahan as he climbed out.

JD hooked an arm around my waist and Cody's waist and pulled us protectively close. Then he nodded to Callahan.

Callahan looked up at the smoking building. Then he looked at the approaching fire trucks and police cars and ran a hand through his tousled hair with the air of one preparing for a long night. He ducked back inside his car and brought out a travel mug of coffee. "Okay," he said. "Start at the beginning."

∼

The NYPD, the FBI and the State Department all got involved and we sat in interview rooms answering their questions all night. As dawn broke, JD finally put his foot down and told them that I was only a few days out of the hospital, that I needed to rest, and that I could answer anything else once I'd slept. Cody was already asleep on a couch, curled up under a blanket and watched over by Gina.

We stumbled out of the FBI building into a blindingly bright dawn. The storm had passed and the sky was electric blue: it was going to be a beautiful day. But there was something else...the buildings all looked extra-shiny, the yellow cabs extra-colorful.

Then I realized what it was: I wasn't in danger anymore. I took a breath and it was full and deep: that iron band around my chest was gone.

The rest of the team headed back to the hotel to sleep. JD, Cody and I went to the hospital to check on Danny and to try to persuade Erin to get some sleep. When we crept into his room, we found her curled up asleep on his bed, warmly snuggled to his side. Danny groggily opened his eyes, glanced down at Erin and grinned, then mimed *shh*. We nodded and backed silently out.

Our next stop was the penthouse, to pick up some clothes and other essentials before we joined the team at the hotel. When we'd each packed a bag, I stood in the living room for a moment, looking around at the devastation. I kept a firm hold of Cody's shoulders, paranoid about him wandering too close to one of the gaping, empty window frames.

JD put his arm around me. "Sorry," he rumbled. "Must be tough, seeing it like this."

I looked up at the hole where I'd fallen through the ceiling, at the drifting grains of safety glass being blown around by the wind. "It should be," I mumbled. "It should be, but..." I shook my head. I couldn't put it into words. Then I looked out at the rising sun and my stomach lurched. "Crap," I said. "It's morning."

JD looked at me blankly.

"Today's the day the company runs out of money," I told him. We couldn't pay salaries. We'd have to close down and let everyone go.

"Someone else can handle it," JD told me firmly as he guided me into the elevator.

"It's my responsibility. I should be there."

JD put his hands on my shoulders. "You need to *rest,*" he growled.

"It's not your fault, mom," Cody told me.

But it felt like my fault. I should have been better, smarter, more ruthless. I was about to go down in history as the CEO who took over a world-renowned company and ran it into the ground in a matter of weeks. The least I could do was give all those people a face to yell at.

We reached the parking garage, the elevator doors opened and we started forward. Then we stopped short. Right in front of us was a Rolls Royce...and standing beside it, Van der Meer. JD glowered and started towards him.

Van der Meer put his hand up. "No need for that." He came a little closer. His skin was still pale and he looked exhausted but he still had that arrogant swagger. He looked at me for a long time, as if weighing things up, then sighed. "The bank has reopened your credit line."

I felt my eyes bulge. We could pay everyone. We'd survive until the money came in from the dam. I stared at him, bewildered. "*Why?!*"

He sighed again and frowned. "Because you saved my life. And I might be cruel but I'm not a complete asshole." He turned around and got into his Rolls Royce and they swept away.

"Does that mean everything's gonna be okay?" asked Cody.

"Yes," I said, my voice shaking and my eyes beginning to shine. "*Yes*, that means everything's going to be okay."

At the hotel, I made some calls to the senior executives to reassure them that we *weren't* going out of business, that the threat to me was over and that everything was going to be fine. Then JD plucked the phone from my hand. "Now handle things yourselves for a few hours," he told them. "The woman needs some sleep." He ended the call and slid my phone into his back pocket. "You can have it back later," he told me in that voice that I couldn't disobey. "Right now, you're getting your ass into a hot shower and then into that bed."

I relented. A hot shower chased the chill out of my bones and the smell of diesel smoke from my hair. I pulled on a nightshirt, then fell into bed and was out before my head had stopped bouncing on the pillow.

When I woke up, it was past noon. "Where's Cody?" I asked.

"Next door, getting introduced to classic rock by Colton," said JD. I listened and made out crashing drums and wailing guitars soaking through the wall. JD handed me a cup of coffee. Nothing had ever smelled so good.

He had the doors to the balcony open and we went out there, both of us leaning on the stone parapet and looking out over Central Park as we sipped our coffee. "Guess we'd better talk about what happens now," he said, eyes crinkling as he gazed at the city. "You don't need guarding anymore."

My whole body tensed.

He turned to me, his voice like iron. "But I'm sure as hell not letting you go."

I pressed my lips together hard, melting inside. Then I threw my arms around him and hugged him so tight that he knew I wasn't letting go of him, either.

"Did some thinking while you were asleep," he told me. He

looked out at New York and grimly shook his head. "I ain't sure I belong here. But you and Cody are here. So…"

I stared at him, stunned. "What about Colorado? What about the team?" I looked at New York and then I looked at JD. He'd put on a clean white shirt and his blue jeans and boots, the same outfit I'd first seen him in, and he looked amazing. And just as out of place in New York as he'd always been. "You'd move *here?*"

He looked at me seriously. "I'd move to Mars if that's where you were."

I bit my lip. I was sure he could get a job here: private security firms would be fighting each other to get him. But I'd seen the bond he had with his team. I couldn't split them up. But Cody was in school here and I had the company and all my projects. I felt it all tearing at me, overwhelming…

Then JD put a hand on my shoulder and, immediately, the warm solidness of him grounded me. I took a deep breath. "We'll figure something out," I told him.

He nodded slowly. "I got a notion how we can start."

EPILOGUE
LORNA

One Month Later

"You got the steaks?" asked Esther Taggart.

"Yeah, ma," said JD gently.

"The wine?"

"Yup."

"The bacon, for the morning?"

JD patted a bulge in one of the bags.

"Well, alright then. You three have a good time."

I beamed at JD's mom. I'd only known her a day but I felt so blissfully relaxed in her company, not at all like when I'd met my ex's family. Maybe it was because she was so much like JD: warm and uncomplicated and mainly concerned that her little boy had enough to eat. "See you in a few days," I said, waving.

"Not if I see you first," JD's dad, Jack, shot back. He was nice, too, although he wasn't big on conversation. He spent a lot of the time sitting on the porch, staring out at the landscape, only coming inside for meals. One wheel of his wheelchair squeaked something awful and was bent inwards in a way that made my engineer's brain wince, but he wouldn't let me, JD or anyone else take a look at it for him, claiming it was fine just the way it was. Danny had been right: JD had learned his stoicism from his dad. When we got back from our trip, I was going to ask if he'd at least let me improve the wheelchair ramp so it didn't keep sliding away from the porch, leaving a crevasse that trapped his wheels.

Right now, though, I had other things on my mind. Like trying not to fall off my horse.

"Ready?" asked JD. "Nice and slow..."

He made a noise in his throat, some magic word that only country folk know, and his horse set off obediently. Cody's horse followed and then—*ulp!*—my pony lurched into motion and I clung onto the saddle for dear life. It was only my second time on a horse. JD had given Cody and me a basic riding lesson that morning but while Cody had turned out to be a natural, I was still getting used to the feeling of being atop the big, gentle creature.

"You're doing great," JD told me. He made it look effortless, bouncing and swaying as if he was part of the horse.

"Doesn't—*whoah*—doesn't feel that way," I told him as my horse decided to speed up a little. I was way out of my comfort zone but in a good way, bemused and fascinated and only a little terrified. There was something wonderfully physical about being on a horse: it balanced and grounded me, just like JD. I tugged gently on the reins and my horse came to a dead stop and refused to start again. "I'm literally the world's worst person at steering a horse."

"You've never seen Erin ride," said JD seriously. He gave my horse a look: *what are you doing?* And my horse snorted, shook itself in a kind of horse shrug, and walked on.

We cleared the gate of JD's parents' ranch without me falling off and I breathed a sigh of relief. As the ranch dropped behind us, the landscape rolled out around us, vast and wild and very, very quiet. To each side of us were wide, rolling plains, a warm wind washing over the pale grass until it looked like an endless, foaming ocean. Ahead of us, the land rose into gentle hills lush with trees, and overhead the sun blazed down from a deep blue sky dotted with fluffy white clouds. JD had given Cody and me cream Stetsons to keep the sun off us. Neither of us had ever really worn hats before and we loved them: we kept tipping our brims to imaginary people.

JD dropped back so we could all ride side by side. "Did I pass?" I asked him. I was very aware that Jillian, his first wife, had been a Texas-born country girl, and I was anything but.

He looked at me seriously. "That was never in any doubt. My folks love you."

A warm bomb went off in my chest. This trip had been a good idea. A couple of days meeting JD's folks and seeing the ranch, then two days of the three of us camping out in the wilds. Cody, who'd lived in New York his entire life, had already learned how to saddle a horse and tonight JD was going to teach him how to build a campfire and cook on it. Cody kept staring up at the huge Texas sky in wonder and it was the most relaxed I'd seen him since this whole thing began. He was seeing a therapist in New York and she was great but I had the feeling this was the best therapy, right here.

I'd taken some time off work, made much easier by the fact that I wasn't CEO anymore. Miles was out of rehab, clean and doing great, and a week ago we'd completed the transition to him as CEO. The team at the dam in Poland had finished the work and the government had paid us, so the company's finances were looking much healthier. Miles was already closing deals and solving disputes, proving himself to be exactly the leader I'd always known he could be.

We followed a winding trail that led up into the hills and over the next few hours the scenery just kept getting better and better. The dirt track we were on began to hug a river, so as the sun began to sink lower in the sky and light up the clouds in shades of delicate peach, salmon and finally deep, boiling scarlet, we got to see it all twice. I'd never known Texas was so beautiful.

We made camp, cooked steaks and, when Cody was snoring inside the tent, JD and I sat by the embers of the campfire, sipping red wine. The temperature had dropped fast once the sun went down and I was glad we had the blankets Esther had insisted on. But for now, I was sitting between JD's legs, he had his chest pressed against my back and his arms wrapped around me and I was as cozy as a person could be.

We looked up at the sky as the stars came out. First it was just one tiny pinprick of white in the middle of the deep blue. Then another, then a flurry and suddenly, they were coming too fast to count. I looked up in wonder as they spun a tapestry of silver overhead. I'd never seen the Milky Way before.

After a long time, I said, "I keep wondering how my dad could do it. Burying the baby, substituting me, covering it up all those years."

"Maybe we shouldn't be too hard on him," said JD. "He'd lost his wife and child." His voice grew rough and I knew he was remembering his own pain. "The poor guy was in agony and he dealt with it the best way he could."

I nodded, reached up and hugged his arms with mine, letting him know that I was there for him. And I felt his body relax.

I gazed up at the stars. I'd been doing a lot of thinking over the last few weeks. I'd finally realized what I'd been feeling, when I'd looked around at the wrecked penthouse. It didn't feel like home anymore. And that had been weirdly freeing.

When I married Adrian, I'd had a dream of setting up my own architecture firm. I figured I'd work at my dad's company for a few years and then, when the time was right, I'd strike out on my own. But then Adrian walked out on Cody and me, my confidence hit rock bottom and my life had gotten stuck on hold. I'd moved into the penthouse my dad built, one floor up from the company offices. Living and breathing McBride Construction every day, I'd gotten sucked in. I was just grateful to be able to do what I enjoyed and with a child to raise, my own dreams had taken a back seat. It had taken becoming CEO to remind me that, unlike Miles, it wasn't the business that I loved: it was designing buildings. At the same time, I'd come out of it more confident, more able to deal with people, and with a little more faith in myself.

Maybe it was time to revisit my dream.

I took a sip of wine. "What if..." I began.

~

Two Months Later

"Thirteen, fourteen, fifteen, *here*," I said triumphantly, finishing the last pace and marking the spot with my toe. JD pushed a stake into the ground and Cody hooked red marker tape around it. We all took a few steps back.

In the center of the field of long grass, we'd created a blueprint, rooms and hallways drawn life-size in shining red tape that shone and danced as the wind played with it.

"So that's the living room?" asked Cody, pointing. "And what's this?"

"That'll be a porch, running all along the side of the house, so we can sit out at night."

He ran along one of the hallways, excited. "And this room?"

"An office, for me," I said. "So I can work from home."

I'd take the leap and gone solo, opening a one-woman architecture business here in Mount Mercy. I'd still have to travel to New York sometimes to check in on projects like the hospital, but there'd be less and less of that as time went on. I was already getting interest from people in Mount Mercy and the surrounding towns and I'd said I'd look into some improvements for the team's base. I was going to be busy. And then there was the most important project of all: overseeing construction of our new house.

"And *this* room?" asked Cody.

"Entire room is devoted to Legos."

He ran over and hugged me.

JD and I had bought a plot of land on the edge of town and I'd designed a ranch-style house that would have great views out across the mountains. The same house I'd glimpsed in my dream, on the plane on the way to Poland.

JD adjusted his Stetson, put his arm around my shoulders and pointed to the area in front of the house. "Figure I can run a fence down here, divide it into two pastures. Then build a stable over here, nothing fancy..."

Cody's face lit up. "We're going to have *horses?!*"

JD grinned, picked him up and swung him up onto his shoulders, then walked him around where the horses would live. I noticed the gap that had opened up between Cody's pant cuffs and his sneakers: he was going to need new pants *again*. He'd really started to shoot up in height, over the last few months, just in time to start at his new school in Mount Mercy in the fall. Moving from the city to this tiny, quaint little town was going to be a big change but he seemed more excited than scared. He'd grown in confidence so much since he met JD. Working for myself, I'd be able to set my own hours and see a lot more of him.

I heard the sound of an engine in the distance. "That'll be them," I said. "We should head down there."

With Cody still on JD's shoulders, we walked through the pastures, towards the trees that marked where a creek ran across the bottom of our plot of land. It was August and the sun blazed down from a cloudless sky, baking us. It was a relief to get under the shade of the trees.

A big black SUV rumbled along the dirt track that edged our property and pulled onto the grass. The doors flew open and people started spilling out: Kian and his girlfriend Emily, Bradan and Stacey and Gabriel and Olivia. Another black SUV followed at a discreet distance: Emily's Secret Service protection.

The back of the SUV was full of coolers and we all helped with the unloading, setting up folding tables and laying out food. There were platters of thick-cut, hearty sandwiches, crispy bacon and slices of roast chicken peeking out between lush green lettuce and juicy tomatoes. There were salads: kale with creamy mozzarella, tomatoes and wild rice, a white bean salad wrapped in lettuce leaves, pasta salad with flaked tuna, sun-dried tomatoes and herbs. And then the sweet dishes started arriving: Poke cakes and lemon drizzle cake, an enormous pie of some kind and trays of cookies. *That's a lot of food.*

Stacey beckoned me over. "Can you give me a hand? There wasn't

much space in our SUV with six of us, so most of the food had to go
with the Secret Service."

Oh.

A Secret Service agent opened the rear door of their SUV and I
stared. There was at least twice as much food again: more
sandwiches, chips and dips, cold meats and a cheese board, three
more salads and two trays of baked, sweet treats that smelled
amazing. *We can't possibly eat all this!*

But then Cal and his girlfriend Bethany arrived with Rufus, and
Danny roared up in his vintage Jaguar along with Erin and Gina and
that made fourteen of us. As Erin set up a wireless speaker system
and hung lanterns from the trees for when it got dark, I helped
Danny unload the drinks from the trunk of his Jaguar. There was a
cooler filled with beer and pitchers of orange iced tea and three sorts
of *aguas frescas*, Mexican fruit coolers: watermelon, peach and mango.
Danny grunted as he hefted the cooler. "You okay?" I asked. I still felt
guilty that he'd gotten shot protecting me.

He gave me one of those winning Danny grins. "Yeah, I'm alright.
Got a wicked new scar from it, too." He undid a few shirt buttons and
showed me the ragged mark where the bullet had entered. Then he
rubbed his pec. "It's just a bit stiff, sometimes."

"You know what'd help with that?" asked JD, sauntering over.

"*Don't* say yoga," Danny told him firmly.

"Yoga." JD was a convert. We did a session each morning and his
back injury didn't bother him anymore. He put an arm around me
and pulled me close. "Changed my life."

"I'm not wearing Lycra," said Danny. "Or saying *Ommm.*"

"It's not like that." JD clapped him on the back and led him away.

Erin started the music playing. I checked on Cody, who was
happily playing with Rufus, then wandered over to where the women
were talking. When I'd first visited Mount Mercy a few months ago,
I'd been nervous about meeting them. But they'd been nothing but
warm and welcoming. It helped that we were all in the same
situation. We might come from very different backgrounds but we'd
all moved to this small Colorado town to be with our men. We hung

out at each other's houses, went for drinks in the town's quirky, German-themed bar and supported each other when the team was away.

As we all started talking, I noticed something weird. Gabriel's girlfriend, Olivia, the ER doctor who'd saved my life remotely when I was poisoned, was...not *nervous*, exactly, but definitely different. She was smiling, which was a little unusual in itself because she was always so serious. But it was more than that.

I started talking to Erin, who was full of plans for a trip to Texas. "Ever since you and JD visited, my mom's been demanding to know when she's going to meet *my* guy." She looked across at Danny, who was talking with the other men. "I think Danny's nervous about meeting my dad. We're not sure how he'll react to a Brit."

"Jack was really nice to me," I told her.

"Yeah, but JD's his son. It's different, with daughters. You should have seen what JD was like when he found out I was seeing Danny, and he's just my *brother*. Texas guys can be a little over-protective."

"Talking of trips," said Emily, "That trip to New York got me thinking: we should go somewhere." She looked around. "All of us. Just us girls."

Everyone leaned forward, intrigued. I looked at Olivia again and narrowed my eyes. Everyone looked excited but Olivia looked like she was going to burst.

"I'm ready for a break," said Bethany. "This year's been pretty tough." She was redoing her second year of med school. "Where are we talking?"

"Somewhere hot?" said Erin. "With a beach?"

"Are we inviting Gina?" I asked. I looked across to where Gina was talking to Cody, quizzing him on parts of a helicopter. For someone who claimed to hate children, she looked happy. Then she saw me looking and did her best to look grumpy.

"Of course!" said Emily. "It'll be good to spend some time with her." None of us knew Gina as well as we knew each other because she was usually away with the team.

"What if we got cheap flights to Europe and—" began Stacey

"Gabriel asked me to marry him," blurted Olivia, then looked apologetically at Stacey.

We all swung around to stare at her. *"What?"* I asked all of us.

"Last night," said Olivia. "He took me for a drive, up in the hills, and we got lost...or I *thought* we were lost. We walked into these woods and suddenly the trees all started lighting up...he'd put fairy lights everywhere, like the whole *forest* was made of light. And then he drops to one knee..." She put a hand to her chest, her eyes suddenly swimming, "and asked if I'd make an honest man of him. Or as honest as he can be." And she held out her left hand. The ring was gorgeous, a delicate web of silver that held two oval sapphires and one large, round diamond in the center. We all *ooh*ed.

"It's beautiful," said Emily. "Looks old. Is it vintage?"

"It's from the 1700s," said Olivia. "A pirate gave it to his lover when he settled down and married her in London: there's a whole story. It bounced around the world for years. Then a few years ago, some really unsavory drug trafficker in Colombia got hold of it. Gabriel, uh...*liberated* it to give to me. I think he sees himself in that pirate."

"And what did you say?" demanded Stacey.

"Yes! Of course yes!"

We all hugged her at once, and that got the guys asking Gabriel what was going on. He blushed as he told them and then they were all punching him on the arm and slapping his back.

Stacey, always the planner, started asking Olivia about what sort of wedding she wanted. She seemed lighter and more relaxed, since we all got back from New York. She'd shared, over drinks one night, that Bradan was doing much better. He was sleeping soundly and seemed to have made his peace with his past. I saw him and Cal talking a lot, so maybe that had something to do with it. I looked around at the group of women and smiled. After never having many female friends growing up and then having my BFF turn on me, I'd suddenly found myself with a whole group of women I really liked.

There was a rattle of metal and the pop of an engine misfiring. Colton's ancient pick-up truck swung around the corner and clattered noisily to a stop. Colton jumped out, then had to jump back in, cursing, because the truck started to roll. He reset the parking brake, scowled at it as if daring it to slip again, then climbed out and slammed the door.

Danny shook his head. "You've got to replace that thing," he told Colton.

"There ain't nothin' wrong with it," insisted Colton. He opened the passenger door and Atlas lolloped out. The others had told me that when Colton rescued him, the bear had just been a cub, small enough to hold in your arms. But now he was close to a year old and already he was over eighty pounds, more than Rufus. He was no less adorable, though. He padded over to us and we all started stroking him. Then he got interested in the food tables and we had to distract him before he tipped the whole thing over.

People filled plates and started to eat and the afternoon passed in a warm haze of good food and good company. We threw a frisbee around, planned more of the girls' trip, went into full wedding planning overload with Olivia (while JD, Danny and the others talked to Gabriel about his bachelor party) and got soaked when Rufus and Atlas both decided to take a dip in the creek and then shook themselves dry right next to us.

As the sun went down, the lanterns Erin had put up began to glow. Gabriel took Olivia's hand and started to dance with her, and then Danny and Erin joined in. Suddenly, I felt an arm slip around my waist and JD was there, pulling me close against him.

I checked on Cody and relaxed when I saw he was being tutored by Cal and Colton on how to make a backwoods fishing pole. He'd gone from having no father figure to having a really great one in JD, plus six protective uncles of varying talents.

JD led me over to where the others were dancing and we started to move to the music. The first song was light and fast, and as JD twirled me around and smiled down at me with those amazing, prairie-sky eyes, I realized how much he'd changed, since that first time I'd met him. The pain had been a weight that crushed him down, robbing him of his sense of humor. He was more jokey, now, and more relaxed with the team.

The second song was slower and more romantic. JD pulled me closer, one big hand holding mine and his other arm around my waist, just like at the ball. But now I didn't have to just fantasize that we were together. He was mine and the look he gave me made it very clear that I was his.

The third song was even slower, a love ballad. JD pulled me even closer and rocked me against him. I watched over his shoulder as the other couples cozied up, too. Cal pulled Bethany into the dancing and she leaned against his chest, a happy grin on her face. As I looked around the pairs, I realized Colton was now the only Stormfinch man still single. *We need to find him someone.* And Gina, she needed to find someone, too.

I looked at Cody, who was now petting Atlas. JD so obviously adored him and was going to make a great dad. Our little family was complete. And we'd become part of a bigger one, too, one that was fourteen strong plus a dog and a bear, and growing fast. A weird, quirky family but a family nonetheless. One that nothing could tear apart.

I looked around at everyone, then off through the trees towards where our house would be, then finally down to the town of Mount Mercy. "I think we're going to be happy here," I thought. Then I realized I'd mumbled it out loud.

JD put his finger under my chin and gently tilted my head up to look at him. He was grinning. "I think so, too," he said. And kissed me.

The End

Thank you for reading! If you enjoyed *Guarded,* please consider leaving a review: every one helps!

Colton's story will be next. Sign up to my newsletter at helenanewbury.com and I'll let you know the second it's out.

. . .

This is the third of my *Stormfinch Security* books.

Gabriel and Olivia's story is told in *No Angel*.

Danny and Erin's story is told in *Off Limits*.

Kian and Cal have their own books, too. Kian becomes the bodyguard for Emily, the President's daughter, but winds up falling for her in *Saving Liberty*.

Bethany saves Rufus...and in turn is ferociously protected by both him and Cal in *Deep Woods*.

Finally, Kian and the rest of the O'Harra brothers rescue Bradan from the cult in *Brothers* (the ebook of which is free when you join my newsletter, a paperback is also available).

The story of how geeky girl Hailey had plastic surgery and swapped places with the glamorous girlfriend of Russian mob boss Konstantin is told in *The Double*. Agent Callahan also plays a role.

Callahan gets his own book, and finds love, in *Hold Me in the Dark*, in which he teams up with a reclusive genius to catch a serial killer.

All my books are available in paperback and can be ordered from any bookshop or requested from your library: there's a list of ISBNs on my website.

9 781914 526244